PRAISE FOR

"*Love and Other Brain Experiments* is brainy, fun, deeply relatable… I guarantee it will take up all the bandwidth in your head and heart"
Elena Armas, *New York Times* bestselling author of *The Spanish Love Deception*

"No one loves fake dating like I do, and this one elevates my favorite trope with emotionally vulnerable characters navigating their way through a truly heartfelt and hopeful love story"
Annabel Monaghan, *New York Times* bestselling author of *It's a Love Story*

"*Love and Other Brain Experiments* was a brainy delight. Brohm's writing is cheeky and self-aware, but warmed by an undercurrent of sincerity and real heart… I was left charmed and delighted"
Brigitte Knightley, *New York Times* bestselling author of *The Irresistible Urge to Fall For Your Enemy*

"Smart and addictively romantic, *Love and Other Brain Experiments* is the perfect read"
Peyton Corinne, *USA Today* bestselling author of *Unloved*

"*Love and Other Brain Experiments*
is the intellectually seductive, trope-perfect, lanyard-
melting debut of the year… I couldn't get enough
of the gorgeous writing, delicious academia backdrop,
and heartwarming main characters"
**Clare Gilmore, *USA Today* bestselling
author of *Never Over***

"Attention all STEM romance lovers: this smart and
poignant debut will make you swoon, fan yourself, and
wonder how neuroscience could be so sexy"
**Victoria Lavine, internationally bestselling
author of *Any Trope But You***

"A just-one-more-chapter, heart-palpitatingly
romantic delight of a romance… Frances and Lewis are
totally delicious, and had me invested from the first page.
It's so good I'm pretty sure it altered my brain chemistry!"
Cressida McLaughlin, author of *A Cornish Love Story*

"Brohm weaves a beautiful tale of self-worth,
patience, and hard work through fake dating chaos,
the slow realization of romantic feelings, and a brilliant
woman-in-STEM. Smart and sexy…
An absolute knockout!"
Chelsea Curto, author of *In Stormy Weather*

"A totally charming read,
Love and Other Brain Experiments is the sweetest romance…
I loved this brilliant debut and I can't wait to see
what Hannah Brohm comes up with next"
Laura Wood, author of *Let's Make a Scene*

"Sexy, heartfelt, and bursting with charm. Lewis and Frances will take root in your brain and heart just like they do each other's… This is pure academic rivals-to-lovers catnip"
Katie Naymon, author of *You Between the Lines*

"Smart, beautifully written, and teeming with delicious romantic tension… *Love and Other Brain Experiments* is a dopamine rush from start to finish"
Ellie K. Wilde, author of *If Only You Knew*

"A whip-smart, flirty and fun debut! Frances and Lewis's witty banter and sizzling tension had me hooked from page one. This book changed my brain chemistry"
Annabelle Slator, author of *The Launch Date*

"Smart, tender, earnest, and masterful, this debut does STEM romance right. I'm no scientist, but my study's results say that *Love and Other Brain Experiments* needs to be on your bookshelf"
Georgia Stone, author of *The Friendship Fling*

Love and Other Brain Experiments

HANNAH BROHM

An Aria Book

First published in the USA in 2026 by Atria, an imprint of Simon & Schuster LLC
This edition first published in the UK in 2026 by Head of Zeus,
part of Bloomsbury Publishing Plc.

Copyright © Hannah Bernhard, 2026

The moral right of Hannah Brohm to be identified as the author
of this work has been asserted in accordance with the
Copyright, Designs and Patents Act of 1988.

All rights reserved. No part of this publication may be: i) reproduced or
transmitted in any form, electronic or mechanical, including photocopying,
recording or by means of any information storage or retrieval system without prior
permission in writing from the publishers; or ii) used or reproduced in any way for
the training, development or operation of artificial intelligence (AI) technologies,
including generative AI technologies. The rights holders expressly reserve this
publication from the text and data mining exception as per Article 4(3) of
the Digital Single Market Directive (EU) 2019/790.

This is a work of fiction. All characters, organizations,
and events portrayed in this novel are either products of
the author's imagination or are used fictitiously.

9 7 5 3 1 2 4 6 8

A catalogue record for this book is available from
the British Library.

ISBN (PB): 9781035919673
ISBN (E): 9781035919659\

Interior design by Lexy East

Printed and bound in Great Britain by Clays Ltd, Elcograf S.p.A.

Bloomsbury Publishing Plc
50 Bedford Square, London, WC1B 3DP, UK
Bloomsbury Publishing Ireland Limited,
29 Earlsfort Terrace, Dublin 2, D02 AY28, Ireland

HEAD OF ZEUS LTD
5–8 Hardwick Street
London, EC1R 4RG

To find out more about our authors and books
visit www.headofzeus.com
For product safety related questions contact productsafety@bloomsbury.com

Julio,
Remember when you came up to me and asked
what statistical model I used in my Bachelor thesis?
Favorite moment of serendipity, right there.

This one was always going to be for you.

Chapter One

Murphy's Law
/ˌməːfɪz ˈlɔː/
noun
a supposed law of nature, expressed in
various humorous popular sayings, to the effect that
anything that can go wrong will go wrong.

I've always been skeptical of Murphy's Law.

As a scientist worth her salt, I know that it's all about the probabilities. With the thousands of actions we take every day, it's just extremely unlikely that so many of them go wrong. But honestly? After sleeping through my alarm, barely making it to the airport on time despite Lennart's—my sister's husband—shortcuts and misplacing the allergy pills that make me drowsy enough to keep my flight anxiety at bay, I'm starting to believe that Murphy's Law might actually be a thing.

It's seemingly not enough that I have to be awake on this flight, visualizing what feels like a million different ways that this plane could crash. The seat belt signs on flight UA 963 from Berlin to Newark Liberty International Airport have barely been switched off when the universe decides to throw an emergency into the mix.

"Your check-in data say you're a doctor. Is that correct?" asks the flight attendant with the black polka-dot headband. Right after boarding, when I asked the crew for some pills, she gently pushed me back into my seat, which shouldn't have come as a surprise. I'm well aware that the crew isn't allowed to hand out pills just like that, even if it's over-the-counter medication. They probably don't even have them on board, but with mine out of reach, I was desperate and thought it was worth a try, no matter how unreasonable the request.

Now, the flight attendant is staring at me with big brown eyes, polite smile plastered onto her round face, while I'm too panic-stricken to respond, tongue thick in my mouth and heartbeat heavy against my ribs. She leans over the man sitting on the aisle seat next to me—the one with the thick, caterpillar-like eyebrows—to tap on my shoulder and try again.

"Excuse me? Ma'am? Dr. Silberstein?"

Caterpillar Eyebrows decides this situation is more interesting than his doorstop of a thriller and slots his finger in between the pages of his book. On my left, the woman is still fast asleep, tie-dye hoodie scrunched up between her head and the window, and one leg tucked up onto the seat.

"Could you confirm if you're a doctor?"

Murphy's having a field day with me today.

As I force my vocal cords to work again, I cringe into the pleather of my seat. Five years ago, freshly graduated with my PhD, it had struck me as a good idea to register my new official title in my passport. To show it to the world and rub it in everyone's face. Yes, I'd TAed almost as much time as I'd spent in the lab because my stipend wouldn't cover my monthly costs, and yes, grad school and the ensuing breakup with my ex had sanded down my self-confidence. But at least I had something to show for it. I could skip past the *Miss* and *Ms.* in the drop-down menus, and demand to be called *Dr.* instead.

"I am. But not that kind of doctor" I mumble awkwardly. When she tilts her head, I blabber on, "Not the medical kind.

I have a PhD in neuroscience. I can't help with any emergency, unless it's a statistical one."

"That should do," she says cheerfully. "Can you bring a thousand-word abstract down to five hundred? It's due in two hours."

My gaze pinballs from her face to my neighbor, who raises those thick eyebrows at me. The woman on my other side stirs as I shift in my seat. Did I mishear? Maybe the flight attendant *did* give me pills after all, and they're giving me surreal dreams?

Unless the abstract is about neuroscience or anything remotely related, I won't be of much help, but I'm desperate for any kind of distraction. "I guess I can try," I reply. And from how she snaps into action and gestures for me to get out of my seat, I begin to suspect that she's being serious. That this is not some cosmic joke.

"Let's get you to your new seat then, Dr. Silberstein," she prompts.

My neighbor has already swung his knees into the aisle to let me through, so all I can do is get up and get out. "Just Frances is fine," I tell her, stumbling out into the aisle and trailing her, my oversize tote bag bumping into my thigh with every shaky step.

As ridiculous as the request sounds, I feel for this person who's racing to meet an abstract deadline. It's a rite of passage in academia; one we've all been through. With the experiments, heaps of teaching, grant proposals, peer reviews of colleagues' papers, and other admin work we have to do, conference prep—like abstracts—tends to be an afterthought, tacked on to train journeys, slotted between meetings, or, like yesterday, preceding my younger sister Karo's wedding. Already dressed in my bridesmaid's gown and waiting for the nail polish on my left foot to dry, my fingers whirred over my keyboard to put together the interactive code I need for this week's workshop.

What a glamorous life.

Ahead of me, the flight attendant weaves effortlessly around other passengers down the aisle. "I've never been called for any emergencies before," I tell her, grabbing onto headrests left and right. "I'm not really the useful kind of doctor."

"The desperate man in 44L will find you plenty useful, I'm sure," she replies as she picks up someone's trash from their tray.

Seat 44L. We're still only at 30. I scan the rows in front of me, trying to spot the person who didn't understand the concept of an abstract—summarizing a study or a set of studies in a short paragraph, like a sort of preview—and wrote half an essay instead.

"And don't worry, if it had been an actual emergency, we would've used the intercom," she informs me. "I'm just bored, is all."

I can't help but be intrigued. "You help out desperate academics when you're bored? What else do you do? Match up seat neighbors based on their interests?"

"Darling, have you ever flown long haul before? It gets real boring real quick." She looks at me over her shoulder, while also helping a short, elderly lady grab something from the overhead bin before stepping around her. "Especially if the back galley chat is stuck on the same old topic. Kimberley's wife just had a baby so that'll be all they talk about today. Don't get me wrong, lil' Jonah is cute, but I'll survive without seeing sixty more photos of his wrinkly face by the time we land."

We pass through the mid-cabin galley, where the other flight attendants are preparing the drink carts. One of them bumps into me.

"We sing birthday songs or participate in people's proposals," she continues, pulling me out of the way by the cotton of my white T-shirt. "Nothing as exciting as that going on today, so I thought I'd help someone out. I've always had a soft spot for nerds." She crooks her palm over her mouth, voice pitching lower. "And it helps that he's cute." Glancing at the seat numbers, she stops. "Here we are. I told you I'd find someone who can help you," she chirps, turning to the people sitting in row 44.

I size up the three people in the row. In the aisle seat is a guy about my age with the most enviable shade of strawberry blond hair and a blush tainting his cheeks. Next to him, there's a nondescript white middle-aged man with a sports cap that screams sitcom dad. A teenage girl with pointy cat ears attached to the band of her headphones has the window seat, an open bag of saltines in her hands. The flight attendant's comment implied it was a guy, which rules out the teenager, plus she said he was cute. Unless her criteria for cuteness include a dad bod, it's down to Blond Guy.

"You really didn't have to," Blond Guy says.

Bingo.

I'm not a native English speaker, but based on the accent, he's American, maybe even from New York. He bites his bottom lip, but there's a flash in his blue eyes. He looks bashful. Definitely cute.

"Well, it's your lucky day," the flight attendant responds, her words a different kind of slow now. With the way she leans toward him, I wonder if he flirted her into this absurd search for a nonmedical doctor.

"And mine," Sitcom Dad adds. The flight attendant steps to the side, letting Blond Guy and Sitcom Dad stand and file out of their row, before she guides Sitcom Dad to a free aisle seat a few rows down, leaving me face-to-face with Blond Guy and his receding blush.

"One thousand words, huh?" I mock.

"It was a joke." He shrugs, almost apologetically.

I glance back at the empty middle seat I vacated. "So you're not over the word limit by five hundred?"

"I am," he hurries to say. "That part's true. But she asked if there was anything she could help me with and I said I had this abstract deadline, and I didn't think she'd take it so literally and—"

"Look, do you want to get in?" A passenger behind me grumbles and we jump back into action. Blond Guy steps aside so I can slide into the middle seat.

Before I manage to settle in, though, there's a bump underfoot and my pulse skyrockets. I reach out to steady myself. For a moment there, I'd forgotten that planes are lethal.

"Are you okay?" Blond Guy wants to know.

I wait for another bump before responding, and when it doesn't come, I straighten. I rarely get manicures, but for my sister's wedding I carved out time, and now my nails are an unfamiliar berry-red against the backdrop of Blond Guy's soft flannel.

Whoops. It seems like the solid ridge my hand reached for wasn't part of the airplane fixtures after all.

"Sorry," I stammer, dropping my hand from his biceps. A corner of his mouth flicks into the blink of a smile.

I push my leather tote under the seat in front of me, and by the time I'm sitting upright again, he's already back in his seat, his arm brushing mine. The sleeve of his flannel is pushed up, exposing a tanned forearm with golden hairs that dust up toward his elbow.

He clears his throat. "So."

I blink up to his face, to the set of blue eyes and the scatter of freckles plotted over the bridge of his nose. His hair is parted at the side, and the soft waves fall to the tips of his ears. Something about him makes it impossible to look away. Is it the knowledge that he's an academic who happens to look hot? Is it that I'm finally away from my desk long enough to appreciate it? Or is exposure to fearful situations correlated to a heightened attraction to people?

Someone should run a study on this.

"The abstract," he says.

"Right. Let's see what I can help you with. I'm Frances, by the way."

He holds out his hand in the cramped space between us. "Lewis. Nice to meet you." His fingers close around my hand briefly, then let go—and that's when gravity decides to make another entrance. It pulls us down like we're on the world's steepest roller-coaster ride, only we're not, we're in a freaking plane, and there's nothing below us except the green fields of Ireland or the vast expanse of the Atlantic Ocean and we're plunging toward them and—

"Hey."

When I open my eyes, the lights of the cabin are too bright. People are chatting, someone is giggling, and it grates against my ear. Blond Guy—Lewis—shifts and blocks out my view of the cabin with his shoulder. I look down to find his hand in my lap, sandwiched between mine.

"Breathe with me," he says and maneuvers our hand sandwich to his chest. My breaths are a dizzying harmonic of his, short and quick, and I force myself to focus on how his lungs expand and contract against the sides of my fingers.

"Frances? Are you—"

"I'm a little afraid of flying," I choke out between clenched teeth.

"Ladies and gentlemen, this is the captain speaking," a tinny voice comes over the speakers. "You've seen the seat belt sign come on. We're encountering some turbulence as we enter the airspace above the ocean, so the ride may be a bit bumpy for the next fifteen to twenty minutes. Crew, please return to your jump seats."

"Fuck," I hiss. It's been ages since I witnessed the hours between takeoff and landing. Usually, I'm well knocked out at this point, allergy pills working their magic. But then again, usually my pills are tucked into my carry-on, ready for me to take right before boarding, and not out of reach in the pocket of a pair of jeans I decided to wear last night only to change my mind this morning because who wears jeans on a long-haul flight?

Lewis's long exhale reminds me to breathe. "You're doing great," he encourages me over the captain repeating his announcement in German. I drag my eyes up his clean-shaven jaw to his bottom lip that's slightly larger than the top, the set of lines that brackets the corners of his mouth up to the wings of his nose. He nods as I draw in a breath and slowly let it out again.

"Did you know that it's the lift around the wings that gets planes off the ground and keeps them in the sky?" he says. "Turbulence is really just a perturbation in the air that interferes with the lift, but the wings balance it out, see?" He nods to the window, in front of which the teenager has inexplicably fallen asleep. Behind the tinted glass, the wings are violently swinging up and down. "It won't break the airplane apart. Turbulence is dangerous because it jostles people around, but since we're safely strapped into our seats, we should be okay."

I know he's just trying to distract me, but unfortunately, throughout his speech, my mind has found a new image to latch on to: a GIF of a plane snapping in half. Rationally, I know this is very unlikely to happen, but my brain has abandoned all logic, letting panic steer my thoughts. "Our plane might break apart?" I whisper.

He tugs at my hand. "It won't. I thought the science might comfort you, but let's talk about something else."

The plane shudders, and my stomach decides it's time to ignore anatomy and climb into my chest. The rapid up and down reminds me of my parents' house outside Berlin, where the last stretch of the road was paved decades ago with large and irregular cobblestones.

But unlike there, where I'd get out of the car and walk the last hundred yards to avoid motion sickness, now there's no way out as we plummet toward earth. The seat belt digs into my thighs. Panic taps on my shoulder. I burrow my face into Lewis's flannel, and he immediately stiffens.

"Oh god, I'm sorry." Mortified, I pull away and press the crown of my head into the back of my seat. His scent—woodsy and warm—reminds me of that time Karo joined me after a conference and we canoed the lakes of Central Sweden. "I swear I don't use everyone I meet as a human comfort blanket."

He squeezes my hand. "It's fine." After another moment, he clears his throat. "You can use my shoulder, if you think that helps."

I wince and press my eyes closed as another jerk goes through the plane.

"Tell me about yourself," he prompts, his voice quietly confident. If the memory of him freezing when I nuzzled into him weren't quite as fresh, I'd hug him in gratitude for his attempt to distract me.

"I'm a postdoc," I tell him. Since he's an academic, I don't go into the usual spiel of explaining that it stands for postdoctoral researcher and describes the time of fixed-term research contracts after grad school until you finally make it into a tenured professorship—or, the more common outcome, leave academia for good.

I force myself to continue talking through the blood rushing in my ears. "I'm from Germany, but now I live in the Netherlands. Although I don't know for how much longer."

"Is your funding running out?"

Ouch. "Dead center, Dr. Lewis. Or is it *Professor*?"

"I'm a postdoc like you, and just Lewis is fine. I'm sorry for bringing that up."

"It's okay." I take a deep breath and his scent unwinds something in me. "But yeah, my funding is running out, and my lab doesn't have money to extend my contract. Which means I'll be out of a job soon, unless I find another open position somewhere else. I've applied for grants to extend the funding myself, but that's not a guarantee. Well, you probably know the drill."

He sounds wistful when he says, "I do. Makes me question why I don't just leave and get a cushy job in industry."

It's Karo's favorite question, whenever I tell her I've been working at all hours to make a paper revision deadline or when yet another one of my fixed-term contracts ends and I gear up to find another job with an expiration date. The reasons are numerous, or they were at first: Because I love working at the forefront of discovery and my mind switches off when my fingers type out lines of code. Because I have so many questions and I can't bear to leave them unanswered. Because one day my work might help someone in this world. Because there's nothing better than seeing a student get passionately interested in something I explained to them. But with every passing year and being nowhere closer to achieving the long-dreamed-of job stability that would allow me to fully focus on my research, it gets harder to answer Karo's question.

I'm glad for the opportunity to be the one asking it, for once. "Well. Why don't you?"

"I don't like to be told what to do, so I don't think I'd last long in a company." He hums, low in his throat. "But no, truth is, I love it too much. I was that kid who annoyed the hell out of everyone with all my questions. I wanted to understand how everything works. That never changed, except now I get paid for it."

It's not only his words that trigger an immediate sense of connection, but also the way he says them. Lewis's voice softens as he talks about being an academic, like it's the most precious thing in the world.

"What about you?" he asks, squeezing my hand, which I

guess I should take back soon, but I can't make myself pull away just yet. Though it does give me the courage to open my eyes and find his gaze.

"I guess . . . I want to make a difference," I tell him. "And I know, don't we all. I don't mean it in the 'I want to find a cure for Alzheimer's' way—although, don't get me wrong, I hope we do find it at some point. But I'm working in this tiny niche of science that is sort of far away from anything that can be applied in the real world. I love my tiny niche of science. And I love chipping away at it, and maybe, somewhere, at some point it will make a difference?"

I'm surprised that I'm sharing this much with him, but he's easy to talk to. Maybe it's the fact that I'll never see this stranger again, or the fact that, as a fellow academic, he understands the strong pull of those unanswered questions and doesn't need justifications like my sister does. Or maybe it's the fact that he hasn't let go of my hand, either.

After a beat of silence, Lewis shifts around to face me fully, leaning his temple against the headrest. "And what brings you to New York? Summer vacation?"

I push out a laugh. "I wish. I just got done with a paper revision that took ages, so a holiday sounds tempting, but no. There's this summer program that I'm attending. I thought it would be good for some networking, collaborations. Maybe to see if anybody would hire me if my grant application gets rejected."

"It sounds like there's a *but* there," he notes.

Of course there's a *but*. A giant one. One that made me glad I'd missed the taxi when I woke up this morning, and tempted me to stay in bed rather than race down the quiet corridor of the country estate my sister got married in. But the dread of having to quit my research and leave all my questions unanswered got me up those stairs to the honeymoon suite, where I banged against the wooden door until Karo's fiancé—*husband*—Lennart opened it with a rumpled look on his face.

It's a *but* so personal that I'd usually not get into it, not even with Karo. Then again, I've already shown this guy my deepest irrational fear so what's there to lose?

I take a deep breath, focusing on our linked hands. "The Sawyer's Summer Seminars I'm attending—if that tells you anything—is organized by my ex. We were together when I lived in New York, but then I left and we . . . Well, we didn't part on good terms, and I'm not at the point where I thought I'd be when seeing him again."

"You're not over him?"

I look up and find Lewis scrutinizing me. Shame burns in my throat, a phantom reaction as Jacob's words from five years ago come echoing back.

"I'm sorry," he starts. "That was a personal question."

"No, it's okay. I'm one hundred percent over him, it's not that." I swallow thickly. "But at the end he told me I'd end up unsuccessful and alone."

Lewis's cringe mirrors the feeling that's buried deep in my stomach. Naive younger me was convinced Jacob had no clue, that his retaliation was only meant to hurt me, but in the days counting down to this flight, and at the prospect of seeing him again, doubt has crept in. He's always been good with people, and he knew me more intimately than anybody else.

What if he was right?

"I don't care so much about being alone," I continue. "It makes the nomadic life of academia a little easier. But I'd pictured myself starting the tenure track by now. Job security. Staying in a city for more than a year or two. More high-impact publications. Something that would make it all worth it. Something to show him how wrong he was."

Although it's only half of the *but*, off-loading my worries to someone is freeing. Vulnerability is not my strong suit, but Lewis makes me feel at ease—and knowing that I won't see him again makes it easier to open up.

The other half of the *but* is a little more complicated. It involves a know-it-all scientist who goes by the name of Theodore L. North. Once upon a time, I thought we could be friendly colleagues, but then he tore it all down with a paper he published, making it clear that his life's mission is to sniff out any and all weaknesses in my academic papers. I don't know what I did to him, because while he loves scrutinizing me, he seems perfectly generous with the rest of the scientific community on social media. He makes his data sets openly available, hosts online panels to amplify researchers from underrepresented communities, and every month, he dedicates a day to giving online advice for people who are starting out. Although we both work in memory research, we've never crossed paths. But I know he'll be at the Sawyer's, and I'm not sure if I'm looking forward to finally putting a face to the name, or if I dread having to fight our battles in person.

"Well, for what it's worth," Lewis says, tilting down his head so he can look me straight in the eyes, "this ex of yours sounds like a douche. Good that you put your career first and don't let yourself be intimidated by him."

"Thank you." I smile at him. They may be a mindless offer of kindness, but his words ease something in me. Maybe Murphy's Law is a lie after all. Without this seat change, I'd be freaking out all on my own. "Now, please tell me you have nicer reasons to be traveling."

"To be honest, I'm also torn about my trip." His eyebrows pinch together. "I'm traveling to the Sawyer's as well, which is exciting."

Columbia University is hosting this year's Sawyer's Summer Seminars, with topics ranging from the neuroscience of memory to personalized medicine and antimicrobial peptides. I'm about to ask which one he's going to, when Lewis continues, "But I also have family in New York, and I should probably make an appearance at a few things that are happening there."

"Like?"

His gaze swivels past me, and for a moment he looks lost in thought. Then he focuses on me again, and his voice is low as he responds, "My little brother's college graduation."

"That's exciting."

"Yeah, well," Lewis replies, as if it's anything but. "He doesn't even know I'll be in the city, so I'm not sure I'll go."

He sounds like it's normal to skip a sibling's graduation. To me, the thought of missing any of the big events happening in Karo's life feels wrong. When she got promoted to her current job as social media manager at a publishing company, I felt sad for a whole week because I was too tied up at the lab in Phoenix to fly out and celebrate with her, and although we live on the same continent now, the seven-hour train ride that separates us still feels too far.

"What's holding you back?"

Instead of answering, he tips his head to the ceiling. "Looks like we're finally in the clear."

There's a blank screen where the seat belt sign used to be. A flight attendant wheels a food cart down the aisle, and the plane seems mercifully steady. Enough for me to finally lower my shoulders.

I'm burning with curiosity about his relationship with his brother, but it's obvious he's in less of an oversharing mood than I was so I don't push. "Thank you," I say instead, and give his hand one last squeeze before I let go. "Should we look at your abstract then? The deadline is in a few hours, right?"

"Noon—the conference is in Auckland, so midnight in

their time zone. It'd be nice to go. I've never been to New Zealand." While Lewis pulls his backpack out from under the seat, I bring myself into work mode and tie my hair into a bun. The back of my neck is still slick with the traces of my panic. "But first, I need to shorten it massively. I'm not sure what your area of expertise is, Dr. Frances . . . ?"

"Silberstein," I supply. Lewis's laptop slides out of his hands, and I catch it against my thighs. "Actually, my name is Franziska, but I go by Frances ever since I moved to the US. Lived in the UK, for a bit, too, which is why my English is all over the place. Anyway. My area of expertise is cognitive neuroscience. I investigate the mechanics of memory in the human brain, so I'm not sure how much I can help with your physics stuff."

He frowns. "Physics?"

I wave to the tinted window, where the clouds pile up behind the tip of the wing. "I assumed. Since you gave me a quick rundown of aerodynamics."

"Um, I'm not a physicist. Just a bit of a nerd, that's all." His cheeks redden again.

"What's your research about then?"

He seems strangely nervous, his Adam's apple bobbing up and down the column of his throat. "I'm a neuroscientist. Cognitive neuroscientist, to be precise." He pauses and fumbles with the crew neck of his T-shirt. "I think . . . we've exchanged a few emails."

I shoot him a questioning look. "I'm pretty good with names, but I don't remember a Lewis."

A corner of his mouth ticks down. "I also didn't remember a Frances. Lewis is my middle name and what my friends call me. But I publish under my first and last name."

Because he's clearly stalling now, I narrow my eyes at him. "Well, what's your name?"

Lewis clears his throat, and just then, Murphy throws me his finest curveball. "You probably know me under the name Theodore L. North, and I'm afraid I may have just submitted a comment discussing your recent paper on detecting neural replay with fMRI."

Chapter Two

A laugh bubbles out of me. "You're kidding, right?"

He frowns. "Why would I be kidding?"

"You have to be."

I know it doesn't make sense, but it's the only explanation I can reach for in this moment. Because there is no way that I just poured my heart out to my academic rival, all while holding his hand. How long has he known for? From the moment I sat down? Was all the gentle care and distraction a farce to coax out my insecurities? I know how methodical he is, so it's not far-fetched to think he'd come up with a complicated plan to sniff out my weaknesses like this. Less far-fetched than the alternative, more logical explanation: that I got asked to help a random stranger and ended up next to my academic nemesis on the *one* transatlantic flight where I'm not knocked out into slow-wave sleep, only for turbulence to hit and push me into a panic spiral that made me overshare.

What are the odds, really? Or maybe, Murphy was onto something.

I feel exposed, unexpectedly naked, like when your T-shirt

rides up while taking off your jumper and suddenly, you're showing off your threadbare bra. No matter how fast you pull your shirt back down, the image will be etched into everyone's mind. Even if it's only a short glimpse, they'll know that you should have gone bra shopping a long time ago, that your belly button looks weird, and that you have a little birthmark right under your left boob.

My job struggles, my not-quite-broken-but-bruised heart. All there, on a silver platter.

And as if that's not enough, I'll have to sit next to Dr. Theodore North for the next—I want to wail when I see the clock on the in-flight entertainment screen—seven hours. I want to gather up all of the secrets I spilled and stuff them back into the dusty closet of my brain.

See, I want to shout at Karo. *This is why we keep that door firmly closed. This is why we don't open up.*

Dr. Theodore Lewis Know-It-All North, or, as he likes to call himself on social media, @theoretically, studies human memory with rare invasive recordings directly from the human brain. I'd kill for the data he has—and he knows it. Once upon a time, freshly out of grad school, I thought we could build a collaboration, exchange hypotheses on our experiments and eventually build up big-scale projects, but he popped the bubble of that dream a long time ago. Since then, all he's ever done is drone on about the inadequacy of my scientific work and make my life difficult.

Fuck. Fuck squared. Fuck to the power of three.

This is a disaster.

Our thoughts seem to be tracking opposing patterns, because he holds his hand out to me. The one that's been my stress ball for the past thirty minutes. "I'm not kidding. But it's nice to finally meet you—"

"Do you know," I push through gritted teeth, "how many

fucking months you shaved off my life with that revision process you put me through?"

I press my fingers against my forehead. As if on cue, the nervous twitch that has haunted my eyebrow for the last three months is back. Although we've been at each other's throats about our work for the past four years, his most recent review of my research took it a step too far. Not only was it hypercritical of every last detail, but also filled to the brim with snide remarks, like he truly wanted to tear me down.

Lewis drops his hand and with it, his pretense of friendliness. A challenging gleam enters his eyes. "How do you know it was me? Peer reviews are anonymous."

"Oh please. 'Before resubmission I would advise a more thorough understanding of the references mentioned,'" I quote him. "'Particularly North et al., *Science*, and North and Chaudhury, *PLOS Biology*.' Those comments were reeking of you."

Unfazed, he opens his laptop. "It's generally advisable to know your sources," he notes. It drives me mad that he's not admitting to writing the review, especially because this one was so much harsher than all the ones he wrote for my previous papers.

"I know my sources well, thank you very much," I retort. "You were just begging me to cite you some more."

"Knowing you, that reviewer probably improved your paper. You have a tendency to exaggerate the implications of your findings, which only undermines your research."

"Are you calling me flashy again?"

"No." A corner of his mouth turns down, as if he's tasted something sour. "But you don't need to sell your results like that."

Heat shoots up my torso and burns over my collarbone all the way to my cheeks. "That's how scientific publishing works!" He ignores me as he navigates through the files on his laptop.

"Nobody cares about your meticulously designed experiments if you don't have a story to tell."

Eyes firmly fixed on the screen, he juts out his jaw. "If you want to tell stories, maybe you should write a book."

"Well, good luck with your abstract then," I snap.

Scratch my earlier evaluation of him. He's prickly, and much worse in person. I cross my arms in front of my chest, bumping my elbow into his side.

"How are things going? Are we making any progress here?" At the quippy tone, our heads whip around. The flight attendant is back, waving a paper flyer in Lewis's direction. "I thought you might need the info for the in-flight Wi-Fi."

"It's going swimmingly. Thank you so much." He beams at her, and in the blink of an eye, friendly Lewis is back.

"We're going to serve the food soon. Do you maybe want yours later? After your deadline?"

Once he's assured her that *yes*, he'll let her know if he has a problem logging into the Wi-Fi, and *yes*, we would be grateful if they'd serve our food last, the flight attendant flutters her fingers at him and walks away.

"If you need someone to type for you, she'd probably be happy to help," I comment as soon as she's out of earshot.

He throws me an icy look. "I'll be okay," he says and turns to his laptop, lowering the contrast all the way down so I can't make out anything on the screen.

Pulling on my headphones, I navigate through the in-flight entertainment system and settle on a movie about a linguist saving the world from an alien invasion.

But my focus drifts to Lewis's movements.

So this is what he looked like while typing out snide remarks about my choice of statistical test. Shoulders a little hunched, mouth tucked up like he's fully aware of his own ingenuity. Even his stupid hair, and that wayward curl in his forehead, is a major flex. After being confronted with the finished products of this laser focus for so many years, it's strange to see him in action. His fingers bounce off the keys, hitting the space bar with a little flourish that sends a spike of anger down my nerves.

"Shouldn't you be deleting words, not adding them?" I ask him drily, but he ignores me.

As I watch him, I get mad all over again. At him, at myself, and how naive I'd been, four years ago, when I mistook our email exchange as a discussion between like-minded colleagues and didn't understand it for what it really was: a competitor looking out for himself, grabbing for those valuable publications that would increase his chances for future grants and eventually a professorship. I should've known better—it wasn't the first time this happened to me, after all.

The cooped-up space of the airplane is like a catalyzer for my anger and humiliation, and my nerve endings feel jittery, my face hot.

I jump up, eager to not let it overwhelm me. "Can you let me through?"

Lewis drags his thumb over his trackpad before he closes his laptop and gets up.

Slowly.

I swear this man breathes to provoke me.

Once I make it into the microscopic bathroom of the airplane, I splash my face with cold water. I'm not sure if it's the unflattering light in here or my tiredness, but I look washed-out. Frizzy white-blond hair in tight curls that would corkscrew down to my elbows if it weren't piled into a messy bun atop my head, gray eyes underlined by deep circles, and a tiny muscle in my left eyebrow that spasms every so often. Without my morning touch of mascara, my lashes are practically invisible, and my cheeks have lost their usual rosiness, leaving my face as pale as the rest of my body.

I look like the ghost of a mad scientist—if mad scientists were ever portrayed as female, that is.

As I stand there, a wobble underfoot has me grip the sink and reminds me of how far away I am from my tried and tested methods to calm my nerves. Some laps at the community pool, a few sets at the climbing gym. When I get this frazzled, anything that makes me feel the edges of my body helps, but up here, with Lewis out there, the Sawyer's ahead, and the reunion with Jacob looming, I need to steel my nerves some other way. I take deep breaths and try to focus on the reason I'm on this plane in the first place.

The Sawyer's Summer Seminars is a yearly event spanning all the scientific topics under the rainbow. It's organized by scientists for scientists, and with talks that are at the forefront of the field and networking events that bring together researchers across all generations, it's the type of academic gathering leading researchers look forward to even after decades of attending conferences—at least that's what the website says. There seems to be a grain of truth to it: I've seen colleagues return from previous installments not only with an enviable gleam of inspiration in their eyes, but also newly formed collaborations or invitations to job interviews.

The Sawyer's gets hosted by a different university every year, with topics varying according to the location. In my more than ten years of studying and then working as an academic, the Sawyer's has edged around my research interest, with topics that were adjacent but never close enough to my own focus to warrant an application. So when the email announcing a seminar on the neuroscience of memory as one of this summer's topics landed in my inbox before Christmas, it was like a dream come true. I had to close and open it twice, but when I finally believed my eyes, they registered the catch—Jacob was organizing it. It set up a whole new cycle of rereading the email and hoping I'd gotten something wrong. Because as much as I wanted to avoid Jacob, I knew I had to risk a shot at one of the limited spaces. A talk at the Sawyer's meant new ideas and having all these high-profile scientists from my field to network with. I couldn't pass it by.

As I rifle through my bag for eye drops, then lip balm, I try to remind myself of the resolve I felt when first applying. I yank the scrunchie out of my hair and pile my curls into a fresh bun, giving myself a little pep talk along the way. It's not that I've never dealt with asshole colleagues in my life, it's just that they've never been able to push all my buttons the way *he* does.

Back in our row, as I squeeze past him, Lewis hovers his hand over my shoulder, stress written all over his face.

"What?" When I scowl at him, his gaze darts away.

"I could actually use some help," he admits with a sigh. "Your help."

Huh. So much for laser focus.

"You're not afraid it will end up being too flashy?"

He frowns, as if those weren't literally the words he used to describe my work in his last review. Yet another quip I try to breathe through.

"As long as it's within the word limit," he tells me.

"Can I quote you on that? Print it out and hang it up in my office?"

He glares at me. "Will you help me or not?"

The satisfaction that he needs my help is almost enough to make me say yes. But not quite. No way am I going to let him take advantage of me again. "You didn't have the decency to credit me when I helped you back then," I point out, narrowing my eyes.

His mouth ties into a dissatisfied knot. "Do you want to be on the abstract?"

It needles me how the same person who just talked me

through my panic can say this so carelessly, as if he's joking about his action that brought on our rivalry. Even if being credited on a conference abstract for the minuscule help of cutting down on words is laughable, he's failed to credit me for my work before.

"No. But—" As I sit down, different options shoot through my head. Access to the data of that paper he published last spring, a truce on social media, a formal apology for what he did. But the truth is, I barely have enough time to analyze the data I've been collecting, and as annoying as our public discussions are, they put me and my papers on people's radar. As for the apology? He just showed how little he cares about his actions four years ago, so it's highly unlikely I'd get an apology even if I spelled it out for him. "I'm not sure yet. But you owe me one."

His eyes swivel to the corner of his screen and he grimaces as though he realizes how little time he has left until his deadline. "Alright," he finally agrees and angles his laptop so I can see the mess on his screen.

The flight attendant wasn't kidding: 1,045 words.

"Did you write this while you were asleep?" I scoff, skimming through the text.

"You're enjoying this, aren't you?" he grumbles.

"Why all of these details?" I highlight three sentences and delete them with a satisfying smack on the backspace key. Lewis's fingers twitch as if to restrain my hands. "Doesn't feel so great to have your work criticized, does it?"

"Without introducing this concept first, the rationale won't make any sense."

"Theodore—"

His gaze sharpens murderously. "Don't call me Theodore."

"What should I call you then?" I hiss out a laugh. "Your friends call you Lewis. Don't you think describing us as friends is a gross misinterpretation?"

"We can make an exception."

Lewis. The name gets stuck somewhere between my vocal cords and my lips. Lewis is the man who kindly let me squish his hand through a panic attack and who smells of pine needles and blushes easily. He of the incredible hair. Definitely not the person who pulled that stunt four years ago, and whose idea of a fun Saturday night is to tear apart every piece of work I produce in long threads that make me wonder if I'm cut out for this career.

Lewis. I try again.

Nope, not going to happen.

"Dr. North," I settle on instead, to which he turns his eyes to the ceiling. "In its current form, nothing in your abstract makes sense. Save all those things you have to say for your lecture."

"I know what an abstract is and isn't supposed to do."

"Well *duh*, Dr. *Nature Neuroscience*. But this abstract is too long, and it needs to be accepted first. And for that we'll need to spin it into a nice little story." I smile sweetly.

"Jesus." He winces, pinching the bridge of his nose. I pull two sentences into one, then condense an entire paragraph into a relative clause. Next to me, Lewis takes a deep breath. "Fine. Do whatever you need to do."

Forty-five minutes later, with three minutes to spare, Lewis uploads his abstract, now at 498 words—499, if you count hyphenated words as two. Now that we've finally stopped arguing about whether he violated one of the commandments of science (correlation is not causation), the hum of the airplane seems quiet.

Lewis slips his laptop into his backpack, folds up his table, and reaches up to fiddle with the controls of the AC outlets. This close, I notice the curve of his biceps and my fingers twitch as if remembering the firmness from accidentally touching it earlier.

"Wake me up if there's turbulence," he tells me, sinking against the headrest. It takes me by surprise, how he has slipped back into this thoughtful version of himself—which is inconveniently also the one that slowly chips away at my base of anger and frustration.

His eyes look droopy, like he can barely keep himself awake, but only when I nod does he blink them shut.

How is it that only a few hours ago I was racing to catch this flight, and now I've worked with my competitor and get to watch him sleep, after hand-holding and entrusting him with my deepest vulnerabilities?

A blush climbs into my cheeks as I tear my gaze away from the softened expression on his sleeping face. I pick at my veggie stir-fry and distract myself with the movie playing on my screen, but I'm still mortified about the fast-track intimacy with Lewis when another bout of baby turbulence hits, so I take deep breaths on my own and let him sleep.

At the airport, Lewis gives me a micro-nod when we get off the plane and I lose sight of him when I queue for immigration. I'm relieved to have him out of my sight, but the confusion about our encounter dominates my thoughts. With my passport freshly stamped, I wait for the air train as I activate my international data plan and scroll through my contacts until I find Karo; her picture showing a white beach and sparkling blue sea in the background, smiling gray eyes, and curly hair in the red dye she's been using since she was nineteen. I snapped the photo on St. Lucia thirteen months ago. Our last holiday together, between dreamy beaches, seafood buffets, and refills of rum. Or, in my case, fresh coconut water because

I'd get up early the next morning to draft the paper I was writing at the time.

A paper Lewis no doubt thinks is *flashy*.

My brain has been looping over the ways I could summarize this strange flight to her, yet all I get out when she picks up the phone is, "I ran into *him*."

"Who?"

The train rumbles onto the platform and when the doors open, I push my suitcase into a car that's already occupied by a woman with a stroller and a man in a suit. I switch to our native German whenever I talk to my sister, though English terms for words spanning the scientific and academic realm remain pebbled throughout.

"Academic enemy number one," I clarify. "The one I complain to you about, like, every other week. My reviewer two."

The latter is probably the most useless descriptor to my nonacademic sister, who, unlike me, hasn't gone through the peer-review process more than twenty times thus far. Whenever I submit papers for consideration to a journal, other experts in my field evaluate the quality of the work to judge whether it's worthy of publication. There's always one who errs a little too far on the side of nitpicky and rude, and although the reviews are anonymous, I know that in the review process of my last paper it was Dr. North—Lewis—who pointed out all the shortcomings with an extra pizzazz of snark. Sometimes, the words "uninspired and lacking any substantial contribution to the field" still echo through my dreams at night.

And that's not even the worst of what he did.

His snotty review comments are just the cherry on top of the pie. The base is a chunky layer of anger and resentment that formed after he failed to credit me on a paper I helped him with four years ago.

"*Oh.* That guy!" My sister's voice grounds me in ways only

few other things can. A neat line of code, an empty lane in the swimming pool, a warm, perfectly pressured shower after a long day in the lab. I saw her this morning, but it feels like a lifetime ago. The turbulence has shaken up something in me, and meeting Lewis has, too. "What was his name again? Theodore . . . West?"

"North," I say before she rattles off any other cardinal points. "Anyway, we sat next to each other on the flight."

"Oooh," Karo coos right as I hear something clanging in the background. "Goddammit. I'm kind of busy packing. But I can talk to you while I finish."

"When's your flight?"

"Tomorrow morning. And I can't find Lennart's stupid sleeping bag. Anyway, go on, I'm listening."

"Well, I had to sit next to him, for seven hours. Ended up helping him with his abstract, even though I probably shouldn't have, with how he made my work hell these past months. Or years, really."

"You work too much," is all my sister has to say about that. She's right, but how else am I going to solve the puzzle—or at least a tiny piece of it—of how our memory works? I've been sifting through the pieces for so many years that I'm not going to stop now. Even if it means moving every two years, skipping dates because I had a breakthrough in my analysis, and taking my laptop with me wherever I go. She knows why it's so important to me.

The air train pulls into the next terminal. I squeeze into a corner of the car as a family with three blond children gets on, and I watch the youngest of the kids drive his palm-size toy car up and down a metal pole, over my knee and his brother's back.

"Not *on people*, Damian." His mother makes a desperate grab for his T-shirt.

I cup a hand around the mic of my phone to shield off their voices, pressing the phone closer to my ear, to hear Karo ask, "What's he like in person?"

Lewis's annoyingly attractive face pops up before my eyes, while the feeling of his hand between mine ghosts over my somatosensory cortex. I push them aside. "As expected."

It's a lie so blatant that I'm happy the older kid in the family decides to rip the car out of his brother's hands. Damian's ensuing screech and the scolding by their mother makes it impossible to carry on with the conversation, so I tell Karo to call me when she's landed in California for her honeymoon before we hang up.

Hours later, as I ride the train into the city, drag my suitcase through Penn Station and onto the subway uptown, my cheeks still heat up over Lewis's unexpected kindness, when he was just a stranger on a transatlantic flight.

I knew Dr. Theodore L. North and I were bound to meet at some point, but I'd never thought it would happen like this. In a lecture hall maybe, in a symposium at the Sawyer's, where we'd argue about science and exchange a tense handshake after, glad to go our separate ways. Not on an airplane, where panic made me frazzled and he was the only one with the instruction manual to slow my racing heart.

I'm not sure what's more disconcerting: that I'd let someone in in the first place, or that it was Lewis who'd pulled down my walls with patience and empathy, making me question why I didn't open up more often. He listened and cared, coaxed me into breathing normally. Even his voice, warm and deep, was hard to reconcile with the clipped tone in his emails.

He was *nice*.

And I don't know what to make of that.

Chapter Three

My drive to understand human memory goes all the way back to a ski trip my family went on during my senior year of high school, when a snowboarder drove into Karo. Although her concussion was minor and she was otherwise fine enough to be released from the hospital after a few days, her memory got wonky. We would sit with her and recount the accident, but her memory reset whenever we left the hospital room. I'd get back with a glass of water, a bag of chips, or after a visit to the bathroom, and she'd be confused about who I was and why she was stuck in a hospital bed. It was scary, disconcerting, and worrisome—until I started looking into it back home, on the bulky desktop computer we shared as a family.

Googling concussions brought me to amnesia, to a structure in the brain called the hippocampus. I didn't get half of what I was reading, but I was eager to understand everything, even after Karo recovered. So instead of studying computer science in college, like I'd planned to, I applied for psychology with a minor in computer science. Undergrad taught me that despite decades of advances in uncovering the mechanisms of the brain, we still couldn't draw clear conclusions about how any of these structures *really* worked. More studies were needed. Neuroscience was lagging behind the older sciences like physics and chemistry and it didn't have the clarity of medicine. As a species we'd been on the moon, but we didn't understand the tiny universe right inside our skulls. Over and over again, I read about how future research should study this and examine that, and I decided then that I would be the one to fill these gaps in knowledge. At this point, Karo had long recovered from her temporary amnesia, but I knew there were countless people who weren't as lucky.

Helping those people became my objective. To get there, I studied harder, went for a semester abroad to Edinburgh, landed a summer placement in Denmark, and finally asked two professors to write me outstanding recommendation letters, which got me an international grant for grad school in the States. Now, my battered suitcase carries stickers of all my stops from the past decade: six years of grad school at Columbia, a postdoc in Zurich for eighteen months, then a year in Singapore, six months at my old lab in Denmark, a year in Phoenix, and then another in the Netherlands.

Thanks to the unstable funding academia is based on, I've completed more international moves than first dates. It's not just that dating is hard, but even friendships are hard to build if your time in a place has a clear expiration date from the get-go, determined by the local funding agency or the fixed-term contract of your university. Add to that a research question so compelling that it blurs the boundaries of my workday and consumes my weekends more often than not, and maintaining those relationships becomes almost impossible. The few friendships I've managed to sustain are with other researchers—those I can count on running into at various conferences throughout the year, those who understand what it's like.

I've forgotten how much New York feels like home. But just like back then, the city welcomes me in a hot and humid embrace. After I drop off my luggage at the studio I rented in Morningside Heights, I head to Broadway and queue at one of the bagel places that kept me fed throughout grad school. Equipped with an iced coffee and a bagel, I walk around the neighborhood, sun-dried tomato cream cheese melting onto my hands as the sights, scents, and sounds bring me back to being an underpaid grad student in one of the most expensive cities in the world.

Five years. I've been gone nearly as long as I lived here, but suddenly the time away feels like the blink of an eye.

There's the building that I had my first apartment viewing in, only to realize that I wasn't earning enough to even be considered for the lease. The musty smell coming from the street drain reminds me of the summer I wrote my first publication, sucking on ice cubes and frozen raspberries to cool down. The bar where I had my first date in the city has been replaced by an Italian restaurant, though the laundromat where I cried for a full wash-and-dry cycle after my breakup with Jacob still exists.

So many things have changed, and yet one thing is the same. I'm still fending for myself and flailing to find a lab I can stay in permanently. Constantly surrounded by the politics of academia and now with memories of Jacob sprouting up, it's hard to remind myself of all the progress I've made: ideas and what-ifs that were a faraway dream when I left five years ago, now implemented into neat experiments and algorithms that have gotten me—and the research community—a fraction of a step closer to understanding human memory.

It should be enough. In an ideal world, one where I'd have a secure position, I'd continue plugging away at the question that lies at the core of it all and be happy about each tiny grain of knowledge, but in reality? I spend a lot of time fighting for the money that is necessary to make leaps in understanding. In the hierarchy of academia, some people, like Jacob, end up at the top, with tenure and a name that almost guarantees getting more funding to finance their research in the future, but as much as I code and solve and explain, my name is far from being recognizable. Which means that job security is still far out of reach.

With my pending grant and the opportunity that participating in the Sawyer's brings, I'm hoping to level up soon. I just need Dr. Theodore L. North to stay out of my way.

I pick up groceries on the way home, then spend the rest of the day unpacking and catching up with emails I missed in the lead-up to Karo's wedding until jet lag knocks me to sleep. The next day, a Sunday, I prepare my materials for the workshop I'm giving at the Sawyer's and unwind with a long rock-climbing session before I head to attendee registration at Columbia. My rental is only a few blocks away from the Morningside campus, but when I arrive, the sun has drawn sweat to my skin. The campus is busy, white tents with registration booths for the students pebbling the green and flocks of Sawyer's students milling down the paths. As I walk between the imposing buildings, I rein in my mind from dousing itself in memories from my time here. But motor memory kicks in and guides me to Schermerhorn Hall, home of the psychology department. Empty corridors and closed doors greet me at the department, including the one reading *Prof. Dr. Jacob Bellingham*.

Of course, he's not here. He wouldn't lower himself to do the work of his secretary. Relieved to have one more day to pump my confidence before seeing him, I try the secretary's door at the end of the corridor again. It's locked, despite the email on my phone saying attendee registration would be open from 11:00 a.m. to 6:00 p.m.

Resigned to wait, I slump against the wall and open social media. It's been a few days since I logged on, with Karo's wedding keeping me busy and the surprise encounter with Dr. North—Lewis, whatever—making me avoid my phone. I couldn't stomach scrolling through the platform and seeing another cheerful *happy to share our new paper on effects of brain stimulation on spatial navigation skills*, cementing the point that everyone around me is Discovering Things and Proudly Contributing to Science.

Given my inactivity, the quantity of notifications surprises me. But then I see who they're from; the profile picture of a mountain landscape with a man facing away from the camera and the username @theoretically. Just as he informed me on the flight, Lewis has mentioned me in a post, uploaded two days ago.

I'm puzzling through his arguments against the implications I drew in my last paper when a shadow falls over my screen. Gray suede sneakers with a green stripe at the edge of my view, an inconveniently pleasant pine scent.

"Dr. Silberstein."

"Dr. North," I murmur without looking up. "You've had, what, five hours to sign up and yet you show up when I'm here. Did you miss me?"

"So much. I've been dying to see your scowl ever since we got off the plane yesterday," he shoots back as he looms over me and my phone. A smirk appears on his face when he registers what I've been reading. "Don't let me interrupt you."

"You're good. I was just standing here, being unimpressed."

He steps around me and props his shoulder against the wall, his hair, once again, falling perfectly. "You don't look unimpressed. You look angry."

I glare at him. "I do, because you're putting words into my mouth. All this text, and it's just random pieces of information that supposedly provide evidence against statements I supposedly made in the paper."

"Supposedly, huh?" he echoes. It's only been a day since we arrived, but his accent is thicker now, all vowels leaning into *a*s. "Sounds like you're not very good at taking criticism."

I'm not, but that's not the point.

"If it was actual criticism, then fine. But you're arguing against things I never wrote. I don't know where you got this from." I zoom in and highlight the sentence that gave my pulse a jump start. "Here. Would you please enlighten me on where I claim that we found evidence for memory replay using fMRI?"

"Gladly." His voice is infuriatingly unfazed as he pulls his phone out of the pocket of his navy shorts. How can he stay so calm? After seeing him blush over the smallest things on the plane yesterday, this surprises me. Is it only me who gets worked up when discussing science, or is he simply better at not showing it?

After a moment of tapping around on his screen, he zooms in on something and says, "*This* is what I mean." He turns the phone around for me to see and I reach for it, but he lets go too soon, and it slides out of his fingers. I lower my hand in a desperate attempt to stop it from shattering on the ground.

"Got it," I yelp. But it seems he has, too, because his hand is suddenly wrapped around mine. We both freeze. The calluses on the pads of his fingers and the strength of his grip transport me back to yesterday. The flight, turbulence shaking us, his skin warm on mine. I lift my gaze to find him looking back at me, the sharp focus in his eyes replaced by something else. Something softer. Something that makes my throat so parched that I need to swallow. He tracks the movement as his hand tightens around mine, and it sends prickles shooting up my arm and blooming in my rib cage.

"I—" I start without knowing where this sentence is supposed to lead.

What were we talking about again? My phonological loop has been swept empty. The corridor, the Sawyer's sign-up, and whatever we were arguing about retreat to the background, put on standby by the blue of his eyes, and the memory of whispered words of kindness on a transatlantic flight.

I'm still looking into his eyes when the stab of heels echoing farther down the corridor yanks me back to reality. "Hi there! I'm so sorry you had to wait." The voice is high pitched and has a slight accent that I can't pinpoint. I manage to drag my gaze away from Lewis and spot a slender woman wearing a dark green satin skirt and white blouse. About half a head shorter than me, she has curly black hair that is swept back and pinned at the nape of her neck. As she comes to a stop in front of us, her dark brown eyes dance over me, then Lewis, and finally come to rest on our clasped hands.

Her eyebrows inch up in surprise. "Ah, but at least you didn't have to wait alone," she notes, the smile on her face deepening.

Lewis seems to regain control of his body first, and pushes off the wall, then drops my hand as a blush creeps up his cheeks.

Even then, my fingers still tingle from his touch, but I shove the sensation aside. I smile at the unknown woman, ready to tell her that the hand-holding was a consequence of trying to save his phone. "Hi, I'm—"

"You're Frances!" she exclaims, and foregoes my outstretched hand, pulling me in to kiss the air next to my right and left cheeks. Awkwardly, I pat her shoulder. Who is she? Was she in my grad school cohort? I don't remember anybody dressed so elegantly, except for that one computer scientist who'd come in wearing suits. The rest of us traded personal style for maximum comfort: hoodies, flip-flops, leggings, washed-out tees, oversize shirts. Anything that was loose enough to not remind us of our bodies while we got into the workflow.

When she releases me, she shakes Lewis's hand and I watch as he introduces himself as Theodore "but please call me Lewis" North.

"It's so very nice to meet you. I'm Vivienne. Vivienne Duchamps," she introduces herself, her French accent fully coming through now. Her name gives me a much-needed lightbulb moment. She's a postdoc in Jacob's lab, the one who sent most of the Sawyer's emails, but I'm not sure why she recognized me so quickly. "I've heard so much about you, Frances."

Her easy familiarity confuses me. "Oh, from who?" I ask.

"Jacob," Vivienne says casually before dipping into the secretary's office, as if she hasn't frozen me in place with one word. When she emerges with a stack of papers, she motions for us to follow her down the corridor. "I'm so sorry again that you had to wait. Regina, our secretary, had to leave early because of a family emergency, and then there was maintenance on the 1, so it took me a little while. I hope you haven't been waiting for long. I'll do the sign-in for you," she says, a few paces ahead already, "and we'll have you out of here in no time to enjoy the rest of your evening. Did you have a good flight?"

"Turbulent," I answer at the same time as Lewis pipes in, "We made it work."

Vivienne throws us a look over her shoulder, lifting her eyebrows. "Are you familiar with New York, Lewis? I know Frances knows it well."

Oh?

"I was born and raised here," Lewis replies as I try my hardest to figure out why Jacob talks about me to some random postdoc.

"Wow!" she says cheerfully. "Well, I'm glad this trip has given you an excuse to get a family visit in, too."

Lewis murmurs a noncommittal, "Hmm."

Inside what I assume is her office, Vivienne points to the round table in the left corner with four chairs around it, and suggests, "Why don't you sit down while I get everything together."

Vivienne's is like any textbook academic office: crammed bookshelves, department-issued desk pushed against the window, and two large monitors, one of which is turned to vertical for better code visibility. Unlike my desk, though, Vivienne's is organized and clean: no discarded coffee mugs, no Post-its strewn around, and no mess of papers containing everything from student reports to printouts of scientific articles. Instead, there are two wooden paper trays, neatly stacked on top of each other. As I look around, I'm surprised she gets an office to herself as a postdoc—usually this honor is limited to more senior researchers. I'm on my way to perch against the lip of the table when Lewis pulls out a chair for me.

"Here are the flyers that include the program for the next two weeks, the contact information from us organizers and all the speakers' information. You already received your time slots via email, right?" She hands each of us a brochure, waiting for our respective nods, before continuing, "You're, of course, welcome to join any of the other program points, except for the wet lab–based practicals. Those have limited capacity." She taps on the page Lewis has opened, where it says *Neuroanatomy*.

She shifts her neatly manicured index finger to the program point reading *Using Virtual Reality for Human Memory Research*—the workshop I'll be giving—and adds, "In the computer lab classes there should be enough space."

Lewis flicks up his eyebrows at me. I'll personally see to it that there won't be enough space for him to join my class.

The first week of the Sawyer's Summer Seminars tends to be geared toward the younger cohort, with students joining workshops and small panel discussions, often led by early career researchers, like Lewis and me. Then, toward the end of the first or beginning of the second week, the big names will arrive to present their newest cutting-edge research.

"The official program will start tomorrow at 8:30 a.m. with the welcoming lecture. I suppose you'll be staying for the full two weeks since you're both leading sessions on the last day," Vivienne guesses and we both nod as she stacks more items on the table. A sheet of paper, a laminated badge, a lanyard sporting both Columbia's and Sawyer's logos for each of us. "These are your visitor passes. And here's a map of the campus, though you probably won't need that, Frances."

I want to know why Vivienne knows so much about me when she's just working for Jacob. It's not like I've told any of my colleagues about him, not even the ones I grab a drink with after work or travel to conferences with. In fact, the only people who know about him are my family and, thanks to my moment of vulnerability on the plane, Lewis. Perhaps in the future I'll tell a boyfriend about Jacob, but at this point it seems unlikely given how low dating ranks on my to-do list.

My stomach drops.

Dating, past relationships. Could Vivienne and Jacob . . . The thought is so jarring it's hard to finish it even in the confines of my brain. Could she be more than just his postdoc? More than a friend?

I zone back in to the conversation when Vivienne finishes with, "I think that covers everything for now. Do you have any questions?"

I do, but none of them are related to the Sawyer's program. Like, why is Jacob in a relationship with someone from his lab again? Someone working *for* him, no less. Did our breakup teach him nothing? *Do you know what you're getting into*, I want to ask her, *by dating your boss?* I hope Jacob doesn't take her for granted the way he did me. I hope she doesn't put all her brilliant brain cells to an end goal that will serve only him.

She claps her hands together. "And that's it for the official details."

Thank god we're done here. I need to get out of this room so I can process this new worst-case scenario, the one my brain couldn't even fathom when picturing this trip.

Dropping the stack of materials into my bag, I lift the corners of my mouth into a smile. "It's all pretty clear," I say, "thank you for checking us in."

Lewis zips his backpack shut. "Yes, thank you so much."

"Of course," Vivienne chimes and we all stand up. But instead of saying her goodbyes, she blurts out, "Oh, one more thing." Her eyebrows draw together, and as she fumbles with something on her left hand, she opens her mouth, as if to talk, then closes it again. "Jacob and I are hosting a dinner tomorrow at our home," she finally says. "It's not included in the program, because it's an informal event for all speakers, but we'd love to see you there. We'll email all the details sometime tonight."

Dinner? At *their* home?

Her words confirm my suspicion. There is no way that they're living together as friends. Not when I know that Jacob has always despised roommates and could afford his own two-bedroom even back when he was a postdoc, thanks to his family money. But this also means that Jacob and Vivienne aren't only dating—they're serious enough to have moved in together.

"Sounds great," I bring out and press my hands into my thighs, palms suddenly damp with sweat as I track the million details of her that exude elegance and put-togetherness and maturity. The subtle and symmetrical eyeliner, the whiff of cologne that's flowery but not too sweet, the fact that she's co-organized something as huge as the Sawyer's, and is now calmly telling her boyfriend's ex about their relationship.

I know I'm not competing with Vivienne. I don't want Jacob, not anymore, and won't gain anything if I hate her out of pettiness. But it still hurts, seeing how he's come out of our breakup unscathed and not only built a successful lab but replaced me with someone better, too.

"Sure." Lewis's voice sounds far away, drowned out by the rush of my blood. "Thank you for inviting us."

Vivienne says something that I barely register, something about wanting to talk to me and something she needs to get over with, and then she waves her hand through the air, only to catch it in front of her again and that's when I see what she's been fumbling around with all this time.

There's a ring on her finger, one with a fine diamond that catches the sunlight slanting in through the windows. One she starts twirling again, and before she even opens her mouth, I know what's about to happen.

"Jacob and I—we're engaged," she says, her tone hesitant despite the smile blooming on her face.

Something feels phenomenally off.

I try to breathe past the dizzying hurt stabbing at my lungs, but oxygen has gotten rare in this room, and my pulse shows no signs of slowing down. Like on the plane, except now I know I'm not objectively in any danger. I'm in an office with my academic rival and my ex's fiancée, not a metal can that could fall out of the sky at any moment.

And yet lights flash in my brain telling me to get out of this room *now*.

I'm frozen as they both look at me, Vivienne expectantly, Lewis with an expression I can't quite read, but softer than a moment ago. Like, he's sorry? I don't need him to feel sorry for me. There's nothing to feel sorry about.

Wiping my clammy hands against my jeans, I force my vocal cords into action, yet all they manage to croak out is a weak, "Um."

Fuck, I didn't know my heart could even beat this fast.

I'm contemplating how I'm going to finish that sentence when of all people, Lewis comes to my rescue. He steps around his chair to stand closer at my side, and when his fingers graze against mine, I grab his hand, desperate for a tether to reality.

"Congratulations. We have to check if we're free tomorrow, but thank you for inviting us," he says, keeping his eyes on her face as he squeezes my hand. His words from the plane come back to me, a quiet and reassuring *breathe with me*, and I focus on counting the ins and outs of my breath while pretending Vivienne's news hasn't just shaken me to my core. Though my pulse keeps thudding maddeningly, my inhale for two, exhale for four has finally channeled enough oxygen to my brain to attempt stringing a few words together without sounding completely out of breath, and I bring out a low, "I'm so happy for you."

My response seems to be convincing enough to Vivienne, because relief settles on her face as she crosses the room toward us. "Please, if there's anything I can do, let me know. I was really excited to meet you and now that you're here—well, I hope we'll have some opportunities to talk. If you would like that, too, of course."

I'm so focused on masking the panic that has whirred my organs into chaos that I barely listen to what she's saying, instead taking the path of least resistance by nodding along. I hope that whatever is happening on my face resembles a convincing smile. "Sure."

Lewis clears his throat, and as he steps toward the door, he pulls me with him. "We need to get going."

"Of course!" Vivienne rushes to say. "You must be jet-lagged. I'll see you tomorrow—if not at the conference, then at dinner." She squeezes my shoulder in goodbye and when she looks at our joined hands, she gets the same expression as when she spotted us outside her office, the lines around her eyes crinkling with the depth of her smile. Then she gives me a conspiratorial wink. "Frances, I'm so glad we finally got to meet. It makes me feel better, knowing you won't be coming alone tomorrow, but in the company of someone as lovely as Lewis."

My body still on autopilot with the only goal of finally getting me out of this room, I do my nod and smile again, and even manage a weak-sounding "Yeah."

Then, Lewis tugs me out of the office and pulls the door shut behind us.

Chapter Four

Jacob and I started dating well into my second year of grad school. He was a postdoc in the same group, and though we worked on different projects, I'd sat across from him for many lab meetings and admired him from afar for publishing papers in the big journals and seemingly running the lab whenever our advisor was traveling. But one evening, I ran into him as I was catching up with paperwork for a study. He'd stayed in the lab late to test out new equipment, and took pity on me, asking me to grab a bite for dinner.

What started with me complaining and Jacob giving me advice soon became a tentative friendship over a shared love for the grilled cheese sandwiches in the deli around the corner. At first, we didn't act on the attraction between us, but then, after weeks of talking in and out of the lab, and finding excuses to spend time together in the evenings and on weekends, it bloomed into full-on love.

Where I used to rarely come up for air from my research and only quickly catch up with fellow grad students, my time at the lab morphed to a companionship of two. I'd drop by Jacob's office to steal a kiss after TAing, share glances with him during lab meetings, or stroll with him across campus to pick up a triple-shot latte at the coffee cart on Broadway that would snap me into the focus needed for my data analysis.

As a second-year PhD student struggling with my place in the world of elite academics, Jacob drew me in with his easy confidence. He wasn't stingy with it but extended it generously, handing out the compliments I was so eager for. After being at the top of my class in undergrad, my confidence had plunged when I got into grad school, where I met the limits of my knowledge and capacity daily. I was far from home in a new, loud, and busy city. I wasn't the only one—several students in my cohort quickly dropped out, spiraling into anxiety and self-doubts. But in the crowd of postdocs and professors with their paradigm-shifting papers and opinionated social media posts, Jacob's trust in me was soothing. Not only did he see the person and scientist I yearned to become, but he also inspired me with the high expectations he set for himself and everybody else around him.

The intellectual and supportive bubble of our relationship made it easy for me to ignore the double standards we were being held to: the interns who whispered behind my back but not his, the sly looks I got from professors at conferences while he was being congratulated for his newest achievements, the comment I got from another grad student that my paper had only been accepted by a prestigious journal because of Jacob's name on it.

But through it all, I held steadfast to the belief that their view of our relationship was wrong. Nobody was *taking* anything, advantage or otherwise. We were only adding, giving so we could both grow into the best versions of ourselves. Long days at the lab were bookended by nights helping him out with the grant that would go on to get him his professorship. Dinners would get swallowed up by discussions to strengthen his proposal. On weekends, I'd find pockets of time between my own research to transform his ideas into clear, colorful figures. I was all in, helping him pave the way to his future. I thought he'd be willing to pave mine, too, if I ever needed his help.

I thought that this was what romance between scientists looked like.

It was only when he got the grant and explained how he had neatly slotted me into his future that I understood he'd taken me for granted. Between the shelves of all-purpose flour and maple syrup at Trader Joe's, he told me how perfectly I fit into his plans. According to him, it was a win-win situation. He'd hire me as a postdoc once I graduated, so we could stay together, and he'd get a computational neuroscientist in his lab that he trusted. Job security fresh out of grad school, *Isn't that what you wanted?*

Except, no. I did not.

I wanted to find my own path in life and identify the gap in knowledge that *I* could fill. To change some tiny thing in this world, to be the one flipping a switch from *unknown* to understanding.

Not with Jacob or for Jacob.

For myself.

When I suggested doing long distance so I could build my own career, he called me selfish and egotistical. Naive for thinking I could make it in science, with the small number of publications tacked to my name.

Job change after job change, and rejected grant after rejected grant, I told myself that he was wrong. That I had what it took, and that the last thing I needed was a man by my side to get there.

Except, maybe all that confidence was just a shell to hide behind.

Maybe I've been wrong all this time. Maybe Jacob was right, and I really don't have what it takes. The thought spins around and around in my brain while my lungs work overtime.

Because I'm still as unsuccessful and alone as Jacob predicted, while he has moved on big-time. I'm miles behind where I thought I would be, pushed to the sidelines and watching everyone else race ahead while my feet are stuck to the ground.

Outside, on the corridor in front of Vivienne's office, Lewis looks at me, dumbfounded. I stare back, my heart tumbling over itself and skin slick with heat while I tell myself to breathe.

Instead of ripping his hand away like I expected him to, Lewis ducks his head lower to match my eye level. "Frances?"

"Something . . . I . . . Something's wrong," I stammer, guiding his hand up to where my heart is *this* close to sprinting out of my sternum. He flattens his palm over it, as if to catch it. When my own hands drift back to my sides, they're trembling.

"Are you in pain?" he says, voice low but urgent, and I manage to shake my head.

"Okay." He swallows as his eyes flick between mine, down to my hands, and up again. "If you're not in pain, you might be having a panic attack."

Over something like my ex being engaged? Something that should be insignificant? The way I'm taking the news makes me feel even *more* inferior—

"Frances, come back here," Lewis orders gently. "Let's try to get you out of your head. You're breathing, that's good. Keep doing that but, hey, look at me." He takes an exaggerated deep inhale, then lets the air out again. "Slow it down."

I cling to the sounds of his breaths as I watch his chest expand and deflate slowly, his thumb drawing grounding circles over the collar of my T-shirt. Whenever my mind drifts off, I tell myself to focus on the warmth of his hand, the prick of air against my nostrils.

Lewis stands by me silently as I ride out the tail end of my panic. I'm not sure how long it takes, but gradually my breaths even out, and my pulse slows, leaving my ears to pick up the chatter of students drifting in from outside, the sound of a keyboard from Vivienne's office, and the creak of a door somewhere in the building.

"I think I'm okay now," I finally whisper, using the heel of my hand to wipe the sweat off my forehead.

"Are you sure?" Lewis scans my face, as if to check for himself, before he moves his hand away from my breastbone. "Have you gone through something like this before?" he probes, worried.

"I haven't. Except maybe on the plane yesterday? But I'm okay now." I gulp, and when I realize that he's become my human comfort blanket for the second time in just as many days, a blush heats up my cheeks. "Thank you."

"You're welcome," he mutters. "Can I get you anything? Some water? Do you want to sit down?"

"No, I'm good—I brought my own." I dig through my bag for the bottle of water I carry everywhere.

"Are you sure you're okay?" he asks as he observes my every movement.

"Yeah. I'll just have a sip." I give him a brief smile, hoping it convincingly portrays that I'm fine. I'm mid-swig when my capacity for rational thought returns, and I finally absorb what just happened.

What I just did.

Because it sounded like Vivienne thinks Lewis is my boyfriend. And, instead of clearing up the misconception, I seem to have confirmed it.

My eyes widen. "Did I just . . ."

"Yep," he confirms, popping the *p*.

"Shit," I say under my breath, then look up at Lewis. Anger brews in the dark of his eyes, the depth of his frown and the twitch in his jaw.

The human brain is a mysterious, awe-inspiring organ, really, because mine makes a split-second decision and rattles off motor commands to the muscles in my limbs before I realize that Lewis has just uttered the words "So now that you're okay, let's talk about—" much too loud and echoing for this awfully empty corridor. But at that point I've already clamped my hand over his mouth and pushed him toward the staircase, decidedly not willing to let Vivienne hear any discussion we're about to have.

When we've reached the stone plaza in front of Schermerhorn Hall, he shakes me off.

"What were you thinking?" His voice is quiet but deadly.

"What do you mean?" I ask, feigning nonchalance. With my two hemispheres exhausted from flashing danger at me *and* stuck processing the news about Jacob's engagement, I don't have much mind space to guess which particular part of this clusterfuck of a situation he means. Not to mention that minor part of my brain that is trying to build a true-to-life sensory memory of Lewis's soft lips against my fingers, the stubble of his jaw against my skin, the warmth of his thumb through the cotton of my T-shirt.

He dips his head toward the entrance. "First," he hisses, "that you basically told her we're a goddamn couple. Second, the way you brought me out of that building like a human trash bag." A strand of his hair comes loose and falls onto his forehead, interrupting the neat hairline. He pushes it back with a forceful movement, but it's this side of too short to be held behind his ear, tumbling forward again.

"It's not like I did it on purpose," I bite back. "I didn't know about them."

He grimaces, and some of the intensity in his eyes melts away. "It sucks to hear the news like that. I'm sorry."

I cross my arms in front of my body, the sudden warmth in his voice taking me by surprise. "Regarding your first complaint—I didn't *actually* say we were together. I just didn't correct her."

Lewis mirrors my pose, his stare turning unyielding again. "Seriously?" he calls out what might have been an excuse so flimsy it's practically see-through.

Internally, I wince. But I'm not ready to go into the full postmortem of what I did and why, embarrassed by how the looming reunion with Jacob seems to have turned my ego into a cardboard box labeled *Fragile*.

"I still don't get what gave her the idea that you're my boyfriend," I say, though I'm pretty sure I know what it was. Some weird brain glitch that made us hold on to his phone, and each other's hands, for longer than necessary. The same glitch that is now bringing back how he looked at me right after, his gaze open and—

Not the right moment.

"Right," he scoffs, catching my bluff.

"You're welcome for not having to buy a new phone," I grumble.

"I'll be in your debt forever, Dr. Silberstein." His tone is icy as he shifts his jaw. "The fact is, we were literally holding each other's hands when she walked up—and inside her office, too—and both of those instances have a clear, rational explanation. What doesn't, though, is you agreeing with her that we're together. Besides the fact that you hate me," he says and uncrosses his arms, "why would you do that?"

Because Jacob has always made me feel small, and I doubt

myself when I measure myself against him. Because we're not even playing in the same league of *Who's better off without their ex*. Because instead of landing a stable job and getting to do my research, I'll be unemployed soon, and my love life is so far off track it's not even worth mentioning. Because, with a panic-addled brain, all I could do to get out of that room was to switch into autopilot and go along with what Vivienne was saying.

Before I can try to explain, though, Lewis's phone starts ringing, saving me from admitting how much the news about Jacob and Vivienne has shaken me. "I have to take this," he says, frowning at the screen. "But we're not done here. I'm sorry about the position this puts you in, but first thing tomorrow, you need to tell her the truth." And with that, he disappears around the corner of the building, leaving me behind wondering what fresh hell I've gotten myself into.

Back home, I flip through the leaflet I got from Vivienne, until I get to page thirteen. Opposite Jacob's photo is the profile of Rosanna Alderkamp, PhD, Professor of Integrative Neuroscience at Amsterdam University. At barely forty years old (I may have checked her CV some years ago), she's the second youngest keynote speaker behind Jacob.

When her presence at the Sawyer's was announced, I knew I had to be a grown-up and apply despite Jacob organizing it—her research on memory was the reason I decided to go to grad school. Throughout the years, with every paper she's published and talk she's given, my admiration for her has only grown.

Rosanna Alderkamp is a powerhouse of a scientist, the kind I aspire to be. It's not only about how well recognized she is by the community or the lab equipment she has at her fingertips, but about how much she's contributed to the scientific field of memory. She is known for a meticulous but pragmatic approach that has improved diagnostics and symptom management in people with Alzheimer's or dementia.

It can't have been easy for her to become a professor at her age, and as a woman no less. Academic tenure is notoriously hard to get, and though wealth, confidence, luck, and a Y-chromosome help, there is no guarantee you'll ever get there. I'm sure she has her own list of wildly inappropriate behaviors she had to deal with, like advisors recommending her to freeze her eggs so she doesn't slow down her career. Sometimes I want to ask if her colleagues also thought her night shifts on a year-long project were only worth mentioning in the acknowledgments while the cocky intern got first authorship to help him with his PhD applications. Or if she, too, has worked in departments where she had to cross to the other side of the building to use the bathroom, because while scientific progress happened in these halls, they certainly weren't built for a societal one.

Point is, I would love to meet her and get to talk to her, about her research first and foremost, but her experiences in academia, too. It would be a dream come true if I could establish a connection with her so we can collaborate whenever I get my own grant.

But it dawns on me that I jeopardized that dream by lying to Vivienne.

Why, Frances. *Why?*

In the spur of the moment, all I could think of was fleeing that room before anybody could see how badly I was taking the news. But now she thinks Lewis and I are dating, and while it would be unpleasant to have Jacob know just how unsuccessful I am in both my love life and work, being deemed a liar by my colleagues would be detrimental to the career I've so painstakingly built. If Vivienne or Jacob—anybody, really—were to learn the truth, everybody else at the conference would find out soon after. It would tank my reputation. Worse, with attendants sitting on scientific editorial boards, hiring committees, and grant panels, I'd get skipped over for open lab positions and my research wouldn't get funded anymore.

My phone vibrates from where I tossed it onto the couch, giving me a short break from mentally kicking myself for my irrational behavior. Karo has messaged the family group chat that she and Lennart have landed safely in San Francisco, ready for their honeymoon to begin.

Finally. I flop onto the couch, tap her name, and press call. "I need your help."

Airport noises fill the other end of the line, a last call for a flight to Tulsa.

"Franzi, are you finally asking me for that list of beach reads I've been preparing for you every year?"

"Nope. But you're much better with social situations—"

Karo's laugh interrupts me. "May I remind you that I'd pick an evening with a book over any social outing anytime?"

"Yeah, but you're better at understanding people."

"Fair. We're on the way to pick up the rental car, so I don't have a lot of time," she informs me. "Wait, did you run into Jacob?"

"No, not yet. Thank god." I loosen my hair out of its bun and comb through it with my fingers. "But I need your advice on something."

"Okay, shoot." Karo doesn't even hesitate after years of operating as my second opinion on problems spanning the social, professional, and sometimes also academic realm. She's given me advice so many times that sometimes I forget I'm the older sister.

"How bad would it be if someone at your office mistakenly assumes you're together with your colleague . . . let's say the one with the pizza socks—"

I hear Lennart giving directions in the background. Then, Karo: "Adam?"

"Yes. That one. Let's say you didn't correct them, but agreed, thereby making it sound like you were together. But both Adam and you know it's not the truth and you don't even like Adam—you actually really, *really* dislike him—and now you need to explain to the people in your office that you're not together, even though you literally agreed that you were. What are the chances of others thinking you're unprofessional and a liar?"

For a moment, the line is silent. Then Karo asks, "Is that a trick question? Because we both know you're the numbers whiz, but it seems pretty obvious that the chances would be very high."

Well, isn't that great.

I squeeze my eyes shut. "I did something really stupid," I finally admit.

"Like making someone think you were dating a colleague of yours?"

"Precisely," I grumble, grinding my heel into the armrest of the couch. "She saw us holding hands—"

"You were holding hands?" Karo gasps. There's some commotion in the background, then I hear Lennart ask, "What, your sister?"

"We weren't holding hands," I correct. "She thought we were."

"Is he at least cute?"

"What?"

"Is he—"

"No, I heard what you said. Why on earth would that be relevant?"

"Well, if someone put me in a relationship with a rando, I'd hope they were cute. So. Is he?"

The moment that set off this terrible chain of events flits across my mind, Lewis's and my hands linked and our gazes locked for longer than any stranger can justify. From a scientific standpoint, purely objectively speaking that is, he does have his attributes. I guess with his swooping hair and those clear blue eyes, strong arms and bashful smile, you could even call him cute. Not that any of that matters, because, cute or not, he screwed me over four years ago, he continues to criticize my work, and he annoys the hell out of me just by existing.

"If you like constant fighting and know-it-alls, I guess you could call him cute."

"Sounds just like your type."

I groan. "You know, if you were standing next to me, I'd push you into the wall right about now. But really," I say, growing more somber by the second, "I don't know what to do."

"You could tell the truth?" Karo suggests over the noise of a car door shutting.

"I should." I sigh. "But lying is not just a bad character trait—for someone whose work is reason and figuring out the true mechanisms behind how the world works, it's the *worst* trait. Not to mention that the most important people from my field are at this conference. It's a small community, and word travels fast. I'd be judged big-time, something I absolutely cannot afford, especially now when my funding is running out." I rattle off the flowchart from bad decision to sudden career death that I've plotted out in my head. "I'm still waiting for the outcome on that big grant, and what I did doesn't exactly speak for my integrity—scientific or otherwise. I need my colleagues to know they can trust me, not to make them wonder what else I'd lie about."

"Crap, okay." Karo hums. "You're right, it doesn't sound like telling the truth is the best option." When she falls silent on the other end of the line, I get up and start pacing from the couch to the kitchen island. Illustrated postcards and photos from trips across the world are tacked to the sunflower-yellow kitchen cabinets. The studio I'm staying in is small but more welcoming than my place back in the Netherlands, where the rooms are empty save for the content of two suitcases, mismatched secondhand pottery, and the furniture that came disassembled and flat-packed from IKEA.

"What are the odds that this person didn't tell anybody else?" Karo pipes up. "That they ultimately don't care who you do or don't date?"

"Given that she's Jacob's fiancée," I say, "I'd gauge that those odds are pretty low."

"Oh, *Hasi*." Bunny. Her tone is soft, and I hate how small it makes me feel.

"She's really nice. Considerate. Wanted to tell me the news in person. Probably also extremely smart, otherwise she wouldn't be working for Jacob."

"Hold on, she works for him?"

"Yeah. It feels like déjà vu. Or more like an upgrade, really." I go on to tell her about Vivienne's invitation to dinner, which brings me back to the big question: What am I going to do?

"Well, you know there's always the option of fake dating," Karo shares offhandedly.

"There's what? Fake data?"

"No, don't worry." She laughs. "Nothing as bad as that. I said *fake dating*. It's a thing in romance novels. Or romantic comedies, for those of us who don't pick up books for fun."

I roll my eyes. Karo is a social media manager at a publishing company and likes to nag me to read more, but honestly, after spending my days with words like *hemodynamic* or *bootstrapping*, or *multivariate pattern analysis*, my concept of free time doesn't involve *more* words.

"I'm not following."

"Fake dating is something people do, for mutual benefits. So . . . famous people may do it for some media buzz, other people to get meddling relatives off their back, others to win back their exes—"

"I don't want to win him back," I interject.

"You don't?"

"I don't."

"Well thank god." She sighs. "I already thought Lennart and I would have to skip the road trip and stage an intervention. The guy was a dickhead."

"He was," I concur. "So. False dating."

"*Fake* dating. Yeah. It's a popular concept, though I've never met anybody who has fake dated in real life."

Outside, an ambulance drives by, and I wait until the howling siren fades into the distance. "But how do people do it?"

"It's as simple as it sounds. You make others believe you're in a relationship." The line crackles, like she's switching the phone from one ear to the other. "It has to be a mutual thing—you can't just tell people that you are in a relationship. The other person has to be in on it and you'd have to be seen together enough for people to believe it's true. We've established that he's cute, but how likely is it that he'd help you out?"

Not very. Lewis regularly makes it onto the list of people I want to throw my desk at. As kind as he seemed when he soothed me on the flight and again in front of Vivienne's office, I still don't trust him after the stunt he pulled four years ago. But he does owe me.

Did I think I'd use his favor for more academic purposes when I agreed to help him with his abstract? Sure. But I also thought I'd be on the tenure track by now, have a publication in a prestigious journal, and the luxury of planning more than one year ahead.

What has grad school trained me for, if not finding creative solutions to tricky problems?

"I think I can find a way," I say. "What do people do when they fake date?"

"They behave like, well . . . like they're in love. Some fake couples set an end date, some make a sort of contract, like an agreement to establish how you're allowed to interact and touch each other in public, fake nicknames for each other, which social engagements you accompany each other to. All sorts of things, really."

"Like a social transaction?"

"Sort of."

I don't like the idea of having to rely on Lewis to help me out, but so far, it sounds like the best option to get me out of the dilemma I created for myself. It would allow me to reclaim some of the control I so wildly lost in that meeting with Vivienne.

And how hard can it be, really? It can't be more complicated than doing a PhD. Something that probably wouldn't require much acting, given that a fight with Lewis tipped Vivienne off. I might not even have to pretend I like him. We could just carry on being our hateful selves, and she'd interpret it as chemistry.

Before I can get too far ahead of myself my scientifically trained brain kicks in. Maybe I should do a little more research.

"And people do this in books?"

"Books, movies, series. As I said, it's a popular concept."

"Can you send me some titles of books that include false dating?"

"*Fake*—never mind. I'll send you a title I think you'll enjoy. You can download it on that audiobook app I gave you a voucher for last Christmas."

"How do you know I haven't already used it?"

"Because I know you."

"Fair." I bite my lip, uncertain if Karo has just helped me claw myself out of this hellhole of an impossible situation or handed me a shovel to dig my own grave. "Do you really think this could work?"

"Honestly? I'm not super sure. From what I've read, it's a messy thing." After a beat, she explains, "People develop feelings, Franzi. Because they spend so much time together and pretend they're a couple, the boundary with the real thing gets blurred. For sure there's some psychological explanation behind this, which you'd know more about than me, but the point is, you put your feelings on the line."

Falling for Dr. Theodore L. North? The chances of it are so low that I don't even dwell on Karo's warning. "I don't think that's going to become a problem," I tell her, relieved that this is the only thing she's worried about. "What will be hard, though, is not going straight for his throat whenever he says something wildly obnoxious."

From the program leaflet on the kitchen island, the flat stare of Jacob's photograph follows me as I pace by for what's probably the hundredth time. I try to focus on Rosanna Alderkamp's warm smile instead, visualizing what I'd be doing this for. Convincing Lewis, pretending to date him for the duration of two weeks.

It's nothing compared to the decade of work I've put in to understand what happened to my sister on that skiing trip. Even though Karo's amnesia was temporary, the fascination it triggered in me wasn't. Her accident and how it jump-started my obsession with science has become a bit of a code word in my family, ever since my research became too detailed and complicated to explain.

How's work going? my father would ask when we'd all be at their house at Christmas. I'd complain about my model not running properly, or celebrate a fresh paper publication, or this really cool idea I had, and they'd ask me what it *meant*. I'd tell them about my attempts to translate results obtained from highly controlled environments with lab animals to safe and noninvasive settings in humans.

In those animals, each and every memory seems to have something like a fingerprint, a unique code for the place, timing, and emotional undertone of the memory. If I could detect that fingerprint in humans it might help me solve where Karo's brain got scrambled after that skiing accident. But not only that—it could be a launchpad to help people with longer-lasting memory issues, ranging from post-traumatic stress disorder to Alzheimer's.

I'd try and fail to explain, until it was time to cook dinner or light the Christmas tree, and revert to the surface-level explanation: *I'm just trying to solve Karo's amnesia.* I'm just trying to understand how memory generally works, because only then can we come up with scientifically grounded ways of diagnosing or treating it when it fails.

That's all I'm really doing this for. The moment of panic in Vivienne's office? It was nothing more than a blip, a snafu, that, luckily, has a solution.

I stop the pacing, strengthening the grip around my phone and steeling my voice as I say, "As messy as it could become, fake dating might be my only option if I don't want to risk jeopardizing everything I've worked for."

"Then"—Karo inhales—"you'd better get that other person on board."

Chapter Five

"You're late." I cringe inwardly at my own words as soon as they're out of my mouth.

That's not how I wanted this to go. I sound like a headmaster scolding a student on the first day of school, not like someone who's desperate for their academic rival to go along with a lie that puts their integrity at risk.

But really, how can he be this late?

The first day of the Sawyer's Summer Seminars on the neuroscience of memory officially started at 8:00 a.m. with coffee and mingling. After catching up with Peter, who I shared an office with during my time in Zurich, I excused myself to find Lewis, assuming he'd be here early, too, only to wait close to the doors, nursing a cup of bad coffee, and repeatedly pulling my phone out of the pocket of my blazer to check for updates on my submitted grant until he finally showed up.

His pine scent is going extra strong this morning, like he just showered and shaved. At my greeting, a frown etches into his face. "Good morning to you, too, Dr. Silberstein," he replies, and for once, he sounds neutral. Not angry neutral, just . . . neutral. Maybe it's too early for him to be annoyed.

"We need to talk." I push the—now cold—cup of coffee I've been saving for him into his hands. It almost sloshes over the edge, but he tilts the cup, avoiding disaster and sparing his crisp blue linen shirt.

Admittedly, it's not my smoothest moment. I had pictured it differently: guiding Lewis to a corner of the room, instilling a sense of gratitude for the gesture with the coffee before diplomatically telling him that we really cannot fix the misconception that has arisen, or else I may as well kiss my career prospects goodbye, and finally laying out my much better alternative solution. But instead, I can't rein in my animosity.

He eyes the coffee suspiciously. "What is this?"

"Is it so inconceivable that I picked up coffee for you?"

His gaze ping-pongs between me and the coffee. "If you want me to retract that comment on your paper, my answer is no."

I bite my lip at his arrogant tone. Breathe in and out, and remind myself of the presentations I've given in front of funding committees. This is no different. A proposal with perfectly deducted reasons.

"It's just coffee," I insist.

He takes a sip and immediately winces.

"Still conference coffee, though, and thanks to you being late, probably cold by now," I add. Capitalizing on the moment and the fact that he's busy swallowing the horrible coffee, I touch his elbow to steer him away from the busy door. "Let's move over there."

But before we can make it anywhere, Vivienne steps in front of us, holding a tablet to her chest. "Frances, there you are! I've been looking for you." She's wearing a mustard-yellow wrap dress that's a splash of color in the muted blues and grays of the room. "Lewis, good morning!"

Fuck squared. If Vivienne is here, Jacob cannot be far behind. And as much as I need her to believe that the obnoxious scientist at my side is, in fact, my boyfriend, I first need to convince said obnoxious scientist to play along. Preferably before Jacob walks up to us and witnesses how far Lewis and I are from being a couple.

"Good morning," I respond, forcing cheer into my voice to gloss over my nerves.

"Hi, Vivienne," Lewis greets her and then seems to note her flustered state. "Are you okay?"

"Yes, thank you, Lewis. Just in a bit of a rush, because . . . Well. We have an issue with one of the workshops planned for this afternoon," she explains while I scan the room for Jacob. "Dr. Rosenbaum was supposed to have a class on memory testing in clinical populations today, but her flight got canceled so she'll only be able to join us later this week. We're trying to reorganize the program so everything still fits in the schedule. I'm not sure how far along you are with your material, Frances, but I was wondering . . ." Vivienne trails off, and it takes me a moment to parse that the last sentence is addressed to me.

I tilt my head, piecing together what she's not asking. "You want me to switch sessions?"

Vivienne smiles in what I assume is agreement.

Despite my new pair of prescription lenses, I can't make out the details at the far side of the room, so I'm not sure if the tall man bending over the tea selection really is Jacob Bellingham, but the possibility that he could be charges through my veins. I tense. At my side, Lewis quizzically arches an eyebrow, not only making me aware I've never let go of his elbow but also that my fingers have tightened around it.

Right then, Vivienne glances from my hand around his elbow to Lewis's face and—crap, his frown and puckered mouth is miles away from the adoring boyfriend I made him out to be. If she uncovers my lie now, I can flush my hopes for the Sawyer's—and my grant and, oh wait, my career—down the drain.

"I'll do it," I say quickly, trying to get Vivienne's attention before she looks at him too long. I'd counted on a few early mornings this week to finish the interactive code for my workshop session on Thursday, but I'm far enough that I can cobble the last things together while the students attend this morning's lectures.

Vivienne's eyes are firmly fixed on me now. Mission accomplished.

"Oh, Frances. Thank you." With gratitude plain on her face, she scribbles something on her tablet. "Thank you, really."

"Don't worry about it," I tell her, and I mean it. Just the thought of organizing a conference as big as the Sawyer's makes me stressed, and I admire Vivienne for how calm she seems through it all.

"The computer lab down the corridor is free the whole morning. You can use it to finish your things if you want. And I don't know—maybe Lewis has the morning to spare, too." She looks back at him kindly.

It takes everything in me to pull the corners of my mouth into a smile. Blood pumping in my ears at how close we are to being uncovered, I note Lewis freeze against my side, the confusion on his face obvious as he realizes I never told her the truth.

If only Vivienne wouldn't have been so considerate to tell me about her engagement in person. If I would've seen it in some social media post ("I said yes to the biggest collaboration of my life!"), or heard it from a colleague, I could've pulled myself away and quietly battled the existential crisis, rather than doing something irrational and mortifying. Like pretending I was dating my biggest rival. Whom I can't even be with in the same room for two seconds without arguing.

"I'm sure he'll be happy to help," I say as I pinch into the soft skin of his underarm. He moves his arm away, and in a snap second I see the future playing out in front of my eyes: The slow shake of his head as he tells Vivienne that it's not true, that he doesn't know why I'm pretending that we're a couple. Her incredulous look, and the rumor spilling out slowly, until I can't face the people at this conference anymore. Rejections trickling into my inbox that cite issues of credibility and a lack of professionalism.

But Lewis doesn't say anything as he looks at me with an expression I can't interpret. Instead, I feel his arm—the one he just pulled away—snake around my waist. Relief surges through my body as his face contorts into something that, with a lot of goodwill, might be interpretable as a smile.

Vivienne doesn't look at his face too closely, though, seemingly already distracted by the next thing on her long to-do list. "Anyway, I should head inside—check if everything's ready for the opening lecture." She zips off, leaving me next to Lewis, who plucks his arm away within nanoseconds.

We stare at each other for a beat of silence.

He didn't sell me out.

But he also doesn't seem fine with what just happened, what with his lips pressed together and the crease etched into his forehead.

"I think we should talk," I rush to say before he can second-guess himself and chase after Vivienne to tell her the truth.

He cocks up an eyebrow and drawls, "You don't say, *darling*."

"Let's— Please." I gulp, his pointed tone almost making me lose my nerve. "Can we go over here and just . . . Just let me explain. Okay?"

When we're finally tucked into a quieter corner, and the murmur of voices in the hall has died down, I take a deep breath. So far, I've managed to float in that gray zone where Vivienne thinks we're a couple and Lewis doesn't fully play along, but it's only a matter of time before more people find out. I wish, I really wish I could dial back to yesterday and stop myself from going along with Vivienne's misconception, but time travel isn't my area of expertise, let alone scientifically plausible, so all I can do is mitigate the hell out of this embarrassment of a situation. Starting with phase 1; getting Lewis on board.

Lewis looks at me, then the stairs to the lecture hall, and his impatience gives me the push that I need. As much as I despise opening myself up to him *again*, I sense that my only chance of convincing him is bone-deep honesty. "Remember what I told you on the plane, how I was scared of coming back here and running into my ex?"

His eyes don't ease their squint, but he nods at me, almost imperceptibly.

"You know by now that that person is Jacob Bellingham." I want to drop my gaze, avoid the pity in his eyes that will undoubtedly arise with my next words, but I force myself to keep my chin up. "He's a professor, leading his own lab, and, to top it all off, also happily engaged. I didn't think it would hit this badly, but learning how well he's done for himself in all aspects of life, while I'm nothing but the walking confirmation of his predictions, made me panic. I think I shut down. I wanted to get out of there, and fine, perhaps a tiny part of me felt better when Vivienne implied we were dating. But believe me, I know how stupid that was—I'm probably more ashamed of the whole thing than you are."

"It's not stupid," he says after a pause, the softness in his voice giving me a glimpse of the man who has now anchored me twice through my spiraling thoughts. He looks like he's on the brink of saying something else, too, but then he bites it back, crossing his arms in front of his chest. "But surely you know we can't keep this up."

Here goes nothing.

"Actually . . . I was hoping we could?"

He's quiet. Too quiet, for too long, like he's gearing up for another one of those cool but sharp outbursts. But then I spot the crinkles around his eyes. "You want me to pretend to be your boyfriend so that your ex-boyfriend who's now engaged to another person . . . does what exactly?"

His right eyebrow flicks up.

Is he *teasing* me?

His mouth twitches, like he can barely hold back a laugh. As the measured, professional woman that I am, I clamp down the urge to wipe the grin off his face, and school my features. "I want him and Vivienne and everybody else, really, to not think less of me for lying and putting my career and any prospects for my future at risk."

"Right, I see," he says hesitantly, and lets me wait for what feels like an eternity. Then, finally: "So you want us to fake date?"

"*You* know what fake dating is?"

"I do."

"You do?"

He shrugs. "I have an older sister who was a teenager right around the peak of the early 2000s rom-coms."

I didn't expect him to be so relaxed about this, as if it's normal to be asked into a fake relationship by your colleague. Could this turn out to be easier than I thought it would?

"Good, so I don't have to explain."

"Not the concept, no." He shakes his head, a muscle in his jaw ticking and eyes sparkling with what I now understand is silent laughter. Laughter at me because he thinks I'm joking. How could I not be, with this ridiculous proposition?

"I'm serious." I drag my fingers through my hair, tugging on my scalp to ease the slosh of anxiety in my veins. If this doesn't work out, I'm out of ideas. I'll have to consider a career change for real. Apply to some company, hoping academic gossip doesn't travel into their world and bide my time as a data analyst while dreaming of the days when I tried to uncover the mysteries of human memory.

Lewis scans my face from narrowed eyes. "What even makes you think we could pull this off? All we do is argue."

"It didn't used to be this way," I remind him, expecting him to brush it, and me, off like he did all those years ago when he published that paper. The one that made his career, and could've made mine, if not for his actions—or lack thereof.

But to my surprise, he winces, "I know." His voice sounds tight. Together with the lowered eyebrows, I'd almost say it's apologetic, if I didn't know him any better.

"It doesn't really matter, though," I go on, pushing his puzzling reaction to the back of my mind and focusing on the matter at hand. "We might not even have to stop arguing, since whatever fight Vivienne saw yesterday, she took it for chemistry." I skip over the fact that we might've held on to each other's hands just a little too long, but the thought sticks, and a flush creeps into my cheeks.

Thankfully, Lewis doesn't point it out, either. He just shakes his head as he bites his lip. "Who on earth could mistake *this*," he points at himself, then at me, "for chemistry?"

"But that's what makes this easy. We wouldn't even have to do that much. We're at a summer school where nobody expects us to be all touchy-feely with each other. We can sit next to each other in lectures, do a few cute things like pick up coffee for each other, and you'll put on a smile when you see me."

He snorts, as if this is the singularly difficult aspect of the plan.

It takes everything in me not to roll my eyes and force my voice to stay level. He needs to understand that I'm serious about this. "I know you hate me, but it can't be that hard."

"What?"

"To smile at me. Here, I can show you." I lift my hands, threatening to pull up the corners of his mouth manually, but he takes a step back, catching my wrists midair and ducking his head away.

"You really have no idea," he mutters, close enough that his breath ghosts over my cheek. A prickle slinks up my arms, all the way from the hot grip of his fingers.

I shake him off, but the feeling on my arms lingers. "We don't negate when people imply that we're dating. That's it. It involves zero effort, but it would help me a great deal."

As he pushes his hand into the pocket of his jeans, he frowns at me, the way he did on the plane when I told him to cut a part of his abstract he seemed particularly attached to. The way I'm discovering he does when he knows that I have a point but tries to come up with a counterargument, just because.

"And here I thought you think so little of me that you can't even stand to be in the same room as me," he observes pointedly.

"As I'm sure you'd understand, I can do almost anything when it comes to science," I retort. "Including pretending to like you. Besides, it's not for long. Two weeks, and then we can go back to verbally destroying each other's papers and hating each other."

"That's what you think I was doing?"

"Uhm, yeah." I swipe out my phone, about to open my inbox and pull up his scathing review. "I'm not sure how short-lived your memory is but I can *show* you—"

"Aren't you worried, though?" he cuts me off. "About the optics of dating a colleague?"

Once or twice, or maybe a thousand times, it has crossed my mind that outwardly, our fake dating will look like real dating. Which means risking my professional independence once again. A blurring of lines between Lewis's and my work, to the point that my achievements could be seen as his, which is far from ideal, but less bad than tanking my reputation altogether. Even if I don't like putting myself back into this position, at least it would allow me to get the resources I need to continue with my research.

His question is surprisingly thoughtful, though, given that the optics would be worse for me than for him.

"It's not *that* uncommon," I cite the counterargument I've used to rationalize myself out of my doubts. It's the truth—from fellow students back in grad school, all the way up the hierarchy, academics date each other all the time. Probably because it's the easiest way to find someone who understands the drive to ponder the tiniest and trickiest of questions, and the long hours needed to get there.

It doesn't seem to be enough for Lewis though. "That's not what I meant," he says, shaking his head. So, he *is* worried for himself?

"The alternative would be much worse," I point out. "I'd rather have people think you had something to do with any good piece of work I do than be seen as a liar. Remember that whole paragraph on directionality of replay you made me put into my discussion in the last paper? The one where I suggest using probabilistic classifiers in future research?"

His nod sends his hair toppling onto his forehead. "Yeah, that was an important point," he concedes, but then catches himself. "Though may I remind you that the peer-review process—"

". . . is anonymous, yes," I finish. "I still know it was you. Anyway, that point? I can only do that future research if the grant I submitted works out, or if another lab takes me in and lets me work on my own projects. If word gets through and people doubt my integrity, I won't be able to answer anything."

I pause and wait for his rebuttal, but when it doesn't come, I go on, "It's not just about my integrity, though, but my professionalism in general. Day in, day out, it's a balancing act. I try not to speak my mind too freely and avoid firm boundaries because then I'd have an attitude problem. But if I'm too quiet, I get passed over. Maybe if you were the one who'd slipped out a lie, it wouldn't matter so much." I shrug. "Boys can be boys, right? But if people learn I lied about this one thing, who's to say I'm not equally dishonest in my research when it suits me? A change of labels in my data here, a little p-hacking there."

When he wrinkles his forehead, no doubt thinking of the many fights we've had about whether I'm flashy or not, I quickly add, "I know you have your qualms with how I do my research, but I'd never do anything unscientific. But letting Vivienne know about my lie would absolutely harm my reputation, and I can't risk that. Not when I'm waiting on the outcome of that huge grant I applied for, and not ever."

Four years ago, we built an easy connection over email, which he then went on to destroy. Ever since I met him on the plane, his empathetic side has gleamed through the cracks of our conversation, and it's that part of him I speak to, when I catch his gaze and say, "I know that what you took away from all our emails four years ago was something else, but you must remember how much my work means to me. Please. I can't lose this now."

Lewis stares back at me, and something shifts in the blue of his eyes, like maybe he's actually contemplating my words. But then he breaks his gaze away. When he lifts a hand to push his hair off of his forehead, he presses his eyes shut for a moment, looking almost as exhausted as I feel. I know I'm probably the cause of his exhaustion, having chewed his ear off and kept him out of the first lecture of a summer school he traveled across an ocean for.

He turns away but stops himself before walking off and sighs. "I don't think I can lie for you, Dr. Silberstein."

As he ambles toward the heavy doors of the lecture theater, I call out, "Dr. North."

He throws me a glance over his shoulder.

"You . . . you owe me one," I remind him, though I know what I'm asking of him is nothing compared to the few hours I spent editing his abstract.

He pinches his lips. "I'll think about it."

It's not the answer I was hoping for, but it's not a *no*, either. I let out a long breath—maybe there's still a chance he'll turn around. My eyes flit to the large clock embedded into the paneling high on the wall. "I need to get started on the workshop materials." I try to sound calm as I hook a thumb over my shoulder, but I know some of my desperation is seeping through. "I'll be in one of the computer rooms. Find me there if you change your mind?"

Lewis gives me a curt nod before he disappears into the lecture theater.

A few hours later, I hack at my keyboard in panic as the clock ticks away at what has to be double its normal speed. How could I ever believe I'd get the workshop materials ready within a few hours? And why did I think Lewis would help me now, after everything that happened four years ago?

I should've known better—no matter how good he was at talking me through my panic, this man is not to be trusted. He seemed nice four years ago, too, when we started following each other on social media, reposting each other's new publications and commenting on other groups' new research findings. He seemed nice when we started emailing back and forth, sharing our struggles as newly minted postdocs and our hopes and dreams for our research.

We both thought we'd have it easier once we graduated, and we bonded over the many ways in which we didn't. Lewis had just moved to a lab at Oxford, where he worked on a massive project, for which he had to coordinate between different, stubborn professors to make progress. I confided in him about all the extra work that got piled on me but not my male colleagues. Like organizing lab meetings and other social outings, checking in on all the internship and thesis students, even if I wasn't the one supervising them, or presenting at internal conferences that weren't worth putting on my CV, while being skipped over for prestigious talks.

But what made me truly look forward to each *ping* of my inbox was how Lewis made me feel less lonely, when it had only been a year since my breakup with Jacob. I loved science more than anything else, but as the only postdoc in a small lab with a professor fully engaged in teaching, I barely had anybody to share my passion with. Our emails not only made me hopeful that self-absorbed Jacob was the exception to the rule of collaborative, well-meaning scientists, but also reassured me that I'd made the right decision in leaving him to go after my own future.

Lewis patched up my loneliness, until he excavated it even deeper.

For months, we exchanged long email threads discussing future directions in memory science and volleyed replies back and forth that culminated in sudden silence on his side. Then, a few weeks later, an opinion paper on a preprint server came out. It held the arguments I'd provided Lewis with over the course of our exchanges. He hadn't copied my emails word for word, but half of my rationale was there, the references I'd suggested, the whole paper an echo of our conversation, except it only read

North, Theodore L. on the author line, along with his professor's name at the University of Oxford.

My name was nowhere in sight.

Postdoc life can be akin to *The Hunger Games* (Karo's words, not mine, but she has a point). In the few years after you graduate with a PhD, you have to publish incessantly, preferably in respected, high-impact journals, and build a list of good publications because those will land you the recognition needed to transition from underpaid, fixed-term contracts into a faculty position. Publications can make or break your career, because grant panels and hiring committees like to see papers in renowned journals and with a high citation score. Academia is full of people with great ideas, but those aren't worth much if you can't reel in the money to test whether those ideas actually work.

My dream of using computational models as a fine-grained template to uncover the fingerprints of memory could only come to fruition if I had the money to pay for all the research expenses, and didn't need to worry about applying to new labs every year. It wouldn't have cost Lewis anything to list me on that publication that carried half of my thoughts. Because, really, people got included in papers for much less than that. He used my thoughts, but not my name, and while his career skyrocketed as a result, mine was left behind. As attentive, understanding, and outraged on my behalf as he had seemed whenever I told him about the challenges I faced, he finally showed his true colors with that paper. Instead of becoming a companion in this lonely system, he treated me like everyone else: a rung on his ladder to success. Useful, until I wasn't.

I waited for an email from him, for some kind of reasoning behind why he left me out of the paper, but my inbox stayed empty. Several months later, when I came upon the published paper in a prestigious journal, I raided the minibar of the hotel room I was staying in and decided never to waste my energy and intelligence on collaborations with idiotic men again.

For the next four years, throughout long threads of arguments on social media and nitpicky peer reviews of each other's papers, the only reminders of Lewis's human side were the things he posted online to make himself look good, like public access to the data he collected and the monthly Q and As to mentor younger academics.

But then the flight happened, and the news about Jacob and Vivienne, and my panicked decision to nod along. For a moment, I thought the man who held my hand to slow down the chaos might help me this time around.

But his lack of a reply proves what I should have known all along: he didn't help me then, and he won't help me now.

Granted, it's only been a few hours since I asked him to be my fake boyfriend, but each minute cements my lie further into reality. I picture him out there telling people the truth and taking down my career in one swipe. My fear seeps into mistyped lines of code, switched up words in my instructions, and mixed-up version copies.

"Goddammit!" My outburst is met by the whir of dozens of computers on standby and the impatient blink of my cursor. Closing my eyes, I breathe into every frazzled nerve end. I need to get myself and my interactive code together, otherwise it won't be my lie that makes people doubt me. I grab my empty coffee cup and speed down the corridor, hoping to gain some liquid focus. But the coffee only adds another layer to my spiral of worry, and churns in my stomach as I insert the last screenshots into the instruction documents and load my scripts into the cloud.

By the time the first students filter into the lab, it's been four hours since I've last spoken to Lewis and I've come up with, and discarded, six different excuses to skip the faculty dinner. His absence all throughout the morning tells me that he's not willing to help me out. Instead, Vivienne breezes into the room, and that's when it gets truly hard to tamp down my panic. Either she's here to tell me there's no space for me at the Sawyer's anymore because Lewis has divulged the truth, or . . .

What *is* she doing here?

"Vivienne, what a surprise," I say, trying to keep my voice light.

"I've read about the task you use in your experiments in your last two papers, and I've been wanting to see it for myself. This is going to be so exciting," she singsongs and claps her hands together as she heads to a workstation in the third row.

Huh. Vivienne really *is* just here to learn. Apparently, and very much to my relief, it looks like Lewis hasn't given me up yet.

Maybe he decided that the truth can wait until after my workshop. Pressing my back into the lip of the desk, I survey the rest of the now-packed room. A few known faces have dropped in: a postdoc from Japan who I met at a conference in Vienna two years ago, a girl wearing a LEGO *Star Wars* T-shirt who started her PhD when I left the lab in Singapore, and a tall, gangly guy who interned with me in Zurich for a summer.

I check the time on my phone, slide off my blazer, and clear my throat to get everyone's attention. "Welcome," I announce, "and thanks for joining this session on virtual reality for researching human memory processes."

Few things glue my attention to the moment like teaching does, and as I introduce myself, this morning's tension dissipates. By the time I get started on today's topic, my shoulders have melted down.

"You might wonder what computer games have to do with neuroscience research in general, and memory research in particular." I begin to pace the front of the computer lab. "After all, a lot of memory research has been done differently. Give people lists of words to learn, for instance. Those experiments can show us how new associations are built." I use my fingers to count as I speak. "Which brain regions are involved in learning. We can also look at what goes wrong when we don't remember. There's an issue though."

I give the class time to absorb my words and take a few steadying breaths. No matter what Lewis decides, this is what I came here for: learning and teaching, networking, meeting Professor Alderkamp. A shot at carrying on my research after my current contract expires.

I almost manage to convince myself, but then a latecomer pushes through the door, nods tightly at me, and strides down the rows of the computer lab. Lewis, tearing down my fragilely constructed confidence as he sinks into the last available chair next to Vivienne.

Chapter Six

I blink at the spot in the third row where Lewis and Vivienne murmur something to each other, suddenly feeling too hot despite the blasting AC.

"What's the issue, Doc?" someone pipes up. A guy in the first row who wears his hair tied into a thick knot at the back of his head.

The issue is rather obvious. My academic competitor has sat down next to my ex's fiancée, in a perfect position to dish to her about the insane plan I concocted to remediate the misconception I should've cleared up when it first arose. My throat is heavy with humiliation.

"List learning is more of a semantic memory process, right?" someone else calls.

I clear my throat. "What?"

"The issue that you mentioned. I thought you wanted us to guess?" Same voice. It belongs to a girl with a purple-dyed undercut and a pink T-shirt that reads *Babe with Power*. She blows a bubble with her chewing gum, and as it pops, I snap back into myself.

Right.

I have a class to teach.

Behind my back, I pinch the soft flesh between my thumb and index finger. "Correct," I say, my voice less steady than I'd like it to be. "Except for when we're learning for vocabulary quizzes in school or trying to remember our grocery lists, a lot of our memories are formed as by-products, without intention. Take today, the first day of this summer program."

And maybe the last for me, if Lewis tells Vivienne that her assumption about us was plain wrong. That I lied to her face and have been lying ever since. A glance tells me they've stopped talking to each other, and instead, Lewis is leaning forward, elbows on the table and crystalline eyes boring into mine, as if whatever I have to say is riveting.

Maybe he did change his mind?

I focus on the hope curling in my chest and clear my throat. "Sure, you came here to gather new information about the brain. But throughout the day, you'll pick up so much more: names of the people around you, the layout of this building. The encounters you've had today. Your brain saves all these bits of information from your day-to-day life without any conscious effort."

Most students have their heads down, scribbling on paper or typing on their laptops, but I spot the bob of several heads nodding in agreement.

"The truth is, everyday life is much more complex than what we investigate in our carefully controlled experiments in the lab, and we need to bring them closer together. Because, after all, the memories you form throughout your life . . . They are what really makes you *you*, right? That's where virtual reality and computer games come in, because they allow us to bring lifelike complexity into our experiments."

Out of the corner of my eye, I see students drawing forward, impatient to get started.

I clap my hands together. "What do you think, should we try out some code?"

"Do you have a moment?"

Lewis leans against the side of the instructor's desk, where I'm getting out of my chair and packing up my bag in a very determined attempt to keep calm and not hope too hard that he might've changed his mind. With the workshop over, chattering voices and shuffling students have replaced the sounds of scraping mouse wheels and key taps of the past two hours.

"Sure," I answer, and slide my water bottle into my bag. I'm going for nonchalant, but then I realize that this is it—the moment that decides how the rest of the Sawyer's, and my career, is going to go. The bottle falls with an ungracious *thunk*.

Lewis glances down at where his fingers are drumming a rhythm into the tabletop next to my laptop. "Your desktop is a mess," he notes.

I continue closing the open applications on my laptop, before snapping it shut. "Are you here to criticize my work style or did you actually want to talk to me about something?"

"Vivienne asked if we had any food allergies or preferences. For tonight's dinner."

I don't have any allergies, but as my boyfriend, he would know that I'm a vegetarian. But he's just a colleague, and who knows what he told Vivienne. While I contemplate whether I'd eat meat to keep up the ruse, I peer at him, but his face betrays a whole lot of nothing.

I bite my lip. "What did you say to her?"

"No fish or meat for you." Relief untangles right between my shoulder blades. When I don't say anything, his eyes search over my face. "Right?"

Does that mean what I think it means? He could've told Vivienne to ask me herself if he really wanted out of this scheme.

I wave goodbye to the last students leaving the room before turning back to him. "How did you know?"

"Your meal on the plane."

I shouldn't be surprised that he's observant, not when it's literally part of our job. But so far, he's only ever used his attention to detail to point out my shortcomings, not to learn more about me. I busy myself with packing up my laptop and zipping my bag shut, hoping he won't see the heat climbing to my cheeks.

"You didn't tell Vivienne I lied," I state, keeping my voice even. After our conversation this morning, I didn't think he'd turn around at all, never mind so quickly. "What made you change your mind? You said you wouldn't lie for me."

"I said I wasn't sure if I could," he corrects with a glint in his eyes, but he keeps his reasons for agreeing to himself. "And that I needed some time to think," he adds, crossing the room to shut the door. Then he pulls something out of his back pocket: a small journalist's notepad with the stub of a pencil tucked into the metal loops at the top.

Perched against the door, he crosses his legs in front of him. I stare at his long fingers as he removes the pencil and flips through the pages. "You brought notes?"

"They help me think," he says distractedly.

"What else is in there? A running list of arguments against fMRI research? Quotes from my papers that you found offense with?" I deepen my voice in imitation of his. "*How do you know that your effects are not driven by blood vasculature artifacts? Maybe you're just measuring the throbbing of a big-ass vein.*"

He snorts. "I don't generally tend to think about big

throbbing veins, but no. It's more for personal stuff, decisions, mind maps. Things I need to see laid out on the page."

"Really? You journal?"

"Yes." He sighs. "Essentially, I journal." Finally at the page he was looking for, he glances up, as if to check if I'm listening. "I'll be your boyfriend—*fake* boyfriend—under a few conditions."

Air rushes out of my lungs. I haven't been able to breathe this deeply since I arrived here. "Thank you, thank—"

"First," he goes on, eyes shifting between his notes and me. "No espionage about projects we're working on. Or any upcoming papers."

I grimace at him. Funny request, since he was the one who piggybacked off of me with that paper four years ago, and not the other way around. I force myself to relax my jaw. He's building a bridge here, and I don't want to burn it down.

"Good luck finding anything." I try to sound jovial. "You just said it yourself, my computer is a mess."

He bites the inside of his cheek.

"Fine," I say. "Consider it done. Though I'm still allowed to complain about past projects of yours, right?"

He ignores me. "Second, and this one worries me a bit more. We'll need to exclude each other as potential reviewers from all future papers." A sigh escapes him. "Even if it's fake, we'll have a conflict of interest, since supposedly we'll have a close social relationship that precludes an unbiased opinion."

"Did you just quote the reviewer guidelines?"

"I looked them up before I came here," he explains. "Don't look at me like that. We have to consider these things to every last detail."

Is this another one of his hidden jabs at how much more detail-oriented I should be? *Building bridges, building bridges*, I remind myself in an attempt to let the comment slide. "Well, I don't mind. In fact, I'm looking forward to you not being able to tell me what to do with my statistics anymore."

"And here I thought I was helping you make the best out of your publications. Anyway, I also need *your* help, which brings me to my third and last point."

"I'm all ears."

He tucks his notepad into the back pocket of his chinos and pushes himself off the door. With hunched shoulders he wanders to the opposite wall and taps a hand on one of the tables, before he turns around to me. "Do you have any formal clothes? Here?"

Odd. "I brought the dress I wore at my sister's wedding before coming here."

"Your sister lives in Berlin? That's why you were on that flight?" He squints at me, waiting for my nod, before he continues, "Wednesday evening—it'll be my brother's graduation. And I'd like you to come."

"As your date?"

"As my girlfriend," he clarifies.

Wow. Things must be bad with his family if he's willing to pretend to be my boyfriend and risk his career in the process just so he doesn't have to go to this graduation alone. But also, who am I to question it when he's agreeing to help me out.

"So you decided to go, after all?"

"Let's say . . . The decision was made for me," he answers, cryptic and half-hearted, like it truly is a chore to see his family.

"Shouldn't I know a little more about your family if I'm to act as your happy girlfriend?" I make another attempt at puzzling out what can be so bad about them, but he doesn't take the bait and just stands there with his cuffed shirtsleeves and muscular forearms, the unanswered question bothering me like an incomplete line of code. I'm going to accept all of his conditions, of course. It's a no-brainer. But I'm also dying to find out what the deal with his family is—and with that defined body shape of his. Between putting my research under the microscope and working on his own, when does he have time to work out?

He presses his fingers to the bridge of his nose. "I can't believe we're doing this. That *I'm* doing this."

I rise to meet him at the windows, the nervous tone in his voice tapping into some unknown reserve of confidence within me. "It's going to be fine," I say. "And fun, maybe. And helpful for both of us."

"I'm not so sure about that."

I force some cheer into my voice. "Well, I am. P-value smaller than 0.001 sure. Bonferroni-corrected sure. This Sawyer's will be a blast, you wait and see."

But doubt is etched into his features, mirroring the unease I feel deep inside.

Chapter Seven

From the curb, Vivienne and Jacob's townhouse in the West Village looks like any of the other ones on the street. White, brown, or red bricks, iron fire escapes snaking down the fronts, large windows that let in the light and frame glimpses of life: corners of bookshelves, edges of cushioned armchairs, the terra-cotta red of potted indoor plants.

Back when we were dating, Jacob lived closer to campus, on the Upper West Side, in an apartment his parents bought back in the seventies when his dad was in med school in the city. Unlike me, who functioned on a tightly calculated budget in which every last cent was accounted for, Jacob had the luxury of a wealthy family background that afforded him a two-bedroom apartment on his own—when I was sharing with two, sometimes three, roommates (one of which would often "accidentally" eat my emergency ramen)—and a safety net if science didn't work out. Not to forget about the trump card that was his father, a medical director at a hospital in Hartford, whose tennis partners and colleagues and Yale secret society members hold sway over the country's most important research foundations, either by donating to them or sitting on their boards.

It's not that Jacob isn't also a capable, smart, and meticulous scientist, or that his work hasn't furthered our understanding of pattern separation in the hippocampus. But the leap to discovery is a little less scary if you have a soft place to land.

I scan over the set of names on the doorbell panel, spotting theirs at the bottom. *Duchamps & Bellingham*. Like the author line on their recent paper in *Computational Biology*, which I read on the way over, only here it signals their private life together. Their shared home.

"There you are." Lewis appears behind me, his hand hovering in the air as if he was about to tap me on the shoulder. In the short time between the end of this afternoon's program and now, he's changed into a white T-shirt and dark blue jeans. A gray blazer dangles over the crook of his arm, and his mouth is pressed into a tight line.

"Dr. North." I wick away the bead of sweat that trickles down my hairline and waffle between the greeting options. Step into the arc that his arm forms in the air? Or give him a peck on the cheek? I have no clue. Why did we fail to talk about the etiquette for saying hello to your fake boyfriend, and waste our time with useless research-related stuff?

He takes a step back. "You're late," he says, aggravated, as I sink back onto my heels. If I know anything, it's that this greeting was a few degrees too cold to pass for an authentic relationship. A peek over his shoulder tells me the sidewalk is empty, and the panel beside the door is old-fashioned, just an intercom and no camera. Nobody here to witness our awkwardness.

"Sorry. I was on the phone to my parents. What are you doing out here?"

"Waiting for you. I figured it's not quite convincing if we arrive separately."

I close my eyes. Have I been single this long to forget relationship 101? "Right."

"I also picked up a bottle of wine," he continues and lifts up his navy canvas backpack, "so that one of us keeps track of basic decency."

This time, I can't stop my face from sliding into a scowl. "I'm getting this really crabby vibe from you. Is there anything you want to talk about?"

"Well yeah, you're late, we didn't exchange numbers, so I had no clue where you were and I didn't want to go in there"—he nods at the door—"and make up random excuses for why my pretend girlfriend wasn't showing up." I shush him at the word *pretend*, but he carries on ranting. "Which makes me wonder if this 'easy' plan of yours"—he uses his index and middle fingers to swipe angry quotation marks into the air—"doesn't need a major revision because you clearly failed to account for some very important details."

My brain spools off flashbacks of his pages-long reviews, spelling out every tiny gap of logic in my research papers. "So, you're calling me careless? Again?"

He sets his jaw, but even his silence is answer enough.

Ouch.

As my spine stiffens, I take a breath and remind myself we're not competitors but collaborators now. We can't risk our colleagues seeing through our act. So, as much as his jab hurts, for once, he's right—we should've planned this better.

I fiddle with the tips of my hair that I left loose and falling to my elbows today, and force myself to not rise to his bait, but to breathe it out like the poised thirty-two-year-old woman I am.

"I'm—" I blurt out at the same time as he says, "Sorry."

I nod at him. "You go first."

For a moment, he peers down at me, then quickly blinks

away again. His Adam's apple bobs up and down and a blush forms at the tops of his cheeks, like maybe he's jittery, too? "Look—I'm sorry. All these people in there make me a little nervous," he admits. "I'm not a huge networker."

It's not only his honesty that surprises me. It's his nerves. On social media, he usually moves headlong into arguments with me, and even in person I have yet to see him as anything but confident. His emails read as standoffish and cold, and I know he can be boyishly charming if he tries, like he did on the plane.

But shy?

"If you want to skip the small talk in there, you can just hang on to my arm and look pretty." I push playfully against his chest, but the joke's on me, because he has a very firm chest. Before I can stop myself, a "Well done, Dr. North," slides out of my mouth. I look up at him, eyes wide.

He tenses under me, his gaze locking to the point where my hand touches him. For a moment, all I can think about is holding his hand on the flight, when he was just a surprisingly hot and bashful researcher and not the colleague I'd been engaging in paper wars with.

My throat is working overtime these days, swallowing down all the unwanted feelings. The prickle in my nerves, the awareness of how attractive he is. I already damned myself by opening my mouth, so I may as well keep going. "I suppose this doesn't come from typing up condescending remarks to my research?"

"No," he says, lowering his voice. "It's from programming real hard." It's ridiculous, but also a little bit sexy, the way he drags out those last words, the way his mouth quirks around them.

Is he flirting with me? The thought flits across my mind, but then I remember where we are. What we're about to do.

"Oh, you're getting into character," I note and drop my hand.

Lewis's gaze follows the movement before he swallows. "One last thing. You should probably start calling me by my first name. Unless you want people to think that, you know," he pauses, "we get some kink out of calling each other 'Doctor.'"

It's Jacob, not Vivienne, who answers the front door once we've made it through the lobby. He pulls it open in the self-assured way I remember well and steps into the sliver of hallway space, arm flung wide in what I suspect is supposed to be a welcoming gesture. I stare at the collar of his crisp white shirt, the knot of his ochre-patterned necktie.

"Frances," he greets me in his deep voice. I forgot how tall he is, how he'd duck when stepping into the subway, standing out in any crowd. How I always had to crane my neck to see his face. How utterly and terribly small I felt next to him.

When I meet his dark eyes, my memories superimpose with the present version of him. Then: wide-eyed and excited in the lab, sleepy with his hair sticking up to one side, and, at the end, with disdain pulling at his features. Now with the same dark brown hair, although receding at the edges of his forehead. Same upright posture making him seem taller than he already is, same glasses that look like he picked them up in another decade, the half-frame obscuring his eyebrows. But the tweed jacket with elbow patches is new, as is the mustache. He's leaning harder into the role of classic professor from some private New England college, made of old money and heaps of nostalgia.

He looks like he's trying too hard.

And yet . . .

Yet he also looks like the man I used to love, who pushed me through doubts and insecurities in my career, who made me cinnamon toast when I was racing hard to meet deadlines. Who whisked me away to his parents' sprawling Connecticut home when the noise of the city became too much.

Neither of us has said anything yet and in my case, I know it's because I'm overwhelmed by this reunion. Just as I'm tracking the changes on Jacob's face, his eyes roam over me, too, and I wonder what he notices.

A touch feathers over my back. Lewis. I'd almost forgotten about him. With his fingertips pressing into the space between my shoulders he can undoubtedly feel how my heart's thundering at seeing Jacob again.

Here's the man who broke your heart, I remind myself. *Here's the man for whom you've never been enough. Here's the man who only wanted you to succeed when he was succeeding more.* And then it's as if I've opened a cobwebbed room somewhere in my brain. The memories come tumbling out, stacking up into piles of resentment. Snapshots of Jacob with his tight-lipped expression that last time I saw him. When I dropped off the last of his shirts and toiletries in a tote bag, a few days before leaving the city.

Not to be a cliché of any thwarted ex-girlfriend ever, but suddenly I am glad that Lewis is at my side, even if it's just for show. With his hand on my back reassuring me, I lengthen my spine, until my chin's up and my confidence is back.

Still, I'm not sure how I want to greet Jacob—a hug seems out of place given how we left things, but a handshake feels too formal. So I stay put and say, "Jacob, hi."

"Frances. It's good to see you," he replies after another pause. "Did you have a good trip? Good, uh, first day?"

I didn't know polished and self-assured Jacob was even capable of stumbling over his words, but I guess I'm not the only one who finds this entire affair uncomfortable.

"Yeah, it was, thanks. I gave my workshop, and it went well . . ." I trail off with a shrug.

"I'm glad you could make it," Jacob says, his eyes sticking to me a little longer before he peels them away to a point over my shoulder. "Dr. North, welcome."

"Nice to meet you." Lewis leans around me to shake Jacob's hand, while skipping the routine offer of his first name.

Vivienne's voice pipes up from somewhere inside the apartment, "Is that Frances? And Lewis?" before she appears next to Jacob. The look she gives him is unreadable, but it settles into a smile as she turns to us. "What are you doing, keeping them outside? Come in, come in."

Vivienne greets each of us with a kiss on each cheek, managing to simultaneously grab our bottle of wine and hold on to my arm to guide me into the apartment. With Lewis following close behind, Vivienne whisks me past the coatrack, into the living room that hits the right spot between inviting and understated. With the dark gray couch, the bookshelf occupying one of the walls, and the abstractly shaped floor lamp, it's like walking into an upper-tier furniture showroom, but the stacks of colorful spines, framed art-house movie posters and bric-a-brac on the TV unit make it feel personal and lived-in. Jacob heads past us, through an arched doorway into the kitchen, while Vivienne leads us to a set of glass doors on the far side of the living room that opens up to a patio.

The other guests have gathered outside, where the evening air is balmy and the patio is dipped in shade, a relief after the pressing heat of the day. Vivienne leaves us after asking what we'd like to drink, and I watch the groups of people mill around the space. A wrought iron table holds a dozen steaming food containers, stacks of plates, and glassfuls of silverware. At the back, below a white painted wall, I spot a vegetable bed, thick stems and green leaves rising from crates filled with soil. Potted plants—some palm trees, others flowering in bursts of purple or yellow—dot the patio, and on the floor and the wall, lanterns flicker with warm candlelight.

Vivienne returns with a glass of white wine for each of us, but since Lewis only hovers silently behind me, I have to restart the conversation. "It's beautiful," I say to her as she waves us over to the buffet. I heap my plate with roasted vegetables, a creamy cheese, and a layered dish of eggplant and tomato sauce.

She hums in agreement. "I had to bring a little bit of home with me." Her smile is playful as she clinks her glass against mine, but dims down once she's taken a sip. "It's not always easy being so far away from family."

I nod, knowing far too well what she's talking about. "I haven't lived close to home in ages, but usually it's the time zones that get to me."

"Yes. It's hard to stay in touch when your days are so misaligned," she agrees. "By the time I'm done with work, everyone back home is fast asleep. At least that's something the two of you don't have to worry about," she adds, tipping her head at Lewis.

"Oh, right," he says, as if the thought just occurred to him.

Once Vivienne has drifted into another conversation, I raise my eyebrows at him. "Focus," I mutter. "If we're the loving couple we're pretending to be, you should know that there's no time difference between the Netherlands and Germany."

"Of course I know that," he hisses back. "I've just never been in a relationship across time zones before."

What kind of relationships *has* he been in then? Once it pops into my mind, the thought doesn't let go of me. I shouldn't care this much about his previous love life, but then again, he is currently posing as my boyfriend, and girlfriends usually know these things. Before I can ask though, Peter and some of my other former colleagues from Zurich trickle out through the patio door, and someone says hi to Lewis, pulling us apart.

For the next few hours, the few square feet of backyard work their magic on me, making the kickoff dinner far more pleasurable than I would've imagined. Several people promise to contact me whenever a position in their lab opens up, and I end up giving a newly minted postdoc from Sweden a rundown of things not to miss in New York. She adds me on her social media with the promise to talk to her boss about datasets they could share with me. This kind of networking is exactly what I had hoped to get out of the Sawyer's, and I'm pleased to finally get to focus on it, now that Lewis has agreed to help me.

Later, in search of the bathroom, I accidentally step into what must be Jacob and Vivienne's bedroom. Bleached wooden floorboards, linen curtains, a narrow desk, and a jar of seashells on the rattan dresser opposite the king-size bed. Along the walls hang framed art prints and a giant map of Manhattan. When I look at the dozens of tiny nails holding up the frames, the jealousy finally catches up with me. I'm surprised I've lasted this long.

This could have been mine.

It could have been me, living here, rolling out of bed in the morning, after a slumber under these sheets with a thread count of a million, then picking up a venti latte on my way to the subway. I'd be friends with the owners of the local coffee shop and they'd have my order ready to pick up when I walk through the doors. Because I'd have routines. No, even better. I'd have a five-year plan of where I want my life to go, and a group of gal pals that I got to know through my Pilates studio. I'd have a capsule wardrobe because it's stylish, not because I'm still haunted by the excess baggage fees I had to pay at the airport when I moved countries the first time.

Laughter from the patio snaps me back into the here and

now. *You didn't want this*, I remind myself. *That's why you left. You didn't want to give up your own research interests and work toward someone else's goals, so get a grip, Frances.* I loosen my fingers from white-knuckling the door knob and leave the door at the angle I found it. As I'm pushing open the correct door to the bathroom, Vivienne rounds the corner into the corridor.

Adrenaline charges through my body, but I school my face into a neutral expression. "I was just . . ." I point at the open door to the bathroom.

She tucks away a strand of hair that has come loose from her updo. No signs of apprehension. A minute earlier and she would've found me snooping. What was I thinking? "Come by the kitchen on the way back. I want you to try a special wine from my hometown."

Mortified, I lock myself in the bathroom. Not only have my feelings for Jacob been gone for years, but Vivienne's also been nothing but kind ever since I arrived. She's one of not many women working in computational neuroscience and someone who—like me—has been forced to move around the world in pursuit of her career. Seeing her as a competitor should be the last thing on my mind.

When I have pulled myself together and step back into the kitchen, I find Vivienne loading wineglasses into the dishwasher. She hands me a clean one from an overhead cupboard and pours me a glass. "Are you enjoying yourself?"

"I am." Mostly because I've seen little of Jacob. Somehow, I think Vivienne's to thank for that. She's all innocent questions and impeccable hosting skills, but I've seen her drink her wine cautiously all evening. I wouldn't put it past her that she's keeping an eye on us, nudging us in a way that has us avoiding each other naturally. She must know that Jacob and I didn't part as friends, but I doubt she knows the full extent of why we broke up—which begs the question if she's aware how self-serving

Jacob can be. If she were a friend, I'd pull her aside and make sure he's not giving her the rinse-and-repeat of how he treated me, but I just met her and I barely know her, so it's not like I can outright *ask* if she's okay.

"You have a lovely home," I compliment her, sipping from my glass as I rack my brain for a way to steer the conversation to her and Jacob without seeming like I'm prying.

"Thank you. I'm glad to hear you're having a good time. I hope your boyfriend is, too?"

"Oh, I'm sure he's enjoying himself." Truth is, I don't know where Lewis is. I lost sight of him after we finished our food and he took away our plates.

After she closes the dishwasher and dries off her hands, Vivienne finds my eyes and says, almost whispering, "Honestly, I was a little nervous about you coming, with the situation being as it is." She's twirling her engagement ring around her finger just like she had in her office yesterday. "But I would really love for us to be friends, if that's not too strange for you."

"Yeah. That could be nice," I agree, though I don't think my lie is a good base for whatever friendship we might strike up.

"I was a little apprehensive when Jacob suggested hosting this dinner, because there was already so much else going on," she continues, her smile lighter now. "You know, with a whole two-week summer program to organize. But I'm glad we've done it. It's great to see everyone relax and get some time to chat." She motions me to head back outside and leans in conspiratorially. "Gives us the chance to talk a little more, too. How do you like living in the Netherlands?"

"I like it," I respond as I tuck away the unexpected fact that Jacob planned this evening. Whether he's changed for the better or not, I don't know, but at least he's not leaving everything to Vivienne. "I've only been there for a year, and it's not like I get out much, but I wouldn't mind staying there."

"Oh, I totally get that. I was at the Donders for an internship during my master's and absolutely loved it," she tells me, then points at my glass. "How's the wine?"

"Really good."

We reach the large sliding doors leading out to the patio and I let my gaze drift around, searching for Lewis, as Vivienne says, "Don't let me keep you any longer from your *beau* then. We have another two weeks to talk, but this probably doesn't happen very often."

"What?" I look back at her.

She lifts her shoulders. "That the two of you get to spend a lot of time with each other. I know how busy the postdoc life is."

"Yeah, we don't, um, see each other that often." I can't quite tamp down the hesitance in my voice. Is she truly this invested in our relationship? Or have Lewis and I done such a horrible job and she suspects something?

But Vivienne makes an *ugh* sound, followed by a dry, "Long distance is truly the worst," which makes me, a) wonder what experience she has in that department, seeing as Jacob seems to be allergic to the concept, and b) feel she might actually be genuine. "I need to say hello to some colleagues, but you go and enjoy your time with Lewis," she says and heads off toward a couple of people standing by the table.

It's good that she leaves then, because I'm pretty sure the panic is blatantly obvious on my face. Maybe Vivienne believes us, but I know Lewis and I need to step up our game if we want to leave no doubt that we're in a happy relationship.

Chapter Eight

Outside on the patio, dusk has settled in, streaking the clouds in shades of pink on a lavender sky. I finally spot Lewis at the back corner where, with his back to me, he's talking to a woman with thick, black hair pulled into two space buns atop her head. Every few words, she pushes a huge pair of glasses back up the bridge of her nose. They look like they know each other—closely, I suppose, given the relaxed set of his shoulders and the animated gestures she makes, followed by a hearty laugh. My steps falter as I approach. Faking a relationship in front of random colleagues is one thing, but one of Lewis's friends?

Go and enjoy your time with Lewis, Vivienne's words echo in my mind, making my decision for me.

As I make a beeline for the pair of them, I flip through my options of how I could slide into the conversation in a determinedly *couply* way. Call him a pet name? Or hold hands? We've done that before, and he didn't mind, even when I was crushing his fingers. Although Vivienne's probably looking elsewhere, I need to prove to myself that I can do this. So, I take the leap and stretch my arm into the space between us until my fingertips graze the back of his hand.

Lewis jumps. He snatches his arm back and clutches it to his chest.

A hole in the floor would be nice. Or a collective, very short-lived amnesia for everyone attending.

He turns, eyes wide, and his mistake registers as he sees the chasm of space between us, my pained expression, and the quizzical look on his companion's face. I curb the urge to down my glass of wine in one gulp and force myself to keep looking at him instead of checking if Vivienne—or worse, Jacob—witnessed this little show.

It's fine. It's all fine. It's totally normal for a person to jump at a tender gesture from their girlfriend.

"Static shock," Lewis says unconvincingly. There's a hitch to his voice, as if his body wants to tell each and every person around us that he is capital-L Lying.

Hell, this is not working.

He makes a grab for my hand, but his grasp is so tight that it hurts. I plaster a smile on my face and wiggle my fingers, forcing him to loosen up.

"Hi, I'm Frances," I introduce myself, nodding at Lewis's friend.

As Lewis clears his throat, her gaze shoots to him. "Frances, uh—I don't believe you've met each other. This is my friend Brady. We did our PhDs in the same lab. And this is Frances, my girlfriend."

Her brown eyes grow wide on that last word, then snap to Lewis. "Okay, so while I've been word-vomiting at you about my idea of a small-town AU with Geralt of Rivia as a hot grumpy veterinarian, you didn't think *once* of interrupting me to tell me you are dating? And Dr. Frances Silberstein, of all people?"

She turns to me and, without letting Lewis get another word in, continues, "It's *so* nice to meet you. I've heard so much about you!"

Lewis blushes furiously, as though he doesn't want Brady sharing what he's told her about me and my uninspired, flashy research.

"It's really nice to meet you, too." I smile, although I only understood about fifty percent of what she said, and even that was confusing.

"Brady, um." At my side, Lewis rubs the nape of his neck with his free hand.

"Listen," Brady murmurs, leaning in as she rights her glasses. "You have to tell me everything about how angel eyes over here"—she nods her head in Lewis's direction—"groveled and finally made it up to you because last time *I* heard, you were still very much enemies and far away from being lovers." Her mouth gapes open. "Ohh, or is that your thing? Intellectual sparring as forepl—"

"Brady," Lewis cuts in, exasperated.

I'm so lost. "Um? Groveled?"

Her gaze flicks to Lewis, then back to me. "I mean for that paper he published? The one he left you out of?"

Lewis's hand tightens around mine again.

"Oh yeah, right. He did. Um, grovel big-time." I force my cheeks to hold on to the smile and change the subject. If we start talking about that paper, there's no way I'll be able to pretend to be in love with Lewis now. "So, uh, what do you do now?"

What I really want to ask is: What does she mean, *finally* make it up to me?

It's not like I need to be reminded of what he did four years ago, but both of their reactions confuse me. That Brady knows and so bluntly talks about it and that Lewis stares back at me with what I can only interpret as a painful expression.

"After graduating, I took a bit of a different path, research-wise," Brady supplies. "I'm working on early diagnosis of Alzheimer's now."

I rifle through my mental file on Lewis, wondering where the hell that *same lab* they were both in is based. We only got in touch once we were postdocs, so I'm not sure where in the world they first met. He was in Oxford when we first started emailing, and then he switched to the Berlin School of Mind and Brain two years after. But where did he live before?

A girlfriend should know that, right?

I can't place her accent, but her sentences sound like they're questions—Australian maybe? Hang on, did Lewis do his PhD in Australia?

"That's interesting," I say. "Did you move . . . elsewhere for your postdoc then?"

"No, still in the same place," she tells me, unhelpfully.

I nod and push my thumb into Lewis's palm until he finally catches on. "Brady fell in love with Vancouver from the moment she moved there."

She laughs. "Says the one who went for a weeklong hike to say goodbye to the area before moving to Oxford."

He grins at her. "England is nice and all, but the hikes don't compare."

"Seems like you share a love for the outdoors then." Vivienne glides into our loose circle like a pro. She presses a glass bottle of soda into Brady's empty hands and throws a measuring gaze at Lewis's and my drinks. We've advanced into the next level of our fake dating test way too soon. A good friend of Lewis's *and* Vivienne all at once?

I take a sip of my wine. Despite my hard attempt at confidence, the rim clanks painfully against my teeth. "We surely do."

"Do you have any outdoor adventures planned while you're here?" Vivienne asks.

I consider adapting the two-week-long trip to the Pacific Northwest that I'll embark on with Karo after the Sawyer's. But it's too risky. Vancouver is on our route, and Brady would likely want to see Lewis if we stopped by.

The silence stretches.

How can we be so ill-prepared? I'm considering walking up to Columbia tomorrow and demanding that they take back my PhD, because I'm so many levels of stupid. Analytic thinking, strategic planning, my ass.

"A friend of mine has a cabin upstate," Lewis answers eventually. "It's not the wild outdoors, but it's a nice reprieve from the city. I was thinking we'd spend the weekend there. It was meant to be a surprise," he adds as a last thought, probably to excuse his long silence.

Brady "Awww"s.

"It'll be a nice change of scenery," I note.

Both of their expressions shift into a frown.

Crap. I should probably react to this romantic surprise, shouldn't I?

"Omigod!" I exclaim with a pitch I didn't know my voice could venture into. "We're going to a cabin?" I lay my hand on Lewis's chest and do my best to lovingly gaze into his eyes. They flash in amusement.

"That sounds lovely," Vivienne says, but Brady tilts her head, like she's contemplating how to extricate Lewis from my arms. "How did the two of you meet?"

"It's a funny story . . ." I falter as Jacob casually steps up to Vivienne and sneaks his arm around her shoulder, then swirls the amber liquid in his glass. Whiskey, no doubt. We've advanced to the boss fight, but it's much too soon. I knew I wouldn't be able to avoid Jacob completely, seeing that we're at his house, but I didn't expect him to come hang out with us. Between his curious gaze, Brady's probing questions, and

Vivienne, who I still can't read, my teeth clench so tightly I should probably pencil in a dentist appointment for when I get back.

"It must be," Brady quips, "since I've only ever seen the two of you fight online."

Painfully aware of how I'm blanking, I pull my hand from Lewis's chest and put it on his arm, where I dig my fingers into his skin, hoping he'll get the message: *Help me out here.*

"We met on our way to a conference. The flight was pretty turbulent," Lewis jumps in.

Jacob knits his brow. "That doesn't sound like it'd be funny, especially for you."

I'm not sure how to feel about the fact that he remembers my fear of flying. "It wasn't. But luckily, I sat next to this guy."

"And I had to distract her through the turbulence," Lewis continues. So far, so good. In the back of my mind, I replay our encounter, looking for moments where romance could've sparked.

"You were sat next to each other?" Vivienne's gaze jumps back and forth between the two of us. "Such a coincidence!"

"It was." Lewis takes a long swig of his drink, and I hope it's not as obvious to everyone else that he's stalling for time. "I started a discussion about the role of sleep in memory consolidation. You know, if it has an active contribution or if all it does is to protect the brain from interference of new incoming input."

"Active role, definitely," I state. "The alternative option is ridiculous. During sleep we see a repetition of those same patterns of activity that a rat exhibits when it's learning the layout of a new environment."

"Yeah, but that's not conclusive evidence, is it?" Lewis smirks down at me. "The rat also shows this sort of activity when it's awake and relaxed."

I narrow my eyes at him and that glint in his eyes. "What about strengthened synaptic connections? The fact that memory performance is better after sleep?"

Lewis pats my hand, the one that's gotten far too comfortable on his arm. "And this," he says, turning to the others, "is how she captured my heart."

Brady smiles into her drink. "I can see how that would distract from turbulence."

"Here we are questioning you about all these details. You must feel like you're in a job interview. But we're just very curious. At least I am, for my part. I love to ask couples how they've met, it always makes for such entertaining stories—thank you for telling us yours." Vivienne crouches down and picks up the bottle of wine she left at her feet. "More, anyone?"

My arm shoots out, holding up my stress-drained glass.

Jacob takes the bottle from Vivienne and, angling his arm over her shoulders, tops us up. "I hear you work in Berlin, Lewis? Nice city."

"It's amazing, but the winters are really gray."

"Oh right, you're from Berlin, aren't you, Frances?" Vivienne asks.

I nod. "My sister still lives there, and my parents, too."

"How's Karo doing?" Jacob wants to know as he's raising his glass.

"She's—uh." I study his face, searching for an ulterior motive, but his tone is relaxed and not the fake-friendly kind he puts on when he wants to hide his true feelings. "She just got married, actually. We went to the wedding right before flying over."

"Really?" Brady butts in, gaping at Lewis. "You don't even like weddings."

Lewis smiles good-naturedly. "We don't get to spend a lot of time together. And I get along well with her parents, so . . ."

Oh no.

I register Lewis's mistake the exact same moment as doubt settles into Jacob's face.

I forgot to tell Lewis. And he'd know, too, if he'd actually met them. My parents don't speak English. They learned Russian as a second language back in the days in East Germany and it's not like that'd help Lewis to get to know them, unless he has hidden talents I don't know of.

"That's great. Send them my best wishes," Jacob tells me, then turns to Lewis. "How do you talk to them, if you don't mind me asking?"

In fact, *I* mind him asking. Especially after my parents stammered through a language they barely spoke just to get to know him while he didn't even show a modicum of motivation to pick up a few words of German to make things easier on them. I mind a lot, so much that I need to squeeze my hand into a fist, trying to dilute the sudden anger.

"I'm not sure I understand your question," Lewis says, stepping into what I suspect was a trap on Jacob's behalf.

Of all things, I can't believe that it's my parents' language skills that mess up this entire farce.

"Then again, I speak German to them, same as I do with her," Lewis goes on as he leans into me. *"Nicht wahr, Bärchen?"* His mouth is hot against my ear, the goose bumps on my skin chased by a wave of elation. *Isn't that right, little bear?* It's a cringe-worthy term of endearment, and he butchered it with his American accent, but it gets the job done.

When we finally get out of their place, I'm riding a high, pure enthusiasm flooding my veins. Our first test as a fake couple and we crushed it—especially Lewis's knockout punch that drew a dark look to Jacob's face and made him leave us alone soon after. Granted, it may also be the wine sloshing through my body, but nothing can ruin my mood. The information screen showing major outages on the subway network due to some signal malfunction? The hot, stagnant air? I don't care one bit.

"What a nightmare." Lewis surveys the empty platform and the screen above our heads. The orange LED shows two horizontal bars instead of its usual time estimate.

"I can order us a ride," I suggest. "You also have to go back uptown, right?"

He runs his palm over the back of his neck. "I wasn't talking about the subway."

I stop the search for my phone in my bag and nudge his shoulder. "Come on," I say. "We weren't *too* bad. You knocked it out of the park when you showed off your German skills."

"Uh, Frances? We barely scraped by." Lewis frowns at me. "You do realize that I literally jumped away when you tried to take my hand."

The smile slides off my face when I mentally review the past hours. That gesture should've been normal for a couple. We all but stumbled through Brady's and Vivienne's questions, not to mention Jacob's doubtful expression, as if he was somehow onto us. "Okay, fine, you're right," I concede.

In the silence that follows, I worry that Lewis wants out of our deal. But calling it off is not an option, not with our careers on the line.

He peers over my shoulder, bites the inside of his cheek, and hoists his backpack up. Then he utters five magical words: "We need a better plan."

"Yes," I breathe, relieved. "Okay. We're scientists—we're good at plans."

"Whatever we did so far is not working," he continues and holds out his hand. "Come on, let's walk. We can talk on the way."

I give him a confused look. "Are you not staying close to campus?"

"I am."

"We're on the other end of Manhattan."

"We have a lot of planning to do," Lewis retorts and motions for me to follow him up the subway stairs. "So, a plan," he repeats when we're back outside, on the busy sidewalk.

This close to Jacob and Vivienne's house, there might be inadvertent eavesdroppers, but between the man zipping by on a skateboard and the group of students carrying a couch across the street, I don't spot any familiar faces from the faculty dinner, making it safe for us to talk.

"We should've thought about this sooner," I grumble as we stop at a traffic light and let a car pass by, then cross the street. "Karo warned me. No fake dating without a plan."

"Karo is your sister, right?"

"Yeah."

"Okay, so we're in this madness thanks to your sister."

"I'm saving my career thanks to my sister," I correct him. "Well, and thanks to you." I try to remember the basic ingredients to a fake-dating setup Karo told me about. "Our end-date was kind of implied right? For the duration of the Sawyer's. Which is next Friday." I wait for him to nod, then go on, "And to make things less complicated, I guess we should be exclusive for this time, unless . . ."

"Relax, Frances. I don't have some high school sweetheart hanging around town."

"Good. What about back home?"

He huffs out a laugh. "Maybe this is something you should've considered before you included me in your plan."

Ah, here it comes. Another lecture about how I should be more detail-oriented in research and in life.

But Lewis just shrugs. "There have been women. Friends

of friends, colleagues. But nothing in the last couple of months. Nothing serious, just friends with benefits."

Colleagues. My mind latches on to the word. "Wait, you're familiar with this whole situation?"

"God, no. The absolute opposite. The benefits I'm referring to are—"

"I know what friends with benefits are," I interrupt him. We pass a food cart selling churros and breathe in the air that's heavy with sugar and frying oil. "I meant that you're used to hanging out with colleagues in your downtime."

"If that's what you want to call it, yes."

"Huh."

"Don't sound so surprised," Lewis says. Ahead of us, in front of what turns out to be an ice cream parlor, the sidewalk is clogged with people. I momentarily lose track of him as we weave around the crowds, but then catch the unmistakable swoop of his hair, the set of his shoulders and his canvas backpack. He reaches for me, wrapping his fingers around my elbow, and throws me a look, as if to make sure that this is okay. I nod, trying not to catalog how rough the pads of his fingers feel against my skin, how his knuckles brush against my waist, how his scent envelops me. A whiff of pine trees, a hint of sweat. As we cross another side street, he lets go of me.

"We were attracted to each other," Lewis picks up the conversation again, "and we both didn't feel like dating, but needed a way to," he drops his voice as he leans in close, "decompress after work. It's as easy as that."

The technical term makes me snort. "Decompress. How romantic." How did this whole thing between him and his colleague start? Did their paths cross at the printer? Did she come on to him with a calendar invite? Until three days ago, the thought of stuck-up Dr. Theodore L. North seducing anybody other than a robot would've been laughable.

But now that I've gotten glimpses of his quiet charm, I suppose I can acknowledge that he can be attractive. To some people. Under a certain light, which annoyingly includes the cold neon glare inside planes and the milky glow of the streetlights on Eighth Avenue.

I clear my throat. "And here I thought you were plenty busy with waging social media wars against me and finding the holes in my analyses. And learning German, of course."

"Well," he says, ducking his head, "I'm not that good." As he pulls a steel bottle from his backpack, his ears and cheeks flush pink.

Interesting. He's proud to a fault when it comes to his science, so his humility surprises me. Those three German words he said at the dinner were more than Jacob ever deigned to learn.

"You've lived in Berlin for what?" I backtrack the moment the footnote of his affiliation switched from University of Oxford to Berlin School of Mind and Brain. "Like, a year?" I ask, though I know it's been longer than that.

Lewis takes a swig from his bottle. "Almost two," he corrects once he's swallowed. "Being able to speak German is sort of expected on the job. It's not like patients who just underwent open brain surgery should make the effort to speak English to me. Not that I expect them to in the first place. Speak English, I mean."

"They don't call you *Bärchen*, though, do they?"

He laughs. "No. A nurse I work with is married to one of the neurosurgeons, and that's what he calls him. Not in the OR, but when they have me over for dinner." He angles his shoulders toward me and takes another sip from his bottle. I watch his throat work and get distracted by the droplet of water that clings to his lower lip. "Anyhow, what was that whole thing about?"

"The language thing?"

He nods.

A deep sigh rolls out of me. "Just something we used to fight about. I know it's hard to learn a language that has two more grammatical genders than what he's used to. And I know understanding the difference between the accusative and dative case can be harder than grasping MR physics." I shrug. "But he never even tried to make an effort and learn German to meet my parents halfway. He didn't care enough about me, I guess."

Lewis shifts his jaw, and he looks at me in a weird way, like he's trying to figure something out, but all he says is, "So, what else do we need to plan?"

"Aren't you the expert on fake dating?" I counter.

"Sure, if expertise for you is watching a handful of romantic comedies that are probably considered misogynistic by now."

"Hey," I say, nudging his biceps with my shoulder. There it is again, that humility I wasn't expecting from him. "Claim it with the confidence of a medical doctor who did one credit of statistics in his undergrad but criticizes your choice of nonparametric test."

Sixty blocks, four manholes spewing out questionable fumes, and countless passing ambulance cars later, we've not only come up with a plan, but a blister has formed under my left toe and exhaustion has settled in my bones. Noting my slowing tempo, Lewis motions forward with his chin where, at the center of Columbus Circle, the monument juts out from a circle of water fountains.

I sink onto one of the stone benches. A group of girls sits a few seats down, sharing a bucket of popcorn and lobbing pieces at their friend who wades through the water as she heatedly argues with someone over the phone.

"So," Lewis murmurs next to me. "We've got our schedules down from when we would've seen each other. I'll send you photos of this when I get to the hotel later. As for the next days, we sit together in the lectures, join some of the same workshops, skip some of them to work at the library," he rattles off, and when I turn back to him, he's flipping over a page in his tiny notebook and adding to the list he started on our walk. Our plan etched into reality in his blocky handwriting.

I'm about to make fun of him for taking notes, when he sets aside his pencil and takes my hand. This time, his grip is warm and just right, his thumb drawing a lazy circle over my skin.

"What's this about then?" I nod at our linked hands. "It's okay if you're not into holding hands. We probably should've talked about it before, but if you're uncomfortable with touch, we'll find another way."

"No, it's fine. You know I don't mind holding your hand," he murmurs, reminding me of the times he's grounded me with his touch on the plane and outside Vivienne's office. Lewis meets my gaze straight on, and I glance up, at the wave of his hair. How can it still look this . . . soft and neat after the long day we've had? "I'm not sure what happened back there. I wasn't expecting you to come up behind me like that, and with all those people—" He pulls my hand closer, rests it on top of his knee and emits a deep sigh. "I was nervous."

He said something similar earlier today, in front of Jacob's door. It was hard to believe then, and is hard to believe now. "You're never nervous around me," I point out.

Lewis scratches the back of his neck and for a moment it's quiet except for the lapping water. "Because it doesn't matter. You're not someone who might have a job for me," he says eventually.

What a lovely reminder of my low position in the grand

hierarchy of academia. It's not like it's news to me, but it stings nonetheless.

I tug at my hand, but he doesn't let go, just touches his jaw with his free hand and gives me a small smile. "I'm sorry, that came out wrong. What I meant is that with you I don't have to think about the second layer—if I could be useful for your lab, how we might work together—and that makes things easier. You and me, we can cut to the important things."

"Like the science," I prompt.

He looks at me, eyes dark. Even though we're sitting more than an arm's length apart, it feels too close, and despite the waning heat, the back of my neck suddenly burns. I swallow heavily and his eyes dart to my throat. My heartbeat staggers into a slow, deep *thud*.

"Yes, like the science," he echoes. "For example."

His sentence sounds unfinished, as if he's about to add something else. But he just keeps studying me while his thumb draws electrifying circles over the knuckle of my index finger; tiny ones that make me wonder whether he's even aware of it. I don't know if it's this or his confession or his eyes locked on mine, but I don't like how this shift between us feels like he's reaching into me. Getting me to relax around him, to trust him again.

Earth to Frances. This is Dr. North. The one who asked you to redo a month's worth of data modeling to get your paper "remotely publishable."

Remember?

This is nothing but a collegiate relationship, I remind myself, a pact to keep my integrity intact. It's only natural that he becomes real with me, because I can only pretend to be his girlfriend if I know him well enough. This is practice.

A subway rumbles by underfoot, telling us that the perturbation in the network is resolved. "Well now that that's settled, maybe we can wrap this up." I pull my hand out of his grip.

Head dipped forward, he looks at his hand and, after a beat, says, "Sure." Once he gets to his feet, he slings his backpack over one shoulder and holds tightly onto the strap.

I get up, too, and shift my weight to the foot that is still blister-free. "I guess I'll take the subway."

He nods quietly. "My hotel's just a couple of blocks from here. But I'll walk you to the station."

I'm about to protest, but he's already started toward the subway entrance. As we walk, the awkwardness builds and presses into the space between us like New York's heavy humidity. Then we reach the turnstiles and it's time to part ways, and something makes my brain short-circuit. Like my body is one step deeper into this fake relationship than the rest of me.

I push up to my tiptoes and kiss Lewis on the cheek.

It's chaste, not even a real kiss, just the slide of cheek against cheek.

His hand comes up to tighten on my waist, and for a flash of a second, he holds me in place.

Then, finally, my brain catches on. "Look, you didn't even flinch," I say, a little too brightly. "I think we're good for tomorrow."

As I wait on the platform, loosen and retie my hair, and check my phone for the pending grant application, it's the stubble of his jaw against my cheek that I can't get out of my mind.

Its soft scratch slips into my dreams later that night.

Chapter Nine

About every week or so of my life since I started grad school, in a sober moment when I discover that a participant has moved too much in the MRI scanner for the data to be useful, or when inefficient code burns my RAM, or when a grant proposal I've worked on for the better part of six months gets rejected, I contemplate leaving academia and opening a coffee shop or a plant nursery or a sourdough bakery. Except, I have virtually no skills outside of this insular profession of mine, which makes me wonder whether going to grad school and scraping by on a diet of coffee and grilled cheese sandwiches was such a good idea, because what has it really taught me?

Except now.

Because, as I discover, it has taught me (and Lewis, I suppose) one thing, which is deconstructing complex problems into tinier, manageable bites. Case in point: the potential disbelief in our relationship of Jacob, Vivienne, Brady, and other colleagues caused by the abhorrent performance of our fake relationship at yesterday's dinner. But the plan that we hatched last night seems to be working.

Several pairs of scrutinizing eyes follow us when we enter the lecture hall in the morning, but as Lewis drapes his arm over the back of my seat, they become interested in other things. While the keynote speaker sets up his slides on spatial memory in bats, I steal some of Lewis's takeaway coffee, just to satisfy the last skeptics, but I doubt anybody's still looking. Which works out in my favor, because I grimace hard when I discover Lewis likes his coffee unpalatable (read: black and without sugar), and then it's up to my inhibitory neurons to keep me from spitting it back out. In the five-minute break of the lecture, as my sleep deprivation catches up with me and momentarily makes my eyes droopy, Lewis startles me awake when he runs a warm finger under the lanyard around my neck. He tugs gently until my head meets his shoulder, where I spend the next five minutes pretending to be asleep as my whole body is lit up with his proximity.

After the lecture, we're practically old news. Give nerds an interesting piece of information—Did you know that bats are pollinators, and we rely on them for fruits like bananas and mangoes?—and you'll divert their attention in no time. Whether it's on purpose or because everyone constantly wants to talk to him, Jacob keeps his distance. Which gives me a break from sifting through the constant change of direction my feelings take when I learn something new about his relationship with Vivienne. I didn't lie to Karo when I said I was over him, and our reunion wasn't half as bad as I expected, but his presence has a nasty way of making me question everything: my science, my worth, my decisions, my aspirations.

Just before lunch, Vivienne joins me in line for the bathroom.

"Did you get home okay last night?"

"We ended up walking a good bit, but it was nice," I respond. "I forgot how much I missed the city. Minus the rats, of course."

"And the questionable smells," Vivienne adds as we inch forward in line. "I know what you mean. For the year that I was still in Paris and would only visit every now and then, I missed New York in this visceral way."

Interesting. Jacob must've changed his mind on long-distance sometime after our breakup.

"Speaking of, I've been meaning to tell you," Vivienne goes on. "If you miss New York, you can always come back. They're looking for lecturers in the psychology department right now, and maybe a pure teaching position is not what you or Lewis want, but I know how hard postdoc-ing can be, and to get a permanent contract . . . Anyway." She motions to the cubicle that has freed up.

Her kindness takes me aback. I've encountered enough backstabbing colleagues that my "Thank you," doesn't come out right away. After her interest in Lewis's and my relationship at the dinner yesterday, I wasn't sure if she had some ulterior motive, but the more time I spend around her, the more I believe she actually wants us to be friends. Plus, it's an upside that she included Lewis in her suggestion.

Operation *happy and successful relationship* seems to be back under control.

Until the end of lunch. Lewis and I are hanging out at one of the bistro tables with Brady and Peter, who is distractedly scrolling through his phone. When Lewis leaves on a hunt for the little pieces of individually wrapped chocolate they put out for dessert, Brady sets down her napkin, brushes a few stray crumbs off her Peter Pan–collared blouse, rights her glasses with her index finger, and scrunches up her nose, "Funny that I haven't run into you at our hotel yet."

Friends, welcome to science. If you solve one problem, another one pops up right away.

"What are the odds." I laugh nervously.

She stares into her empty teacup. "Yeah, it's strange. I even saw him arrive on Saturday, but you weren't with him," she notes. My heart starts racing, but I cling to the fact that her voice is neutral, as if she's listing curious observations, rather than exposing a major flaw of our plan.

Peter glances up from his phone. "I got in a little later that evening," I quickly reply. "Still had to wrap up wedding stuff. With my sister."

They both nod, satisfied. While Brady pulls the pamphlet with the Sawyer's program from her tote bag and leafs through it, my jaw clenches so hard it could start a career as a nutcracker. Lewis returns and opens his hand to let the chocolate rain over the table, but doesn't notice my glare.

"Oh, great! Loot!" Brady calls and snatches up a piece of chocolate.

I bite down my annoyance until Peter excuses himself to go to the bathroom and Brady gets approached by a student.

As I trail Lewis to the coffee machine he finally notices my gritted teeth. "What now?" he asks as he sets a cup under the nozzle of the dispenser.

"Tell me why you didn't mention"—I cross my arms in front of my body—"that whatever hotel you're staying in, Brady is, too?"

He stares at his coffee, fingers pressing the dispenser button. Confusion blooms on his face. "What about it?"

"Didn't it cross your mind that it's maybe a bit obvious she never sees me there, even though, you know, we're supposedly staying there? Together? As a couple?"

He picks up his cup and fully turns to me, his body closer than I'd anticipated. Almost as close as in that dream I had last night. After waking up tightly wound this morning, I've tried to push it out of my mind, because who has a sex dream about someone after holding hands for entirely unromantic reasons?

A colleague, who I have hated for four years, no less? But the sensations come slamming back now, how heavy his breath was in my ear as he moved over me.

I palm Lewis's hip before he can take a step back to colleague-appropriate distance. The warmth of his body radiates through his shirt, and it does nothing to shut up my hormonal, deranged brain.

But Brady potentially uncovering our charade does. "Well?" I probe.

Lewis peers at me over the top of his cup. "Do you have plans tonight?"

With Karo still unreachable on her backcountry hike, I'd planned to pick up a poke bowl, open a bottle of wine, go to bed early, and compulsively check my emails for updates on my grant application, but he doesn't need to know that.

"Nothing," I say and shrug. "Why, do you have something in mind?"

And this is how I end up having dinner with Dr. Theodore Lewis North at a romantic Italian restaurant outside the hotel he and Brady are staying in. With its gingham-cloth-covered tables, exposed brick walls, and bottles of wine stacked under the ceiling, it has the perfect setup for a magical first date. Sconces on the walls bask the space in a soft glow, and the white candlesticks and small tables create an intimate environment, drawing in the patrons to converse in a gentle murmur.

Except this is no actual date, and there's nothing magical about it. Lewis has been off since picking me up from the subway stop at Seventy-Second Street. It's hard to believe now that I even felt a tiny bit happy to see him when I spotted him waiting for me in the shade. That feeling vanished rapidly as he only acknowledged me with a nod and then, as we crossed Broadway, pushed up his sunglasses and roped me into a discussion.

Ever since, we've been arguing about the activity-silent versus persistent-firing models of working memory.

This behavior shouldn't come as a surprise from someone who neither bothered to credit me in that paper nor reached out to me afterward, nor cares for salutations or sign-offs in his emails, and has made it his life's goal to question every and any of my scientific convictions. But then yesterday's dinner happened, and our walk after, and I thought things might've changed. That, even though we haven't addressed the elephant in the room, aka the root of my mistrust for him, we'd look out for each other, if only to avoid suspicions about our dating arrangement.

I engage in his discussion as we wait for our table, but it's half-hearted on my side. When we finally hit a lull in our argument, I look around the restaurant. The waiters are dressed in black slacks and white shirts. It's a getup entirely too warm for the humidity outside, but more appropriate to the heavily air-conditioned interior of the restaurant than my short-sleeved off-shoulder blouse. Goosebumps prickle up my arms and down my back. I pull my hair from its knot at the back of my neck and let it fan out over my shoulders, hoping that the weight will provide some warmth.

"This is cozy," I say, hoping to get Lewis out of whatever mood he's been in, and into fake-date mode. We're here to make sure Brady sees us having a wonderfully romantic evening. So far, it has been anything but that.

Lewis peels his gaze off my bare shoulder, only to turn it to my lips. It lingers there long enough that I worry some of the peanut butter pretzels I inhaled before leaving the apartment have gotten stuck between my teeth. Then he finally meets my eyes and shuts down my attempt at small talk with a simple, hesitant, "It's okay."

"Look," I tell him, "I get that all this wasn't part of the plan. That maybe you wanted to have a quiet night at home with your thoughts of why I'm using the worst possible neuroimaging method, but we started this whole thing together, so now we have to see it through. Otherwise—"

"Frances," he interrupts, voice low. "That's *definitely* not what I think about you. And I'm not annoyed about spending the evening with you."

"Then why are you so cranky?"

He sighs deeply. But before he can say anything, a waiter with a crooked nose and a shock of black hair shows us to our table next to the large window front. The ledge under the window holds a set of stained wine crates, planted with an assortment of herbs, and their scent mingles with the heavenly smell of melted cheese wafting in from the kitchen. This really would be the perfect place for a real date—not that I've had one of those in a while. But tonight, Lewis and I are only here to hold hands and get lost in each other's eyes and be conveniently visible when Brady passes by on her evening walk.

After the waiter has served us sparkling water, an oval platter of bread, and a dish of herb-seasoned oil, I scan the menu for vegetarian and, preferably, warm options that can combat the actual and proverbial freezing temperatures in here.

"You know," Lewis starts, "regardless of all those arguments, the current research points to waning and waxing activity related to working memory, and not persistent firing."

I lower my menu so he can fully appreciate my eyeroll. He finally shuts up as the waiter takes our order—ragú, no cheese for him, gnocchi drenched in gorgonzola for me, and half a carafe of red to share.

"You're cold," Lewis observes, nodding at my posture: arms folded in front of my chest, shoulders hunched.

I tighten my arms around me. "I'm okay."

But he clearly doesn't believe me because he leans forward to ghost his fingertips over my collarbone. I shift in my chair, hyper aware of his caress and the shivers that trail it, the unexpected twist deep in my belly.

"Do you want to leave?" he asks.

"Not when operation Brady is still ongoing. And don't think we're done with this conversation."

A smile crosses his lips. "Fine. But take my jacket."

Before I can protest, he's up and shrugs out of his suit jacket, which he then drapes over my shoulders. The fabric is silky, still warm from his body, and the feel of it on my skin is strangely intimate. It smells good, too. Comforting. Like smoky pines and a quiet stay in a log cabin. Lewis's knuckles brush the nape of my neck as he scoops up my hair from where it got trapped under the collar, sending heat zinging through my body that has nothing to do with the warmth of his jacket.

"Better?"

"Yeah," I breathe out. Glad my back is still toward him, I chug my water to wash down the unexpected surge of sensations. "So. If we're saying you're right, which, to be clear, we aren't. But if you were. How's working memory different from long-term memory then?"

Back in his chair, Lewis stares at the candle on our table, the flickering light reflected in his widened pupils. Without his jacket, the outlines of his arms and chest are sharply visible. He folds up the sleeves of his shirt, calmly, like he's getting ready for battle, and I follow the movement, mesmerized by the dance of his tendons and the gold dust of hair on his forearms. Then he wets his lips, looks me in the eye, and launches another attack.

Our food is served, we dine, and the argument keeps rolling. There's something oddly familiar about this situation and the cogs in my head whir as they grasp for counterarguments and hypothetical questions I can toss back at him. I sip on my wine, and that's when it hits me. We've done something like this before. Four years ago, when he took my arguments as his own.

I won't fall for this again.

"Hey!" I hold up my index finger. "I thought no espionage about each other's projects."

His eyebrows shoot up.

"Wasn't that one of your terms? About our arrangement?"

"Yes. What about it?"

"Are you, coincidentally, writing a review and need some help?" I hiss, stabbing the last of my gnocchi with my fork. "Should I pick my words more carefully so that they'll sound nice in your next paper?"

He sets down his cutlery. "Do you mean—"

"Don't be smart, Theodore," I bite out. "You know exactly what I'm talking about."

"Don't call me that!"

I lean forward. "You've done this before. Remember? Four years ago?"

"I know," he mutters quietly, but I'm too far into my rant to care.

"The opinion paper with *your* name on it? The one that should have had mine on it, too, if you'd had the decency to credit me for my work? But instead you used my thoughts, my intellectual property, for your own good just like he—"

"I know," Lewis says, and then again, "I know." And this time it shuts me up, because:

"You know?"

I would've expected anything else: for him to fight back, or to rationalize himself out of it in some way that makes me feel like I'm overreacting. Or even for him to outright deny it. But not to accept my accusation, the corners of his mouth turned down in a perfect expression of regret.

Lewis pushes his empty plate to the side and rests his elbows on the table. "I know."

I set down my silverware with a clang. "That paper made your career. It's been cited—"

"Five hundred sixty-two—"

"Five hundred sixty-*three* times," I correct him, because yes, I checked again this morning, and yes, it's pretty awkward that I know and he doesn't. "It was wildly, vastly unscientific of you to leave my name off of it."

He scrubs a hand over his face. "Listen, I'm sorry. I was then"—he pauses, as if to find the right words—"and I still am. I wanted to tell you, but I didn't know how to, for so long, until I felt like it was too late. I tried making it up to you, instead."

His reaction blew the anger out of me in a gust, but with the bullshit he's serving me now, it's back in an instant. "By requesting me as a reviewer on your next paper? Gee, thank you very much."

"I suggested you as a reviewer because I thought you'd see its worth," he tells me, voice sharp. "It tied neatly into one of the open questions we'd discussed, and I thought it would be good for you, being able to list *Neuron* as a journal you were reviewing for. And anyway, that's not what I meant."

Is he getting frustrated? Great, that makes two of us.

"What *do* you mean, then?" I hiss back. "Because between publicly sharing everything you think I do wrong—"

"I don't think you do anything *wrong*," he cuts in. "I just want to help."

"Help?" I echo, unable to get out anything else while I process his obnoxiousness.

"Yes," Lewis exhales. "Because that's what peer reviews are all about: making the science better. That's what you *should* care about, too. The science and not whether you're seen as successful or not."

I've never engaged in a physical fight, never been kicked, but I imagine this is what it must feel like. The blow hits me deep in the pit of my stomach, pain spilling bluntly, hitching my breath for one, two, three maddening seconds, until the adrenaline kicks in and anger seethes through my chest.

"Oh, the science? That's easy for *you* to say. Also, why even bother." His pages-long review on my last paper is fresh on my mind. "If all I produce is research that—how did you put it?" I tilt my head, "Is 'uninspired and lacking major contribution to the field.'"

"I said what?"

His question confuses me, but I barrel on. "It's a little hard for me to see how any of that would make up for not crediting me in the first place, but maybe you can help me with that, too, since apparently, I'm not fit to produce anything 'remotely publishable' without your contribution."

"Why would I ever say such a thing?"

"What—"

But he cuts me off when he reaches across the table, his expression replaced by a forced smile. He cups my jaw and rubs his thumb over my temple. "I see Brady," he says. "And as much as I get that you're angry, maybe the sight of us fighting would tip her off."

"Oh."

He's shielding my face from Brady's view, drawing lazy circles on the side of my cheek. I lower my eyes and take a few slow breaths to wrestle down the anger. There's another lifelong skill grad school has trained me for. Every time my advisor decided to send a male postdoc in his stead when he couldn't make it to an invited lecture, or when I noticed he only ever responded with "good question" or "excellent thought" when said questions and thoughts came from one of the male lab members. I not only have a PhD but also an unofficial diploma in how to keep the burning unfairness to myself to not disadvantage myself further as a woman by appearing emotional in the leagues of oh-so-rational male scientists.

"How did you know she'd pass by at exactly this time?" I ask, when I can trust my voice to sound level again.

"Brady is a creature of habit," Lewis explains. "She has dinner on her walk home from the Sawyer's, then goes to her room to write fan fiction. After about two hours of that, she goes outside for another burst of inspiration. And here she is."

Right at that moment, Brady notices us. Tote bag over one shoulder and a massive bottle of water dangling on a strap from her arm, she stops in front of the window. She waves at us, we wave back like the insanely happy couple that we are, and she continues on her walk. A few seconds later, the pocket of my borrowed jacket buzzes. I hand Lewis his phone.

"Mission accomplished," he declares and angles the screen for me to read. I'VE NEVER LIKED ENEMIES TO LOVERS BUT YOU GUYS ARE MY NEW FAV SHIP, it says.

"What's a ship?" I ask.

Lewis puts his phone face down on the table. "It's a fanfiction term," he says and then pauses, a nick appearing between his brows. "Basically, it's when you want two people—two characters—to be together, whether they're portrayed as a couple or not." His eyes catch mine, then dart away.

"And you know this how?"

He pulls up one shoulder. "Brady's one of my best friends. Sometimes she asks me to give her feedback."

Surprise pulls at my features. Either Brady likes scathing

feedback, or Lewis doesn't go around telling everyone how uninspired they are.

"If she's such a good friend, you could've just told her the truth about us."

"We don't want that," Lewis says with a shake of his head. "I love her, but Brady has absolutely no filter and she's bad at keeping secrets. In our second year of grad school, she was meant to organize a surprise birthday party for me, and it didn't even take an hour for her to spill the secret. She has the best of intentions, but I can see her accidentally telling our secret to Jacob or any of our other colleagues."

"Right. So, are we done here?" Bristling from our fight, I'm eager to get back home, kick my feet back, and open a tub of ice cream on the couch.

His gaze flits over my face. "Look, I'm really sorry. What I said earlier—"

I raise my hand to flag down the waiter.

We finally leave the restaurant after another discussion about who pays for dinner that we settle by splitting the check. Outside, a sharp wind lifts the tips of my hair, followed by a clash of thunder that makes me jump on the spot.

"We'd better hurry up," I mumble as I peel off Lewis's jacket, but rain starts pelting down as soon as I hand it over. Within seconds, we're drenched, our shoulders and arms slick with the quickly cooling water.

He pushes the jacket back at me. "Take it!"

"I'll be fine," I protest and shove it his way. "The subway is close by."

"At least wait until it lets up a little," Lewis calls against the noise of the water hitting the pavement. He covers my head with his jacket and pulls me in the opposite direction, under the green canopy of a hotel's entrance. *His* hotel's entrance. Brady runs down the sidewalk with pigtails plastered to the sides of her neck and her mascara smudged into a raccoon's bandit mask. When she reaches us under the awning, she doubles over, hands on her knees.

Lewis touches her shoulder, brows drawn together in concern. "Are you okay?"

"All good," she pants and gives him a thumbs-up. "Thank Golgi, I stopped to pet this dog and hadn't gotten far yet." When she rights herself, she rummages through her tote bag, the cotton now splotched with water. "Well, thank Golgi, twice," she exhales. "My notes are okay."

"Lewis was just telling me about your writing," I say.

"You're familiar with *The Witcher*?"

"That's the one with the handsome blond guy, right?"

Brady's eyes swerve to Lewis. "It's not like the difference between the books versus the games versus the screen adaptation have been a topic of conversation," he tells her apologetically.

"*Yet*, I hope," Brady mutters. Then, louder, "What are you guys doing out here? Let's go inside!" We have no choice but to follow.

The lobby is welcoming with its low, unobtrusive jazz music. We pass the gray upholstered armchairs and softly glowing brass lamps, our wet shoes squeaking on the marble floor. As we wait for the elevator and Brady wipes the fog off her glasses, I try (and fail) to ignore how indecently Lewis's shirt sticks to his shoulders and his chest.

It would've been easier if he had let me run to the subway in the first place. Now I have to, what? Wait out the rain in his room? Argue with him some more? Though I guess it's good he didn't let me leave, or else we would've tipped Brady off and the dinner would have been for nothing.

I use the sleeve of Lewis's jacket to wipe the water out of my face, then draw it tighter around me by the lapels before I check the weather app on my phone. A massive purple cloud swirls over Manhattan and several warnings crowd my notifications: Flash floods, heavy rain, the recommendation to stay inside.

"I don't think this storm is going to stop anytime soon," I report.

Brady pushes her glasses back up her nose. "Good thing we're safely sheltered. If you weren't already together, this situation would be the perfect setup for my favorite of all tropes—*only one bed*."

I catch my surprised laugh behind my closed fist. Lewis's mouth twists with a barely suppressed smile. If only she knew.

"Anyway," Brady continues, "I've been meaning to say something, but I'm glad you two finally get along now. He's always felt terrible about how things went down between the two of you. He wanted to put you on that paper back then, but his professor made him take it off, wanted to publish it fast, the usual stuff." She shrugs as the elevator doors slide open. "Even paid an express fee. I guess you already know all of this, though."

Huh. Not only is this a clear demonstration of how Brady cannot keep a secret, but also a very interesting piece of information. Maybe the one that finally connects Lewis's uptight and obnoxious side with the bits of thoughtfulness I've seen gleaming through.

We step into the elevator, and as Brady punches the buttons on the control panel, I turn to Lewis. "Is that true?" I murmur.

Sheepishly, he returns my gaze. "Yeah," he confirms as he rubs the back of his neck, his biceps tense under the wet fabric of his shirt. I'm *most definitely* not looking.

"Well," I say quickly and, eager to get my focus elsewhere,

tell Brady, "it was all a giant misunderstanding and I'm long over it," though I'm definitely not. But I should probably hear him out, because it seems there's more to the story than I thought.

"Hold up," someone shouts, and Lewis slots out his knee to keep the doors open. A group of teenagers files into the elevator, filling it with chatter that might be Italian. Matching backpacks with a big logo—they must belong to some kind of class trip or language school. As we press into the back corner, Lewis's shoes touch mine.

"Has he been chewing your ear off about boats, too?" Brady asks as the elevator finally starts moving.

"Boats?" I repeat. Lewis's expression darkens, but before I get to ask him about it, the elevator stops.

"Oh, this is me," Brady calls, gives both of us a simultaneous half-hug, and pushes a path through the gaggle of students. "Sleep tight, you lovebirds!"

Once she's off, I sink back against the wall. After our fight and Brady's revelation, I feel calm, as if I've stepped out of the pool after floating in the water for a long time, grounding me in my body like nothing else can. Except maybe an orgasm, though they're always less effective when achieved solo.

I blink to hide the track of my thoughts from Lewis, but my plan backfires as I once again notice how closely his shirt sticks to his torso. The fabric does a horrible job at hiding the ridges of his chest and the lean muscles of his arms. A drop of water beads from the center of his collarbone into the V of his two undone shirt buttons, and I imagine its progress down his chest and the plane of his stomach.

Lewis flexes his abs and a moment later I hear him clearing his throat. "Frances."

My gaze snaps back up to his face. "Yes?" I say, drawing the word out innocently.

Flushed ears and a flicker in his eyes—it's obvious he noticed me ogling his body. What's not obvious, though, is if he minded. "My floor is coming up."

"Right."

Out of the din of the elevator, the corridor is awkwardly silent. "Do you, um, want to wait out the storm with me?" Lewis raises his brows and hands, as if he's not sure what to do with me. "I mean, I'm happy to wait downstairs with you in the lobby if it's weird to come to my room. Or we can get you a car, although it may not be the best idea to go outside right now."

"What about Brady, though?"

Lewis shrugs. "She's probably busy writing. We can go back downstairs if you want, though you might want to change into something drier." He motions to my drenched blouse peeking through under his jacket. I pull it tighter around me to shield off the cold, suddenly self-conscious under his gaze.

He notes my discomfort. "Or." He swallows. "I could give you a set of dry clothes, make some tea . . . We could raid the minibar and watch some TV. If you'd like," he adds, a tentative smile playing around his lips.

Catching a ride home or even waiting out the storm in the impersonal hotel lobby would probably be the best idea, but my wet pants are starting to chafe against my thighs and, fine, maybe Brady's revelation has made me a tiny bit curious about the things I might have gotten wrong about Lewis and what happened four years ago.

"Where's your room?" I ask.

With a small smile, Lewis leads the way along the carpeted corridor. "What a useless bunch of academics we are," he says over his shoulder. "Going to this tasteful restaurant and debauching it with a nuclear discussion that exactly N equals two people care about."

I peel my eyes off of Lewis's thighs, which look strong

under the hug of his wet chinos. "What else would you have wanted to do there? Share a plate of spaghetti and tell me the three magical words?"

"Three magical words?" He laughs. "Why, I don't know what you mean."

I swat his back. "Don't be coy."

"Oh you mean *those* words!" He stops in front of a door, slides an arm around me, and fishes something from the pocket of his jacket. A charge flits through my chest as he dips his mouth toward my ear. "Accepted without revisions."

And with a *beep*, he unlocks the door to his hotel room.

Chapter Ten

"Is that how you seduce your colleagues?" I snort as Lewis pushes the door open. "'Accepted without revisions'?"

He waves me inside, lifting one shoulder into a shrug. "If you think about it," he says, toeing off his shoes, it's kind of what real love is."

I bend down to pull at my soggy shoestrings as he starts padding around the room. I've never had a scientific paper get published without being asked for a million revisions, so these three words surely hold some magic. But real love?

"I think you have to explain that one to me."

"I mean . . ." He steps up next to me and fumbles with the thermostat. "What's more loving than telling someone you accept them the way they are? Annoying quirks, and all? That it doesn't matter if they hate public speaking, that they cannot figure out emojis for the life of them, that they use scientific discussions as a way to ignore their feelings? Because you love them anyway?"

While Lewis sets the kettle to boil, draws the sheer curtains in front of the smudged and darkening skyline, and dips into the closet, I'm rooted to the spot, his words on playback in my mind. He does have a point, even if I'm not willing to ever tell him that.

As I let my gaze wander around the room, I second-guess my decision to come up here. The room is by no means small, and it's not even really his room, just a temporary one, impersonal in the way housekeeping has no doubt tidied it up and made his bed this morning, but still. It feels intimate, knowing that he sleeps right there. That he was probably preparing his lecture for later this week before he left to pick me up. There's a thick book on the night table closest to the window whose title I cannot see, and a pair of climbing shoes pushed under the bench in front of the bed.

I cross my arms, unsure what to do about this new thing we have in common. "I didn't know you climbed, too."

"I do. A little top-rope, but mostly bouldering," he says, his voice comes from behind the open bathroom door. "Helps me take my mind off things."

Huh.

I guess that explains the callused fingertips, the corded tendons on his forearms, the sculpted chest.

Lewis steps out of the bathroom. "You do, too?"

I nod. "Only once since I've arrived here, though."

"Me, too. It's not like we've had tons of free time. Here." He places a stack of fluffy white towels into my hands, topped with a pair of maroon sweatpants and a forest green T-shirt. "You can shower if you want to, and I'll see if I can get a second set of towels. These are clean, don't worry. They changed them this morning."

"Don't worry about—"

"Frances," he interrupts and nudges me to the open bathroom door. "It's no problem. Fake girlfriend or not, I don't want you to get sick."

I open my mouth to protest some more, but Lewis gives me a stern look. "How are you going to give me a 'more of a comment than a question' remark at my lecture on Thursday if you're home in bed with a cold? I've been looking forward to this all year. Don't let me down."

Fifteen minutes later, I'm showered, dried off, and finally warm, my hair tied into a damp braid, and my skin smelling like a forest full of pine trees. I cuff up Lewis's sweatpants and pull on his University of British Columbia tee, the fabric worn soft over the years. As I catch my own eye in the mirror, I wonder how I've gotten here, into the bathroom and the loungewear of my academic nemesis, but the warm water has lulled me into an easy state of mind and the thought dissolves easily.

The rain hasn't let up when I get out of the bathroom. Lewis sits on the floor with outstretched legs, back propped against the wall opposite his bed, a mug of tea in his hands. He gives me a lopsided smile, his eyes following me as I cross the room. I deposit my ball of wet clothes in the laundry bag he's laid out and retrieve the mug he left on the table for me.

"Great—"

"This is—"

We speak at the same time, and he nods for me to go on. "This feels much better, thanks. You were saying?"

He blushes. "Great shirt."

"It is," I say, ignoring the way my belly warms up under his attentive gaze. "Very comfortable."

Lewis pushes to his feet, sets down his mug, and grabs a stack of clothes from the duvet as he heads toward the bathroom. "Don't get too attached. It's my favorite."

The door clicks shut behind him. Under the rumbling thunder, I nurse my mug of peppermint tea and check my purse to find its contents have thankfully stayed dry. My phone is devoid of new messages, the grant committee is still undecided, and Karo is still hiking through the phone-free wilderness of California. What would she say about this situation? This weird blurring of battle lines between Lewis and me that is not quite collegiate anymore, but too fresh to be considered friendly?

Behind the bathroom door, the shower stops running and minutes later, Lewis pads out. "We should talk," he says as he towels off his hair. From my cross-legged position on his bed, I grant myself a look at him. Just one, even if it's a long one. Hair damp and curling against the nape of his neck and feet bare, he's wearing black sweatpants and a sleeveless sports shirt that shows off the full glory of his shoulders.

Suddenly feeling parched, I drain the rest of my tea in one scalding gulp. "What do you want to talk about?" I ask.

He clears his throat. "Us."

Anxiety zips through me. Did he notice the way I just looked at him? At his hair, his eyes, his arms? I'm grasping for some smart comment to deflect, play the ball back into his court and watch him flush, when I note the serious set of his eyebrows.

"It's true what Brady said." He presses his lips together. "About my advisor. About not crediting you on that paper."

"Ah," I exhale, relieved. Lewis is talking about *us* as in colleagues. As in, the giant clusterfuck our communication has been thus far. The revelation that maybe he didn't mean for things to go this way.

He sits down on the far edge of the bed and I watch the cream duvet ripple under his weight. "That paper, four years ago . . . I should've handled that whole situation differently."

"You should've," I agree.

"I wanted to include you, but the professor I was working with needed it out quickly, for an important grant he was preparing. And you know, more coauthors mean longer delays to get the paper out, since everyone whose name is on it gets time to read, comment, and needs to give their approval. All of that takes time—time my advisor convinced me we didn't have." Lewis sighs. "I should've fought harder. I suspected it the moment I submitted the paper, but then it got so much traction even before it was officially published, and I knew. It shouldn't have mattered what he said and wanted, I should've put you in regardless. But by then it was too late."

"Why didn't you say something?"

"I wanted to get in touch and tell you how sorry I was, but everything I typed out seemed so callous. No matter what, no matter how I tried to make up for it in other ways, I had still made the wrong decision to go ahead with the publication, and I couldn't change anything about it." He pinches the bridge of his nose. Like back at the restaurant, the guilt is etched into his upturned eyebrows. "So let me tell you now, Frances. I'm so sorry."

It's an apology I didn't ever think I'd get. It doesn't make it okay what he did, but his serious tone loosens something in me. A knot, right between my shoulders, one that has been tightening for the past four years.

The falling rain outside and our quiet breaths are the only sounds in the room as I loop back through his words. "Hang on," I finally say, hugging my legs to my chest, "you think dissecting my each and every turn of scientific thought is a way to make up for what you did?"

"I don't. But I do like to understand you and your experiments, which is why I like to ask questions and discuss with you," he states, as if it were as simple as that.

"But you scrutinize my work. Publicly. All. The. Time."

"Yeah," he says, quietly. "Because it makes others more aware of your work."

"Because your name is on it? That's how you were 'helping' me?" I ask, offended by how patronizing he sounds.

"No." Lewis gulps. "It's not about my name at all. You know people reshare each other's work all the time, because it helps get more reads and more citations down the line. That's what I was doing this for. I think your work is brilliant. It's worth sharing, so that's what I did."

I scrunch my eyebrows together as I flip back through the last years, my memories reshaping with this new perspective. "It felt like you were singling me out. You seemed so nice to everyone else on social media, reposting and participating in all these mentoring events, but with me you went in deep, like you really wanted to show everyone how inadequate I was."

"I went in deep, Frances, because I wanted to learn from you," he clarifies. "All of these questions, the scrutiny, they were a way to figure out what you really meant, to understand the step-by-step of it. Plus, if I'd only reshared you wouldn't have replied. This way, you did. This way, at least I got to talk to you."

"What about that review on my last paper? Back in the restaurant, you said—"

"That wasn't me," he finishes my sentence.

"But . . ." I trail off in disbelief. "You like to criticize me for the implications I draw from my results. And there were so many points about putting in references to your papers that it could only come from you. I was trying to figure out what I'd done to you, why this one felt more like a personal attack than your usual reviews."

"I have reviewed your papers, even your most recent one," Lewis tells me, meeting my gaze with earnest eyes. "But calling you those things? 'Uninspired'?"

"Flashy, too," I supply him with another haunting word from that review.

"That's anything but constructive." Appalled, he furrows his brow and pulls out his phone. "Here," he says after he taps around on it, and shows me an email addressing the journal editor from my last paper. While his review goes on for pages and meticulously details all his notes, it's objective but not rude.

I gape at him. "You were the *other* one? The one that was perfectly reasonable?"

He nods. "Your paper was really good, and so were all of your other ones. I'm sorry my behavior landed so wrong with you. I messed up when I didn't credit you, but everything else was really only coming from a place of intellectual discussion and constructive criticism." He shrugs, a blush tinting his cheeks. "I was really only ever trying to push you to be better."

I break my gaze away, needing a quiet moment to mull over his words.

As a scientist, I've internalized making analytical, objective decisions. I've been trained to look at the same thing over and over again, to consider it from all angles, and to pivot when the data demands it. Lewis has just supplied me with a whole lot of new data. He made a mistake, but he regrets what he did. He hasn't been out to get me this whole time. In fact, looking back, I can see how I've let resentment seep into my perception of him. While he was trying to push the science further, I twisted his genuine feedback into personal attacks. And that last review wasn't even him, but some other anonymous scientist who chose to be outright rude.

Ever since meeting him on the plane, I've been struggling to fit the two versions of him together; the condescending Dr. North that only cares about himself, and the considerate Lewis who agreed to fake date me even if it was a risk for him. But maybe Dr. North is an image forged by years of bad communication and bitterness, and the real Lewis is the one sitting in front of me, the one who has learned from his mistakes and wants to do better.

I decide to pivot.

"I'm not sure I'll be able to forgive you for leaving me out of the paper," I finally tell him, still looking down at my hands. "But hearing your side of the story helps, and your apology does, too. I think I resented you so much that I was only too happy to jump to conclusions, but maybe I've judged you too quickly. You seem too kind and thoughtful for the egocentric asshole I painted you out to be."

I look up at him to see that the tension has melted from his face. "I'm sorry for judging you."

"It's okay. I'm just glad we finally got to talk," he responds softly, giving me a small smile.

"Me, too," I say, though I suspect it'll take some time for his apology to fully sink in.

Lewis glances out of the window, where the rain is still pounding hard. "Now, do you think you can tolerate my presence for another hour or so?"

I let out a laugh, grateful he's found a way of lightening the mood. "Only if you share your snacks with me."

"You pick." Lewis lets me root through the minibar and rifle through the basket of surprisingly nice snacks that come with the room, as he sets up camp on the side of the bed I've left empty. He seems more at ease now, one arm propped against the wall behind his head, so that his caramel skin pulls smoothly over the landscape of his biceps and—

Enough, I scold myself.

My prefrontal cortex really has to get it together.

I grab two cans of premixed gin and tonic, a bag of salted cashews, and some fancy dark chocolate thins. Lewis switches on the TV as I spread my haul out on the duvet, making sure they form a nice, obvious line between our halves of the bed. The chatter of the show host washes over the room and folds into the noise of the raindrops drumming against the window. We catch the end of *Family Feud*, followed by a rerun of a trivia quiz show where college teams compete for a spectacular spring break trip. Next to me, Lewis mutters his answer to the first question and I shout an alternative into the room, although I have no clue what the Production Possibility Frontier even is. Lewis twists his mouth triumphantly when the show host reveals the correct answer.

And the competition is on.

Though I barely scrape by on a question about relativity physics, the science questions are a no-brainer for both of us, and the challenge is really about blurting out the correct fact before the other does. My specialty is world geography (all that moving has to be good for something) and sports (I religiously watch the Olympics whenever they're on). Lewis, annoyingly, aces all the boring questions: names of obscure presidents throughout history and details about the US tax system. When he correctly names all fourteen golf clubs in a set, I can't help myself any longer.

"Wow, you truly *are* a treasure trove of useless information." I pretend to yawn as I dramatically fall back into the pillow.

"You," he says, glaring at me out of the corner of his eyes, "are just jealous I got one of your sports questions right."

"You," I counter, mimicking his clipped tone, "are losing all popularity points that you've just gained. *Golf*—really?!"

Lewis laughs, and nudges my shin with his bare foot, setting off a prickle up my leg. "Shush. Look at what a great team we'd make. I think we know where to go if we ever need funding for a lab."

I swallow thickly. For me, *ever* is more like right now. The familiar anxiety bubbles back into my chest, prickling and sickening like a fizzy drink that has been shaken too much. It's always there, simmering somewhere below the surface, but it spikes when I remember that soon I'll be out of a job.

Lewis must remember what I told him on the flight, because he amends, "I'm sorry about that. I'm guessing you haven't heard about the grant yet?"

"Nope." I take a breath to dislodge the ball of nerves in my throat. "It's driving me crazy. Everyone always complains about how they dislike writing the grants. Like, yeah, putting in all this work for something that most likely won't get funded sucks. But I find the waiting worse. When you're writing, at least you're doing something."

Lewis sighs. "I know."

"How do you deal with it?"

He shrugs. "To be honest, I don't think about it much. Once a grant's submitted, the work's done for me. I don't like the writing, so I'm usually happy to get back to whatever data I was analyzing before."

"Lucky you."

"I could introduce you to some people, if that helps," Lewis suggests.

I shake my head. Getting propelled forward in my career by the man at my side, fake or not, makes me feel cheap and incapable. It's the trigger that blazed off my relationship with Jacob.

"No, thanks," I brush him off. "I don't need your help."

He bites his lip and then, as though he's sensed his offer might've come across wrong, clarifies, "I know you don't. But if you think it would be useful, just say the word."

"Thank you." Now I actually mean it. "But I need to figure this out on my own."

We lapse into silence as an upbeat jingle of a commercial chimes from the TV.

"Hey, do you want to know how I know all these boring facts?" Lewis asks after a beat, his secretive tone luring me closer. "In a previous life," he murmurs, "I studied economics and was a member of a kids' golf club."

"Yeah, right," I drawl, "and then you decided to turn your back on multinational corporations and become an honest man, so you went into academia."

Rolling my eyes, I lob a cashew at him. Lewis tries to catch it with his mouth, but it bounces off of his chin and falls into the collar of his shirt, where it nestles up against the smooth skin of his neck.

He peers at his chest. "Here," I say and point at my own throat, but he only stares at me quizzically. I lean into him, fishing the nut out of its hiding place. My nails brush against his throat, and as his exhalation prickles over my jaw, heat flickers low in my belly.

I only realize how close I've gotten to him when I feel the warmth of his body radiating against my skin.

"I—uh."

I should lean back.

Do I want to lean back?

My brain abolishes the motor plan when I catch his eyes. His pupils are blown large, his lips parted ever so slightly. He doesn't look like he wants me to lean back, either.

"Found it," I say lamely and hold up the cashew. My voice doesn't sound like it belongs to me.

Before I can force myself to pull back, Lewis curls his hand around my wrist and draws forward. Eyes pinning me, he lowers his mouth, slowly and carefully, until he closes his lips around the cashew.

A tendril of want licks up the base of my spine. It's the heat of his mouth and the scrape of his teeth against the pads of my fingers; the pine scent of his skin and the smolder in his eyes. It's the press of his thumb at the inside of my wrist, sensing each and every thudding pulse, even when he sits back and leaves my fingers feeling cold.

As I shift my hips, the comforter rustles, and the noise snaps me back into reality.

What just happened?

The gin must be getting to me, or the unexpected apology, or maybe it's the fact that I haven't been in the proximity of an objectively attractive male body attached to an objectively smart and, accordingly attractive, brain in a long time.

Whatever the reason, my synapses seem to be going haywire.

Lewis lowers my hand onto the empty square of comforter between us, runs his fingers over my knuckles once, and then, eyes flashing at the darkened window, says, "I think it's stopped raining," as if we're in the midst of a regular conversation and not at the tail end of a strangely intimate moment that colleagues, even if they're in a fake relationship, shouldn't be having.

His touch echoes against my skin. My insides are molten with the memory of his gaze, and now the room feels even smaller than when we entered it, like a tiny little shoebox that is too small to allow me the arm's length at which I like to keep him, apology or not.

I have no clue how to define what just happened, which is why I need to get out of here. Now. I surge from the bed and pace across the room where, to my relief, the rain has indeed stopped drumming against the window.

"I should go," I announce, rummaging through my bag for my phone.

"Sure. Should I order you a car?"

"Already on it." My thumb flies over the screen, and I'm glad for the excuse to avoid looking at him. "It'll be here in a few minutes." I keep my head down as Lewis slides his legs over the edge of the bed, his sweatpants riding up to reveal a bare ankle, and dear god, I need distance to talk some sense into my hormonal brain. "You don't have to walk me downstairs," I rush to say, my voice panicked.

"I—"

"Please."

I must sound desperate enough, or maybe he notes my choppy movements as I pull on my sneakers, still wet from the rain, because he stops insisting and watches me instead as I tie the laces. "You know, it wasn't a joke."

My head whips up. "What?" I swear I can feel the beat of my heart against my vocal cords. What just happened didn't feel like a joke to me, either, but I'd still rather not talk about it.

Lewis clears his throat but pauses long enough for me to grab my purse and the bag with my wet clothes. When I straighten, he looks down at his feet. His eyebrows slot toward each other. "The stuff about studying business and playing golf."

Back in the elevator, the same generic jazz music that was playing when we walked into the hotel washes over me, but I know something monumental has changed since Lewis and I rode up to his room together.

Now, I'm wearing his clothes, wrapped up in his scent.

Now, I'm relieved, intrigued, and confused where the shift we've undergone tonight is going to take us.

Chapter Eleven

When I walk up Broadway the next morning, Lewis is waiting in front of the Korean grocery store and drinking his takeaway coffee with the devoted attention of someone who hasn't had a full night's sleep in years. A pair of sunglasses sits in the cushion of his hair, and he's paired his tan chinos with a white-and-blue-striped shirt, the collar crisp and, to no one's surprise, the top two buttons undone.

Does he even know about the existence of those two buttons?

I spot him before he notices me, and as I approach, my brain slides right back into the spiral it started last night, when I shot him a simple *I got home okay* text and didn't hear back. All night, I'd gone back and forth over the events of the evening. It'd felt so good to finally vent my anger at him, hear his apology, and understand he'd wanted things to go differently, too. I know all of this should be more important than what happened after, but it was the pressure of Lewis's lips and the nip of his teeth that burned in my memory and kept me tossing and turning in bed until early morning.

Why did he do it?

And why did I like it?

"Frances," Lewis calls and waves, though at this point I'm already standing in front of him. It's as if his limbs are operating at a ten-second lag. "Hi."

I switch my bag to my other shoulder. "Hi," I echo, and he leans forward as if to kiss my cheek, and I stretch out my hand to hug his shoulders, but in the end, we just hover around each other.

"Uh," I say, wondering if smooth Lewis, who ate straight out of my hands yesterday, was a figment of a few misfiring neurons.

Lewis clears his throat and blushes. I resort to plucking his coffee out of his hands, if only to end this horrible moment, but he shifts back, sending my fingertips to brush against his stomach. At the contact, my belly loops into a somersault.

"Uh," I repeat. Believe it or not, I have a PhD.

Our awkward dance doesn't end there. Lewis tries to pick something up from the floor but fails to account for how closely we stand together, and his chin hits my shoulder, while his nose skirts over my skin in the V of my silk blouse.

Mind stuck, all I get out is another, "Uh."

If he'd turn his head slightly, if he'd put his ear to my chest, he'd hear the way my heart tattoos its pattern of unforeseen attraction into the underside of my skin. Maybe he even senses it from where he froze in his movement.

"Sorry," he stammers, and then we finally manage to reconfigure. Once I take a step back, Lewis retrieves a tall takeaway cup from between his feet. "Brought you something."

Grateful to have something to wrap my fidgety fingers around, I cradle the cup to my chest. I already had coffee at home, but after the short night and the tally of sleep deprivation I've collected over the past weeks, I'd probably need an IV drip of caffeine to feel properly awake.

I smile up at him. "Thanks." The drink he's brought me is toothachingly sweet and topped by a layer of froth. In short, delicious. "What is it?"

He shrugs. "I asked the barista for something that wouldn't make you grimace like a regular cup of coffee does."

The drink settles warmly in my chest. "Thank you." I drain my cup at record speed as we trek up the hill to campus, if only to help me endure the heavy silence.

With Lewis's brother's graduation party coming up, we have no time to waste to get some more facts about each other down. Even if my academic integrity isn't at risk tonight, I know next to nothing about Lewis's family, or why he wants me to pose as his girlfriend. But the stakes must be pretty high, given that my company tonight was his main condition when he sealed the deal.

"So . . . Golf?"

He glances at me. "Yeah."

"Econ?"

"Yeah." He sighs again. When I don't say anything for a moment, he spreads out his hands. "Come on. Let me have it."

The air is finally fresh enough to not break into a sweat first thing in the morning, and the light is different after the rain, too. It glints in the puddles on the sidewalk, catching the golden strands of Lewis's hair.

As I consider him through narrowed eyes, I thumb the plastic lid on my takeaway cup. "It explains why you dress like a prep school boy. But I'm more curious as to . . . why?"

A corner of his mouth strays sideways, pulling his face into a grimace. "If you'd met my family, it wouldn't come as such a surprise."

"About that," I note. "What's the deal with your family? I'd say you don't have to tell me, but you kind of do. At least enough for me to get what's going on at the party tonight."

"Right."

Lewis bites the inside of his cheek and blinks his eyes shut for a moment, as if he needs to steel himself. Then, when he opens them again, he says, "I'll give you a rundown," and something in him has changed, like he's slipped into another version of himself.

I learn that Lewis has an older sister, Ada, short for Adeline, who works at his dad's firm and has been married for eight years to John, who, according to Lewis, is a textbook himbo, but has all the emotional intelligence Lewis and Ada never learned from their dad. They have a daughter, Alice, who Lewis has only met three times in person but often video chats with. Then, there's the youngest of the three siblings, Ben, short for Benjamin, whose graduation will be celebrated tonight, and their mother, "who can be nice if my father is not around." Last, and very much least, there's his father. From what Lewis says, I picture him as the quintessential money-hungry investment firm CEO shark. Lewis laughs when I tell him, and says grimly, "Not too far off."

All morning, I keep pushing my luck, asking questions about his family and surprisingly, they don't make Lewis shut down anymore. I suspect he welcomes my curiosity because it keeps us from getting into how we ended up with his lips on my finger last night. Whatever it is, I'm happy to finally learn more about him.

Between lectures, Lewis tells me how he grew up in a high-rise luxury apartment on the Upper East Side with a slew of au pairs, a meticulously planned-out week of extracurriculars, weekends in the Hamptons, and the persistent expectation to eventually take over his father's real estate investment firm. He mentions a year when he was shipped off to boarding school somewhere in the South of France, summers in some second (or third?) home on the Mediterranean coast, and winters in the Alps or the Rocky Mountains. His voice is offhanded, almost bored, and I notice how he sticks to a neutral retelling, sketching out a timeline and skirting over the details.

"Hey." He nudges my side as we make our way to the front of the coffee line, huddled together to keep our voices from drifting. With his arm draped around me and fingers drumming a distracting rhythm into the dip of my waist, he's so close that the plane of his chest shifts against my side whenever he breathes. Despite reminding myself that our embrace is only to keep up appearances, I find myself leaning deeper into it. I should be tired after the short night. But even now, as the double dose of caffeine is wearing off, my skin feels charged with the proximity of him. "This shouldn't be a one-way street. I know you have a sister . . . who just got married . . ." With his free hand, he passes me a clean mug, then takes one for himself. "Karo?"

I stare at him for a beat longer and miss that the line has advanced ahead of us. I'm impressed that he remembers Karo's name when I've only mentioned her once or twice.

"Yeah," I murmur as Lewis nudges me forward and grabs a sachet of sugar for me. "She stayed in Berlin for her studies, has been dating the same musician since high school, now works in publishing, and, as you correctly remembered, got married last week."

He lets go of me, and puts our coffee mugs under the dispenser, one after the other. "Is she older than you?"

"Younger. But she's the one of us who's better at the whole adulting thing."

"How so?"

I shrug. "She's just better. Her fiancé—no, husband—Lennart and her have it together. They have multi-seasonal plants on the balcony, and they get their picture frames custom-made. A few months ago, I helped her paint her living room wall."

"Okay." He narrows his eyebrows. "Sounds cozy?"

"It is," I agree. "My point is, she's settled. Stable. She knows she'll be living there for the next however many years, so she can afford to paint the walls of a rental, drill holes, and hang up pictures, and, well, do all the stuff you do when you have your life figured out."

Where I was antsy to explore the world, moving from our small town outside of Berlin to the big city was enough for Karo. I used to think she was playing it too safe by staying close to home and settling down with the boy she met in high school, but I'm not so sure anymore. More security in my life, fewer unknown variables? It doesn't sound that bad.

Fresh coffee in hand, Lewis leads me through a throng of students to a free high-top table. "Sounds like you two are close, though."

"We are. I don't know what I'd do without her. She's more like a big sister, really." I stir the sugar into my coffee. "She's the one constant I have, with all the moving I've done in the last few years. Though my parents have been supportive, too." He asks me about them, and I tell him how they met (as summer camp counselors when they were nineteen), how I grew up in a farmhouse that they renovated themselves, and how Sundays were a reliable routine of a long walk in the woods, followed by an elaborate home-cooked meal and one of my father's favorite vinyls playing in the background.

While he's listening to me Lewis sets his elbows on the table and traces the rim of the coffee cup with his index finger. As a strand of his hair flops forward, a forlorn expression ghosts over his features, and in response, something contracts in my chest. Something that makes me want to brush the golden strand off of his forehead. He grew up with money in a way that I only know from the TV shows of my teenage years, but it's not that. Although my family doesn't understand what I do for a living, much less why I'm willing to pack up my things and move across the world for it, they've never wavered in their support. What must it be like to be constantly pushed by your parents, to fulfill some image they draw based on a perfect idea rather than their child's personality?

Lewis lifts his gaze, and some of my sympathy must show on my face, because he blinks and pushes himself to his full height, as if to shake off his family's weight.

"Tell me about your time in Singapore," he prompts.

I look up at him, confused, until the coin drops. Just like I've tracked the changing universities under his name on academic papers, he's paid attention to mine, too, to the journey that has taken me across three continents. I tell him how I fell in love with the mountains in Switzerland, the street food markets in Singapore, the easy accessibility by bike in Denmark, and the blissful winter sun in Arizona.

After another set of back-to-back lectures, we eat lunch at the deli on Amsterdam Avenue. Lewis orders a chicken salad. The grilled cheese is as good as I remember, a thick layer that's perfectly melted in the middle, the bread crispy but not too oily.

I nudge my plate across the table. "Do you want some?"

Lewis shakes his head without looking at my sandwich. "Lactose intolerant."

The deli is tucked into the basement unit of a Columbia housing building, and from our vantage point at the window, we can only see the feet of people walking by. The Crocs of hospital staff at the end of their shift, the white sneakers, the leather sandals showing off freshly manicured nails. Only two other patrons are in the deli and, from the scrubs they're wearing, I deduce that Lewis and I are safe to catch up without tipping off any Sawyer's attendants.

Gradually, throughout the morning, my body got drunk on the pressure of Lewis's fingers, the warmth of his breath, the blanket of his scent. I'd hoped I could breathe a little deeper now that Lewis isn't glued to my side anymore, but my intoxicated state shows no signs of disappearing. There's something awake in his eyes, an unwavering focus, when he listens to me talk. I feel his attention like a touch to my temple, a nudge to my chin, a physical connection that grounds me in the here and now.

"So, what about your brother?" I ask. "You've only told me about Ada so far..."

Lewis stabs at his lettuce. "We're not really close because I've been living abroad for so long," he explains. "He's eleven years younger, so by the time he started being a person, I was already on my way out."

"Wow, that's difficult to imagine."

"I know," he says and wipes his fingertips on a paper napkin. "We share genetics, but not much else." He takes a sip from his water, the corners of his mouth weighing down. "I wish it would've gone differently, but I couldn't stand being around my parents and their expectations for my life anymore. I was tired of pretending for them. So I left."

His words from last night come back to me.

What's more loving than telling someone you accept them the way they are?

They were uttered in passing, but now I understand that there might be a deeper layer there, something Lewis has wished for but never gotten.

"Is that when you moved to Vancouver?"

He shakes his head. "Nah, that was later. This was still in undergrad. I was bored out of my mind in my econ classes, dreading the summer internship they'd arranged for me at my father's friends' firm. I realized it would never end—if I fulfilled one of the plans they'd set out for me, it would trigger the construction of the next." He drops his napkin into his empty bowl. "No satisfaction, no words of appreciation, no end point. It would go on and on. All for something I didn't even want." He's silent for a moment, following the path of a skateboard gliding across the pavement. "Which is why I broke off contact with them, changed my major, and finished college."

My heart squeezes together as I try imagining that kind of distance between Karo and me. "That sucks, I'm sorry. What's it like being around them now?"

He shrugs. "I don't know. Except for Ada, I haven't seen them in ten years."

I almost choke on my water mid-sip. "Jesus." I gape at him. "So I'll be part of the joyful family reunion today?"

Lewis grimaces. "Something like that."

"But they know I'm coming, right?"

"Something like that," he repeats. "Ada does. Maybe Ben, too? She told him I'd be in the city, though I explicitly asked her not to since I hadn't decided if I was going to the graduation party or not, and after the earful I gave her about that, I'm not sure she relayed the information about you."

We fall into silence as we walk back to campus, but a sense of unease swells inside me. We'll have to perform really well tonight if we want Lewis's family to believe us. Even if they've never bothered to know him for who he truly is, they haven't seen him in years. They might be more attentive than our fellow academics, who would rather think about new control conditions to add to their experiments than a relationship between colleagues.

Lab-based workshops are on the schedule this afternoon, so Lewis and I decide to skip the regular program and work in the library instead. After swiping our IDs at the entrance, we quietly make our way down a carpeted corridor between tall bookshelves.

"Are you sure you want to get back in touch with your family with a lie?" I whisper, searching for a free table to set up camp. "Karo would kill me."

Which reminds me that I haven't even updated her on our fake dating agremeent yet. I'm not sure if I'm looking forward to her call when she's back from the first hike of her honeymoon, or if I'm dreading the concern she'll no doubt express. It was her suggestion to fake date, but a growing physical attraction to my fake boyfriend is something she'd definitely consider *messy*.

"My parents can think whatever they want. I don't care," Lewis murmurs. "But yeah, it's not ideal for Ben and Ada. It'll make things easier, though. We just have to be really good."

"Why are you even taking me?" I ask. "I'm not having second thoughts, but seriously, couldn't you just go on your own?"

"You're foreign and new and my father is polite to the people he doesn't know," he says. "Image conscious. He won't make a scene. And since the whole thing is going to go down on a cruise, it's not like I can escape whenever I want."

I stop walking. "Hold up, what?"

A few steps ahead of me, Lewis turns around and clenches his jaw. "Yeah. We have to be at a pier downtown by seven thirty, from there the boat will cruise up the Hudson." He sighs. "I don't want to make this about myself, but it very much feels like someone deliberately chose a location I could not leave whenever I want to. Anyway, if you're afraid of boats, too, we can cancel?"

"Too?" I ask.

He tilts his head. "You don't like planes."

I swallow. "Boats are fine. So, I'm basically there to hang on to your arm and look pretty?"

"You're there to keep me sane." Lewis motions to a miraculously empty table in an alcove between two shelves. Behind it, a window stretches to the ceiling and lets in the pearly afternoon light. "But if you want to make my father uncomfortable, you could tell him how you've been renting for your whole life."

"Or that I've been putting all my money into a savings account?"

He snorts. "Good one."

I pull out the chair across from where Lewis unpacks his laptop and notebook. While I go through my inbox (zero grant updates), Lewis falls into an impressive rhythm of smacking keys on his keyboard and ticking off items in his notebook that, upside down, I can't decipher.

"Is that why your emails are like that?" I wonder, opening the first in a string of messages one of my master's students has sent me.

The rapid-fire key tapping stops. "What's that supposed to mean?"

"Oh . . . you know," I mutter, skimming through the wall of text in which the student spirals into borderline desperation over messing up a line of code and having to redo all her analyses.

Lewis clears his throat. "I don't?"

I close the email and find him looking at me over the edge of his laptop. "You come across a little cold in emails, messages . . . take your pick. But that's not news to you, is it?"

He frowns at me, then his screen, and I consider myself dismissed when he starts typing again. But halfway through reading the riveting tale of how my student fixed her code and thinks *It's okay now??? You're not gonna fail me for this, right?!*, my inbox dings with a new email.

Dear Dr. Frances Silberstein,

In clearing up misunderstandings between Silberstein et North, I feel like I owe you another explanation. You may have noticed how easily I get wrapped up in discussions about science. Looking at the data, my short way in written communication is likely a side effect of this excitement, and this can be narrowed down to three causal pathways:

1) I was very focused on condensing my observations and notes as precisely and compact as possible and,
2) I was often pressed for time between teaching classes and testing patients, but too eager to hear your thoughts to wait until I was back at my office, so I disregarded common etiquette and just fired them out.
3) I'm a bit of a texting grump.

I'm sorry for the disrespect this may have caused and the impression this may have left.

Kind regards,
Theodore Lewis North, PhD

His email is silly, formatted like a response letter to a paper submission, yet something like excitement races across my chest as I reread his words about me.

"Better?" he asks from the other side of the table.

"Better," I agree, bumping my knee into his leg. "Though if you compliment my brain one more time, it might go to my head."

He catches my gaze for a second. "Good," he says, and bumps back, causing sparks up my thigh and a sentence so nonsensical that I need to rewrite it for a third time before I send the email off to my student. I lose complete track of what I was doing when Lewis's knee brushes mine again, softer now, and then stays there. But his face is impassive, fingers flying over his keyboard again.

"Seriously?" I grumble.

Lewis keeps typing. "What?"

"You were all against digging into each other's current research when we made this pact, but then you resort to . . . cheap tactics of manipulation and distraction to keep me from doing my work?"

He peels his eyes away from his screen. "What?" he repeats, dumbfounded.

I draw back my leg, and as I knock it into his, he must finally understand, because he frowns and sits up.

"Sorry, I didn't realize." Seconds later, though, his face morphs into a smile, and he cocks up a brow. His sole taps against the side of my shoe. "So, you're saying this distracts you?"

I glower at him over the edge of my laptop. His eyes dip, no doubt tracking the flush that climbs up my throat.

"Don't be smug," I bite out. "And don't tell me you're not doing it on purpose."

"Doing what?" Eyes wide, he runs his fingers along his hairline, drawing my attention to another extremely attractive feature about him. At this point, I find everything about him attractive.

Physically, that is.

"This." My voice echoes loudly in the silent library, and I quickly bend forward to mutter, "All this teasing you're doing."

He mirrors my posture, and although there's still half of the table between us, he feels provokingly close.

"And why," he wonders quietly, "would I be teasing you?"

Under the table, his knees slot around mine. The pressure triggers a flash of electricity deep in the pit of my belly.

"Explain it to me," he insists as his hands spread wide over the surface of the table. The muscles in his forearms flex and shift, and when I look up again, I catch the glint in his eyes.

Playful. Challenging.

"You're nervous," I state. "About tonight. You're nervous about seeing your family, about pretending in front of Ada, and lying to Alice, but you're deflecting."

His eyes are unwavering, but the air feels heavier now, as if my observation has pulled it tighter around us.

"I'm right, aren't I?"

He works his jaw.

"You know, you could just tell me that you're nervous," I say. "And we could take care of it. Prepare better for tonight, make up a secret code so I can drag you out of any inconvenient situation."

His gaze slides to my mouth. "Yeah? How would you do that?"

I could kiss you.

The idea slams into my mind, unforeseen, but so blazingly clear that I have difficulty thinking of anything else. I tug at my collar, my skin lit up by his attention. It takes me a moment to realize that he *is* touching me, that he's lengthened his finger to drag it from my wrist to the knuckle of my middle finger.

My eyes, hell-bent to lead this conversation without me, dip to his lips. God, the set of his mouth should be forbidden.

He smirks when he recognizes my intentions. "You wouldn't dare," he says in a deep rumble that prickles down my spine.

His challenge stokes the fire in me. I want to show him how much I *would* dare. I want to see how far he lets me go in our weird new ceasefire friendship.

My chair scrapes over the floor as I stand and round the table. Lewis catches my hand—to keep me away or to pull me closer, I don't know.

"What are you doing?"

"You just dared me."

A blush dusts his cheeks. "I meant later. At the party."

I press my hip against the edge of the table, let the solid wood dig into my skin to yank me back to reality. "I'd do it if you want me to."

"Okay," Lewis says, voice grating over the word. He still hasn't let go of my hand, and there's that blond strand again, messing up the neat line of his forehead.

His hair—

My fingers tingle with the wish to touch it, tidy it, mess it up.

"But," I hear myself say, "based on our past performances, I'm not sure that kissing you would be the best idea. We're not very good actors, remember? What if you jump away once I get closer to you?"

"That's true," Lewis comments. "Although unlikely at this point," he adds, quieter.

"Right. To avoid that from happening again, let's consider what we're both good at."

He smirks. "Stomaching bad conference coffee?"

"The other thing."

A wrinkle appears in his forehead. "Science?"

I nod and step closer, until my knees almost brush his. "We should approach this methodically. If we decompose romantic relationships into their building blocks, we have, among others, emotional and physical intimacy."

"So?" Lewis asks. "I'm still not following."

"So, that's how we convince ourselves to make this relationship seem real. We've been telling each other about our lives all day, but that's not so different from what friends would do, right?" I bite my lip, cringing at the eager lilt of my voice.

His fingers, locked around mine, tighten.

"What's really missing is the body contact. The intimacy."

That's not quite the truth though. We've been touching for the better part of the day and are holding hands right as we speak, but somehow, it doesn't feel like enough. Somehow, I cannot stop thinking about the rough slide of his tongue against my thumb. Somehow, I keep wondering how it would feel dipping into the corner of my mouth.

"So essentially, you're hypothesizing that a kiss now..." he spells out my chain of logic, "would trick our bodies into the right mindset for later?"

"Precisely." Holding his gaze, I bring our hands to my hip and when he spreads his fingers, his thumb drags over my hip bone.

His eyes follow the path of it. "Yeah? You think it's that easy?"

"I've given you the hypothesis," I inform him. "Maybe you should test it."

One corner of his mouth ticks up. "Right. Any other steps you've thought about? The experimental procedure?"

With how tingly my entire body feels, I'm surprised I'm not visibly shaking from his touch at this point. "I'd say this is more of an exploratory study, though I know these don't quite match your high scientific standards—"

Suddenly he's up and crowds me against the lip of the table, arms bracketed around me.

"Will you shut up." He cups my chin with one hand to tip up my face. His gaze is dark and probing in a way that should make me feel vulnerable, but all I feel is the thrill of anticipation, a whisper of longing. With the heel of his hand on the base of my throat, he keeps me at a narrow distance, sensing my racing pulse. The air between us grows heavier with every passing breath, and I'm waiting, yearning for the tipping point.

"For practice?" he murmurs.

"For practice," I breathe.

Lewis runs his hand up my throat, and when his thumb skims over my bottom lip, some sound must rip out of me, because he quickly moves in and catches my whimper with his mouth.

His lips against mine are coffee sweetened with a hint of mint, and I discover that Lewis kisses just like he does everything else. Carefully, measured, and meticulous. I can't decide if his languid pace is infuriating or deliciously right, and when his fingertips skid against that sensitive spot behind my ear, they tug the barest whisper of a sigh out of me. The flutter behind my rib cage morphs into a heavy thud.

I rise to my tiptoes and brace myself against Lewis's chest. My hands roam up over the nape of his neck, the corner of his jaw, the places that have been out of reach all this time, but that I've been dying to touch. Desperate to get him closer, I hook my fingers through his belt loops, and then, finally, he brings his hips flush with mine. His hands trace the outsides of my legs, where they hesitate for a breath. I curve into him, frustrated by the last pockets of distance that remain between us, and he lifts me onto the table, bringing our heads to the same height and crowding into the space between my legs. Satisfied with the new angle, Lewis coaxes my mouth open with the tip of his tongue. His teeth skid across my lip and—

More.

I want more.

It's a singular thought flashing through my mind. Want claws its way down my body, and, hungry for the pressure, I tighten my thighs around his hips, sighing as I feel Lewis heavy with need against me. His next breath is audibly ragged, and it sends a pulse of heat low into my belly.

Before I can sink my hands into his hair and urge him to kiss me deeper, somewhere something heavy clangs to the floor. The shrieking sound of laughter hits my ears, and then I remember—we're in a library. Behind those shelves that shield off our little alcove, there are students. There might be *colleagues*.

What were we thinking? What was *I* thinking?

Clearly, nothing at all.

I pull away, and under my mouth and fingertips, I can sense the awareness gradually returning to Lewis, too. A slow wave of stiffening limbs, a shuddering breath, a shift backward.

"I . . ." I falter, mortified at how breathy I sound. How turned on I am.

"Frances," Lewis rasps, eyes blazing, lips bruised and raw. The gruff sound of my name and the disheveled sight of him make the desire spike up again, but it's narrowly chased by a grounding realization.

I just kissed Dr. Theodore Lewis North.

And even though I try to convince myself that it was merely in preparation for tonight's meeting of his family, the urge to get back to it tells me that it was more than practice. That, somehow, inexplicably, I liked it.

Chapter Twelve

I wrench my hands from Lewis's shirt like it's on fire, as awareness of what just happened singes through my veins.

"I—"

"We should probably—" Lewis says at the same time and drags a heavy hand through his hair. The collar of his button-down is crumpled, and my fingers tingle with the memory of messing it up. I shove them into my hair and scrape my curls into a bun so tight that my brain gets forced out of its dazed, horny state, then remind myself that this kiss was in preparation for tonight. So he can focus on reconnecting with his brother.

"Okay, so the data . . ." I try to revert back to scientific language while I tell my reward centers to stop demanding more, more, *more*, but my voice sounds breathless.

Lewis's brows flick up as he echoes, "The data?"

"Yes, the data. The kiss." I clear my throat. "We hypothesized that, uh, some physical intimacy would make this relationship seem real." I can't tell who of us I'm reminding. With his lips against mine and his hands on my thighs, the kiss felt dangerously close to the real thing.

Real desire.

Which it can't be, because we're only doing this for a specific purpose: protecting my academic integrity, and helping Lewis reconnect with his family. Everything else is secondary, so I need to get over how my body still hums with his proximity.

I try to get off the table, but while Lewis has pulled back, he hasn't left the place between my open legs, which makes me slide down his body until I'm eye-level with his mouth.

"*Fuck*, Frances," Lewis growls, stopping me with a palm on my hip, inadvertently trapping me between him and the table. His hardness against my abdomen leaves no doubt that he must've been into this kiss, too.

All my blood collects in my cheeks. I didn't think this through.

"Could you, please . . ." My hand *trembles* as I motion for him to move out of the way.

"Oh." He glances down at the sliver of space between us. With his head tipped forward, I get a whiff of his hair and a front row view of the blond strands. It's not helping. "Right." But our lanyards are tangled up in each other, keeping us chained together. Knuckles brush as we hastily work ourselves free. When he finally steps back, his hip catches against a chair and topples it over.

Desperate to put some distance between us, I rush to the opposite side of the table where my laptop is propped open. Lewis picks up the chair, then meets my eyes with a sheepish expression, one corner of his mouth tucked up. "I—I think we should talk about this."

A sticky, uneasy feeling prickles over my skin.

Talk?

Absolutely not. We don't need to. Nothing's amiss, because this kiss was meant to make us more convincing as a couple. The way it set me alight doesn't mean anything. It cannot.

We're colleagues, and those are better off not fooling around, not kissing, and, most especially, not dating.

I force a smile. "No need to talk. We agreed it was practice, right?"

One kiss is hardly enough practice, my lizard brain supplies as my eyes get caught on Lewis's lips, still swollen from being pressed against mine. I need to get out of here before I find an excuse to kiss him again. Shoving my laptop into my bag, I yank it over my shoulder. As I reach for my water bottle, it tips over and rolls toward the edge, but Lewis catches it before it falls. I debate whether I really need my bottle back or if I can leave it behind and get a new one, when Lewis holds it out.

"Here," he says, and I'm not sure if I'm imagining the resignation in his voice. "Text me your address, okay? I'll pick you up later."

The afternoon rushes by in a flurry of getting ready for the graduation party tonight, all while downplaying to myself just how horny that kiss made me. I'm angry and annoyed that after years of having meaningless flings, it's not a random friend of a friend who made me feel this way but Lewis, who is decidedly off-limits as a colleague.

I'm also scared he'll want to talk about the kiss when I see him again, no doubt to tell me what a big mistake it was. But it turns out that in light of the upcoming reunion with his family, he isn't very interested in talking anymore. He's quiet when he picks me up, a stoic figure poured into a three-piece suit that's such a deep blue it brings out the color of his eyes. For a moment, at the door, his gaze drifts down my face and snags on the halter neckline of my dress. The lilac chiffon fabric hugs my body close and exposes my back. But then his expression closes up again and he stays quiet for the entire taxi ride downtown, pulling on his cuff links with his thumbs and radiating nervous energy.

"Here we go," are the first words he utters, after paying for the taxi and guiding me down the pavement to Pier 11. Before us lies a yacht that's as big as the ferries leaving to Brooklyn or Staten Island from the neighboring piers. People wearing tailcoats and evening gowns spill out of the two-story cabin onto the deck, while the tasteful soundtrack of a jazz band sweetens our wait. The tinkle of a piano, the croon of a saxophone, the excited chatter of the party guests. Our names are checked, and then we're walking up the short gangway. It bobs with the sway of the waves, and I wobble in my strappy high heels until Lewis grabs my arm.

Inside, a seamless window front encloses the salon on the lower deck, revealing a view of the soaring skyscrapers to one side and the majestic Brooklyn Bridge on the other. Beyond the opulent setting, wealth is apparent in the shine of people's hair and their smooth complexions, the sleek ties and glistening necklaces.

"Is this your family's? Why didn't you tell me they owned a freaking yacht?" I call over my shoulder, the air a cool relief from the heat outside. "They do own this thing, right? Are you sure you don't want anything to do with them anymore?"

When I turn around, I catch Lewis's gaze snap from my back to his wrists. The shells of his ears have turned pink and he's nervously fiddling around with his cuff links again.

Before we can make our way farther into the room, I pull Lewis into a nook under the stairs that lead to the top deck. But despite my heels putting my eyes almost level with his, I'm not strong enough to womanhandle him, so we stumble into the alcove, which is smaller than it looked from afar. My face gets squished against the smooth skin of Lewis's neck.

"What the fuck," Lewis hisses into my temple as he trips over my toes. The alcove's original inhabitant, a potted palm tree, leaves little space for us.

"Sorry—"

To stop us from falling over, he clamps an arm around my waist. His hand lands on my spine, now exposed by the low dip of my dress.

Warm.

Firm.

I inhale sharply at the sudden contact. The air hitting my lungs is ninety percent log cabin with an afterthought of oxygen. I breathe him in again, once, twice, before I weasel a hand between us and peel myself off his neck.

"Why—"

"It's not how I'd planned it. But. Here." I maneuver him around, shielding us from view by the width of his shoulders. The wall is a grounding weight at my back, allowing me to recover from the onslaught of feelings his proximity has triggered. They only feel more intense now, after we kissed. Practice or not, that kiss in the library was a terrible idea.

Lewis brushes the fanning leaves of the palm tree out of his face. "Christ, what was *that* for?"

"You seemed nervous," I say. "Are you okay?"

"Before you shoved me into a wall, I was."

I narrow my eyes at him, at his face cast in shadows in the dimly lit alcove. "You were not," I insist. "You started getting all flushed again."

"Jumping to conclusions, are we?" He studies me and heat blooms wherever I notice his gaze, spreading from my shoulders over my neckline and up my throat. "Maybe it wasn't nerves. Maybe I was just mesmerized by my pretend girlfriend."

"Yeah right," I scoff. "You looked more like you're already

missing the wrinkled shirts and elbow patches of our dear colleagues."

"That, too." He gives me a small smile that disappears as soon as he sneaks a glance out of our hiding spot. "This place brings back so many memories."

I raise my eyebrows. "So, this yacht is like your family's party boat?"

"I've never seen it, so it could be borrowed from a family friend? But no, I meant the . . ." He gestures over his shoulder. "Crowd. The vibe. I left for a reason, and being back is weird. I keep wondering—if this is how my brother celebrates his graduation, do I really want to meet him? It seems more like something my father would do."

His sigh tugs something loose in me. I know I can't make this situation with Lewis and his brother right, but I can try my best to support him through it. "Jumping to conclusions, are we?" I parrot him, imbuing his words with all the gentleness I can muster, lest he take them as an attack. "Look, unless you want to make a run for it in the next thirty seconds or so, we're here now. Maybe give your brother and this whole event a chance?"

I flatten a crease in his collar and smooth the pad of my thumb over the lines of worry etched into his forehead. Lewis blinks at me, but I'm as surprised as he is at the sudden contact.

If only I hadn't kissed him, maybe it would be easier to keep my hands to myself.

It's alright, I tell myself. This has nothing to do with wanting to touch him again. I'm getting into character. *Supportive girlfriend, remember?*

"Besides, if there's one thing I learned recently, it's that people can surprise you," I continue, "and maybe he can, too."

When Lewis reaches for my hand, my belly tumbles into a

little swoop, even if all he does is tuck my arm into the crook of his elbow. I really need to get a grip, mind over matter and all that stuff, otherwise the next ten days will be an exquisite form of torture for my touch-deprived body.

"As much as it pains me to say this, Dr. Silberstein, I think you may be right. Shall we?"

Leaving the alcove on his arm, I widen my eyes in fake astonishment. "Look at you, agreeing with me for once! Who would've thought that he, the man they call Dr. Theodore Lewis North, the one who's always right, was capable of uttering those words."

He lets out an exasperated sigh as he tugs me closer. "Jesus, maybe I do want to make a run for it."

Chapter Thirteen

"What do you think? Fourth marriage or fifth?" I whisper behind my flute of champagne, tilting my chin in the direction of a middle-aged guy with a thick gray mustache as he shuffles by. "Or first, but secret, affair with the help?"

Lewis coughs mid-sip, and I remove my hand from his arm to softly pat his back. The boat must've departed more than fifteen minutes ago, yet Lewis doesn't seem like he's in a hurry to look for his family. As we toss down glasses of sparkling wine and sample the various bites, I resort to guessing the attendants' scandals, hoping this will soothe him ahead of the inevitable reunion.

When a tray with bite-size puff pastry pockets floats by, I pluck one off and pop it into my mouth. Across from us, an older woman talks to what must be one of Ben's friends, judging by his age. "Interesting . . . a lady friend," I observe as she squeezes his shoulder. Based on what Lewis told me, the personal drama in these social circles tends to be a little less juicy than what *Gossip Girl* has led me to believe, so it's likely she's simply the mother of a childhood friend. But he's finally loosening up, so I keep the outrageous ideas coming.

Lewis hands his empty glass to a waiter. "She actually dealt drugs when we were in school," he notes, tipping his temple toward a woman in a modest two-piece suit. The brown color of her ensemble makes her look unfavorably pale, but I do another take at the down-turned corners of her mouth.

"Really?"

The glimmer in Lewis's eyes tells me he was joking. I'm relieved he's finally relaxing, but before I can respond, a small shape hurtles at us and collides with his legs.

"Uncle Teddy!" the girl exclaims. I check if anybody is with her, but she seems to be on her own. She's maybe six or seven years old and her sparkly outfit makes me like her instantly. Velvety green trousers, a white shirt, deep purple patent leather shoes, and, my favorite detail, a black-and-white-striped top hat. She looks like she whisked here after her shift as a circus magician.

Lewis folds himself around her, bending at the hip to lift up the girl. "You're so much bigger than in the camera!"

She wrinkles her nose. "Not enough."

"Has Dani grown taller than you, again?" he asks her.

"One inch," she grumbles. Her hair is the same shade as Lewis's, although much curlier, and their smiles are identical, if you ignore her two missing front teeth. She must be Alice, his niece.

"Where did you leave your mom?" Lewis clutches her with one arm, removes the hat, and deposits it on his own head.

Alice flaps her hand toward the window front. "Somewhere over there." When she spots me, she twists around in his arms, blue eyes zeroing in on me. "Who are you?"

"Frances," I introduce myself and hold out my hand. She considers it skeptically. "I'm your uncle's girlfriend," I say, to which she puckers her lips.

Tough crowd.

"Girlfriend," she repeats and turns in Lewis's arms. "Why do you have a girlfriend?"

He sets her down and the way he crouches to her height warms me up from within. "Because she's wonderful," he says.

"Hm."

"And smart," Lewis continues, squeezing her elbow. "And I like spending time with her." He sounds almost sincere enough to convince me, too. It tickles a small smile out of me.

"Okay." She frowns at him. "Is Miss Frances in danger?"

"What? Why would she be in danger?" Then, he cups a hand around her ear, and leans in to whisper something I can't catch.

"Ooh, okay. Well, Mom said *Doctor* Frances must be part of a witness production program—"

"Witness protection program?" Lewis interjects.

She glares at him. " . . . because you've never told us about her."

"I'm not in danger," I hurry to say.

"Okay . . ." She takes my hand very hesitantly.

"And what's your name?" I ask her, though I already know it.

"Alice. Do you also read brains, like Uncle Teddy?"

"Yeah I do," I say, fighting a grin, and look up at the man in question. "Teddy?"

Before he can reply, the music stops, the conversations in the room louder now that they're not carried by a blanket of melodies. As the dull sound of someone tapping a mic echoes through the speakers, Alice pulls me closer to a stage in the corner of the room. I guess she's accepted me as her uncle's girlfriend.

Lewis, still wearing Alice's much-too-small top hat, rolls his eyes. "I've always been Teddy to my sister. Al took it over from her."

Alice tries to catch a glimpse of the microphone on her

tiptoes until Lewis scoops her up again to give her a view over the crowd. She grabs the back of his collar, and their familiarity takes me by surprise. After Lewis's rundown of his family situation, I wasn't expecting a kind welcome, but then again, he mentioned staying in touch with Ada and her daughter while keeping his distance from everyone else.

The commotion turns out to be a toast. "There's Grandpa," Alice whispers excitedly, but only gets a tight nod from Lewis in response. Although he prepared me earlier today, up until now his issues with his father have felt insubstantial. But his tension and his reluctance to say hello catapult it into reality.

"Welcome, welcome," Mr. North greets the crowd with outstretched arms, and the resemblance to his son is uncanny. He looks like an aged version of Lewis: same shock of hair—though his is shimmering silver at the temples—same square jaw and clear eyes. But where Lewis tends to smile reluctantly, with only a corner of his mouth, his father shows off his whitened teeth in a confident smile. His voice is a little rougher around the edges and deeper than Lewis's, as he invites Ben to join him on the small stage. Half a head taller than his father, Ben has the same winning smile, though it's softened by his boyish looks; the dimple to one side of his mouth and the curve of his chin.

Mr. North launches into a speech about Ben's studies at Princeton—Mr. North's own alma mater—and how he's graduating with honors, showing off the discipline and dedication that is inherent to the North family name. "For the most part," Mr. North adds, and from Lewis's sharp intake of breath, I gather that it's another stab of resentment aimed at his other son.

Mr. North goes on to name-drop several companies and programs for which Ben has interned and volunteered over the past years, and ends his speech with a formal welcome to the best company of them all, North Star Investments. At its mention, a cluster of older men hollers.

"Jesus," Lewis exhales next to me.

Ben, who's been smiling good-naturedly through the entire speech, runs a hand over his buzz cut and raises his glass for everyone to cheer. "Thank you all for coming!"

As applause thunders through the room and the crowd disperses enough to open up paths for the waitstaff, Lewis sets down his niece, snatches up another flute of champagne, and tosses it back in one gulp.

I'm about to ask him if he wants to head outside when Alice grabs Lewis's and my hands, hauling us through the room with no regard for the people standing in her way.

"Al, hold up."

But Alice doesn't listen. She keeps pulling us through the crowds until she stops right in front of a man and a woman, fits my hand into Lewis's, and lets go. Standing tall, she announces, like a courtier in a throne room, "Uncle Teddy and Dr. Frances. His girlfriend."

The woman, who must be Alice's mother, Ada, pulls me into a hug. Even in her heels, she's half a head shorter than me. "So, you're the long-guarded secret and the reason Teddy's been too busy to drop by these past days. It's so nice to finally meet you. And you," she adds, voice sharper as she's turning to Lewis. "If I'd known that all it takes to get you here is a scientific conference, I would've chaired one years ago."

Lewis stoops down to greet his sister with a kiss on one cheek. She has the same upturned eyes as her brother's, and her thick chestnut curls are pulled into some complicated half braid. The man at her side introduces himself as her husband, John, enveloping my hand with both of his in a warm handshake.

As we get offered another drink, I pick it up gratefully,

only to realize that I should eat something solid. I crane my neck, but all I can see are square plates with dollops of colorful pastes and tiny glasses with tails of grilled scampi hooked over the rim. The vegetarian bites I sampled were delicious but do nothing to soak up the—three? four?—flutes of champagne I've downed.

Lewis seems to be following my train of thought, because he leans close to my ear, stirring my heart into a quicker pulse. "I think tiny food is all we're going to get," he murmurs. "I'll get you a slice on the way home."

As he leans back, a tall figure flings itself into our circle and I immediately recognize it as Ben. "Ada, have you seen Mom—Oh." He stops short in front of us, eyes wide and fixated on Lewis.

"Hi, Ben," Lewis says hesitantly, opening up his arms as if to hug his brother, but somewhere midway he reconsiders the movement, falters, and leaves them suspended in the air. "I— well. We . . ."

His awkwardness is painful to watch, like at Vivienne and Jacob's, but a hundred times amplified. It takes him a moment until he becomes aware of his arms again, lowers his elbows and yanks the back of his collar. Neck and ears flushing, he throws me a helpless glance.

I step up next to him. "Congratulations. I'm Frances, Lewis's girlfriend."

Ben smiles and shakes my hand. "Hi, thank you for coming," he greets me politely, but then his eyes stray back to his brother's face. "I didn't think you'd come," he says, words sounding a lot more clipped than when he was talking to Ada or even me. "Ada told me you were in the city, but I didn't . . ." He breaks off, tilts his head. "And now you're here."

Lewis inhales deeply. "I am."

I have the urge to grab each of their shoulders and shove

them together, to make them hug, and stop being this stiff with each other, but instead, I resort to pushing my index finger into the center of Lewis's back. The gesture felt reassuring back at Vivienne and Jacob's place when he did it to me. It told me I had someone in my corner, and I hope it'll tell Lewis the same now.

"I mean, of course I had to be here. I didn't want to miss any of this," Lewis says to his brother and holds out his hand to him. "Congrats."

After what feels like a million moments too many, Ben finally takes Lewis's hand. "Thank you."

Once the band wraps up and a DJ takes over, the party quickly picks up speed, a skittering beat replacing the classy jazz. John and Ada get roped into a conversation by another couple, and after many attempts at stimulating some conversation between the brothers, they are finally chatting about the trip to Europe Ben is planning for later this summer. Lewis tells Ben about his favorite places to visit in and around London, and as someone stops by to congratulate Ben, Lewis squeezes my hand and finds my gaze.

"Hey, why don't you ask Alice if she wants to dance?" he suggests, nodding over at his niece. Alice sits cross-legged against one of the windowed walls, face pulled into a bored pout. Behind her, the setting sun bruises the sky.

"Are you sure?" I check, remembering how he wanted me as a buffer around his family.

"Yeah, I'm good here." Lewis gives me a brief smile just as Ben turns back around.

I crouch down in front of Alice. "Will you dance with me?" I ask her, to which she nods enthusiastically. After a quick look at Ada, who signals that she'll find us upstairs shortly, we make our way to the dance floor on the second deck. It only takes me half a song to understand that Alice and I have decidedly different energy levels. My heart thunders in my chest as I try to keep up with her jerking dance moves, pulling her back when she jumps out of our safe perimeter and into a circle of Ben's classmates. Ada and John join us after a few songs, and we take turns bopping with Alice and recharging with cold drinks. I'm having so much fun dancing with them and spotting all the similarities with Lewis that I almost forget that I'm not here as his real girlfriend.

At some point, the boat's horn vibrates to signal the yacht turning back toward Manhattan. Lewis remains out of sight, and I picture him finally talking to his brother. I know they won't make up for a lifetime of distance in one evening, but perhaps they can lay a foundation to patch up their communication. But then I spot Ben's tall frame weaving through the crowd and stepping up to the bar on his own. The way he drops his head into his hands while he waits for his drink tells me I've made a mistake. Even though Lewis asked me to, I shouldn't have left him alone.

I hurry down the stairs to the lower deck. Outside, the sky has darkened, and the windows reflect the interior of the lounge. Orbs hang at different lengths from the ceiling, basking the room in a soft glow and creating enough light for me to finally spot Lewis, his father by his side and, with her back to me, a woman with dark, shoulder-length hair. I let out a breath when I see how casually they're conversing. Mr. North laughs at some point, so surely things can't be going too badly.

Except then I get closer and see how rigid Lewis is holding himself, how his hand is clenched into a fist at his side, knuckles white and thumbnail pressing into the side of his finger. And then I catch his father's words, "... It's not ideal, but I'm sure you picked up *some* transferable skills in your studies."

Yikes.

I make a move to step into their circle, but Lewis catches my gaze before I can close the distance. I lift my eyebrows and nudge my head to the side, hoping he'll read what I'm trying to communicate: *Do you need me?*

He gives his head the barest of shakes, like he's got it—like he wants to give his parents another chance on his own. "I'm here for Ben, not for you," he then says, surprisingly calmly. "You don't need to mine my résumé for any transferable skills, but thank you for *such* a generous offer."

I'm proud of him for standing up to his parents when— from the little I know—it's probably one of the few times he's done so, but that doesn't mean he should feel alone. Deciding to stay by his side while respecting the space he asked for, I perch on an empty stool close enough to let me listen in on the conversation and come to his rescue whenever he needs.

"Richard, dear, let him be." The woman—Mrs. North— puts a hand on her husband's arm.

"But how much time does he need for this phase to be over?" he asks her. "Ben and Ada were able to grow up ..."

Mrs. North leans closer to his ear and says something that I can't catch, but it seems to appease her husband as he pats her hand and smiles down at her. "You're absolutely right," he hums in agreement.

"A phase?" Lewis spits out. His voice sounds a million degrees colder than when we fight about measuring neural replay, and more than a few curious glances snap his way. "My research isn't a phase to build character until I'm ready to be your perfect son again."

But they keep talking about him as if he's a somewhat

difficult twelve-year-old rather than a fully grown and independent man with a PhD and a career in neuroscience.

"How's your German?" his dad asks when he finally turns back to his oldest son. He hovers his hand in the air as if he's about to give him one of those painful-looking finance-bro slaps on the pec. "The office in Europe isn't doing so well these days, so perhaps . . ."

"That's a great idea," Mrs. North agrees with an enthusiastic nod.

"Jesus, do you ever listen to anyone but yourselves?" Lewis exclaims.

Uh-oh. The group closest to us turns their heads at the raised voice, but Lewis doesn't notice, or he doesn't care. "I'm not going to dick around in some sleek boardroom, and push money from rich people to other rich people. Not here, not anywhere. Besides, you have Ben for that now."

"Don't make a scene, Theodore," his mother shushes him, throwing a glance over her shoulder, and it's then that Lewis's mask slips. Just for a second, his withdrawn look becomes one of exhaustion and the lines around his eyes turn deep and tired and resigned, like he knows and has always known that he's on his own. That there's nobody on his side to stand up for him. And when he stands up for himself, the people who should care the most don't even listen.

It makes my heart *ache*.

Before I know it, I'm walking toward him. Not to help his family save face, because I couldn't care less about the gossip-hungry people around us, craning their necks and snickering in mock embarrassment. Not to satisfy his mother, who gasps indignantly as I move past her and slide up to him. Not to convince his father, who thinks his son isn't good enough.

I just want to get Lewis out of there.

"Hi," I say brightly, and force myself into their circle. "Mr.

and Mrs. North? It's *so* nice to finally meet you. Lewis has told me all about you and, you know, how you helped him build his character so he's become one of the most promising scientists Germany has to offer. He's humble about it, so I'm not sure he's told you." I lean closer and say, "But only last year he was awarded a prize by the German Academy of Sciences to honor the groundbreaking research he produces, and honestly, they were right to. He's absolutely brilliant at what he does. I've watched his career for four years now and he's not only meticulous and ambitious, but he looks out for others, too—shares his data, helps where he can. And all thanks to you and how generously you let him pursue his passion."

I finally pause to catch a breath and look at Lewis, whose gaze is sharp as it tracks over my face. Lips parted slightly, his eyes burn up my cheek until they meet mine. "Hey, you." At his rasp, a charge flicks in the pit of my belly. I see a flash of us between the library shelves, his touch at the pulse of my throat, fingers curled against the underside of my jaw. When he looks at me like that, like I'm the question he's most eager to investigate, I almost get the feeling he could want me, too.

Too?

What the hell, Frances?

That cursed kiss really shouldn't have happened.

Someone clears their throat.

Right.

His parents.

The ones who have been stunned to silence by my impassioned speech before I got distracted. I need to focus. I came here to extract Lewis from this situation, not to remember how he kissed me, and yearn for an encore while standing right in front of his parents. I'm here as his pretend girlfriend and confrontation buffer. Which is *why* Lewis looked at me like that. He's doing a better job at faking this than I am.

Mentally, I tip a bucket of ice water over my face, forcing my thoughts back on track. Physically, I shove my hand toward Mrs. North first, then Mr. North. Both have rearranged their faces into polite smiles.

"Anyway. Congratulations on your son's graduation!"

Mr. North grips my hand confidently. "Thank you. We're very proud of our Benjamin." By now I've seen enough of this man to understand that the side-eye at Lewis is fully intentional. I really have no time to lose to get us out of the perimeter of Lewis's perpetually disappointed parents.

I smile sweetly. "I can see that. It's a very . . . grand celebration. If you go all out for a BSc, it makes me wonder what you would've done for Lewis's PhD. It's probably good that you weren't even talking to him when he graduated."

Mrs. North covers up her cry of surprise with a cough. Mr. North releases my hand and the grin stays on his face, except it's looking a little tight now. "You must be the girlfriend that Ada told us about. Miss . . ."

"Silberstein," I inform him. "Though that's *Doctor* to you." When I turn, a smirk plays around the corners of Lewis's mouth. I rub the tip of his shirt collar between my fingertips. "Wanna dance?"

He blinks at me, catching my hand and pressing it against his chest. Through the three layers of fabric, I feel the quickened beat of his heart. "Yeah, I do."

Once we're out of Lewis's parents' sight, I suggest taking a breath outside. My legs are tired after all the dancing with Alice, and Lewis's pensive expression tells me he'd rather talk than twirl me around to the beat of an eighties power ballad. With a hand on the small of my back, Lewis guides me through the clusters of party guests to a corner of the stargazing deck, and I have a hard time trying not to think about the charge that circles around his touch.

Lewis lets go of me and leans his back against the railing. As he takes a deep breath of the night air, he closes his eyes, like he needs to process the encounter with his parents. I leave him to it, glad to have a moment to collect myself, too.

It feels like I've stepped into a dream. I don't know if it's the alcohol I've consumed, or the waves that lap against the bow and drown out the noise from inside, but the world seems a little smudged around the edges. There's a salty wind toying with the hem of my dress, raising goosebumps on my skin, and blowing Lewis's hair onto his forehead. The gentle sway of the boat nudges me to take a step forward, to get closer to Lewis, who looks all levels of handsome framed by the twinkling lights of Manhattan's skyscrapers.

As if he's sensing my proximity, he opens his eyes. "I'm such an idiot." He sighs, pinching the bridge of his nose. "Making you go to this stupidly fancy party, then I barely even talk to my brother, and I end up trapped with my parents pulling the same stunts they always have."

I give him an encouraging smile. "You made an effort to see your family and showed Ben that you care. I don't think that makes you an idiot."

Lewis ducks his head to catch my gaze. "Thank you for saving me in there. And for everything you said."

"That's what I'm here for," I say, distracted by how he reaches to tug at the knot of his tie, then slides the top two buttons of his shirt open. "To convincingly pose as your girlfriend."

With his tie undone like that, hair ruffled, and frown etched into his brow, I finally admit to myself that me being convincing is not about my acting skills anymore. I feel tingly and lightheaded, as if I've downed too many glasses of bubbly.

Something soft and giddy at my core makes me want to run my fingers over the lines of worry on Lewis's forehead.

No, Frances, no.

I give myself a mental shake. There's no need to touch him now, when nobody out here needs to be convinced of our relationship status.

The kiss and all this play-pretend are messing with my head.

"If it was only about that," Lewis remarks, eyes roaming over me, "you wouldn't have had to say all those things. You could've just interrupted and pulled me away."

I could've, but it didn't occur to me then. Instead, all I wanted was for him to understand he had someone looking out for him, and maybe that's even more worrisome than the lingering attraction in my belly.

"Or maybe I should've kissed you instead," I retort, knowing it'll make him blush. "*That* would've shut them up."

As predicted, his cheeks redden, but he looks unfazed by it, his mouth cutting into a knowing smile. "Must've been a good kiss if you're still thinking about it," he observes drily.

He looks smug as he tracks the heat that now rises into my face, too.

I make an attempt to steer the conversation into safer waters. "How do you feel about tomorrow?"

He knits his brow. "Why?"

"Your lecture," I clarify, and Lewis's expression tightens, one hand coming up to fiddle with his cuff links again. Remembering his revelation that he's shy in front of crowds, I ask, "Do you want to go through it?"

"Here?"

"Why not." I shrug. "We still have some time to kill until we're back at the pier, right?"

Lewis nods darkly, throwing a glance at his phone. "Just under an hour."

"Right, then we have plenty of time. You can tell me your outline, what you're unsure about. Or just . . ." I trail off when he pulls his notebook out of the inside pocket of his suit jacket. Of course he brought it along.

"I'm okay once I get to the part about my research," he says, "but I'm not sure my intro will help the students make sense of it. I want them to be able to understand it *and* give them the tools to critique it."

For the next twenty minutes, Lewis shares his lecture with me, seemingly having memorized the whole thing. As the wind flaps through the pages of his notebook, I give him pointers on things he can skip (a long-winded timeline of electroencephalography research that would fit into a History of Psychology class) and the ones he should expand on. Lewis takes notes and then murmurs the newly workshopped text to himself.

"It's funny to think that only a week ago, I was at my parents' place, with all the chaos of last-minute wedding preparations," I muse when he slips his notebook back into his jacket. "And in the middle of it all, I was trying to finish the slides for my lecture and interactive code for the workshop."

He laughs. Not that dry kind he gave his parents, but a mellow one, its warmth trickling down my spine.

"And now I'm standing here," I continue, "playing make-believe with my annoying reviewer, at his brother's graduation party, working on his lecture."

"He wasn't so bad, was he?" He pushes his hair back, mouth relaxed and eyes twinkling.

With the newfound knowledge that he wasn't, in fact, the mean reviewer, I find myself smiling when I say, "Yeah, turns out he's actually a somewhat decent human being."

There it is again, that smooth rumble of a laugh. "Decent enough to ask me to fake date you for two weeks." Lewis crosses his arms in front of his chest and takes a measuring look at me. "What was it that made you fall in fake love with me? My horrible abstract-writing skills?"

"I figured you couldn't be that bad when you held my hand through a panic attack," I admit, surprised at my own honesty.

I wait for him to remind me that I technically maimed his hand, but he just hums softly in agreement. "What made *you* change your mind, though?" I ask. "To agree to fake date me?"

"Well." Lewis stares at our feet. When he taps the tip of his shoes against mine, I realize that we've slowly inched toward each other. "I'm responsible for stalling your career in one way, so once you explained how detrimental it could be if anybody found out about us, I knew I needed to help. I meant what I said yesterday, Frances." He pauses to finally look back up at me, and the glimmering skyline reflects in his eyes. "It's never been about tearing you down. I want to see you succeed. Plus, it meant squabbling with you from less distance, so . . ."

Once again, his true intentions grate against the image I've constructed of him over the past four years. "And here we are, not even bickering anymore," I say with a smile, resting my arms on the railing next to him. The air is gritty on our cheeks, the slosh of the water loud in our ears, and, for the first time since arriving in New York, my thoughts aren't rushing elsewhere. They're anchored here, as we watch the matrices of half lit-up skyscrapers glide past and talk about everything and nothing. The places we've lived, the most outrageous excuses our students have come up with, the niche knowledge Lewis has acquired about *The Witcher* after reading Brady's fan fic for so many years.

I feel at peace, until we round the tip of Manhattan and the Brooklyn Bridge comes back into view in all her lit-up glory. Until Lewis lifts a corner of his mouth and mutters, "I like us more like this."

I look up at him as my heart balloons with hope, though

I know it shouldn't. It should stick close to the ground, and to get it back there, I pinprick it with the reality of the situation. Lewis and I have a pact with an end date, he's a colleague, we live in different countries. He was talking about us as allies. Teammates, collaborators, maybe friends. Nothing more. I have to keep reminding myself of this as we fall silent and look out at the water.

As the boat docks at the pier, the vibration of the motor stops underfoot. "Can I take you out for that slice of pizza now?" Lewis asks and hooks a thumb over his shoulder.

An ambulance howls down the FDR and I wait for the sound to pass. "Please," I say, though I had completely forgotten I was hungry. Because all I can think about is that I like us more like this, too.

Maybe a little too much.

Chapter Fourteen

Lewis makes us stop at his favorite pizza place in Hell's Kitchen on the way back uptown, one of those hole-in-the-wall places that are cash and standing-room only. Even under the stark, fluorescent light, with his tie flapping open around his neck, Lewis looks a million times more at ease than back on the boat. We eat our slices crowding around a tiny sliver of the bar table, his a marinara and mine with vodka sauce, and then he takes me back home, offering a softly spoken "Thank you for coming today" when he says goodbye at my door.

And my heart does that weird buoyant thing again.

Which it shouldn't. Because while our history goes over four years back, I've only really known him for five days, and for most of those, I thought we despised each other. But his apology yesterday flipped everything around, and I can't stop thinking about how good he felt pressed against my body in the library, how well his hand fit on the small of my back, and how, even though he already answered so many of them today, I have a million more questions I want to ask him.

I don't want to think so much about him, and yet it feels

like my brain is starting to dedicate an entire lobe to him. I try to remind myself that it's natural. The kiss predictably triggered a cascade of biological processes, including a heavy dose of hormones, and they're the real reason for why my feelings for Lewis are amplified.

It was biology that caused those glitches on the boat today, where I felt like my neurons fired a little harder, just for him.

Upstairs, I peel my dress off, hang it on the shower rack, wipe off my makeup and slather on moisturizer, all while oddly specific details about Lewis loop through my mind. The dimple in his chin, the freckles on the bridge of his nose that have multiplied since Saturday, the top two buttons of his shirts that he always leaves unbuttoned and, worst of all, the parsing look in his eyes in the library before he moved in to kiss me.

Since it's just biology, the good news is that all I need is a little time away from him to recalibrate.

The bad news is, I have to get through another forty-eight hours with Lewis before the weekend.

Less if I tell him to head to campus tomorrow morning without me. Even less if we don't spend the evenings together like we have for the last few days, which I'm sure we don't need to, since Lewis didn't mention any more family obligations, and our colleagues at the conference seem convinced of our relationship status.

Really, I have sixteen hours to get through. Sixteen hours of having Lewis close enough to track how the blue in his eyes changes depending on the light, sixteen hours of his presence and the potential it has to rewire my entire nervous system.

Sixteen hours, and then another five days, but that's a problem for future me. For now, I just have to get through these sixteen hours.

They say you should never meet your heroes, probably because it's incredibly hard living up to those mile-high expectations we form of them. While I never thought I'd agree with the statement, what happens on Thursday morning makes me reconsider.

Coming out of a toilet cubicle, I spot Professor Rosanna Alderkamp touching up her cherry-red lipstick and start babbling.

"Professor Alderkamp, hi! I'm such a huge fan. I've actually been waiting for you to get here. I mean, not this toilet but *here* here, the Sawyer's. Oh, I'm Frances, by the way. Frances Silberstein." I thrust out my hand to shake hers. Just then, I realize that a) said hand is unwashed and, b) the person whose papers I've been reading, disseminating, discussing, and praising for the past twelve years has listened to me pee.

Yeah.

So much for meeting your heroes.

"Oh god," I say when my prefrontal cortex comes to the rescue. I take two large steps to the only other free sink and deposit my hands under the faucet. "That was . . . I'm sorry."

Professor Alderkamp has barely had the time to turn around and face me throughout my avalanche of words, but she smiles kindly. In the mirror on the wall behind the sinks, her large brown eyes find the lanyard with my name tag around my neck. "Silberstein . . ." She tilts her head pensively, as if the last few seconds didn't happen. "Where have I heard that name?"

Her voice is lower and smoother than the one I've come to know through my tinny laptop speakers when watching her recorded lectures. She's deep in thought as I rip a paper towel out of the machine and quietly die of mortification.

Behind me, she snaps her finger. "Silberstein, that's it! I read your latest paper on the flight over."

"You did?" I hate how insecure my voice sounds.

She stows her lipstick in her big navy leather tote, unclasps the clip in her hair, and finger-combs her thick salt-and-pepper curls. "I did." She gives me a wide smile in the mirror. "Very impressive, although I can't say I understood all of it. But then again, I'm not a modeling wizard like you. But you have your session today, right? I was hoping to stop by."

"Uh, no. It got swapped with another one, so I already had it at the beginning of the week. But I could send you the slides and the code?"

"That'd be great." Her phone starts ringing in her bag and she rummages around for it. "Anyway, I need to run, but we should have lunch together while we're here."

It'd be wildly unprofessional to pinch myself right in front of her, but all her praise has me wondering if I'm still asleep and dreaming. Or did Rosanna Alderkamp really just compliment me? My overanalytical brain provides the much-needed reality check: Maybe she's being polite.

But before she dashes out of the restroom, Professor Alderkamp turns around and adds, "I'll be looking out for your email, and from there we can set up lunch. Oh, and please call me Rosanna."

My heart sprints with euphoria. Not only did my idol recognize my name but also wanted to stop by my workshop, found my paper impressive, and called me a *modeling wizard*. I wish I could call Karo to share my excitement, but she's still off the grid, finding peace in the California wilderness. My second instinct is to run to Lewis and gush to him about it, but I ignore that one, too.

I need to tell someone to let the adrenaline out, though, so when I spot Brady down the corridor, I beeline toward her. With her bubbly enthusiasm, she strikes me as someone who'd get how starstruck I am right now.

"You survived the boat!" she greets me and pockets her phone.

"I did, and I also just met my idol—in the bathroom, of all places, but she was so great," I tell Brady, the words tumbling out of me.

"Look at you go," she squeals and gently bumps her fist into my biceps. "Who was it?"

"Rosanna Alderkamp! I've been dying to meet—"

"Frances, there you are!"

I don't get to finish as Vivienne rushes down the corridor. Brady throws me a confused look, but before I can ask her about it, we both turn to Vivienne. Dressed in a shimmering green dress and black flats today, she looks effortlessly elegant as she drags her pencil over her tablet. "Brady, hi! I'm so sorry to interrupt, it'll only be a minute. Frances, there's something I need to run by you."

"Sure."

"Perfect. So, we'll have our *Growing Up in Science Q and A* tomorrow evening, but the bar you were supposed to have your session in canceled the reservation. Something about a problem with the pipes."

The event she's talking about is a casual evening out during which students get to ask questions about life as a scientist, grad school, and making it in academia. I think back to the moment when I signed up to mentor a session, wondering if I qualified since I hadn't yet made it in academia, with my grant pending and the persistent worry that I might not even have a job a few months from now.

"Which is unfortunate," Vivienne continues. "I need to do a bit of juggling now to get a new place booked for you, but there's space at the bar I booked for Lewis, so I was wondering if you'd be fine joining him? I normally wouldn't do this, but obviously you're dating, and a lot of students requested to speak to both of you in their forms anyway, so it might even be a good opportunity for them."

Well, shoot. Vivienne and Brady both wait for my reply, oblivious to the fact that they're adding two, maybe three, hours of Lewis to a system that's already near the breaking point.

I put my new plan in motion this morning when I told him to head to campus without me, but instead of enjoying the few extra hours in bed after the many late nights, I lay there, nearly spraining my thumb by updating my inbox for (still absent) grant updates. I have yet to see him this morning, and my anticipation is building like a tidal wave that will not be helped by additional hours with him tomorrow night, but I don't have another option. I guess I'm signing up to spend more time with the person I desperately need time away from.

"You can put our sessions together," I tell Vivienne.

She breaks into a smile. "*Super.* I'll email you the details later!"

"Golgi, she's so nice, isn't she?" Brady says, watching Vivienne walk away. "I thought it was fake at first, but she's always this kind. We work together on this massively complicated project I'm heading. It involves a ton of different hospital departments back in BC, plus collaborators around the world, and she always does more than she needs to, just to take some work off my plate."

Though I haven't known Vivienne that long, her questions about Lewis, commiserations about long-distance relationships, and her effort to let me spend more time with him all seem so genuine. I can only hope Jacob has learned from his mistakes and values her kindness, too.

Brady heads off to the bathroom, while I look for Lewis to tell him about the change of plans and to see how he's doing ahead of his lecture. As excited as I was about having run into

Rosanna Alderkamp, that giddy feeling has died down now that I know I'll have to figure out how to spend an extra few hours with Lewis tomorrow. I find him in the empty auditorium, a lone figure at the lectern getting ready for his lecture. For a moment, I watch him through the window panel of the closed door, ignoring how my heart squeezes in on itself. While he scrolls through the slides, his other hand alternates between fumbling with the lapel of his jacket, the laser pointer, and the back of his neck. The giant projections flip behind him, from the squiggly lines of a hippocampal ripple, to the pink and wrinkly surface of an exposed brain, and a black-and-white diagram I recognize from his latest commentary. When he seems to be done, I push the door open and his head snaps up.

"I see you got rid of your not-so-brief introduction to psychology. Flashy suits you," I tease, pausing in the doorframe.

"What can I say. I've had some last-minute help from the best," he responds as one corner of his mouth tugs up.

My smile feels inevitable. "I hope you're not sick of me yet."

He watches me as I cross the floor toward him, and I'm surprised my body doesn't short-circuit. "Hardly."

"Because Vivienne just put the two of us into the same Q and A session tomorrow."

"Okay," he simply says, still staring. Something must be weird with my face, although it looked fine in the bathroom mirror.

"How are you feeling about your lecture?" I ask, patting my cheek self-consciously. A wooden plank creaks under my shoe, echoing in the quiet.

"Good, I think. Definitely better after you helped me yesterday. Hey, these are new," Lewis notes when I reach his side. He brushes a strand of my hair aside to tap the frame of my glasses, which I guess I'm wearing for the first time in his presence today.

"Yeah, turns out that late nights and all that wind are not great for my eyes." It's a bit of an understatement. My eyes feel dry and gritty, like someone's scrubbed them with sandpaper, and though it's only been a half hour, I already feel the urge to apply eye drops again.

"They look good on you. Although . . ." He plucks the glasses off my nose, the world around me turning blurry. "Hold on."

I can just about make out the shape of Lewis tugging up a corner of his shirt, revealing a caramel-colored blob that must be the skin of his stomach.

"What are you doing?" I'm not sure if I'm more annoyed at Lewis for stealing my glasses or at my crappy eyesight for keeping me from getting a good look at Lewis's torso. Then I realize what he's doing. "Are you cleaning my glasses?"

"Just making sure you can see my lecture okay," he teases. He holds the glasses up to his eyes. "I'm surprised you made it here without walking into a wall."

"I could see fine, thank you very much. Unlike now."

He greets someone over my shoulder, then steps closer, his facial features sharpening in the process. I can finally see the cocky grin on his face, the tiny freckles on the bridge of his nose.

"Better?" he asks, his breath warm against my forehead.

He's standing close enough that I wouldn't even have to step forward to kiss him. Which I won't, obviously. Humankind didn't decode the genome by giving into its each and every impulse, so I won't, either.

"Well?"

"A bit," I tell him, my voice coming out all croaky.

"Good, I wasn't sure if you were far- or nearsighted."

As Lewis slides the glasses back onto my nose, the world shifts back into focus in a dizzying flash. His knuckles brush my temples, and a prickle spreads over my skin where he touches it. "Here you go."

"Thank you." I take a step back and barely catch sight of Jacob's receding shape, and suddenly Lewis's behavior makes more sense. He was only teasing me because we had an audience.

I push my disappointment aside as he turns to the lectern and join Brady, who waves me over. Lewis is getting too good at this, with his little gestures and lopsided smiles, the snagging gazes and casual touches.

So good that even *I* am beginning to believe there might be something there.

A quiet hush settles over the auditorium as Jacob introduces Lewis, listing the steps of his academic career and the young investigator's award he received from the German Academy of Sciences. Lewis's blush is strong enough that I can spot it from my seat in the third row, though now I know that his lack of a smile and the tense set of his eyebrows are not because of a stick up his ass, but because he's trying to rein in his nerves. What's worse, now I also feel those nerves bubbling in my stomach as I witness him speed through the first slide of his lecture. The only reason I can keep track is because after last night's rundown I know what he's talking about, but a glance over my shoulder tells me some of the students are struggling to follow his introduction.

I push my hand up and clear my throat.

He pinches his lips together, either annoyed or amused that I've barely waited a minute to butt in. "Yes, Dr. Silberstein?"

"Could you go back to this theta-gamma coupling you were talking about?" I ask, then continue with a question he already explained to me in detail yesterday, one that will hopefully slow him down enough to get everyone else back on track.

When he's done answering my question, the redness has faded from his face, and he blinks back at me with an expression I can only interpret as gratitude. From then on, his lecture goes smoothly, and people's arms go up to ask questions stemming from curiosity rather than confusion. I hold myself back until the last moment to make good on the "more of a comment than a question" remark he requested, which makes him break into a grin. And then his lecture is over, and it's easy to imagine the relief he must be feeling, because the tension melts from my muscles, too.

The only thing that gets me through the afternoon workshops is the prospect of a long climbing session in the evening to release all the energy Lewis's presence stokes in me. For a moment I consider inviting him to come with, but that would defeat the entire purpose of going.

At the gym on 125th Street, with my hands dusted in chalk and my mind puzzling through the different bouldering problems, I gradually start to put Lewis out of my mind, but on the subway ride back, I see a new paper that makes me want to call him.

Academia is a marathon of obsessing over the most minuscule questions, the ones you tackle deep into the quiet hours of the night with only your computer at your fingertips. It can get lonely inside your brain. Too much time there can fill you with doubts, but then, sometimes, occasionally, a cool result, a new insight, feels like the most potent drug in the world.

When Jacob and I broke up, I didn't only lose my boyfriend, but the person I considered my scientific partner in crime. The person I called whenever any of those breakthroughs happened, that were so far and few between. Before Lewis failed to include me in that paper four years ago, our emails were on course to fill the gap Jacob had left—not that of a boyfriend, but of someone I could share my thoughts and passions with—and now I want to reach for my phone again, to forward him this article and hear what he thinks.

I make a split-second decision. Right before the tunnel swallows my signal, I press send.

Lewis's call comes through as I'm stepping out of the shower a half hour later, his words racing like he's just finished reading. "They got such good coverage of the hippocampus. And the whole design? It's so fucking elegant."

I'm already whirring with excitement, but I get an extra boost from his enthusiasm. As we discuss the paper, his voice sounds a little deeper than in real life, and I can't stop myself from pressing the phone closer to my ear. I curl my toes to release the electricity buzzing under my skin, but it doesn't help.

After we hang up and I lie down in bed, my brain colors in the map of my body with all the new places Lewis touched today. It tucks away the new pieces of knowledge I learned about him, then calculates the hours until I'll get to see him again.

And as much as I want to stamp it off as surface-level attraction, blame the kiss and some overdose of hormones, I know that whatever I'm feeling runs deeper than that. I'm starting to like Lewis. I want to kiss him again, but I also want to keep talking to him past the eight hours I spend glued to his side daily. I want to learn everything there is to know about him.

This is what Karo had warned me about when she said fake dating would be messy. Now I know that instead of ignoring her, I should've listened.

Chapter Fifteen

After another day packed to the brim with science, the only thing that separates me from my Lewis-free weekend is the Q and A session with the students, which takes place at Second Draft, a microbrewery-slash-bar located in East Williamsburg. Once Lewis and I get there, we push through the crowd of patrons with mustaches and rolled-up jeans, all the way to the back where, below one of the huge factory windows, most of the students are already seated at a long beer table.

Too focused on pushing down my inconvenient feelings for Lewis, I don't pay much attention when one of the staff members explains how our beer tasting will proceed. I make sure to put a few students between our seats: François, who lifts his head whenever someone calls my name; Selin, who's a first-year PhD in Lewis's lab; and Daina, who's outgoing enough to start asking questions. Everyone else seems a little shy.

I smile at them encouragingly, the encounter with Rosanna Alderkamp—and how much it meant to me—still fresh in my mind. In the grand scheme of things, it hasn't been that long since I stood in their shoes: nervous about talking to anybody more senior and experienced than me, wishing someone would notice and reach out to me. I hope I can do the same for them now. Soon enough—and perhaps with some liquid courage—more students join the conversation, and while we taste test through the menu, we drift off into small groups. I pinball back a few of the questions to get an idea of this new generation of scientists, and all the while, I marvel at the fact that this is also my job: mentoring and encouraging the younger students, paying forward the favor that enabled me to get to this position in the first place. As much as I love typing out code and exploring my data, this social side of the job is what keeps me going. It's why I want to become a professor eventually, with my own lab, advising students and helping them figure out their passion within research.

Throughout the evening, the groups mix and rematch, until our conversations drift away from science. At some point, as I survey the room, I find Lewis looking back at me. He holds my gaze across the table, drawing warmth from my core all the way to my cheeks, and it makes me feel like we're in this together, for real. *This is temporary*, I remind myself. But after the I-don't-know-how-many-glasses-of-beer I've had, I don't care. Even if it's temporary and only pretend, I can enjoy it, if just for this evening.

Daina—PhD student at University College London—is sharing their favorite brain-related fun facts they usually unpack at family parties, when my phone vibrates in my purse.

My heart starts to pound. News on the grant?

But no. It's Friday night, past 8:00 p.m. here, and the middle of the night in Central Europe. Academia is brutal, but not that brutal.

I chance a glance nonetheless. It's Karo. "I need to take this," I apologize. The restrooms are packed, and smokers cluster outside the bar, but a few steps beyond, the sidewalk is empty and quiet enough, now that the stores and cafés in the surrounding buildings have closed for the night.

The hot and humid night air presses in on my skin as I lean against the brick wall. "You're back! Finally! Did you get back okay?"

Karo laughs. "It's only been five days, but yeah, we did get back okay. Probably with a few more mosquito bites than physically tolerable, but we're good."

I'm soothed by the sound of her voice, the knowledge of her presence, even if it's only virtual. "No bears then?"

"Actually, we saw some bears, but from far away," she adds before I can let out a gasp. "It was amazing, really." She sounds high on fresh air and endorphins from all the hiking. "Listen, Franzi, I wanted to ask you something."

A dark shape exits the bar, and when it steps into the cone of streetlight in front of me, I recognize it as Lewis. "Everything okay?" he murmurs. "I missed you in there."

"Give me a second," I tell my sister at the same time as I nod at him. "All good. I'm talking to Karo, but I'll be back in a second."

"Alright. I'll see you inside." He squeezes my shoulder, and something uncurls at the base of my stomach. Without thinking, I lift my fingers and graze the back of his hand in a gesture that feels intimate, just right. That is, until his eyes snag on the point of contact.

Maybe this is a little too much for friends who are helping each other out.

Confusingly, his eyebrows slot into a frown at the same time as the corner of his mouth flicks up. When he returns to the bar, I'm left behind with a thudding heart and the realization that while my attraction to him is growing by the day, I really have no idea what he's feeling or thinking. A concerned fake boyfriend may have come outside to check on his girlfriend, but the shoulder squeeze? The warmth in his eyes? That lopsided smile and the fact that he told me he missed me?

"Hmm." Karo's voice crackles through my phone speaker. "Sounds like more interesting things than science are happening at that summer school of yours."

"I— Well. Yeah . . ."

"I see," Karo purrs.

"No, no," I tell her. "That was Lewis. Dr. North. He was just—"

"*The* Dr. North?" Karo cries.

"Ye—"

"Hold on, is he the one you had to convince to fake date you?"

"Karo—"

"And he let himself be convinced?"

I think that she's done then, but she still doesn't let me get in a word.

"I thought we hated him!"

"We did," I agree, "but it turns out there's a little more to the story than I thought."

After a beat, she teases, "I told you that know-it-alls were your type."

"Stop it," I grumble. I kick a pebble out of the way and watch it skip down the sidewalk. "It's not like that. He's helping me out."

"Helping you out, but missing you, too. O-kay," she says, lingering on the vowels in a way that lets me know she doesn't believe me at all.

"Listen, there's something I did want to tell you. I talked to the professor from Amsterdam."

"Oh! How did it go?"

And so I tell her about the successful conversation with Rosanna Alderkamp that made me hopeful I could collaborate with her using the money from the grant I've applied for.

"I know I'm getting ahead of myself." I sigh. "We didn't talk for long, and in the bathroom, of all places, but still. I've been wanting to work with her for so long . . . and she was so kind." Which is probably what excited me the most. Smartness is a given among academics, but not everyone chooses to be kind.

After we hang up and before going back to meet the others, I check my inbox. It's become such an automatic thing by now. Swipe left, tap on the little icon at the bottom of the screen. I delete the usual three spam emails and one reply-all from a department-wide email.

But there's one more email sitting in my inbox: the response to my grant application.

The thing I've been agonizing over and anxiously expecting. My last shot at securing more funding before mine runs out in under three months. My hope for stability so I can finally plan my research long-term. The one thing I need to work out if I want to avoid packing my bags again to look for a new lab somewhere else in this world.

The Dutch Young Investigators Starting Grant.

The subject-line doesn't reveal any decision, and I tap on it so hard that my phone almost tumbles out of my hands. The message opens to a short text and an attached PDF. I read through everything, the attachment, then the text again.

The sidewalk and the street lights start to swirl around me.

My world tilts on its axis, just like when I enter a high field MRI scanner, except now it's not the strong magnetic force scrambling up my vestibular system. I feel like I'm gliding down a waterslide headfirst, taking turn after turn into the unknown.

Thank god there's nobody else on this sidewalk to see me lose control like this; hands shaking and breaths coming in choppy. I make the mistake of looking down at my phone that's still bright with the words *we regret to inform you*. The hurt flares up, buckles my stomach, and clenches my chest tight.

Slow it down.

Lewis's words come back to me, and I force myself to count to two on my inhale, four on my exhale. Once I manage to keep that up, I lengthen the intervals of my breaths and focus on the feeling of the humid night air when it passes through my nostrils.

Breathe.

In and out, and in and out again.

I think of the days, nights, weekends, months I spent writing this grant. I think of the four subprojects I planned out, each one essential to take the findings of my last research paper a step further to track how we encode memories in real time. I think of having to pack up my apartment into boxes again, another cycle of *keep* and *toss*, departing from yet another town with people I don't know enough to keep in touch with.

When I feel like I have control of my body again, I head back into the bar. My throat is parched after the quick rasps of my breath, and I stop at the bar counter to ask for a glass of water. I know I need to get back to the students, but I also don't trust myself around them yet, with their bright eyes and open faces, their drive and motivation.

Ten years of tirelessly trying, and why the fuck is it still not enough?

I gulp down the water and head back outside, telling myself it'll only be for a moment. Five minutes. That's all I need to get my head on straight again.

"Frances," someone calls. Lewis comes running up behind me as I shove through the door. Out on the sidewalk, he stops me with a warm palm on my shoulder. I turn around.

"What's going on? Are you okay?" he asks, his eyes scanning my face.

I wipe my damp forehead with the sleeve of my shirtdress.

I don't want him to be perceptive now. Not when I need to bury all of this sadness and self-doubt and dejection down, or else I won't function for the rest of the evening.

"What happened?" he insists.

"It doesn't matter." I shake my head and walk farther down the sidewalk, if only to put space between him and me. "I just need a moment."

"Oh, but it does matter," Lewis says and follows close behind me, even when I take a turn into the alleyway that leads to the brewery behind the bar. Caged industrial-style lights line the wall above us, and under their dim glow, his gaze skirts over my face again only to settle on my eyes. "If it's about the grant, there are other options."

He brings up the grant like it's nothing. Like I didn't spend all winter camped out behind my computer writing the damn thing, schmoozing professors to see if they'd put their names on it, then asking people for feedback to get even more of a competitive advantage. Like I didn't cut my Christmas holidays short to help my boss with exam corrections, only so he would scrutinize the grant down to the last hypothesis.

I shouldn't be surprised that Lewis handles a failed grant so casually. All my resentment for him and the advantage that his opinion paper gave him come bubbling back up. Apology or not, the fact is that he's miles ahead of me in this rodeo.

"What would *you* know about other options?" I bite out. "Maybe to you, all of this comes easy. Maybe it doesn't take you ages to work on revisions for a paper, months to come up with the right hooks for grants."

"But that's just—"

"You and I?" I interrupt. "We operate in different leagues. You publish higher. You have all your collaborations, your advisors who network to get you hired or mentor you through whatever hurdle you need to take next. But guess what? I don't. And this Sawyer's—I wanted to meet people here, to connect, to see if I could be useful in any other lab, but *god*." I'm long past the point of lowering my voice, suddenly realizing how furious I am, above all, at myself. "One tiny blip of judgment, and suddenly instead of doing what I came here for, I am obsessing about faking a relationship because otherwise my career would truly be over, never mind how low my chances are at this point at making it in academia. Everyone knows that—"

"That's not—" Lewis tries to interject.

I raise my voice over him, "Which is one more thing I'm mad about, because, once again, I care too much about what other people think, when I should be more like you." With the anger coursing hot through my limbs, I rake my fingers through my hair.

He takes a step forward and tilts his chin as if to measure me up. "And you think that'd do you any good?"

"Yes! You're this insanely driven scientist. You don't let anything come between you and what truly matters," I yell.

"And neither do you," he yells back, and reaches up as if to pluck my hands from my hair. "Otherwise, why would we be doing any of this?" Mid-movement, he stops and stretches his arms sideways instead, encompassing the alleyway, the city, us.

"Frances, let me talk here. You're nothing like me," he continues, and something desperate spans his expression and his voice. His hands bridge those last inches, until he closes his fingers around my wrists and pulls our arms down into the space between us. "You're not and that's a good thing. My only brother is basically a stranger to me and why? Because I have fucking unresolved daddy issues. If I were you, with an ex-boyfriend who's a superstar in our field, organizing this summer school, and—surprise—has also gotten engaged, I wouldn't even have come here. But you, you swallow your pride and pack your bags and get on your way. Because the science matters more to you than any personal stuff."

I open my mouth, ready to argue back, until I track that he's pivoted into complimenting me. I feel outsmarted. *"What?"*

"Also, this stuff about not having what it takes to make it in academia? It's infuriating that this broken system makes you doubt yourself that way and believe me—I know I've played my role in this." His gaze bores into mine as he faces me head-on. "You know what should matter for making it in academia? That you like to pull other people up, that you're brilliant and smart and driven and that you have good ideas—I should know because I've been admiring your work for *years*. So, one decision by one grant committee?" He breaks off his rant with an exasperated laugh. "Screw them."

He has admired my work for years?

As I look at Lewis his words echo through my mind, a loop of *brilliant* and *smart* and something about *having admired my work for years*?

I think back to the evening in his hotel room when he told me that he scrutinized my papers because he wanted to understand me. The email he wrote in the library where he said he's always been eager to hear my thoughts. All his cryptic comments whenever I made assumptions about his opinion of me.

I want to see you succeed.

The memories pull at others, too; how he confessed he liked us together on the deck of that yacht after the graduation party, the way he said, "Hardly," when I asked him whether he was sick of me yet, even the playful nip of his teeth when he nibbled that cashew off my finger.

Understanding sinks in and sends a heart-racing, palm-tingling, core-clenching twist through my body.

There's a different feeling nestled against the bite of anger now. It still makes me want to get into his space, but now I want it differently.

From the way he shifts against me, I think he does, too. So, before I can convince myself that this is a bad idea, I push onto my tiptoes and press my mouth against his.

Chapter Sixteen

I realize my mistake when our mouths meet. Sure, there's the fact that it's an ungracious kiss, that my glasses get in the way of Lewis's nose and the metal digs into my temple. But what's worse is that he freezes—literally freezes with his lips stock-still against mine. It's mortifying. I must've imagined the way his gaze snagged on my mouth and how he swayed in my direction.

Those compliments? Probably just a way to cheer me up.

That rant? A way to show empathy.

Because we're friends. Or, well. *Were*. For a very short amount of time. Because whatever nonsense I just did doesn't seem conducive to any kind of friendship. All these years of studying brains and yet I keep reading him all wrong.

"Oh my god," I blurt out, breaking away from him.

"Frances." Lewis's hands fly to the nape of my neck before I can put more distance between us.

"I thought—" I start, but then falter because clearly, I thought wrong. "Never mind. I'm sorry."

Lewis rests his forehead against mine, fingers tangling into my hair. "Hey," he whispers, breath fanning over my cheek. "I'm sorry. It's not—"

"Not me?" I push out a laugh. "Right."

When he draws in a breath, the movement shifts his chest against mine and reminds me how close we are. Then he steps back and places a kiss on the top of my head. It's the kindest of letdowns, but another rejection nonetheless, and the back of my throat burns with how they've been piling up over this past half hour.

"We should head back inside," Lewis says against my hair and swipes his thumb over the edge of my jaw, up to my cheeks that are aflame with humiliation. "I'll buy you a drink later and then you can rant about science all you want. I promise." His lips bend into a not-quite-smile. "But let's wrap up this evening first."

For the next hour, I answer more questions, all while Lewis keeps checking in on me, glancing over with soft eyes and curved lips. Every time he does, something inside my chest glows. All the rejections tonight, including his, should make me feel far from glowing, but still, inexplicably, I do. In under a week he's turned from the person I could not stand to be around to the one whose presence makes me feel better, and once that realization takes hold, the glow hardens into a tense ball of nerves.

The Q and A was scheduled to last until 10 p.m., and soon after, the first students leave the bar. Lewis and I say our goodbyes, and he guides me to the exit. "You promised me a drink," I protest once we're outside in the sticky heat.

"Unless you want the students to eavesdrop, I'd suggest we go somewhere else for that drink."

Halfway back to the next L stop, I slow as I spot a dive bar across the street, but Lewis keeps walking. "I have a better idea," he says enigmatically. "Trust me on this?"

My confusion only grows the deeper we rattle down the tunnels and under the East River. Lewis keeps his eyes on me, brows curved into lines of worry, but instead of looking back at him, I take in the Friday night crowd; the group of girls in glittering miniskirts, the two guys blasting hip-hop on a portable speaker, and the woman finishing her cat-eye with a hand so steady a surgeon would kill for it. When we reach Union Square, Lewis pulls me out of the subway, up the steps, across the street, and down Broadway.

We pass the shuttered doors of the Strand, the red flag of the book store flapping above us in the nightly breeze. The courtyard of an old church interrupts the tall buildings looming over us, and I still have no clue where we're going. "Are you taking me to NYU? To vandalize some lab or something?"

"Don't get any ideas." Lewis shakes his head, stopping in front of a lit-up shop on the ground floor of a high-rise. In the window, a neon sign blinks *Donut worry* in pink cursive. The first *o* is a doodle of a donut. "Here we are."

"Donuts?" I wonder. "How is this better than a drink?"

Lewis holds the door open and waves me in. "Wait and see."

Inside, I'm hit by the sweet scent of butter and sugar. The shop is pink and bright, with a checkered floor, and a bar counter stretching down the long, narrow space. Behind the counter, shelves carry trays of donuts in a plethora of options: powdered, glazed, covered in chocolate, or topped with a dollop of cream. A few couples and some lone patrons sit on the stools lining the length of the counter.

"Um." My eyes are glued to the stacks of donuts, their bright, happy colors unfastening the knot at the center of my chest. "I'm going to need some time to decide."

Lewis hunches over to nudge my shoulder with his. He points to a free set of metal stools midway down the room. "Have a seat," he tells me, "I'll order for us."

I wander over to the stools and sink onto the pink pleather cushion, hooking my feet up and swiveling from side to side. With each half-turn, the words of rejection from the email crash back into my mind. The *we are sorry to inform you*, the *no support in funding*.

"Hey." Lewis drops two greasy brown paper bags on the Formica countertop and pushes one closer to me. "Eat these, it'll make you feel better."

I peek into the bag. "What's this?"

"A bit of everything." He slides up next to me, and his aftershave melds with the sugary smell. I want to turn my head and follow his scent, press my nose into the hollow of his neck, but instead I watch his long finger as he points at the donuts one by one. "Boston cream, apple fritter, old-fashioned, and salted caramel."

As he pulls back, I inhale another whiff of sugar and pinch a bit of the glaze off one donut, savoring how its sweet saltiness melts on my tongue. Lewis's gaze follows my movement with intense eyes, intense and soft, and entirely confusing. How can he look at me like that and then reject me?

"Go on," he says, still observing me. "I want to see if I'm right about what you like."

As we dig into our bags, Lewis doesn't make any conversation but lets me stew over my thoughts in silence. I'm in the middle of my last donut when I start crying. It's the ugly kind, the wheezing, shoulders-shaking, tears-running-down-my-face kind, and it hits right when I'm eating the only donut that doesn't have a nicely solid topping. My heavy breaths disperse the powdered sugar, sending the white dust flying up in a cloud from where it floats down onto my face, and my fingers, and Lewis's shirt. My sneeze turns the scene into a full-on sugar blizzard.

Tears at full force now, I drop the half-moon of my donut back into the bag, and my instinct to cover my eyes with my hands smudges up the lenses of my glasses. Cramps twist in my chest, hack away at my breath, and push more tears from my eyes.

"What do they put into these things?" I sob. "I wanted to drown my feelings, not drown *in* them."

"Titanium dioxide—you know what, never mind." Lewis offers me a napkin in his right hand and the open palm of his left hand. I take the napkin and stare at him questioningly, until he plucks my glasses off my nose and starts polishing them.

As I wipe the sludge of tears and dissolving sugar off my face, I release a few more sobs behind the protection of the rough napkin. "You have to stop cleaning my glasses for me," I protest.

With a shrug he hands my glasses back. "Why don't you tell me what happened?" His gentle tone threatens my tear ducts once more.

I drop my gross napkin onto the glittering counter. "Why are you being so nice to me?" Taking care of my messy outbreaks is most definitely not part of our fake dating agreement.

"Because I care," he says. "Tell me what's going on." The simplicity of his words and his gently commanding tone are a flashback to when we first met on the plane, and again, something about his level of calm and control soothes the flood of emotions I'm bombarded with.

"You were right earlier. It's the grant. I got the email outside the bar, after I finished talking to Karo." The curious tilt of his head and the unwavering attention of his eyes make it easier to open up to him. "I've applied for grants enough times to know we get rejected all the time. I swear I'm not usually this bad. But with this one, I had my hopes set so high." I glance up at him. "The grant was good, really. It was strong. With a clear vision, a good hook."

He lifts a corner of his mouth. "Frances, *I* don't need convincing. I'm sure it was good."

"It's just . . . My funding is running out and the lab I'm working in has no money to hire me for longer, so this grant was my last shot at staying put. At not having to move again. And it's a big grant, too, one that would've finally given me the chance to level up, away from the grind of postdoc life and into a position where I have more freedom to shape my own projects and supervise students to work on my questions, too. I thought I could finally make a difference . . ."

I feel his eyes on the side of my face; his focus fully on me while my gaze jumps through the café, because it's too much if he sees into me while I open up to him like this.

"Frances. You're already making a difference," he tells me. Before I can ask what he means, he continues, "But I get you. It's tiring to have to move from one lab to another, where you constantly have to figure out how you can work on your own questions while also keeping your advisor happy."

Lewis's words are such an accurate description of what I'm feeling it's as if he has plucked them right out of the downward spiral of my thoughts. Unless you're lucky and your research interests overlap with the lab you're hired in, securing your own funding is the only way to ensure you can work on your own questions, and not somebody else's. My current postdoc advisor has been pretty laissez-faire and left me to work on my own projects, when in previous labs, my boss's research came first. In the first years out of grad school I still had so much to learn, so

I was fine balancing my work around someone else's but now, looking for open postdoc positions on predefined projects feels like a step back.

I might have to leave all of my questions unanswered and that's the part that pains me most. That the thoughts scribbled on Post-its and in my Notes app will remain just that: letters on paper, characters on a screen.

Ideas turning into dead ends.

Who's going to tackle all those questions, if not me? Who is going to care enough? And how many times will I have to uproot my life until I finally get to take them out of the drawer again?

"It's funny, you know," I continue wistfully. "Years ago, when I was in undergrad, and our professors would introduce themselves, they'd name all these universities at which they had worked. All these cities. Doing science *and* traveling around the world? It seemed like the perfect life."

Lewis hums in agreement.

"But now? When I think about my last five years, I get exhausted," I admit. "I hate the thought of doing all the packing and meeting new people in a new city again, knowing that I won't stay there. I'd hoped I'd be able to settle down somewhere. Not the 'having a family' kind of settling down, but you know."

"The 'plant perennials on your balcony and paint your living-room wall green' kind of settling down?" he asks, and I stare at him, puzzled. "Like your sister?"

"Right. Yes. Well." I swallow thickly, some new emotion lodged in my throat because he listened and remembers. He listens and remembers and notices a lot, actually, and that's starting to matter more to me than what he did four years ago. "Maybe not green. But there's this fancy outdoor pool around the corner of my apartment that has a waitlist of a year, and I never signed up for it because I didn't know how long I'd stay around. I go to the community indoor pool, which is fine, but you know . . . It's nowhere near as nice and farther away. Doesn't have a sauna. I know it's silly but . . ."

He nods, like he understands. He doesn't tell me that I will be able to settle down somewhere and I'm glad for it. He knows that we sometimes have to chase our questions around the world, hop from lab to lab, funding to funding. Instead, he flags down a waitress, who has a pierced septum and streak of blue hair, and orders a hot cocoa.

She nods curtly. "Do you want marshmallows?"

Lewis tilts his head to me. "She does."

As the waitress turns away, I realize that the cyclone of feelings the grant rejection triggered has calmed down into a more moderate storm. Still blowing strong, but the hurt, dejection, and anger are much more manageable, all thanks to Lewis. I don't know how he guessed it, but having him listen to me while feeding me sugar is everything I need right now.

"Wanting stability is not silly," Lewis tells me when we're alone again.

"What about you?" I ask him. "How do you handle all of this?"

"I'm not sure it's the same for me. I haven't moved as much as you have. But yeah." Now it's his turn to glance away, and he fumbles with his crumpled-up paper bag. "Some job security would be nice. And, you know, the clock is ticking for me in Germany."

I nod. Germany has the wild system of only allowing fixed-term contracts for a limited period of time, and if you don't land anything permanent by the end of that, you're out of German academia for good. It's the reason I never thought about moving back.

A line carves itself into his forehead. "I'm not in as much of a hurry because I have more than a year left on my current contract but, you know, there's a small part of me that also wants to rub it into my father's face. To have proof once and for all that I excel at something he had no hand in. That I'm good at what I love. I know my logic is totally flawed, because you've seen for yourself how little my father thinks of academia. Nothing I do will ever be good enough for him. But instead of accepting that, I keep hoping that the next milestone will be the one that finally convinces him." His eyes find mine as his mouth cuts into a smile. "So, now who's being silly?"

The waitress comes back and sets a mug on the counter in front of us. "Thanks," Lewis says and slides it over to me. Rainbow-colored marshmallows bob in the dark liquid, and I take a sip, savoring the rich and creamy taste.

"I was thinking..." Lewis pivots on his chair, knees knocking into mine, until he stops himself with his foot hooked onto the metal bar of my chair. The cotton of his chinos rubs against my leg, the part that's covered by the fabric of my dress and a sliver of bare skin below my knee. Warmth spills through me. "I'm going to drive out to my friend's cabin upstate tomorrow. The one I mentioned at Vivienne and Jacob's party. You could come?"

I lower the mug onto the countertop. "I . . . What?"

"What do you think about getting away from here for a little bit? Get out of the city, get some distance to reset."

"You want to spend the weekend with me?"

"Yeah." He lifts one shoulder in a half shrug. "I mean, I don't know if it's the best idea, because this—we—are already such a mess. But I don't think you should be alone right now."

I don't need to consider his suggestion to know it isn't the best idea. This morning, I was counting down the hours to time away from this man, so I could talk some sense into myself. After mauling him with that kiss, it might be too late for that now, but if one thing's obvious, it is that I shouldn't spend *more* time with him.

"Don't worry about me," I tell him, forcing cheer into my voice. "That's not part of your fake-boyfriend-ly duties. And also not something you owe me, to make up for four years ago." Something crosses his face then, almost imperceptibly, but he narrows his eyes and tightens his mouth. "I know it probably doesn't look that way right now, but I'll be okay. You can enjoy your weekend upstate alone, like you'd planned to."

"That's the thing, though," he says, reaching down. With a flick of his wrist, I'm turned around on my stool, legs bracketed by his, his arm on the cushion of my seat. The heel of his hand presses into the underside of my thigh, and I burn with the awareness of how close he is to where I'm aching for him.

He leans in until our faces are separated by what's not even a hand width of distance. His voice is all but a rumble in his throat when he continues, "It turns out, I like spending time with you."

My pulse speeds up, and when I swallow thickly, his eyes flit down, like he can't help himself. If I didn't know better—if Lewis hadn't rejected me earlier—I'd say he's flirting with me.

"And I know I'd rather have you hike in the forest with me than being all miserable here." He tilts his head. "So, what do you say?"

If I was smarter, I'd probably think about my answer for longer. I'd remember how his rejection earlier made it clear that we want different things. But even if he had kissed me back, looking for any sort of relationship with a colleague is a bad idea, let alone the one who betrayed my trust colossally.

But in Karo's absence, I need a friend. And with how expertly Lewis holds my hands through the ups and downs of my anxiety, I think, if nothing else, he can be that.

A friend.

"I'll come with you," I finally say, my heart beating in my throat. I'm not sure if I believe myself, when I add, "It can't hurt."

Chapter Seventeen

"Is this pace okay for you? Or should we go slower?" Lewis asks as he walks ahead of me, a few minutes into our hike.

Despite yesterday's failed kiss and how much I try to convince my brain that he's just a friend, his question triggers images of other pacing-related activities he could be doing with me, because that's where my mind has been all morning: in the gutter. I haven't been paying attention to our speed or the scenery or anything other than him. How his thighs fill out his black hiking shorts. How the muscles in his calves move under his suntanned skin.

The legs stop moving. "Frances?"

"Huh?"

"I was asking if our tempo is okay for you," he repeats.

I force my gaze up and find him observing me. "Oh. Um. Yeah."

He looks at me quizzically. "Why don't you take the lead? I wouldn't want you to miss your step."

"Alright," I say begrudgingly, and as I step around him, the forest finally seeps into my awareness. The ground is softened by fallen pine needles and moss, and the air around us is heavy with the earthy scent of tree bark, the sweetness of dried sap, and a freshness I haven't breathed since landing in New York City. As we hike farther from the trailhead, the noise of the nearby road gets swallowed up by the crowns of the trees. For a while, we walk below a stone ridge, until our path cuts right up the incline and soon, I lose myself in the rhythm of looking for stable footholds, placing my feet, and pushing myself upward.

This morning, when Lewis pulled up outside my stoop in his sister's SUV, I'd been unsure if this weekend was a good idea. Spending more time with the person I'm horribly and unrequitedly attracted to, who also happens to be my colleague, and up until a week ago, my nemesis? It didn't sound smart at all. But Lewis promised me lots of outdoor time to pull me out of my head, and I'm beginning to feel grateful that he urged me to come along.

Halfway up, our hiking path starts meandering parallel to the ridge and we find a small outcrop of boulders in a patch of sunlight. I take a bite of the apple I brought and Lewis hands me a bagel he must've picked up earlier this morning. The sundried tomato cream cheese is already a little runny from the heat, but I'd take this over any starred restaurant. From Lewis's easy smile and the way he leans back onto his elbows, I gather he feels the same way.

Our break is peaceful and unhurried until he whips out his notebook from the pocket of his hiking shorts. I raise my eyebrows. Before we said good night yesterday, we swore to leave our jobs behind this weekend and take a break like normal people would. We even went as far as unlinking our work accounts from our phones and leaving our laptops behind in the city.

"Hey!" I shout as he places the tip of his pencil on the page. "I thought we said no science."

"I had an idea," he says, ducking his head. "For a way of analyzing the data Selin will start collecting."

"Last I checked, this definitely counts as science."

Lewis tucks the pencil back into the metal loops of the notepad. "But this is analogue."

"You went against your own rules," I insist.

His cheeks grow pink, but he meets my gaze with a challenging expression that heats up my body more than the sun-warmed rock underneath my thighs. "Oh, is that right?"

"Remember how you made me desync my Notes app on my phone?"

"Alright." He opens up his arms. "What's my punishment?"

"Truth or dare," I state, because apparently I'm fifteen years old.

"Truth."

Shame. Even with yesterday's rejection, I think I would've dared him to kiss me.

"Okay, let's see . . ." I'm a bit surprised by what my mind settles on when I hear myself ask, "What made you switch over from econ to science?"

He scrunches up his forehead. "Last I checked, *that* also counts as science."

"This is science adjacent. Your origin story."

"Who do you think I am, Iron Man?" He drops the paper wrapping of his bagel into the plastic bag knotted to his backpack. "It's not all that exciting, but okay. I loved my science classes in college, how it was all about asking questions and how addictive that was to me. But when I was interning at my father's firm, I realized that like many other careers, this deep search for knowledge stops the second you graduate. Or maybe it never starts in the first place if you just want to get through your classes."

He shrugs. "That summer of the internship, one of the guys

from my suite, Jerry, was helping out in one of the neuroscience labs. One weekend, I had to pick up some stuff on campus, and I ran into him. Jerry was going to the primate lab, and he invited me to tag along."

Lewis looks up. "When I heard that first sputter of a spiking neuron, that noise, right out of the brain, a cell working on some complex computation we're only really beginning to understand . . . that's when I knew I needed more of this."

His enthusiasm draws out my smile.

"The neuroanatomy labs were a magical place for me, and I tried to spend as much time there as I could the next semester. Practical courses, interning after class." He continues telling me about how he finally felt at home in the dark lab, and how, there and then, he fell in love with the mystery of the brain. "It looked like art. It was wild to me that this is the organic matter that makes us think and feel and *live*." He exhales as wonder lights up his face. "Still is, actually. Sometimes I lose track of it, because the politics of academia get exhausting, or I'm frustrated that my experiment isn't working out the way I want it to. But then it hits me again, how fucking cool it is that our experience of all this"—he draws an arc through the air, encompassing our view of the Catskills, the vast sky, the soundscape of crickets and birdsong—"comes from here." He taps his temple. "It's amazing what a headful of cells and blood vessels can do."

As he looks out at the landscape below, I wrestle down the sense of connection that warms me from the inside. We may have different approaches to playing the game of science and may have gotten here on different paths—while he was squinting through microscopes, I was trying to understand hidden layers of deep neural networks—but we've ended up at the same point. In this weird space where you pick the one question you find interesting, and you don't let go. Even if it drags you to other continents, implodes your romantic relationships, and jeopardizes those with your family. Because it's intoxicating, knowing you're thinking about something nobody has thought about before. Any tiny little question you might answer could help solve something bigger down the line.

Lewis picks up his backpack, and when I straighten to shoulder mine, our gazes meet. "You know, you could've just asked, and I would've told you how I got into science. I'd tell you anything you want to know."

After a couple of hours and a climb so rugged it leaves us breathless, we reach the summit of Sugarloaf Mountain. My legs wobble after the strenuous hike, the air moves hard through my lungs, and the lookout over the valley is humbling. Beyond us, a carpet of green stretches over the lower hills, and a lake shimmers slate gray in the distance. Lewis was right. A weekend out of the city was absolutely what I needed.

"You okay?" Lewis squints against the glare of the sun, forehead glistening with sweat.

"Yeah," I pant, but immediately want to revoke my answer when he lifts a corner of his shirt and passes it over his face, granting me a peek at the hair trailing down his torso into the waistband of his shorts. Temperature-regulating clothing and zip-off pants shouldn't turn me on, but on him, they absolutely, maddeningly do.

Lewis drops the edge of his shirt and waves me over to snap a picture of us together, right next to the wooden sign marking the summit. It's not long until the sharp, ear-whipping wind drives us off the peak and farther on our loop. As we continue our hike, we lapse into a companionable silence, and my thoughts flip-flop between my growing feelings for Lewis and what career options I have now that my grant was rejected. Every now and then, one of us points out something on our route, before we return to the quiet spaces inside our heads. Later that afternoon, we take another break under the canopy of trees on the gentler eastern slope of the mountain.

Lewis spreads out a camp towel on the ground and we both sit with our backs against a fallen log. My body pulsing with his proximity and the exhaustion of the day, I pull my backpack close and search for my stash of granola bars. "Want one?" I offer.

"Nah, thanks," Lewis replies as he unfolds a paper map on his stretched-out legs. Overhead, sunlight slants through the leaves, tinting the forest golden, and a soft breeze ruffles the branches and blows through my hair. While Lewis studies the map, I eat my lemon coconut bar and absorb the peace and quiet I was, unbeknownst to myself, craving after listening to the sirens and the eight million other people in New York City.

"Thank you," I tell him, "for getting me out of *there*"—I nod my head left, though Manhattan could very well lie the other way—"and bringing me here."

He glances up at me. "I'm glad it's helping." His eyes scan over my face like they've been doing all morning, as if he can read the crevices of my skin and the tension patterns of my facial muscles. It's a ridiculous thought; Lewis knowing me this well after only one week, but if there's one thing I've understood about him from the start of our tenuous relationship it is that he's perceptive. Caring, in all his quiet and hidden ways. And that this tough week would've been a million times worse without him at my side.

"I'm also sorry for yesterday and, um . . ." I swirl my hand through the air. "Springing that kiss on you when you clearly didn't want to. That's not—part of our deal. Obviously. And I think pretending to be a couple and spending so much time with you this week got me a little confused. It's not . . . We can be . . ." I take a deep breath, focus on what I want him to understand. "What I'm saying is, thank you for being my friend."

Friend. The word feels out of place after four years of rivalry. It also feels like a lie after a long morning wanting to halt Lewis in his tracks, draw him in by the strap of his backpack, and get into his space. But I know friends is really all we should be, given his rejection and my rule never to get involved with a colleague again.

Lewis looks back down at the map, where I can make out the blue ribbon of the Hudson River, and a furrow etches into the freckles splattered on his nose. I wait for him to respond, but his mouth stays shut.

We've managed to avoid any mention of my clumsy kiss this whole morning. Maybe I shouldn't have brought it up.

"Anyway." I try to sound nonchalant, but the word comes out too high-pitched. "Should we get—"

"Frances, I don't want to be just your friend," Lewis cuts in, his gaze finally straying from where it's been firmly fixed on the map. But instead of meeting my eyes, his skirt over the sun-dappled forest floor.

"Um?" I don't know what to say.

His frown draws tighter. "And I didn't reject you because I didn't want to kiss you."

"Then why . . ."

"I've been thinking about kissing you this whole time." His eyes flick up to meet mine and stay, as if he's drinking me in, all while heat spills through my body and *drip drip drips* into a simmering pool low in my belly. "You have no idea how much bandwidth you take up in my head."

His confession short-circuits my mind, leaving it blank.

"But," he continues, "I want to kiss you—want you to kiss

me—for the right reasons. Not because I'm pretending to date you. Or because you're angry and want to deflect. After the last time, I want to be clear that when I kiss you, we're not hiding behind the roles we're playing."

My pulse starts sprinting and, up in my head, the power goes on again.

I take up bandwidth in his head?

Since when has he been wanting to kiss me?

I want to know everything. If he felt it, too, this connection that pulled me into his orbit and planted me there. If he can pinpoint the moment he started wanting me, or if it was a gradual shift, a sneaking suspicion.

Heart close to dancing out of my chest, I reach for his jaw. It scratches against my fingers, as though he's skipped shaving this morning.

There's one question rising above all the others that crowd my mind.

"What about now?" All I manage is a whisper. "Do you still want to kiss me?"

His throat bobs, and his darkened eyes dip to my mouth for a sliver of a second. "Yes." His voice comes out a little ragged. I want him to say my name just like that.

I lean in, but he only narrows his eyes and shakes his head, his voice surprisingly firm when he says, "Talk to me, Frances."

"I want to kiss you, too," I whisper, dragging my thumb over the shadow of his beard, and watching how he leans into my touch. I've always preferred charging ahead and showing my feelings rather than talking about them, but Lewis said he needed clarity and for him, this—*us*—I want to try. "Not because I'm angry and not because of our deal. I just *really* want to kiss you." My last words come out a little desperate, and, under my finger, his jaw shifts as the traces of a smile curve around his mouth.

I struggle to outright ask him to kiss me now, so I settle for the comforting vocabulary of science instead. "So, um. How about we stop thinking and start executing?"

Lewis arches an eyebrow. "Executing? I'd planned . . ." He breaks off, fisting his hand into the map. The crisp sound of crinkling paper tapers into a heavy silence.

"You'd planned?"

But Lewis doesn't tell me what he'd planned.

He stays still and keeps looking at me. His attention is like a caress on my skin, palpable and toe-curlingly physical. It crosses my mind that a public hiking path might not be the best place to keep pushing this topic. But we haven't seen another soul in hours, and it's been years since I've wanted something this much.

"You know what. Never mind," he finally says, but I already forgot what we were talking about.

His hands come up to track the path his eyes took, over my temples and down my cheeks to the corner of my mouth. Inky eyes hook onto where he's touching my lips, and it's less conscious thought, more reflex that has my tongue dart to his thumb.

Lewis makes a throaty sound.

I lick him again, slower this time, savoring the rough pad of his skin, the salty taste.

His control slips as he finally lifts to his knees and braces his elbows onto the fallen tree at my back, bracketing me in. The scraggly bark digs through my shirt, a forceful contrast to the featherlight tug in my stomach when he lowers his mouth to mine.

His lips are warm, and he tastes like sugar. Like the sports drink we shared on the crest of the hill, but so much better. I want to consume all of him.

For maybe a second, he kisses me slowly, hesitantly. But

then I shift my hands into his hair, pulling lightly at the strands, and his caution gives way. Each time he draws in, he shows his need in different ways. A nip at my lower lip, fingers twisting into my shirt, the tip of his tongue coaxing my mouth open. I feel all of his movements right down to my core, but when his tongue slides into the corner of my mouth, a molten, lush heat bursts between my legs. It drums a lazy rhythm as I pull his face closer and deepens when I trace my teeth along the contour of his jaw.

I'd be embarrassed about how much I want him, how a flick of his tongue and a drag of his fingers can undo me, but the heavy shape of his own desire against my abdomen tells me it's no different for him.

"Frances," Lewis rasps out, and my name on his lips is more exquisite than I'd ever imagined it could sound. I lift my hips, chasing the friction, chasing that choking sound he just made, and he reads my intention, sliding his thigh between my legs.

My sharp exhale comes dangerously close to a moan. "Those thoughts about me," I breathe out. "Did they involve anything other than kissing?"

Lewis pulls back his head, but with his body still pressed against mine, the heavy thump of his heart reverberates against my chest.

His lips tick into a grin. "Wouldn't you like to know."

"I'm pretty much dying to." I scrape my fingers through his hair, noting the catch in his inhale.

"So greedy," he growls.

"So meticulous," I counter.

A pensive expression crosses his face before his mouth hones in on the hinge of my jaw, and the hitch in my breath seems to confirm whatever he was looking for, because he hums in satisfaction.

"Still feel like complaining?" he exhales against my skin.

"Shut— Ah." I whimper as he probes the sensitive spot with the tip of his tongue, and I realize that as much as I love to bicker with Lewis, it's even better when we do it without words. As I bite the tip of his ear, he groans softly. He responds by twisting his hand into the hem of my cutoffs, palm hot on my thigh and thumbnail scraping over the denim inches from where I yearn for him. His languid pace makes me impatient and needy, and I try to shift under him, but he just smiles against my jaw. I'm plotting my next move—his lips back on mine, or should I get us to turn around altogether so I can straddle him?—when I hear a gasp.

High pitched. Distant. Too much of either, to belong to Lewis.

My head snaps up. Lewis sits back onto his heels. A heartbeat and we're untangled from each other, staring into the shocked face of a middle-aged woman clad in khaki hiking gear. Wide-eyed and mouth agape, she's halted in her steps, one hiking pole poised midair, the other one slack at her side.

"Ronald," she calls tightly without turning her head.

"Jodie?" There's a rustle of approaching steps and then a man her age comes up behind her. He's wearing one of those beige safari-style bucket hats with a cord fastened below his chin. "What is it, honey?"

Jodie's eyes narrow into slits as she continues to glare at us. "This is a state park," she says sharply, her hiking pole stabbing into the air in emphasis of her words. "This is public property of the state of New York. It's to be used for recreation—not for *this*."

Her tone is indignant, the slant of her brows scandalized. Who can blame her? She just stumbled upon a pair of thirty-somethings making out like lovestruck teenagers in the middle of nowhere.

A giggle bubbles up my throat. I bite my lips to keep it in, and a glance at Lewis, who's still angled toward me, tells me it's down to me to pacify Jodie. I swallow thickly, hoping my voice won't betray me. "We're so sorry," I manage.

"Recreation," Lewis echoes, dead serious, catching my gaze with a twinkle in his eyes. "That's what we were doing."

I yelp out a fraction of my pent-up laughter, as Jodie presses her lips together. "Unbelievable," she hisses. Ronald, meanwhile, has turned red, his eyes gaping. "This is punishable under the law for public nuisance."

"*So* sorry," I insist and jump up to stuff Lewis's towel into my backpack, then snatch up his map, but the intricate folding pattern is too complicated for my flustered state. "We'll be on our way."

Lewis rises slowly, and under Jodie's watchful eyes, we vacate our spot, the large map fluttering behind me.

Only after we've rounded a bend in the path and are hidden behind a massive boulder overgrown with moss does Lewis pause and take the map from me. "Here, let me," he says. And with Jodie still ranting in the distance, we both burst into laughter.

Chapter Eighteen

By the time we reach the cabin, dusk has fallen. The gravel crunches underneath the tires as Lewis pulls up to an A-frame surrounded by towering pines and a porch out front. Earlier, when we dropped off the cooler of groceries that Lewis had bought in the city this morning, I only got to see the ground floor, a cozy open-plan space with creaky wooden floors, shelves stacked with books and board games, and a gray L-shaped couch piled with cushions in front of a fireplace. On the far side of the room, a wall of windows opens up to the now-darkening forest.

This time around, Lewis shows me the rest of the house, holding my hand as he guides me up the stairs and past the landing to the three bedrooms. One houses a bunk bed, but they're all homey, with wood-paneled walls, mismatched rugs, and bouquets of dried wildflowers. Lewis clocks my gasp when he shows me the room farthest down the hall and insists I take it. Nestled under the eaves, a king-size bed is pushed so close to the window you can see the sky between the tree crowns. On the dark blue canopy, the stars now blink on one by one.

Before he heads back downstairs, Lewis drops off his bag in one of the other rooms, leaving me wondering if we'll sleep in separate beds tonight—and if I want us to.

After a quick shower in the en suite bathroom and braiding my towel-dry hair, I pull on clean underwear, a blue ribbed tank, and a pair of jersey shorts, then pad downstairs to find Lewis. Although it felt good to wash off the sun and sweat from the day, the few minutes away from him have also let second thoughts filter back in. I can't predict with full certainty how this evening is going to go, but after we stumbled through the rest of the hike and stole kisses every turn of the way back to the car, I have a strong hypothesis—and I'm not sure how to feel about it.

Lewis liking me back hasn't made my reservations about him, and us, disappear. Even though I'm feeling sulky at academia this weekend, they're still neatly lined up at the top of my mind: that we have limited time together, that he's a colleague and I don't have a great track record dating those. His failure to credit me four years ago should be up there, too, but it wanes the more I get to know him.

With the looming darkness outside, the large window wall has turned into a mirror, showing me a wooden dining table before it comes into my direct view. It's large enough that not even half of it is decked out. Handcrafted bowls in various sizes hold dips and salads, and sliced bread is laid out in a woven basket.

"Wine?" Lewis asks, setting down a platter filled with more food. Drops of water cling to the ends of his hair, and I wonder how he managed to shower, let alone whip up this meal, in such a short amount of time. He's changed into a white linen shirt that is loose over the slope of his shoulders.

The sight of him scrambles something behind my ribs.

"Sure," I say, pressing my fingertips onto the tabletop. The massive oak slab is a little rough and does nothing to calm down my pulse. "This looks incredible."

Lewis pours the sauvignon blanc into the two glasses set out on the table. The faint bubbles trapped in the liquid shimmer under the soft pendant lights. He slides back a chair for me and lists the items on the table. "I wasn't sure what you'd like, so we have some fresh bread, hummus, baba ghanoush, and a roasted red pepper dip, watermelon-feta salad with a bit of mint, couscous salad, grilled Halloumi for you, chicken breast for me."

"Since when do you cook?"

He settles on the chair across from me and motions for my plate. "There was barely any cooking involved."

I roll my eyes as he piles my plate with food. "Still involves more foresight than ramen or a ready-to-eat salad. So. That counts as cooking to me."

"It relaxes me," he explains and pushes the plate over to me. "*And* allows me to have a more varied diet than whatever you're putting into your body."

"You'd be surprised how many variations of grilled cheese there are," I counter. His low chuckle is a spike for my reward centers. I've gotten greedy for his laughs, all of them: the ones he tucks into a corner of his mouth, and the ones that rumble out of him.

"So many different cheeses," I continue, "and types of bread, for that matter. Mustard, yes or no?" I lean forward, dropping my voice conspiratorially. He sets down his fork and sidles closer, too, the pine smell of his shower gel hitting my nostrils. "When I'm being wild, I put truffle mayo on the outside. Makes it extra crispy and tasty."

His eyes light up, and my dopamine goes off the charts.

Before he invited me to come along this weekend, Lewis told me it'd be good to take some time away from it all, and I know he meant work then, but maybe this should include my qualms, too. Maybe, if just for this weekend, I can forget that he's a colleague.

As we raid our plates, Lewis gives me recommendations for hikes and sights for my trip with Karo to the Pacific Northwest and tells me about local spots for outdoor climbing. From where he's sitting perpendicular to me, his eyes glimmer under the soft lamplight, and when his knee slides against my thigh, once, twice, before he leaves it there, the weight sends torturous sparks up my leg.

I know I should pull away.

I should, but I don't want to. Over the last years, I've always let the *shoulds* win, but after how heavily the grant rejection hit me, I'm beginning to wonder if that was the best course of action. I'm so tired of working toward only one goal, just for the posts to keep moving all the time, and although Lewis is a clear deviation from my path, each tiny step I grant myself is one more burning thought banked.

The unsettling truth is that Lewis makes me feel good about myself.

Isn't that reason enough to skip the *should*, if only for a little while?

I let my leg stay put.

The decision sends jitters down my nerves, and I fold up my napkin to keep my hands busy. "Well. Home-cooked dinner and wine . . ."

"I told you there was barely any cooking involved," he interjects, smiling as he shakes his head.

"Dinner and wine," I repeat, "coming from the man who likes to"—I lift my index fingers—"'decompress' with his colleagues?"

He laughs. "That's rich, coming from the person who told me to 'execute'"—he mimics my tilted head and the wiggling index fingers—"when you wanted me to kiss you."

"Right." The memory of what followed amplifies the flutter in my belly, and I glance down at where I'm playing with the end of my fork. "All I'm saying is that you surprise me, Dr. North."

"What can I say, Dr. Silberstein," Lewis replies with a shrug. "We did establish that you like to jump to conclusions." He presses his knee deeper into my thigh, and it sparks something in my chest, the way he pronounces my last name. Softly, teasingly, with the tinge of his American accent.

I wrinkle my eyebrows as he slides both of our plates off to the side. "Why, I thought that was you, Dr. North."

"Is that so?" He sets his elbow on the table and rests his cheek against his knuckles. "Back to calling each other 'Doctor,' are we? The titles—do they do something for you?"

It's neither the last names, I want to say, *nor the titles. It's all about you, and that softness that slips over your face when I'm being silly. It's about the way the laugh huffs out of you when you catch the joke, the way you search for my gaze before you pinball it back to me.*

Some of the sentiment must spill onto my face, because Lewis halts midway through picking up his glass and pauses to look at me over the rim. Cheeks growing pink, he takes a sip, and when he sets down his wine, he swipes his thumb to catch the drop of condensation sliding down the glass.

My eyes snag on the movement. *Would he stroke me this gently as well?*

He takes his time lifting his gaze back to mine, but when he does, there's something captivating in his eyes. Alluring. Something that I haven't cared about seeing in a man's eyes in years.

An invitation.

"Frances," he murmurs, and the tone of his voice is a gentle caress down my back. "Come here."

I hadn't realized how close we have pulled together as we

talked. With his bare forearms on the tabletop, he's leaning forward, but it's not close enough, so I push out of my chair. A faint voice in my mind observes what a phenomenally bad idea this is, but the wine and the warm lights and Lewis's darkened eyes silence the voice.

I want this. He wants it. It's straightforward, like nothing else ever is.

Under Lewis's watchful gaze, I make my way around to his side of the table, leaning against the edge just inches from where he's sitting with his legs sprawled out and crossed at the ankles. "Seems like it worked," I say.

Tenderness tucks into the corner of his mouth. "What did?"

"You, seducing me over a romantic dinner." My voice is decibels above a whisper.

He leans forward and touches my hip. "That was the plan all along. Before you got impatient on the hike."

"We're back to schedule now, so don't complain."

"I wouldn't dare." We both watch as his fingers spread over my ribs, as his thumb dips into the waistband of my shorts. The flutter in my belly turns into a throb between my legs.

"What's phase two"—I exhale—"of that, um, plan of yours?"

He doesn't move his hand. I try to bring him closer with a tilt of my hips, but his thumb stays where it is, hot and maddening on the edge of my hip bone.

Lewis lifts his eyes to mine. "You tell me."

The unconcealed longing in his face sends my pulse staggering. I pull one foot over his legs, sinking into his lap as his arms curve around my waist. My fingers coil into the damp strands of his hair, and I angle his face up so I can dip my mouth to meet his. I taste him greedily; the wine on his bottom lip that prickles on my tongue, the vibration as he groans and twists his hands into my tank top. Want scorches through me as he yanks me closer. His kisses are slow and a little dirty, tinged with a slip of his tongue, a graze of his teeth, and I find my hips mirroring his cadence with microscopic thrusts that have him grow heavy against me.

Lewis palms my lower back with one hand, urging me to grind into him, his other hand pulling up the hem of my top. His nails skirt over my abdomen, knuckles rippling against the underside of my breast. The echo of his touch is dulled by the fabric of my bra, and when I gasp into his mouth, he feels around my back for the opening.

"Not there," I say, breathless. The lace bralette seemed cute when I took it out of my bag earlier, but now it's all levels of inconvenient. "It doesn't open."

Lewis locks his hands around my thighs, before he lifts me off him and up onto the empty side of the table. He pulls my top over my head, and hooks his fingers into my bralette, but freezes there. "Is this okay?" he murmurs against my shoulder, his fingers tense against my ribs. "We can slow down," he continues, sounding focused. Strained. "Watch a movie. Play board games. Whatever you want. Tell me what you want."

"Fuck, no," I rasp. "I hate board games."

The feathery exhale of his chuckle hits my collarbone. "Alright, no Settlers of Catan then."

"I want this. I want . . . you," I say into his hair.

Lewis's palm skids over my breast as he tugs up the elastic. I arch into his touch, undone by the slow drag of his skin. My reaction distracts him, I think, because he doesn't pull the bralette off, just pushes it high enough that he can glide his thumb over my nipple. My hips tilt forward, lust coiling tightly in my abdomen.

Again, his hand drifts over my breast, but now he studies me with heavy-lidded eyes as if to catalog the reactions in every part of my body. "I . . ." His chest rises and falls with the intake of his breath. "Is it weird if I tell you that I'd hoped phase two would involve something like this?"

"Getting hyper focused on my nipples?" I ask, as he kisses a path down my neckline. Not that I'm complaining, but it's slightly humiliating to be so highly strung when half of my clothes—and all of his—are still on.

"Seeing you naked." His breath ghosts against my nipple, taut after all his attention.

About that.

"Technically," I remark, unbuttoning his shirt, "I'm not. You know, since you're so detail-oriented."

He smiles against my lips as he kisses me, my fingers busy mapping the geography of his chest. And then it's a competition of who can undress the other first, although it's unfair that he has a head start. His thumb finds the button of my shorts, my palms push the linen fabric off his shoulders, he finally drags my bralette over my head.

He wins.

By the time he has me truly naked, I've only gotten his shirt off and the buckle of his belt open. Freckles dot his shoulders, fainter but more densely clustered than on his face, like the point cloud of an imperfect correlation. Muscles and a trail of hair disappear into the waistband of his shorts, which hang low on his hips, bulged out by the clear shape of his desire.

I reach for him, hungry for the pressure of his leg, and when he slots his thigh between mine and pushes me against the table again, I feel a glimpse of relief, but it's short-lived. The index finger of his right hand skirts over my torso, traces over my ribs and to my belly button, but instead of dipping down lower to where I'm unhinged with need, Lewis steps back. And pauses. And looks at me with hunger, slowing my blood down to a crawl.

Then he gently pushes me back onto the table and kneels.

Fingers finding my ankle, he starts a maddening path up the inside of my leg.

"This . . ." he mumbles, and with his cheek against my thigh, I can feel the stubble of his jaw against my skin. It makes me needy. Greedy.

"What?" I gasp out, only noting how my hips have bowed up when he settles his palm over my abdomen and pushes me back to the table. He dips down his thumb, inches from where desire is strumming out a heavy rhythm.

" . . . Was my very faint hope for phase three." He swallows. I take in the soft curl of his hair, the calm focus of his eyes, the puckered lips. "Do you know you narrow your eyes in a very specific way when you're trying to one-up me? You get this little nick on the bridge of your nose. And then you say something smart about fucking basket cells and their contribution to the hemodynamic response. There's nothing more sexy than when you explain things to me."

The confession rushes out of him in a string of breaths against my inner thigh, words slurring as though his discipline is fading. When did I talk about basket cells? Wednesday? I squirm under him, out of my mind for his touch.

Lewis is gentle when he finally strokes me. He slips his hand between my legs, palm and then fingers dragging in one long movement against my clit. His touch sets off quivers everywhere, the tectonics of my body shaking and rearranging even furthest from my epicenter.

"Lewis." His name is little more than a whimper on my tongue.

"Are you good?" he asks innocently, as his thumb draws tight circles over me. "Or would you prefer the board games now?"

My laugh veers into a choking sound when I feel his tongue on me. He moves between my legs the way he kissed me: slow and unhurried, even when I move my hips against his face with impatience. I could stay in this state for hours, drunk on his attention, plied by his fingers and his tongue, but every time he licks my clit, this heavy, empty feeling winds tighter around my spine. It's not enough, not even when he slides a finger into me, and I push my hips into his palm.

My fingers in his hair, on the arch of his ear, bring him to a halt.

"Did you bring condoms?"

Lewis blinks at me, dazed, and I can see his brain reboot in the way his stare loses its glazed-over look and pivots into a sharp focus. "I did. They're in my bag." He sits back onto his heels and runs his left hand over his face, the other still palming the pulse between my legs. After a glance over his shoulder, he rises slowly and walks over to the couch to dig through his duffel bag.

"Is this what you expected for phase four?" I ask him, watching as he steps out of his shorts on his way back to me.

"Shush," he says against the crown of my head, as I hook my thumb into the waistband of his boxers and tug them down. "I did not expect anything. I also brought cocoa powder, vegan marshmallows, bath salts, and a copy of your dissertation." He tears open the packet, then pulls the condom on, fingers twitching once they're wrapped around him. For a breath he's quiet and presses his eyes shut, as if he's holding on to this conversation only by a tether. "It's better to be prepared for everything than end up regretting not bringing the right thing later."

I swallow forcibly, gaze catching on his hand. That edge in his voice does something to my body, makes it feel liquid and molten. His eyes flash back up to me and his chest expands with a deep inhale as he runs his hands over my hair.

"Come here." His voice is soft as he beckons me in for another kiss. He cradles my cheeks, turns my head to one side and bites my earlobe, the underside of my jaw, the curve of my neck.

I lean back onto my hands. Attention unwavering, his hands lift to my ass and slowly, gently, pull me closer to the edge of the table. Closer to him.

"Is this okay?" he chokes out as he lines himself up against me.

Impatient as I am, it takes me a breath to register what he's waiting for. Then another one to get the word out. "Yes."

He holds my gaze and only when I nod to emphasize my words, does he finally sink into me. For a hitch of a breath, the pressure of him satisfies my longing and I let out a moan. But then he stills, and I spiral back into a wide, gaping emptiness. Lewis breathes out a sigh, his eyes closing for one long blink, before they come to rest on my face. I clasp my thighs around him, desperate to increase the tension.

"Is this good?" His words are barely more than a growl.

I nod frantically.

"Frances," he bites out, but he's still unbearably still inside me. "Tell me how to make this good for you."

"Can you . . ." I look at where his hands are splayed on my leg, suddenly shy to ask. "Can you put one hand on my throat again?"

He lifts his arm and follows my request. The light weight of his hand against the base of my throat is even more delicious than the memory of it when we first kissed. I swallow thickly, and his pupils darken as my muscles dance against his palm. My hips roll, almost of their own accord, increasing the pressure, heightening the friction for one mind-bending moment.

We both inhale sharply, eyes flying down to where we're connected.

He looks like he's about to fall apart, face desperate and jaw twitching, until he finally begins to move. I drop down to my elbows and cross my ankles behind his back, chasing the hum that vibrates through me with every one of his strokes, and throwing back my head when it flares into something brighter.

In his hands I feel precious, cared for, enough.

I pant his name as he glides into me again, my voice raw and unrecognizable. It spurs him on as he locks me against him with one broad hand on my back, the other one tracing over my body. Greedily, like he can't decide where he wants to hold on to me, he digs his fingers into my waist, drifts past the swell of my breast and flicks his thumb over my nipples, before he catches my jaw for a kiss. The lick of his tongue and bite of his teeth is a slick echo of the movements of his hips. I can feel myself tremble around him, can feel the erratic in and out of my breath, but even as I arch further into him, the deep, aching hunger doesn't let up.

When I whimper, Lewis slips a hand up my calf. "I've got you," he murmurs against my temple as he opens me wider, then dips his fingers to my clit. His circles grow tighter as he takes me deep and slow, and I curse, sensing how frustratingly close I am to blazing off.

And then he does this thing with his fingers. A tap against my clit, just the right side of forceful.

"*Oh.*" The sudden jolt makes me come with an intensity that shakes my legs, fuse burning and obliterating my nerves. I pulse around him again and again and the jerk of his hips turns into a stutter, like the force of my orgasm has brought him off course and scrambled up his rhythm.

"Put your hands on my shoulders," Lewis orders, and when I curve my arms around his neck, he thrusts into me, once, twice. On the third one he sinks in deep, and presses his thumb into my collarbone. His teeth find my shoulder as the pleasure pools out of him.

Gradually, my moans wane and his muscles slacken under

my hands. He leans heavily against me when the tension leaves his body, and I hug him close. I inhale the warm scent of his skin as he kisses the spot that's tender from his bite and presses his nose into my neck. Curved into each other and breathing the same oxygen, I sift my fingers through his hair and think about how each time I'm vulnerable with him, he makes me feel like it's a good thing.

"I like it when you make plans," I confess into the hollow below his ear.

"Do you?" He trails his fingers up my arm, and I shiver, hypersensitive after his touch. He clasps my hand and lifts it to his lips, mouth swollen from kissing me. "I like my plans, too," he murmurs into my wrist. "Especially when they involve you."

Lewis picks up my limp body and carries me to the couch, where he kisses my forehead before he disappears into the bathroom. When he returns, my cheeks are still warm from his honesty, and with a relaxed smile on his face, he lies down next to me and smooths his hands over my hair. Wrapped up in his warmth, I feel at ease. Like the stress of the last week, months, maybe even years has finally detonated out of me.

"Did you really bring my thesis?" I ask after a while.

He tilts his head. "Do you want me to get it out?"

"I understand the hot cocoa powder, and the marshmallows, probably for drowning my sorrows in chocolate, but my thesis? For what? So we could take a bath together and I'd read you my propositions?" I pause as his mouth crooks up. "Oh my god, is that something that turns you on?"

Lewis watches me silently for a moment. My reaction to the weird mental image of this scenario must play out on my face, because his smirk etches deeper. "No, Frances," he says. "I brought it because sometimes it's good to remind ourselves what we're doing all of this for, and I figured your thesis would be a good place to start."

"Oh," I say. I consider his words once more. "Why do you even *have* a copy of my thesis?"

"I took it the other day. There's a shelf for alumni outside the secretary's office." He rubs his neck. "Yours was there. I was curious."

"Oh," I repeat. His tenderness and thoughtfulness peel back something, an intimacy I'm not yet ready to think about, especially now when my skin is still warm from his touch and heavy with his scent.

Lewis, I've begun to realize, is good at telling from only one look if he needs to shift the conversation sideways or hold the wheel steady and face me head-on. Now, he nudges his knee against my thigh. "But it's also fine by me if you want to take a bath and look at some of your figures together."

Sideways, it is.

"Stop it." I laugh, grateful for his attempt to keep me from spiraling.

"Are you sure? I have some thoughts about chapter four . . ."

Chapter Nineteen

It's the middle of the night, and once again, I can't sleep. The curtains are open, letting in the view of the stars and the moonlit crowns of the swaying pines, but that's not what's keeping me awake. It's the quiet of the night when I'm used to lullabies composed of clinking bike chains, humming motors, and howling sirens. It's the unfamiliarity of a person next to me. Maybe I should've let Lewis pick his own bedroom, but I wanted to stay close to him. He has the exceptional quality of getting me out of my own head, except now he's fast asleep, which means I'm back in there with all my thoughts. The unanimous consensus seems to be that sleeping with Lewis was a very, very bad idea.

My muscles, stiff after the day of hiking, protest when I slide out of bed. I grab my glasses and pad downstairs. My phone is where I left it charging on the kitchen counter and I check it before switching on the light over the extractor hood. No new messages, but when I open my chat with Karo I see that she's online: 2 a.m. here is . . . 11 p.m. in Oregon.

Before leaving this morning, I'd texted her about the grant, figuring it'd be easier that way. I'm glad for it now as I hit call, since it means I don't need to find the words and feel my mouth perform the movements around them.

"Hey," I whisper when she picks up. Several voices reply with a *"Hallo,"* which is when I realize that, instead of picking up herself, Karo has pulled me into the family group call. My parents must be having breakfast, since it's morning over there—after five years in NYC, the time difference to Berlin is practically ingrained at this point.

"Oh, *Hasi*, I'm so sorry," my mother says, and I feel the pinprick of tears in my eyes at her nickname for me. "Karo told us about the grant."

"If they don't want you to solve amnesia . . . their loss," my father adds, voice much louder than my mother's. I picture him at the table, setting his butter knife aside and bending over his phone. The urge to sit with them at the heavy and well-loved dining table hits me out of nowhere. I'd sip *Mama's* perfect latte that she makes with the coffee maker we gave her for her last birthday, watch her and *Papa* bicker over Sunday's crossword and wonder how they were so lucky to find their persons and hold on to them, all through teaching for twenty years at the same high school.

"How are you holding up?" Lennart's voice pipes up.

"I, um . . ." I falter, lost for words, because how do I explain that I've added a whole other set of worries to the ones already occupying my mind? "I'm okay?" I keep my voice low to avoid waking up Lewis. "Catching my breath upstate. I needed to get out of the city for a bit. What are you up to?"

"I was just telling them about our hike, Franzi," Karo jumps in.

"Send us the pictures you were talking about," *Mama* says. "We need to get going."

"Want to take the boat out, it's a beautiful day," *Papa* continues. Ever since they bought a paddleboat two summers ago, they spend their weekends out on the rivers and lakes, sometimes taking camping gear to make it into an overnight trip.

We say our goodbyes, and when my parents have left the call, Karo asks, "Everything alright with you? It's kind of late, right?"

"Yeah." I sigh. "It's . . ." I close my eyes and will the hum of the fridge to ground me. "I think I've made a mistake."

There's a pause where Lennart murmurs something, Karo sighs, and then her voice comes closer to the microphone. "I don't think it's your fault they didn't give you the grant." I hear her walk somewhere, presumably into a different room.

"I'm not talking about the grant, I . . ." I drag my toe over the wooden floor. "He's a good cook. And do you know how I know? Because he made me dinner. Vegetarian dishes with dairy in them, even though he's lactose intolerant and eats meat. How the hell am I supposed to come back from that?"

"As much as I love nonlinear storytelling, I'm going to need a little more context here. Start from the beginning," she demands softly, "and then I'll tell you if it's fixable."

From our last call she already knows that Lewis agreed to fake date me, but now I catch her up with the events of the past week, the evening outings, the first hiccups at selling our fake relationship, the action plan we came up with and how it made our act a little easier and, eventually, not like an act at all.

"Oh no." She sighs. "I told you, Franzi. No extra credits when you're fake dating."

"Our act wasn't good enough, so it needed to be done. Though maybe the kiss was overkill," I muse.

"And this whole weekend, too. But as long as your reputation's safe, it doesn't seem like it was a complete mistake," Karo notes. "And maybe Lewis isn't so bad, either?"

"He isn't." I sigh.

"You sound like that's bad news. Why?"

I hope she has an hour. There are many reasons why.

"We're only in the same city until Friday. He'll go back to Germany, and you and I will go on our trip, which is great, but after that? The best-case scenario would be that whatever lab I end up in is on the same continent as him. But even then, I've only known him for days, so why would I want to start anything as complicated as this?"

"I mean, if you really like him . . ."

I begin to pace the length of the counter. "Karo, we work together. Not in the same office, obviously, but we're in the same field and after Jacob— I can't."

"But to everyone else, you're already a couple anyway," Karo points out.

"I know. But it's not only my reputation I'm worried about, though of course, there's that, too." I take a deep breath, feel for the words that describe best what has me so wide-awake at night. "I lost sight of myself when I was with Jacob. As long as Lewis and I are not in it for real, at least I know that me and my work exist separately from his. Losing that certainty? That's what I'm most worried about."

Karo falls quiet for a moment, then huffs out an exasperated, "Ugggh."

"Exactly," I say.

"Frances?"

I startle and turn around to find Lewis at the bottom of the stairs, one hand wrapped around the banister, the other scratching the back of his neck. My heart squeezes at how rumpled he looks: hair sticking up, creases on his cheek, one eye half-closed against the glare of the light. This side of him, so sleepy and soft, is new to me.

How long has he been standing there?

"Is everything okay?" he asks gruffly and comes shuffling

into the kitchen. It doesn't seem like he overheard my conversation with Karo.

I lower the phone against my collarbone. "Give me a sec." After I promise Karo to call her in a few days, I hang up the call. "Did I wake you up? I'm sorry."

He shakes his head as he touches the small of my back. "Are you okay, though?" His hand lingers there as he opens the fridge door. The stark light illuminates his profile.

I feel his closeness, his warmth, in every nerve of my body, like my cells are rejoicing at having him close again, but that's the problem, isn't it?

I clear my throat. "Yeah, all good."

Lewis studies me for a moment, then puts his hand on my head, palm on my crown and fingers reaching to my temples. "What's going on inside that brain of yours?"

"Hah," I laugh out. "Asked every neuroscientist, ever."

Lewis indulges me with a smile, but it passes quickly. After another long look, he turns to the fridge again, and I use the short break of contact to wander to the other side of the kitchen island and perch on one of the stools. As Lewis rummages in a cupboard overhead, the stash on the counter grows: oat milk, cocoa powder, marshmallows.

"Hot chocolate?" I ask.

Lewis pulls a small saucepan out of the drying rack. "Want one?"

I nod. "This is becoming a sad tradition."

"Having something sweet in the middle of the night and talking to you?" Lewis shrugs. "I could get used to this."

I melt a little inside, until sensible Frances catches up with what's happening. "About that . . ." I trail off. I watch him as he moves through the kitchen, pours the oat milk into the saucepan, switches on the stove, and lines up two mugs on the counter.

"Something sweet? You?" I ask in surprise.

"You're not the only one spiraling after last night," Lewis replies.

"Oh?" Does he regret what happened between us? I pause, giving him the space to elaborate.

"It's . . ." He rifles through the silverware drawer, then straightens with a spoon in hand and says, "It's not . . ." He starts over, only to falter again. A sigh moves through his chest, his whole body. He looks so lost and it makes that tenderness swell up inside me again.

I look at my fingers on the kitchen counter. "But you've done this before. You've decompressed with colleagues, right?"

His brows drag down. "Right. But this feels different." He looks up then, finds my eyes and touches my pinkie. "With you, it feels different."

Heartbeat thundering in my ears, I'm suddenly unsure if him regretting last night was what I was afraid of, or if the truly scary part is how monumental it felt between us, like so much more than just a flicker of attraction.

I lift my pinkie and crook it around his. "Yeah," is all I manage to say. It makes it a little easier, knowing that he's not completely immune to freaking out.

Lewis pulls back with a small smile and measures out two spoons of cocoa powder. He repeats the motions for the second cup, squints at me, and then adds a third spoon.

"Do you want to talk about it?" I ask carefully. He's the one who's held my hand, listened, and told me to slow down, but seeing him this stuck in his head makes me forget about my worries. Instead of answering, he stares down into the cups with his brow all scrunched up, like the cocoa powder at the bottom holds all the solutions to his problems.

"I'm just . . ." He expels a hard breath as he returns the box to the cupboard, then continues, "I'm not sure how to go from here. Whatever this is with you, it feels big and I don't know what to do with that." He swallows, and when his eyes flit to mine, they're glassy with anguish. "I just don't know. I know about other things, like how to mess up. I'm actually really great at disappointing people," he says on a laugh that sounds like it hurt his throat on the way out. "I'm great at doing the one thing that is so bad people end up leaving."

It's the first time I see Lewis at a loss like this. But before I can think of a way to give him comfort, he continues, "Do you want to know why I never emailed you to apologize? Because it wouldn't have mattered." He makes a movement as if to pull out his phone, then, seemingly remembering that he's only wearing boxer briefs and a tee, looks around until he spots his phone on the dining room table. "None of these would've changed a damn thing."

When he returns to my side, his screen is open on a series of drafted emails, and he scrolls and scrolls all the way from one dated a month ago to four years back. I catch subjects and first lines. "Dear Franziska," one says. Another one starts with, "Dear Dr. Silberstein," "I'm an idiot," and "I'm sorry. How do I fix—" And "Tell me what to do."

"None of these matter," he insists with a raw voice. "They won't change anything about the fact that I made a huge mistake when I should've given your career the boost it absolutely deserved."

"Hey." I take his phone out of his hands and push it aside, then shift on my stool to face him. His shoulders are tense when I hold on to them. It hurts to see how bad he still feels about this, when the last days made me see that the real him is so much more than the mistake he made four years ago. When everything he's done since outweighs that one bad decision. When my resentment has evaporated and made space for curiosity and warmth.

"Yes, you did something bad. But what's more important is that you realized and changed your ways and made up for it. Saying sorry doesn't fix your mistake, but it shows that you're willing to learn and change. It shows that you care. At least it did to me," I finish, heart beating fast at my own admission.

In the silence that follows, the lines on Lewis's face even out as his shoulders soften, but they quickly pinch together again.

"What—"

A burning smell hits my nose. "Shit!" I sprint around the kitchen island and turn off the gas, as Lewis reaches around me and swirls the saucepan for the oat milk to cool. Although he looks considerably less troubled than a moment ago, the vulnerability is still plain on his face. He probably doesn't open up like this often. I think of the fraught relationship with his parents, the estrangement from his brother. *What's more loving than telling someone you accept them the way they are?* Does he ever have someone look out for him?

"Hey, why don't you go and sit down." I give his shoulder a gentle nudge. "Let me finish this, okay?"

"Okay." He sets down the saucepan with a tired smile, but before he turns away, his palm finds my waist and he kisses the top of my head. "Thank you," he murmurs into my hair.

After I finish preparing the hot chocolate, I join Lewis, who sits with his legs sprawled out and his right arm resting on the back of the couch.

"Do you want to tell me what's keeping you up?" he asks softly when he takes his steaming mug from me, like he's desperate to turn the focus away from him and restore the balance of shared secrets. And after he let me in so deep, I'm a lot less scared of being honest with him.

I tuck myself into the corner opposite him and cradle the hot chocolate between my hands. "All of this," I say, motioning at him, us, "reminds me of Jacob and how things between us broke." I gulp. "I already told you what he said to me when we broke up, but I think I should tell you the full story."

Lewis takes a sip and nods, so I go on.

I tell him about Jacob successfully winning a huge grant right before I graduated—the grant I'd helped him polish while frantically writing my thesis. How I fought for his dream along with mine and never realized how much of myself I was giving him. The rough awakening when I understood that Jacob mistook my support for lack of a dream of my own and thought that all I wanted was to help him fulfill his career. When he sneered at me for wanting to follow the questions that burned in my mind.

"I didn't want to be his *et al*. My name tacked on to his for the rest of my career," I tell Lewis. "He was so focused on himself and what's worse, I sort of get his ambition, now. How single-minded he was. It's hard to get a professorship, even harder to get there so young, and it takes a lot out of you. I really wish I would've been that focused on myself, too. And I was trying to, after I left New York, but you know how lonely academia can be, especially if you have to adjust to a new city, a new culture, every few years. So, I loved it when you and I started emailing and discussing, because finally, again, someone got me. I felt less lonely knowing you were out there."

When I'm done talking, my mug is empty and my legs are stretched out on the couch. Lewis picks up the foot closest to his thigh and places it on his leg. His expression is tight with anger, but I'm not sure who it's directed at, himself or Jacob. "Until I published that paper . . ." he murmurs.

"Until you published that paper," I repeat. "I'm not telling you this to make you feel bad. I just want to give you context for why what you did hit me extra hard."

"I'm so sorry." He sighs, shoulders slumping forward. "I

let myself be convinced so easily by my advisor back then. I didn't know how much certain publications can shape the rest of our career. When he told me to take you off the list because having fewer coauthors would get the paper out quicker, I did. I thought it was more important to bring the science forward as quickly as possible. I wanted to list it in my next grant application and there was that wish to spite my father, too. All flimsy excuses, really. They don't make it any less wrong."

"They don't," I confirm. "But honestly? I'm not mad anymore. I just wish we could've spared ourselves the years of constant fighting. I wish I had known you weren't out to get me."

"Frances," he interrupts, his brows inching together, "it has never been about that, or getting your research up to my standards, or attaching my name to it. Your research is insanely good, period. Whenever you publish a new paper, sometimes it takes me days to fully trace your steps because they're so inventive." He sits up straight before he continues, "Your research is so *so* good. The questions you dare to ask, they push me to do better, every day. And they spark some of my own, so I add my comments and give my suggestions and hope you see some merit in them, too. But you don't need me to be the best."

I shake my head, the words already out before I can reconsider. "The funny thing is, I think I do need you to be my best," I admit, staring down at my hands and the sludge of melted marshmallows at the bottom of my mug. "I'm humbled and inspired by anything you put out there. Whatever I work on, I know you're there to perceive it. If my curiosity is my drive, you're the one riding shotgun."

When I lift my head, Lewis stares back at me, wide-eyed and with a spark in the blue of his eyes that makes my heart stutter. His presence is a constant undercurrent of electricity. Addicting and confusing and alarming. After admitting to him how much he has shaped my work from afar, it's even clearer to me why I can't let myself give in to these feelings now.

"So that is why I'm spiraling tonight. The last time I dated a colleague, I let him take the driver's seat. And that's not a mistake I want to make again."

Lewis nods slowly as he runs his thumb down the arch of my foot and up again. It soothes the knot in my stomach that has twisted tight with the memories of Jacob and my conflicting thoughts about Lewis. We lapse into a silence that is permeated by the hoot of an owl, somewhere beyond the darkened window front.

"So where does all of this leave us?" Lewis asks after a while. "I'm not sure how to go from here."

"Me, either. I haven't got a clue," I acknowledge, my chest clenching around feelings that should feel new and exciting.

Lewis rubs the bridge of his nose. "Okay, let's remember the one thing we're both good at."

I huff. "I guess you don't mean stomaching bad conference coffee. But how is science going to help us with this?"

"Breaking down a complex problem into its simple parts," Lewis points out, and something about him bringing science into this conversation makes it feel like he's spanning up a safety net for us to walk over. "I like you, but that makes me nervous."

His admission shouldn't come as a surprise, not when all of his actions and touches have been showing me how much he cares, but still, his words spill warmth through my body and give me the courage to tell him the truth.

"I do, too," I whisper. "And I like spending time with you. But you're also a colleague, and there's still the fact that I don't know where the future will take me. I might be living halfway across the world in three months, with no perspective of where I'll end up long term."

"We have another week at the Sawyer's left to go," Lewis adds.

I swallow past the emotions that have gathered in my throat. "Maybe that should be it, then. Just one week."

Lewis nods along slowly. "One week that we'll enjoy." He squeezes my foot. "Sounds good to me. And it'll be easy as pie. At least, we don't have to worry about faking it anymore."

After talking late into the night, we end up falling asleep on the couch to a rerun of *Grey's Anatomy* and head to bed in the early morning hours. Halfway up the stairs, still entangled in our dreams, Lewis reaches for me, and by the time we tumble into bed, my hands are hiking up his shirt and he's kissing me feverishly. When we finally wake up the next day, it's almost midday and we spend the Sunday lounging, doors and windows open to let in the breeze carrying the smell of dry grass and the sounds of the forest. For breakfast, Lewis makes pancakes that we drown in local maple syrup and sprinkle with cinnamon. Later, we wander to the nearby lake, where Lewis pulls out a chunky book while I swim to the little island off the shore and, sprawled on a warm stone, watch the bobbing heads and neon pink floats of people living in the homes on the far side of the lake.

Later, we pack up the car and drive back to the city with the windows rolled down, the sky glowing beyond us, like the sun tipped a bucket of orange over the horizon. The wind toys with Lewis's hair, lifts the ends of mine, and flaps the sleeve of my shirt against my arm. On the center console, Lewis runs his thumb over the back of my hand. His other hand is loose on the steering wheel, and he looks content; freckles darker than when we left New York, ears a little sunburned, and the lines around his eyes relaxed. Unlike on the drive up when he let me DJ, he's lined up a playlist now, and the melancholic guitar sounds trail us down the freeway.

Lewis is appalled to learn that I listen to music when I work, when he can only focus in complete silence, which is why he stays at his institute late into the night. Something between my ribs goes soft when I picture him walking through a dark corridor, coffee sloshing in a chipped office mug, before he sits down to type out replies to my social media posts.

"Actually, you never told me what it was that got you into science," he notes as he overtakes a truck on the highway. "I told you my origin story. Want to tell me yours?"

I tell him about Karo's ski accident, that a crash to the head was all it took for her to fade right in front of my eyes. How scary it was that she stopped recognizing us, and that the doctors—people I'd seen put my broken finger back in place, sew up open wounds, and manage my mother's diabetes—could only give the advice to wait. To let time pass and see if her brain would recover on its own.

I tell him about studying psychology, and the internships I'd done in clinics with Alzheimer's patients whose personalities were almost wiped away with the loss of their memory. How the quiet, endlessly prolonged grief of their family members unsettled me so deeply that I knew I had to do something about this. How the further I got in my university career, the more I realized how deep the rabbit hole was, how little we knew, how we'd have to start at the bottom of the pit, excavating the knowledge inch by inch until we could grasp the whole of it and come up with proper treatments.

"Have you thought about your plans?" he asks after I finish my story, picking up my hand and placing a kiss on my wrist. The song peters into silence, amplifying the weight of his question.

The weekend away from the city ended up giving me enough distance to surface from what felt like overwhelming disappointment on Friday night, and I used my long swim earlier to come up with a plan for the future.

"I want to try applying for research money again, but I'll need a postdoc to tide me over in the meantime," I tell him. "The Sawyer's will get busier with the big profs this week, which is probably good timing for networking. Surely some memory lab somewhere in this world needs another brain to get some work done."

I don't love the idea of moving again, and I'll probably have to fit my own research questions around whichever project I'm hired on, but I can't see another way. Even if it's hard, I want to keep going, because giving up is even less of an option.

"Anybody who doesn't want you in their lab is an idiot." His voice is warm, convinced, and my ears heat up at his quiet confidence in me. "I know you want to do things your way. But my offer still stands—if you want me to see if any of the people I know have open positions, just say the word."

"Thank you. What about you, though?" I ask back. "Have you thought about seeing your brother again this week?"

Lewis lets go of me, and I watch him swallow as he sets the turn signal. "I don't think I can make sixteen years of no relationship right," he murmurs, then, louder, "but yeah, I'll call him. Seeing Ben for the first time in years with my parents around was probably not the best idea."

"You could take him climbing," I suggest. "Might loosen things up."

"Not sure how Ben feels about sticking his hands in chalk. When I asked Ada about borrowing the car, he was away playing golf with my brother-in-law. *Golf.*" He releases a gust of laughter. "It's like my father's wet dream."

I shift in my seat so I can see his face, only to find a furrow of anger etched into the space between his brows. "But if he enjoys it?"

"That's the thing, though. Does he enjoy it? Or did my father's bullshit work on him so now he's a perfect carbon copy—the version he never got me to be? Because if he is, I'm not sure I want to know him."

A million sentences in Benjamin's defense come to the forefront of my mind: He's Lewis's brother, he's family, so shouldn't Lewis at least try? But the truth is, I don't know him. Neither does Lewis, though. "Maybe he turned out like your father, or maybe he didn't. Don't you at least want to know? He can enjoy playing golf and go into your father's business *and* be a decent person, can't he?"

"He can," he concedes, voice low.

I trail my hand over Lewis's shoulder. "So you'll call him?"

He bites the inside of his cheek, glances over at me. And when he nods, I wonder if life can be like this. Calling each other out, helping each other up, drawing from each other's strength.

But it doesn't matter. I shouldn't waste my time thinking about things I can't have. When we get back to Manhattan, we only have a few days left before we return to different countries, to the east of Germany and the south of the Netherlands, where the future looks uncertain for me. I tell myself that in the ups and downs of life, he can be a tangent. Our paths can intersect for one all-encompassing moment, before they head off in different directions.

Chapter Twenty

On Monday, the concourse in Schermerhorn Hall greets us with a maze of cork boards. My favorite part of any scientific event officially starts today: the poster sessions. Compared to a talk or a lecture, they're less prestigious, but there's always something special about seeing the neat boxes detailing experimental designs, the bar charts and scatter plots showing statistical analyses. The most complicated studies broken down into a few key words and a handful of diagrams.

After a short block of lectures in the morning, I seek out the colorful brain maps in the concourse, figuring that the students' enthusiasm will ignite the spark I so desperately need to court professors for a job. I talk to an American professor who's leading a lab in Tokyo and exchange email addresses with a researcher working in Melbourne. During the coffee break, as I grab a chocolate chip cookie off a plastic tray, I spot Rosanna Alderkamp at the other end of the room and take a deep breath to gather up the courage to approach her. I sent her my workshop materials and availability for lunch after we talked last week and while she replied with a slew of questions about my code and the words "Let's discuss over lunch," she forgot to confirm a date.

"Frances." Lewis's voice comes from behind me. I want to wave him away, but when I turn around, his face is pinched into that nonexpression that tells me something must be going on. After dropping me off at home yesterday, he took the car back to his sister, and I haven't seen him since.

"What's up?" I ask, my hand coming up to cup his elbow.

Lewis's eyes swivel over my shoulder and as they dance around the room, the tension carves deeper into his features. He nods his head to the side. "Can we go outside? We need to talk."

"What do you mean, it's *gone*?" I push out between clenched teeth.

It'll be easy as pie, he said back at the cabin when we talked about the week ahead, and it's true that we don't have to worry about convincingly portraying our relationship anymore, but we both forgot a crucial element in our charade, and the havoc it could wreak if it went missing.

The notebook.

Lewis's notebook. The one that has records on his conditions for fake dating me, the start and end date of our plan, all the steps we thought of on the walk after Jacob and Vivienne's dinner. There's one page that lists the names of all my family members, my teaching schedule from last semester, including weekends when we would've visited each other, and the name of who I believed to be the most influential and invaluable person in the history of psychology, although I'm not sure how the latter fits in with the rest. (I told him B. F. Skinner, which Lewis reacted to with an appreciative hum.)

"How can it be gone?" I hiss at Lewis, who sits with his elbows on his knees and head in his hands on the terraced wall snaking around the raised plant beds in front of Schermerhorn Hall. Despite the midday heat, I'm pacing up and down in front of him, unable to sit down. Since he outlined the problem, the deluge of adrenaline in my veins hasn't let up.

Lewis lifts his head and shifts forward to pat his back pocket. "It's not there."

"But you always have it on you, rain or shine. You even found a place for it in those tight shorts of yours when we went hiking," I point out.

"Dr. Silberstein," Lewis tuts. "Were you looking at my ass?"

I roll my eyes and can't help the laugh shooting out of my mouth. It takes some of my tension with it. I stop in front of Lewis and turn the conversation back to the matter at hand. "Just because the notebook's missing doesn't mean people will read it, right? If I were to find a notebook, I'd take it to the lost-and-found. Or check the first page to see who it belongs to."

Lewis grimaces. "It doesn't have my name in it. At least not on the first page. Nobody would know it belonged to me unless they flip all the way through to our fake-dating plan."

My heart speeds up. If anybody finds his notebook, we're royally screwed. Because no matter how obviously attracted we are to each other, it'll be there, in graphite on white paper, that it all started as a wild plan we concocted.

I gulp and resume my pacing. "Are you sure you didn't leave it in your room? Or at the cabin? When's your friend going up there next, so he can check?"

Lewis shakes his head. "I had it this morning. I noted down a reference."

"I didn't see you in the lecture."

"I was in the back. I got in late because I did the school run with Al this morning."

"Right. Okay, so you had it this morning, which means it has to be *somewhere*. Like the lecture hall, or . . . the bathrooms?"

Lewis nods. "I checked, but no luck. Someone must've found it and taken it."

"Fuck." I groan, as I remember the bad-decision-to-sudden-career-death flowchart that had prompted me to convince Lewis to fake date in the first place. If someone were to leaf through the notes and get a line-by-line breakdown of our fake relationship, the news would spread fast in this small community, damaging our reputations irreparably. And then, who'd want to work with us?

It's not only mine, but also Lewis's career that's at stake now. If we're exposed, he goes down with me.

And *I* roped him into this.

Guilt turns the swirl in my stomach into nausea as a bead of sweat trails down my neck.

"Let's go and check again," I say, voice tight with desperation. "It has to be somewhere. It has to."

Lewis presses his lips together. I take his hand, and as we walk back into the building, I'm not sure whether to laugh or cry at the irony that my looming unemployment isn't my biggest problem anymore.

We look for the notebook everywhere.

We crouch down to search below the rows of foldout seats in the lecture hall. We jog down corridors, dart into empty classrooms, and knock at the doors of the ones that are occupied by groups of other scientists. We scour the restrooms of the buildings. We visit Regina at the secretary's office and the security desk at the entrance to ask for a lost-and-found, and all the while my stomach twists deeper into anxiety. Lewis gets quieter, his face cementing into a mask.

"I'm not sure if it's a good or a bad sign it hasn't turned up yet," I mutter to him as we make our way back to the concourse.

"Definitely bad. It should have been found and dropped off somewhere by now, unless the person who found it kept it."

Instead of picturing whose hands the notebook could've gotten into and what they're doing with that information, I scan the concourse, but it's pure chaos: Crowds of people push around, backpacks are strewn on the floors. Discarded plastic and cardboard tubes.

If the notebook is here, it could be anywhere.

Lewis pulls me against his side as we make our way into the first row of poster boards. A motivated grad student spots us and starts presenting his research, and I nod mechanically as my eyes search the floor below us.

"—actually really hoping to talk to you, Dr. North . . ."

Lewis, seemingly unaware of the question, uses his foot to shift the student's backpack, which sports a Stanford logo.

"Um?"

"I lost something," Lewis says. His eyes jump to mine, then the student, who seems to realize we haven't listened to him at all. Lewis clears his throat, glancing up at the poster. "So. Uh." His eyes squint together. "You really think you can detect hippocampal theta with EEG?"

As they discuss, I peer down the aisle of poster boards as far as I can, but when Lewis is still discussing with the student ten minutes later, I excuse myself. I can't tell if he wants to make up for our rudeness, or if he's actually interested, but I know we'll be quicker if we split up.

I'm about a third of the way down the room, in front of a poster that, in other circumstances, I'd find much more interesting, when Rosanna Alderkamp walks up next to me.

"Frances, how are you?"

The poster's author is nowhere to be seen. I'm kneeling to see if the notebook fell behind the paper bin pushed against the wall. A second later and she would've found me with my hand inside that bin.

"Oh, hi," I chirp and retie the laces of my left shoe, pretending that's what I crouched down for.

"Did you have a nice weekend?"

It takes me a moment to answer. After the mad search that has made up this last hour, the weekend feels like it happened years ago. "I did." I straighten. "What about you?"

She gives me a tired smile. "Too warm, but my wife flew in on Friday and we rented a car and went to a beach in New Jersey, so it was manageable."

"Yeah, the summers here are a little different from the ones in the Netherlands," I say. Which reminds me that, once I'm back in Europe, this might be my last summer in the Netherlands . . . unless I bookmark the search for a moment and try my luck with her. "There's something I wanted to talk to you about. Would you still be up for having lunch at some point this week?"

"Sure. Let me check." Rosanna rummages through her bag, and after she finds her phone, she lifts her glasses to the top of her forehead and taps on her screen. "Thank you for sending me the code, by the way. Is tomorrow okay?"

Other than my data-blitz presentation on Thursday morning, the final social event of the Sawyer's on the same evening, and finding this goddamn notebook, I have nothing scheduled for the week, so I nod. "Works for me. Shall we meet outside the building after tomorrow's keynote?"

"Let's do that." She puts her phone away and brushes her hair over one shoulder. "There's this café on Broadway I walk past every morning on the way here that I've been wanting to try."

"That sounds good," I chime. Honestly, we could be having stale store-bought chips on a bench somewhere and I'd still be happy I get to talk to her.

Rosanna gives me a small wave. "See you then."

As she walks away, my worries about the missing notebook immediately burst back up and I tell myself it'll be fine, that it won't turn up in unwanted hands, that nobody will read what's inside, and I'll get to meet Rosanna and make my case for how well I would fit into her lab if she has any available funding.

Lewis comes to find me not long after, and as we continue our search, Jacob stops us on the way to the seminar rooms. He asks us about our weekend, and through our jumpy, nervous replies, I wait for him to casually announce that he's found the notebook, but he only turns to Lewis and says, "Dr. North, could you resend your lecture slides from last week? I think there's something wrong with the file," before he wishes us a good rest of the day.

With Lewis tense against my side, and my breaths shaky, I steer us out of the building, across the plaza, and into the shade of a leafy tree away from view.

"I'm so sorry," I say.

"What for?"

"We wouldn't be in this mess if I hadn't insisted on this whole charade."

"Yeah, but you'd also still be hating my guts." Lewis runs a hand through his hair, his mouth curving into a hollow smile. "This one is on me. We wouldn't be in this mess if I didn't need to write everything down."

But hearing him take the blame doesn't make me feel any better. "What about the rest of the notebook?" I ask. "Not . . . related to us, but is there anything else in there that'd suck if it was gone?"

"Maybe the last few pages. Everything I wrote down since we arrived, but in comparison, that doesn't really matter . . ."

He doesn't need to finish his sentence.

We both know that if we are found out, our careers might well be over.

Chapter Twenty-One

Lewis's notebook remains missing. After checking with Regina again and dipping into the remaining seminar rooms that were locked earlier today, we give up on our search, trudging back from campus in silence. Lewis heads off to dinner with his brother, and I try to keep myself distracted for the rest of the evening by reading through all the emails that came in over the weekend and doing laundry. On the way back from the laundromat, I pick up a salad for dinner and a tub of vegan Van Leeuwen ice cream.

I don't even fight my impulse to text Lewis a picture. It's only been a few hours since we saw each other at the conference, but I don't want to waste any time we still have together. *Want to come over and tell me how it went with Ben?*

As disconcerting as the butterflies in my stomach are, they're better company than the nervous turmoil that arises whenever I remember our charade is this close to blowing up in our faces.

Lewis's reply blinks on my phone a half hour later. *On my way.* He appears on my doorstep another thirty minutes later, hair tousled like he's run his fingers through it. I drag two cushions and a blanket out to the fire escape, and we share the peanut butter chocolate chip ice cream, avoiding any mention of the notebook. I can tell we both need to get it out of our minds for a while. Instead, Lewis tells me about his evening; the stilted conversation at dinner that flowed smoother the more wine he and Ben had. At some point, Lewis licks the last of the ice cream off my lips and curls his fingers into the hem of my shirt—his college tee that I've been wearing every night to sleep since he lent it to me last Tuesday.

"I was wondering when you'd give this back to me," he murmurs into my shoulder.

"I've gotten kind of attached," I tell him. "You better take it off before it's too late."

We stumble inside, and he pulls off the shirt, making us forget all about our worries, if only for an evening.

They're back in full force the next day, though. Notebook still nowhere to be found, we make it through the morning lectures, jittery and tense, until the break when Lewis leaves to check with central campus security. As I join the line for lunch, I survey the room and can't help but question everyone's glances.

Someone says my name and I find Vivienne two steps ahead, throwing me a worried look as she grabs a clean plate. She's wearing a cream silk blouse and black slacks today, her hair pinned back with a golden clip.

"Sorry. What?"

"Is everything okay?" She picks up a napkin. The woman ahead of me motions me forward, and I slide in next to Vivienne. "You seem distracted."

"I guess I am a little," I admit, tongue thick in my mouth. I could be wrong, but she strikes me as the type of person who'd come right out with it if she found the notebook. Still, it feels like it's only a matter of time before somebody uncovers our act.

"What's going on?"

"Nothing, just . . ." I trail off.

Just what?

Just the potential of my career imploding right here because I panicked and confirmed her misconception that I was dating Lewis? Just the at-once nauseating and exhilarating feeling of falling for a person I shouldn't even be considering, especially not now as my future is so out in the open? Just the confidence-shaking news of a failed grant?

Take your pick.

I go for the last one. I shouldn't—not if I want Jacob to continue living under the illusion that I have my life together, but at this point, what I want even less is to end up unemployed once my funding expires.

"I had another grant rejected. I got the news this past Friday."

"That's terrible." Vivienne's eyebrows draw together in empathy. "The worst kind of feeling, really. I'm sorry."

"Yeah, it's been hard," I admit with a sigh.

She touches my forearm and offers me a small smile. "Those teaching positions I told you about—they're still available. If that helps."

A teaching position might be able to tide me over to whatever is next, but it's not ideal. Not only would my research have to take a step back, but I'd have to move all the way here and then to wherever I found a job next. Still, it's nice of her to want to help.

"Thank you."

"I'll let you know if I hear anything else," she says, and I'm racking my head for a way to kindly and not condescendingly recommend her to make an application herself so she doesn't have to rely on Jacob's funding anymore when I remember.

Amidst the debacle with the notebook, I forgot about my lunch meeting with Rosanna Alderkamp.

Shit.

"I'm so sorry, but I completely forgot I've got to run. Thank you, though!" I toss my paper plate onto the table and race outside, where Rosanna is wrapping up a phone call and doesn't seem bothered about my lateness.

All throughout lunch at a coffee place on Broadway, Rosanna asks questions about the virtual environment I run my experiments in, and seeing her this invested makes me hopeful.

But hopeful doesn't pay the bills.

As she empties three sachets of sugar into her latte, I watch the tiny crystals melt into the foam in her mug and wait until she picks up her spoon.

"I'm glad you're so interested in my code, and that you see potential for applications in it. The thing is," I say, then pause. I don't want to outright beg for a position in her lab, but I also need her to know *how* available I am. Rosanna guides her cup to her lips and nods for me to go on. "My funding runs out at the beginning of October."

Her smile turns tense. "I'm sorry to hear that. Have you applied for any more funding?"

"I have, but none of the grants have come through. I had this idea to use the design of my last study, which was more of a proof of concept, really, and apply it to detect signals of memory reactivation."

She nods slowly. "That's very interesting," she says and pulls her curls back into a knot. "What about a rebuttal, for the rejected grant?"

I thought about this, too. After rejections to grants or papers, it's an option to contest the jury's decision, to argue against their comments and hope for a change of mind, but it's rarely successful.

I shake my head. "I don't think I have a convincing angle."

"I see," she says, pressing her lips together.

"I will try again, I will figure it out, but in the meantime . . ." I let out a long breath and push the worries about someone unmasking Lewis's and my charade aside. "I know it's a long shot, but I am looking for open positions now. Postdocs, lectureships, anything. If any funding becomes available in your lab, I would be interested in working with you." I go on to tell her how I've thought about reanalyzing some of her old data from a different angle. It would be partially out of curiosity, and partially because any publication with her name next to mine would bolster my CV and jump-start my citation index, which might, in turn, increase my chances for future grant applications. I don't say it out loud, but we both know it. It's the nature of the game.

"I can't give you a definitive answer," Rosanna tells me once we're out on the sidewalk. "But it looks like we might have funding coming in. I'll see what I can do. We'll keep in touch, okay?"

My heart jumps into somersaults. "Thank you."

I watch as Rosanna heads to the subway before my hand finds my phone in my tote bag, and I've already scrolled to Lewis's number when my conscience catches up with my lizard brain.

Is it really such a good idea to share my joy with him?

Friday looms ahead, the day Lewis will fly back to Germany. I hadn't thought I'd dread it this much, but after the intimacy of the last days, the pending deadline knots my gut into a tight ball of nerves. Even though I should be occupied with the chase for the missing notebook, my mind also keeps slipping into pictures of the future. Pictures of us, situations where we continue to be a *we*. Detailed answers to *What if we didn't stop things right here?*

Weekends spent hunkered down in bed trying to watch movies but getting distracted by each other. Grilled cheese sandwiches after bouldering, warming my fingers on Lewis's skin after a bike ride out in the cold. Eating stacks of pancakes while we discuss some new paper, our legs tangled on the couch.

They're not going to happen, but a girl can dream, right?

I navigate to Karo's name in my contacts instead.

"What's holding you back from telling him?" she asks me as I trudge back across campus. A brown shape on the side of the path makes me halt in my tracks, but it's just trash. A napkin.

I hoist the strap of my tote higher on my shoulder. "Telling him what?"

"You know what I mean," she says. "You've got it bad."

"I already told you what's holding me back."

"You're colleagues, and you can't risk dating one of those again," Karo rattles off.

"Um, yes," I concur. "Plus, I don't even know where I'll be a few months from now. I've been talking to people from labs all over. Japan, Australia, Canada." All possible, although only if they don't find out about the ridiculous scheme Lewis and I came up with. "Starting a relationship when we're in cities separated by a seven-hour train ride is already ridiculous, given how short a time we've known each other. But time zones and flights? It's insane, nothing less. You know how much I hate flying."

"Please don't tell me you're considering moving that far away again." Karo sounds a little desperate. "I love you and I know you love your job, but isn't it a bit much? Moving to yet another continent for your career?"

The day I got the grant rejection I would've agreed with her, but over the past days, Lewis and the conference have re-ignited my passion for my research. They've reminded me that the pure exploration that's at the core of science has a stronger pull than the comfort of a home. Moving to a different continent is the price I have to pay for getting to figure out how the universe works, even if it's only a tiny, minuscule cog of it.

I sink onto the stairs leading up to Low Memorial Library, the stone warm under my thighs, thinking about how much my life has changed in a little over a week. The grant rejection, my growing feelings for Lewis. Both open up questions for the future I didn't have before. "I want to go back to how it was. I didn't feel lonely until I got here," I admit. "It's like I noticed that something is missing. Some . . . connection. Someone else. But what's the point, really, to yearn for something like that. It's not going to happen for me," I continue, knowing deep down that it's not just *someone* I'm missing. It's him.

I can hear her shrug in the rustle of her hair against the phone. "It's only human to want that."

"But isn't that scary? What about being your own person and all that?"

"Franzi," Karo says. "Are you telling me I'm not my own person because I've been with Lennart for twelve years? Because we're married now?" She doesn't sound offended, but her stern question pulls things into focus. "You can be your own person and have goals in your life and in your career and still want to share them with someone else. And let me tell you, it doesn't matter if you live on different continents or just down the road from each other, if you're in the same career or do something vastly different—fitting two lives together always requires some tinkering and a lot of communication."

I sit in silence, pondering her words. The South Lawn spreads out in front of me, a carpet of bright green grass banked by the stone colonnade of Butler Library, and I watch the crowds of students wander between classes. It's silly, really. I know enough examples of people who lead the lives they want, not alone, but together with another person. And yet, in my mind, success and love are the opposite sides of a coin, two things that are mutually exclusive.

"It's up to you," Karo says after a while, her voice quiet. "But when you talk about Lewis, something in you appears that I haven't seen in a long time. So if he's worth it—and it sounds like he is—maybe you can figure out the rest."

I do not tell Lewis. Every successful conversation with a professor or fellow postdoc on potential openings in other labs pushes me one step further from telling him how I feel. I'm an interview away from getting any of these positions, but the reality is that all are farther away from Lewis than I am now. And no matter where I'll end up, the fact remains that he's a colleague.

But as Lewis and I scour the campus for the notebook between lectures, seminars, and poster sessions, I'm starting to wonder if him being a colleague and the potential of a long-distance relationship truly have to be the barriers I'm making them out to be. Even as I'm worried about being found out, having him at my side makes me feel lighter. With everything that's going on, we work well as a team: We stick together and try to look normal and manage each other's stress. On Tuesday evening, we finally take a break to unwind at the bouldering gym, and then head back to my studio, where I make dairy-free grilled cheese sandwiches as he peppers me with questions about the computational model I used in my last paper. We eat out on the fire escape and as he takes the first bite, Lewis groans with delight. Later that night, when we're tangled up in my bedsheets, I get him to make that noise again. The next day, we're back to morning lectures, but with lab work scheduled for the afternoon, Lewis and I decide to get work done in the library instead.

Brady finds us right as we're about to leave.

"You lovebirds off to skip school?" she chirps.

Lewis huffs out a laugh, holding the door open for her while she catches up with us. The dense heat from outside pushes against my back.

"We're going to the library if you want to join?" I offer, but she shakes her head.

"I'm meeting a student who wants to do a summer internship with me. But I wanted to give you this." Unceremoniously, she drops Lewis's notebook into his palm. I try to tamp down any reaction, but Lewis's eyes widen in shock.

"Vivienne told me Jacob found it in the lecture hall, and nobody knew whose it was," Brady goes on, unaware of the jolt in my nerves.

Fuck. It passed through *all* of their hands?

Next to me, Lewis clears his throat. "Thanks . . . Brady."

"I recognized it when Vivienne and I had to check something for our project. It was on her desk." She playfully swats at his chest. "Remember how I used to joke that someone stealing your notebook of big, bright ideas would be your origin story?" She laughs and adds, with a wink, "I guess we're lucky he didn't turn into the Hulk." Then she turns on her heel, and heads back toward the staircase.

"I guess it's safe to say Brady doesn't know," I point out when she's out of earshot, "seeing as she recognized the notebook?"

Lewis's eyes slide to mine, and for a moment we stare at each other, still frozen in the doorway. "Let's hope the fact that it was just lying there means that Jacob and Vivienne didn't open it, either." He flicks through the notebook back to that first page of our pact. *Conditions for fake dating*, it says on top, and my anxiety spins higher.

The next pages are worse. *Game plan for fake dating. Lewis's and Frances's weekends together.* Neat and organized as Lewis is, he put a heading on every page, leaving an obviously incriminating paper trail. *Frances's pet peeves. Frances's quirks.*

My heart beats faster at spotting those last pages. We didn't come up with those together.

Blushing, Lewis snaps the notebook shut. "If they didn't know whose notebook it was, they can't have leafed through it very far," he points out. "It says both our names on these pages."

"You're right. They probably didn't even open it, so we should be in the clear." I swallow down the burst of nerves the last minutes have triggered. "But still, I don't think I feel like working anymore."

With lab-based classes keeping everyone occupied this afternoon, I have a break from networking, but instead of heading to the library, like we'd first planned, we decide to go to the beach to escape the humid soup Manhattan turns into at this time of year. The promise of distance from the Sawyer's is strong enough to make us brace the long subway ride to Rockaway Beach.

"Would you mind if Ben came?" Lewis asks when we're back at the studio and I'm rolling up a towel to stuff into a cloth bag. Hip against the kitchen counter and legs crossed in front of him, he twirls his phone between his hands.

"Not at all. What about you, though?"

The twirling stops and he tilts his head. "I'd like for him to come." He starts texting and as I walk to the bathroom to search for my swimsuit, Lewis calls, "He'll pick us up."

A half hour later, Ben waves at us from the driver's seat of a convertible that has the roof pulled up. Ada sits on the passenger seat, holding an oversize reusable coffee cup.

"Work meetings ended early," she explains, leaning out of the window to pull Lewis, then me, in for a hug. "Alice is with a friend. I figured I'd take the once-in-a-lifetime opportunity to spend the afternoon with my two brothers."

Ben tips up his sunglasses, revealing eyes that are just like Lewis's except for the current glee in them, and proudly slaps the roof of the car. "Graduation present from Dad," he boasts. I don't have to look at Lewis to know that this will make him shift his jaw, but he keeps quiet as he slides in behind me.

Ben doesn't stop talking as he drives and when we reach Rockaway Beach, we've already gotten all the updates on his European summer tour (sponsored by his parents before he starts working at North Star Investments), the video game he's currently obsessed with, and the *Wired* podcast episode he listened to last night.

"Is Berlin not on your itinerary then?" I ask him.

Ben hoots when Ada points out a free parking spot and maneuvers the car into the narrow gap.

"Just for a couple of hours when I change trains. Dad said there wasn't much to it," he replies as we're getting out of the car. "Gave me some advice on where to go and what to avoid."

Lewis puts an arm around my shoulders. "And, of course, we always do what Father says," he quips.

"Teddy!" Ada snaps.

Ben pulls his aviators off his nose and hangs them in the V of his polo, then lifts an eyebrow at his brother, the gesture eerily similar to Lewis's when he challenges some scientific point of mine. "I'm not doing what Dad says. *He* wanted me to fly between cities because who'd want to sit on trains. But for the itinerary, yeah, I did listen to him. It's not like I could've asked you when I was planning the trip." His tone is level as he says this, more a statement than an accusation, but I feel the jolt of tension in Lewis's body.

The two brothers stare at each other quietly, until Ada nudges Ben to carry the cooler, then rolls her eyes at me.

The tension dissolves gradually throughout the afternoon. Partially because we all skirt around topics that could elicit another clash, and mostly because of the beer Ada slides out of the cooler once we reach the beach. We rent chairs for the afternoon with a perfect view of the bay and the ocean, and I take Lewis's hand as we wade into the glistening waves. When Ada joins us, I decide to give the siblings some time on their own, cutting deeper into the water instead.

Back at our spot, Ben finishes a call and heads toward the shore as we open our beers. "I miss being so close to the sea," I say, shielding my eyes from the sun to watch his shape recede.

Lewis shrugs. "Berlin has nice lakes."

Ada plops down onto the lounger next to mine as Lewis takes a seat in the sand between us. "God, I can't imagine long distance."

"It's not ideal, but we try to see each other about once a month, although really, it's more like every four to six weeks," I tell her, recalling the schedule Lewis and I came up with on that incriminating page in his notebook. Something about the lie tastes bitter in my mouth now. It was easier to pretend in front of his family when I didn't wish so hard for it to be real.

"But we talk on the phone every day," Lewis interjects.

"He calls me in the mornings to get me out of bed."

"And she calls me at night, and we cook dinner together."

"He runs me through his slides before he has to give presentations or lectures." We didn't spell out all of these details before, but with my recurring daydreams, it's easy to imagine what our relationship could look like if we really did try to make it work.

Lewis's lips quirk into a smile. "Sometimes she calls me during work to get feedback on her study designs."

Ada laughs at our back-and-forth. "Okay, you don't make it sound so bad. How far apart do you live again?"

"Seven hours by train," I reply at the same time as Lewis says, "Four hours of combined flight and train."

It's normal that I know this because I have to make the journey every time I want to see my family. But Lewis? He has no reason to know anything about Maastricht, the small Dutch university town I presently call home. He wouldn't know how long it takes and how to get there.

Unless he looked it up.

Our gazes catch and I want to lean into the discovery that, just like me, he has also thought about life after the Sawyer's. It's comforting to know that I'm not the only one, but a wave of sadness rolls in simultaneously. We both live in Central Europe *for now*, but who knows where I'll relocate to at the end of the year?

Though maybe the distance between us doesn't have to be such a bad thing. Maybe it's the one way I could stay true to myself, if we did want to try.

"You know, Teddy's never introduced anybody to our family." Ada peers at me over the rim of her sunglasses, her brown eyes half-moons over the tortoiseshell frames.

"Not true. I brought girls over," he protests, pulling a knee up to his chest.

"Yeah, but you never introduced them to me. They'd slink around the place and dreamily look at your blond locks when you were getting ready to leave for some party. I happened to be there. That's different." She ruffles her brother's hair. In return, he catches her arm and wrestles it down. Ada shrieks, then lifts her hands in surrender.

"This used to be so much easier," she mutters, but the grin on her face tells me she doesn't mind one single bit that Lewis has the upper hand now.

Lewis sits up and wipes the sand off his kneecaps. "Well, any other embarrassing childhood stories you want to share?"

Ada tilts her head to the side and pouts. "I have a few things in mind . . ."

"I better leave you alone for this." Sighing mockingly, Lewis gets up and kisses my forehead.

Unsure if he still needs me as a buffer, I catch Lewis's wrist before he pulls away. "Hey," I murmur. "If you need me, just give me a wave and I'll come over, okay?"

He nods just before he runs down to the shore to meet Ben. I watch the water splash around his legs, and from the corner of my eye I can see that Ada's looking at them as well.

"So?" I turn to her, eager to hear about Lewis's childhood shenanigans.

Eyes fixed on her younger brothers, Ada's smile fades. "What's it like, his life there?" she asks instead, so quietly I barely hear her over the rush of the waves.

I grip the neck of my bottle and snip my thumbnail against its lip, rooting through my brain for a reply. I can't tell her the truth, that I've never seen his life in Berlin. But from what he's told me and what I know about the city, I can piece together some things. I tell her that he loves the way the city comes alive in summers, when he can have lunch in the park outside the institute, that he's charmed all but one of the nurses on the epileptic monitoring unit where he spends a lot of weekends to collect data. That after three years, he's not offended anymore when a native treats him with the cheeky rudeness that's so typical for the city.

"But is he happy there?"

"Yeah, he is," I say, though I can't be sure. All I know is that I want him to be.

She finally looks at me then, running her index finger over the neat arches of her eyebrows. "Listen, I don't know what he's told you about our family. If anything, then it probably wasn't good. But thank you for bringing him here."

"We came here because of the conference," I point out, but she waves me off.

"I know that's what you came to New York for. But this? The graduation party? He wouldn't have come without you. Believe me, I know my brother." She glances at her legs and her lips quirk into a smile. "Just like I know he really must love you. He wouldn't listen to you otherwise."

She says this as the two brothers jog back from the shore, and when they reach us, Lewis's gaze is sharp and intense, focused on me. Lower on the sky now, the sun casts a golden glow over the sand, catching in his hair, and the sight makes my whole body feel like I'm the one who just swam against a strong current. Heart thrumming in my chest, senses hyper perceptive, limbs achingly at peace.

"I'm hungry," Ada announces, and pulls Ben with her to get snacks.

"You looked it up," I state as Lewis crouches down beside me, shocking my sun-drenched skin with the cold water that clings to his body.

He slicks his hair out of his face. "I did."

"Why?"

"Frances." When he picks up my hand, goose bumps erupt on my skin, whether because of the contrast in temperature or the way he says my name, I don't know. Maybe both. "I told you I've admired your work for a while, but it's not just that. For the past four years, trying to understand what goes through your mind has brightened up the shittiest of my days. So, for you to end up sitting next to me on that flight"—he pauses to swallow heavily, and my heart buckles when I see the full-body effect the memory has on him—"and then to put the *you* on paper together with the smart and beautiful and intriguing woman who was sitting next to me. And then when Vivienne assumed . . . You know, when you asked me for help, the only thing holding me back was the idea of lying to everyone, of having to pretend again after I thought I'd left all of that behind when I broke off contact with my parents. It really was a senseless worry, though, since none of this felt fake."

He squeezes my hand then, and, because my mind is blank, all I can do is squeeze back. "I like spending time with you," he continues. "I like whatever it is that we talk about, whether it's nonparametric statistics or the right way to make a grilled cheese sandwich. And I know you'll only be back in the Netherlands for a few more months and then who knows what, but I don't care where we'll be after the Sawyer's ends. I just want to keep talking to you."

His words launch my heart right out of my chest, and while it heads for the stratosphere, I scramble for something to say. "Talking, huh?" I hear myself whisper.

"Talking and everything else, too," he murmurs back, "if that's what you want."

Chapter Twenty-Two

We stay at the beach until late in the afternoon, eating the nachos and guacamole that Ben and Ada bring back from the boardwalk, playing an intense match of beach volleyball, and cooling down in the water. Later, Ben takes us back to Manhattan, and Lewis suggests stopping by Westside Market, where I trail him through the aisles as he fills a basket full of food for a home-cooked dinner. Once we get home to my rented studio, Lewis showers first and then starts chopping vegetables in the kitchen while I head to the bathroom and scrub the sand, salt, and sunscreen off my skin.

And all the while I think about what he said.

And what that might mean.

What I want it to mean.

The last time I'd had an *us*, I hadn't set off from such a complicated starting point and, five years later, I'm still feeling the aftershocks. If Lewis and I tried this and it didn't work out, I don't know how I'd recover. But I want those weekends I've been dreaming of, where he visits me and I pick him up at the station, pedaling through narrow cobblestone streets with him riding on the back of my bike, and I want to see his life in Berlin, too, and hang out on long phone calls deep into the night or day or whatever time zone we might be in.

So maybe, I want his words to mean everything.

Hair wet over my shoulders, I leave the bathroom and find Lewis stirring something on the stove. With all of my feelings collecting at the base of my throat and vibrating against my vocal cords, I catch his eyes across the kitchen island. "Maybe," I push out and he must see how much it is costing me to say—to even think—this, because he puts his spoon aside and switches off the flame.

I just want to keep talking to you. Talking and everything else, too, if that's what you want.

"Maybe . . ." I gulp. "Maybe I think I do want to keep talking—and everything else—too."

I can see the moment understanding hits him and the chain reaction it sets off. Eyes that sharpen, the smile that flares on his face as he rounds the kitchen island in three large steps, his hand that first rubs his chest, right where I imagine his heart to be, and then curls around the nape of my neck.

I'm not sure what I'm more relieved about: finally having said it or his response, but I can feel the beat of my heart through my entire nervous system, and it pushes out all the other things that I want him to know but have been too afraid to say until now.

"I'm so glad I sat next to you on that flight and glad Vivienne thought what she did and even a little bit glad about how I didn't correct her, because otherwise there would've been no way I would've let you talk to me," I whisper into his shoulder.

Then, after he brings me to silence with a long, dizzying kiss, "I had this image of you in my mind before I realized who you were on that flight, but the more I got to know you, the more I learned it was the negative of who you truly were. Everything was inversed."

I lean into his touch as his fingers graze my cheeks and fan over my jaw to pull me in for another kiss, so deep and intense that it reverberates all the way to the tips of my toes.

"I used to think we were so different and yeah, maybe in some sense we are, but most times it's like we speak the same language," I go on, voice still low like I'm letting him in on all my secrets—which I suppose I am. "I like how you listen. How you ask questions. How curious and attentive you are and how you want to learn about everything because there's no topic too boring for you. Except for golf, maybe."

He huffs a laugh into the crook of my neck and my skin pebbles under his breath, sensitive from the heat and wind of the day.

"I like how you keep trying with your family instead of giving up, and how you did with me, too," I confess into the softness of his hair.

He tilts my head to one side, his mouth pushing the strap of my camisole away as he tells me, "That was you. I wouldn't have seen Ben this much if it hadn't been for you."

My hands reach for the hem of his shirt then, and once it's off, he leans into me, warm and solid. Something sparks hard in my chest when our bodies align, separated only by the thin fabric of my top.

"I'm afraid of letting you in and having you take over my life," I admit in a whisper.

Lewis tilts my chin up so our gazes meet.

"Frances," he says, wrapping my hair around his hand, "taking over the wheel is the last thing on my mind. When I'm with you, I want you to drive. I want you to show me the sights, to let me in on how you see the world."

Back in the cabin, I told Lewis I had let Jacob take the

driver's seat in our relationship and losing myself like that was something I wouldn't risk again. Now, I brush my knuckles over Lewis's chest and down his stomach, letting his careful and considerate words warm me up.

He helps me out of my top, then kisses my collarbone. "And when you get tired or exhausted, even then I don't want to take over. We'll just stop and stay for a while, okay?"

My hands find the button of his chinos. "What about you in all of this?" I ask.

"I'm just glad that you see me."

"I do," I agree, "and I don't want to change a thing about you. You inspire me."

"I think we could be something great," he murmurs, and I feel him smile against my throat.

It's different as we undress each other this time, like those whispered words against skin amplify the weight of each touch. Over the past days we've ended up tangled up in each other every night, but this feels like it's about more than two bodies intertwining. It's about meeting someone and finding an unexpected companion. Someone who grates against your nerves in a way you thought could only set you off in anger but turns out to be the one who makes you feel exhilaratingly alive. This is about seeing the discouraging statistics of long-distance relationships and betting against all of the odds.

"You're stunning. Up here"—he taps my temple—"and out here," he says and my skin warms under the perusal of his fingers. Cheeks, collarbone, chest, thighs. When he draws an arm around my back and leans in, I expect him to kiss me in the soft, languid way I learned he likes, but instead, he coaxes my mouth open with his thumb on my chin and licks against my tongue. A jolt zaps down my nerve endings, suddenly and forcefully, like I've held my fingers to a live wire.

We chuckle into each other as the frame of my glasses digs

into both our cheeks, and he pulls back to slide them off my nose, turning his face into a blur of gold and caramel, a flash of blue. I'm annihilated by how carefully he folds up my glasses and keeps them out of harm's way in one hand, braced against the wall behind me.

I pull his head toward mine, until it dips into focus again. I want to taste the swell of his mouth, the dip of his collarbone, but he doesn't let me have my way for long, burning his lips down my throat and thumbing my nipple until I'm aching for him.

It's not only every flick of his tongue, bite of his teeth, and stroke of his hands that coils me tighter and tighter, but also the echo of everything he said.

"I need you closer," I grit out.

He walks me back to the bed, his erection heavy against my abdomen, then turns us so he falls onto the mattress first.

"What are you doing?" I breathe as he hooks his hands under my knees. When he drags me over him, his thigh slides against my core and the pressure rips a moan out of me, but he doesn't stop there, guiding me up and up until his face is framed by my legs.

"Close enough?" The exhale of his words prickles over me, almost enough to set me off.

"I meant—" My breath hitches as he spreads his hand on my belly, right where I glow most strongly for him.

"I know." He kisses the inside of my thigh. "But I wouldn't last long. Let me do this," he continues, "let me watch you when you come." My hips jerk at the low rumble of his words, a depraved sound breaking out of my throat when he drags his tongue over my clit.

I claw my fingers into his hair, a mad grasp for something to tether me. "It's just . . ." I protest, "I want to get to see you, too."

The hand that's been clasped against my calf comes up.

"Here." Lewis sounds out of breath as he slips my glasses into my hand.

"That's not what I meant," I gasp, unfolding my glasses on the bridge of my nose and nearly dropping them when he licks me again. His focus as he works his mouth on me is close enough to break me. Lids heavy, pupils inky in the halo of blue. Tension courses low and hot in my body, until my skin vibrates with it, until it curls tightly up my spine. Until he puts his free hand to use and slips one finger between my legs, then two. When he curls them into a hook inside of me, reality melts.

"There is no limit to the ways I want you." The confession breaks out of me, unbidden.

Lewis curses underneath me. "Look at me," he says, his words a mere exhale against my clit, the gust of air so sensitizing that the next touch of his tongue shatters me.

"Look at me," he growls before I finally obey and the orgasm shudders through me, sudden and hard. His eyes darken as I arch into him and breathe out his name.

When I come back to myself, I reach behind me and drift my hand down his stomach to where his fist is closed around himself. As I pry off his taught fingers and stroke him, I watch the heat turn up in his gaze and then, my hand tightens to tip him over, too. It's my name on his lips, a plea at first, a grunt, and finally a sigh as the orgasm ebbs out of him and his body goes slack.

"Come here," Lewis murmurs after we clean ourselves up, tugging me down next to him. I starfish out on the sheets, my whole body wrung out, the heat in my veins simmered down to a comforting warmth. With his arms around me, I squeeze my eyes shut and will my neurons to hard-wire the moment into the architecture of my memory.

When I open my eyes again, affection softens the curve of Lewis's smile.

"I'm scared it won't work," I tell him, remembering all the ways we said we made space in each other's life. The cooking sessions, the academic discussions, the wake-up calls. I want them to be my reality. I want them to be enough.

He's silent for a moment and I watch the rise and fall of his chest. "I think it's like when we plan our experiments. We can obsess over experimental designs and control groups, run a million pilot studies. But discovery always takes a leap of faith."

"We won't know until we try," I echo and nestle into the bracket of his arm. "Spoken like a true empiricist."

Chapter Twenty-Three

On the last day of the Sawyer's, a big summer picnic for all specializations is held on campus. That morning, when Lewis and I arrive, the grass smells freshly cut, and workers string lights above the paths and drag fold-out tables and chairs to different corners of the green. Still tipsy from the intensity of our confessions last night, I give my data blitz presentation, and though it's not one of the contested full-hour lecture slots but a quick twenty-minute talk, I'm glad I get to talk about my models and how they help me gain a better understanding of memory principles in the human brain.

Afterward, Lewis moderates the discussion round that wraps up the academic program, and Jacob comes to shake his hand at the lectern. As their hands meet, he leans in to murmur something, something that makes Lewis's smile tense, but the handshake passes, the attendees applaud, and the lecture hall begins to empty.

Lewis rushes off immediately to pack his bags for his flight that leaves early tomorrow morning. Rosanna catches me in the corridor on the way out, asking if I could get to the festival early. "I have some exciting news," she gushes, handing me a piece of paper with a phone number in blue ink. "If we don't run into each other, call me."

Back home, I pull on a flowy gray jumpsuit, text Lewis to meet me there, and head back to the Morningside campus.

The greasy smell of fried food hangs heavy in the air as I weave down the paths packed with carts selling German sausages, huge slices of pizza, Korean fried chicken, and crispy tacos. I spot Vivienne and Jacob waiting at a stand selling funnel cake, but before I can make a decision whether to say hello or duck out of sight, someone else calls my name.

"Frances! *Hoi!*"

Rosanna motions me over to where she waits in line for drinks, clad in a purple tie-dye dress. She stands close to a petite woman with deep bronzed skin and dark hair cropped into a stylish pixie cut.

Rosanna touches my elbow lightly when I draw up next to them. "Frances, this is my wife, Maria. Maria, this is Frances, the postdoc I've been telling you about."

"It's nice to meet you," I greet Maria.

"Oh, you're the promising programmer," Maria exclaims as she shakes my hand, her grip firm and confident.

I grimace. "I don't think there's consensus on that."

"She's just gotten a grant rejection," Rosanna supplies.

"Fun," Maria says in a tone that promises the opposite. "I don't miss those days."

"You work in academia, too?"

Though before she can answer, we make it to the top of the line and Rosanna starts rattling off an order. "Here, what would you like?" she asks me. Once the bartender slides our three plastic cups over the counter—watermelon margarita for me, Moscow mules for Rosanna and Maria—we make our way to one of the sit-down areas where Maria manages to snatch a table. Above us, the evening sunlight makes the roofs of the surrounding campus buildings glow.

"I used to. Work in academia, I mean," Maria continues our conversation. "I have a PhD in bioinformatics, but I quit a few years into my postdoc. The environment wasn't for me. I'm not as patient as she is." Maria inclines her head toward her wife.

"And much more pragmatic," Rosanna quips in.

"So what do you do now?"

"I run a small e-learning company." Maria prods the ice cubes in her drink with her straw. "We launched an app a year ago that teaches people how to program and think algorithmically in a playful way. For now, it's aimed at adults, but my goal is to make a module for teenagers."

"Wow. That's really cool." Not that I'm surprised Rosanna would be married to another brilliant woman. I've just never closely met anyone who's made the switch into industry and founded their own company, let alone one that has such a meaningful purpose. "How did you get the idea? And the courage? And the *money*? Sorry if that was too forward."

Both of them laugh, then Rosanna says, "You're talking to Dutchies. You need to try harder if you want something to be too forward."

"When I was still working at uni, I used to teach all sorts of introductory programming classes," Maria goes on. "In computer science and engineering, most students were fine with it. But I noticed that the people in the biology department didn't share those skills, particularly the older faculty. I helped a few people, put together some exercises. Word got around, and soon people from social science and psychology were emailing me for resources."

"I was one of them," Rosanna interrupts.

"She was one of my worst students." Maria laughs, and squeezes Rosanna's hand. "Anyway, at some point I realized that I wasn't that interested in disease modeling anymore. I spent more and more hours of my work trying to optimize instructions and teach people how to express their thoughts in code. It was much more rewarding to me, seeing people make progress. I felt like I had a bigger impact this way, giving people the confidence and skills for their research. Regarding the money, it's not so different from asking for grants. You prepare, you pitch, and sometimes you're lucky."

Rosanna taps Maria's forearm. "You're being too modest." Then, directed at me, she continues, "You should see her pitches. She's a mean presenter."

"Oh, it's mostly luck," Maria waves her off and tucks her hair behind her ear. "So, I heard about the virtual environment you've programmed, and it sounds pretty neat. If you ever decide that the politics of academia is not for you anymore, here's where you can find me."

With that, she slides something across the table. A business card. On white cardstock, a techy-looking font announces Maria Benita, founder and chief executive officer, underneath a bright blue company logo that reads *Codify*.

"Thanks." It's only when I pick up the card that her words fully hit me. I'm not used to being wooed for my skills. I've occasionally wondered what working in industry would be like, but I've never seriously considered that I could make a contribution to the world outside of academia. "Thank you so much. This is unexpected."

Maria shows off a little gap between her front teeth when she smiles widely at me. "I know, but I'm being serious. Think about it."

"Don't poach her from me," Rosanna chides.

Her wife shrugs. "You, my darling, haven't even offered her

anything. And I'm just saying," she continues, studying me. "You have skills that we'd value and . . . Well, our working conditions are a little better, too."

"Don't listen to her, she's overly negative about academia. And speaking of jobs," Rosanna says, a little more serious now. "This is what I wanted to talk to you about. It looks like we do have funds to hire a postdoc in the lab. We hadn't quite planned on this, but the person who was meant to start with us in October got his own funding, and we have money left to open another position."

It takes me a beat to parse her words, and I need to rewind them again to assure myself I heard right. Is it appropriate to pinch myself, right in front of these two incredibly smart women?

"You'd mostly contribute to one of the grant projects," she adds, "but I'm sure there'd be some time for your ideas, too. Like the reanalysis we talked about the other day."

A chance to work with Rosanna Alderkamp—it's a dream come true. A sure way of making a difference, even if it's not with my own grant. Her research is so close to my own, but much more refined and there's so much I can learn from her that it wouldn't feel like working for someone else's goals while putting mine on the back burner.

"Stunned into silence." Maria chuckles.

"Sorry, I . . ." I blink at Rosanna.

"Take some time to think about it," she reassures me. "I also thought about what you said you wanted to do with your grant, about the model you built and the potential this would have to bridge the gap between neuroimaging research and electrophysiology."

I nod, the familiar vocabulary of science pulling me back to reality. "We could use the 7T scanner in your lab, use a fast acquisition rate and . . ."

Behind the two women, a familiar shape pushes down the path, and I wave him over. I need to share the news with Lewis immediately, but as he weaves through the chairs and tables, there's an unexpected tightness to his features.

"I saved you a seat," I tell him when he reaches our table. "Lewis, this is—"

Maria jumps out of her chair once she spots him over her shoulder. The chair topples, and Lewis catches it with a laugh as she draws him in for a hug.

"Lewis! I heard you might be coming over for dinner more often soon," Maria says, and the words make as little sense as her overly enthusiastic way of greeting him. "*Gefeliciteerd!* Congratulations on your grant."

I know something's up before I understand it, like when I pull together all the data after a new experiment but can't figure out the pattern yet. Time slows down as my brain loops through the last two minutes and tags all the outliers in our conversation.

The odd familiarity between Lewis and Maria.

The funding for a postdoc position that magically has become available.

Lewis winning a grant.

Which grant?

My pulse thunders in my ears, my mouth suddenly dry. I blink up at Lewis, Maria's arm still on his shoulder, his eyes transfixed on me.

"The Dutch Young Investigators Starting Grant," Rosanna says to my right. I must've asked my question out loud.

An unreadable expression tints the blue of Lewis's irises. He reminds me of an animal caught in the headlights, frozen and uncomfortable, two things he has absolutely no right to be.

After all, he's the one who knew. He's the one who watched me cry over the rejection of a grant and consoled me through it, all without telling me that he, in fact, did get that funding. From a grant I didn't even know we were competing for. For a project in Amsterdam. To collaborate with Rosanna Alderkamp.

No, no, no.

There's that lurching feeling again, the world tipping sideways, my chest clenching in pain. But anger catches me and plants me back on my feet.

Lewis has no fucking right to be surprised. Clearly, I'm the one who's missing crucial information, because if he's slotted to work with Rosanna? Then the position she told me about depends on the new money that just came in.

His money.

"Thank you, Maria," Lewis says in a tone that doesn't sound the part, coming over to me. "Um, Frances. I've been looking for you—"

What, so you could finally tell me about this grant you secretly won? The one I *was desperate for?* I want to snap but shove it down. I need to get out of here before I do something stupid again and tank my career even more.

"Didn't realize it was this late already," I manage to squeeze past the aggravation building in my throat and pretend to look at the clock on my phone. I shoot up a little too fast and Lewis steadies me, the pressure of each of his fingers feeding into the pool of anger simmering at the pit of my stomach. "I need to get going—I told an, um, student I'd meet them . . . Anyway. Thanks for letting me sit with you. I'll be in touch," I tell Rosanna. "Maria, it was so nice meeting you."

I tell my feet to stay put until they reply, but what they

say is completely lost on me. Once Rosanna smiles and Maria nods, I pick up my cup and stride through the rows of tables. I was so caught up in talking to them that I barely sipped from my drink and now the bright red liquid sloshes over my fingers, cool and sticky.

How did I manage to get here again? Back into the role I've been running from for five years? The place where I watch the man in my life advance his career, wondering what I lack in qualification or grit.

A better colleague would be happy to hear about Lewis's scientific success. A better partner would secure a bottle of champagne and cheer on the move to a new city closer to her. A better scientist would be exhilarated about the prospect of working together on a topic she's passionate about.

Turns out I'm none of the above.

I drain the drink in my cup. It's almost too sweet, but then the bitter aftertaste of the alcohol hits and I'm glad for how generously the bartender filled up the bottom of the glass with tequila.

Lewis comes running behind me. "Frances, please wait. I know what this looks like, but could you—"

Alcohol does nothing to extinguish a fire. You don't need to be a scientist to know that. But when Lewis catches up to me, the liquor is already trickling into the flames scorching my insides.

"*I* won't do anything," I spit out, keeping my voice low to avoid causing a public scene. "I won't wait for you or listen to you, or *work* for you, for that matter."

"Just let me—"

"Explain? Fuck no, Lewis, there is nothing to explain. It's clear, isn't it?" I stab at his chest with my index finger. "You got the funding I wanted, I didn't. In fact, you got so much of it that there's money left over. Not only did you keep this from me while I let you comfort me and tell me the grant committee had no clue what they were doing, but now you want to hire me. Because, apparently, that's the only way for me to get a job. Not because of my skills, my capabilities, but out of pity."

"I don't pity you, I—"

"Just—shut up."

The words break out of me, loud enough for the people at the surrounding tables to lift their heads, a sea of alarmed, sympathetic faces. I turn on my heel and march past the edge of the sitting area to the green, but Lewis overtakes me and steps into my path before I can make it far.

"Whatever it is you want to say, I don't care," I tell him, my words coming fast. "You had plenty of time to make this right. Plenty of time to talk to me. I didn't know you were interested in moving to the Netherlands, but okay. We're scientists from the same field, so it's not such a big surprise that we apply for the same grants or want to work with the same people." I cross my arms in front of my chest. "But what is a big surprise is that you didn't warn me *not* to pursue Rosanna for a collaboration. You didn't tell me your news about the grant. You didn't think it was worthwhile to communicate *any* of this while I was moping about my failures. When did you find out? Friday?"

Silence.

"Did you already know when you got me those fucking consolation donuts?"

My hands shake with the force of my anger, the empty cocktail cup crushed between my fingers. I don't feel anything as I hurl the words at Lewis. I watch them land and wait for the impact to hurt him. His shoulders slump forward, and there's a pink smudge at the center of his chest, right where I poked my finger into the white fabric of his shirt.

"I didn't. Know then, I mean. I also didn't know you wanted to work with Rosanna. I'm so sorry, Frances. Just let me explain." His gaze holds mine hostage, his eyebrows reaching out toward each other across the bridge of his nose. Something ice-cold laps at the flames now, steals the air out of my lungs, and punches my heart into a painful race.

It's too much to take. Too much with all this noise around me, and Lewis *right there*, triggering the alarm centers of my brain.

I shake my head sharply.

I can't. I can't listen to him right now. Whatever he has to say, it won't make this right.

My voice is all but a croak. "Tell Brady I wasn't feeling well, okay?" I say, remembering that we were supposed to meet her.

His eyes scan mine, drop to where my chest is laboring with quick breaths, and after a beat he concedes, "Okay." His Adam's apple travels up and down the column of his throat. "Can you text me once you've made it home safely?"

I nod. "Fine," I say. "Ah and, Lewis—"

"Yes?"

"Congratulations on your fucking grant."

Chapter Twenty-Four

The pleasure of stomping out that little glimpse of hope on Lewis's face is short-lived, and all too quickly replaced by an oxygen-sucking pressure. I weave through the rows of tables, past the islands of laughter and busy food carts, my only goal to get as far away from Lewis as possible.

"Hey, watch where you're going," someone calls as my hands fumble for my phone to call Karo. The news about Lewis winning the grant and keeping it a secret is tearing my chest in half and lighting the leftovers on fire, and I know Karo is the only one who can extinguish this horrible, sickening feeling.

But nobody picks up the phone, even when I try calling again.

"Frances, are you okay?"

I look up from my shaking hands, only to find Vivienne a few paces ahead, untangling her hand from Jacob's arm.

Absolutely fucking brilliant.

Just the people I needed to run into.

"Yes," I say, but it sounds unconvincing.

She closes the distance between us. "Were you looking for the bathrooms?"

"I'm—"

I'm good, I want to say, though I'm not sure my body remembers how to breathe. Vivienne seems to know better. Hand on my elbow, she steers me toward the psychology building.

"You don't have to go for the smelly excuses of a toilet out there." Rummaging in her bag, she swipes a card across the reader and pushes the door open.

I don't have to pee, but I tell her, "Thanks. I'll be quick." My words come out hoarse.

"On second thought," she muses. "I better go as well. Since I'm here already."

The corridor ahead is dark, but the overhead lights turn on one by one as we walk, and when we reach the bathroom, Vivienne stops in front of the paper dispenser. She pulls out a towel and holds it under the faucet, as I wrap my hands around the other sink and take a deep breath.

"Here," she says, and that's when I see myself in the mirror. Strands of hair curling around my face, my cheeks reddened and splotched with smears of mascara.

Have I been crying?

Surely, I would've noticed.

Right?

Come to think of it, my throat does feel raw. Hoping none of my colleagues saw me lose control, I grip the sink tighter and focus on the porcelain against my skin. Solid, cool, grounding.

How is it that I know how the different cells on the human retina transform a visual image into a highly complex electric signal, yet seem to have no idea when tears are running from my eyes?

After what must be a solid minute of breathing in and out to collect myself, I take the towel from Vivienne's hand and scrape it over my skin. Vivienne leans against the edge of the sink, arms crossed in front of her, and quietly watches as I clean the gunk of mascara and tears from my face.

"Didn't you want to go . . ." I trail off, nodding my head toward the bathroom stalls.

She shakes her head. "Look, I know I may not be your first choice when it comes to talking about anything, for very obvious reasons. But if you feel like you need to get something off your chest, I'm happy to listen."

I do need to get something off my chest, a lot actually, but it's not like I can tell her about any of it. My dream job is tangled up in the research funding Lewis got, but so what? Vivienne's working for her fiancé, so that's clearly not an issue for her.

"I don't think you'd understand," I say, disposing my tissue in one of the bins.

Try me, her lifted eyebrows say, and I don't know if it's the challenge, or the fact that my emotion regulation is nowhere near as good as I'd like it to be, but I blurt out, "Lewis's future lab has offered me what is basically the position of my dreams, but there's no way I can take it because it's his money. I can't depend on that. I can't have people thinking I got my job because I slept with the boss, which . . ."

I stop myself there, my brain chanting *Don't get involved* and *It's her relationship*, but I'm too angry at Lewis, at Jacob, at all of them, to even care.

" . . . is your breakup with Jacob, all over again," Vivienne finishes my sentence, and my jaw?

It drops.

"What? You *know* about that?"

And yet you're still with him? I don't say it, but it hangs there in the air, together with the piercing scent of disinfectant.

Vivienne sighs. "Let me help you." Too stunned by the change of direction in this conversation, I let her step closer to me. I stay put when she rummages for something in her purse and then starts dabbing it under my eyes. "A little magic from my *mamie*," she says, her touch on my skin careful and surprisingly soothing.

When she's done, my face is not only clean and practically glowing, but the roil of emotions in my stomach has quieted down a little, too. Except now my head is full of questions.

"Voilà, much better. My grandmother was a stunning woman. A bit enigmatic sometimes. But before leaving the house, she would always put a little dab of tan lotion under her eyes. That was her little trick," Vivienne tells me, pursing her lips as she leans sideways against the wall and finds my gaze in the mirror. "Look, Frances. Believe it or not, I was nervous before the Sawyer's and before I met you. Think about it," she adds when I frown, "you're the only person Jacob has ever been in a proper relationship with. Five years! I haven't even known him for that long, so maybe you understand that I was intimidated by this woman who spent so much time with my fiancé."

Her perspective is one that hasn't crossed my mind at all yet, but as she takes me through it, I see her overfamiliarity that first day and her extra dose of kindness ever since for what it truly was: her way of dealing with her nerves in an awkward setup. She truly was just trying to be kind in a situation that was as uncomfortable for her as it was for me.

"I feel like we have a lot in common," she continues, "but also, and this is horrible, I feel like I owe you? Jacob told me how things between you ended, that he was responsible for it, and I know that may be hard to believe. I can't fault you for that, really. He didn't treat you well, and I so wish you didn't have to go through that.

"But at the same time, *I* didn't have to go through that because you changed him for the better. It's complicated, and," she swallows hard, "as I said, it probably doesn't paint me in the best light, but I'm grateful for it. For you."

I appreciate her honesty, but at the same time, it's salt in a wound that's already burning strong with dejection, and now jealousy, too. Maybe five years from now, I'll run into Lewis's new partner at a conference only to hear how *he* finally learned from his mistakes.

That is, if I'm still in academia then.

"You don't owe me anything," I say quietly, and even though I've been in this bathroom for a year too many, I pull my hair tie out of the frizzy leftovers of my braid and pile my curls into a knot.

"When I saw you with Lewis that first day, it was a relief. It looked like things had worked out for you, too, and it made me feel better to see you'd landed in such a good place." Vivienne pushes herself off the wall before following me to the door. "Though maybe I was too quick to judge."

My heart stops for a moment, fearing she means Lewis and me faking it as a couple, but she adds, "I know it's hard to figure out how to run this beast of a marathon that is academia . . . How to push and pace ourselves, balance ambition with the things that make us happy. It seems like an impossible situation that you're in, but I'm confident you'll find a way."

Out in the corridor, the motion-sensitive lights blink on again as they lead us back to the foyer, where the music and chattering voices from the picnic are dialed up louder.

"I'm not so sure. But thank you," I tell Vivienne, even though, clearly, she resolved her impossible situation in a way that's out of the question for me.

She pushes the button that unlocks the door. "I know you will. You know, Jacob and I were long distance for almost two years before I finally moved here. I refused to work for him—wanted to do my own thing."

"What made you change your mind?"

Ahead of us, the doors open up to the balmy summer night and Jacob, who's waiting for us under a lamp pole, thumb scrolling through his phone. Before she heads back to her fiancé, Vivienne turns and catches my gaze. "I didn't," she says, a furrow on her forehead.

"You didn't what?" I ask.

But her next words don't give me any clarity. "I didn't change my mind," she says, and then Jacob notices us and comes to meet her halfway, and it's too late to ask her what she meant.

Once Vivienne and Jacob have ambled off and I've decided I've had enough of this event, I wander aimlessly around Morningside Heights, my brain flipping through the memories I've formed with Lewis this past week. How long has he known? When we went for our hike? When we slept together that first night? When I opened up to him about Jacob, sipping on the hot cocoa we made in the middle of the night?

I wish I could Control + z my way back to the point when I heard about Jacob's engagement and correct Vivienne. Fast-forward to now, and it'd just be my long-standing rival offering me a position. It would still be a mess, but a more straightforward one.

I try calling Karo again, and this time, she finally picks up.

"Thank god," I exhale.

"Franzi, are you alright?"

"No," I tell her. "Everything's all messed up." The end of my sentence gets jumbled by a sob, but I swallow it down, eager to push out the words so Karo can help me sort it all out. She doesn't say it, but I hear her familiar words in my ears. *Start from the beginning, and then I'll tell you if it's fixable.* "Professor Alderkamp, the job. She offered it to me, but it turns out that the funding . . . it's the same situation with Jacob all over—"

"Franzi," Karo interrupts me. "Are you hurt? Did something happen to you?" It trickles through to me then how tight her voice sounds. Worried. I'd be, too, if I had four missed calls from her. "Or is this, once again, about work?"

Tight. Angry.

Not worried.

Pissed.

"I—"

"It is, isn't it? About work?"

I'm too tongue-tied to reply. I've never heard Karo speak to me this way. Her compressed tone sends my pulse puckering in my fingertips.

"It's the last evening of my honeymoon road trip, and I'm sitting here with my new husband, having dinner at this restaurant we booked months ago because it has a view of the ocean and the sky is breathtaking and the food is to die for, but do I actually get to enjoy it?"

I flinch as she pushes out a brittle laugh. What is happening? It's like I've landed in a different reality and my brain is failing to catch up.

"No," she continues, "because once again, my sister has some job drama going on that is entirely preventable and wouldn't be half so impactful if she wouldn't put her career above literally everything else in her life."

Every syllable out of her mouth is armored with tiny spears. "Karo—"

"If this was a relationship with a person you were in, I would've told you to get out years ago. Don't you see how dysfunctional it is? You give so much of yourself, but do you get anything in return?"

In the short break she takes, plates clatter in the background, cushioned by the soft melody of a piano. A man, probably Lennart, murmurs something I can't hear.

"I know it hurts hearing this, and it hurts me just as much

to say it, believe me. But Franzi, this has to stop. I want you to be happy, but I don't want to solve your problems about work anymore. When has it ever made your life better? You want to become a professor and then what? More sleepless nights? A job on another continent where we get to see you even less? More stress about funding?"

"That's not—"

"No, Franzi," she cuts over me. The wobble in her voice hurts as much as her horrible words. "You listen to me for once." She sniffs. "You're thirty-two years old. You're supposed to be my *older* sister. You're supposed to give *me* advice, too, listen to what's going on in my life. I know you think I have it all sorted out, because my life is more stable, and Lennart is in it. But I have worries, too, which you'd know about if you ever gave me the space to talk about them. I want to vent to you, too. I want to tell you what's on my mind, that I'm thinking of applying for jobs because I can't stand the sameness of mine anymore. That Lennart and I want to try for a baby, and that I'm scared shitless about how our life would change. But I don't get to share any of this with you because you're like . . . a black hole. All our conversations revolve around you."

She's crying now while I am speechless, helpless, too far away to comfort her. Her words are a screw tightening in my chest and knowing that I'm the source of her pain brings tears to my eyes, too. I hear her hitched breathing, and then she clears her throat, "So whatever it is, Franzi, you figure it out. And I will go back to my dinner and the fucking view of the skyline and have this evening to myself."

Chapter Twenty-Five

I never thought I'd be the one to break my sister's heart. Being a sister should be the most natural thing in the world, and yet I've messed it up. I've been so single-minded about my career and relied on Karo holding me together through all the ups and many downs of it that I forgot about her needs. I should've been looking out for her over the last years, too, instead of hijacking any conversation. And to top it all off, I bombarded her with my worries on what should have been her unique and stress-free, once-in-a-lifetime honeymoon.

Here I am, as incompetent in life as I am in my career. Turns out, Jacob was right when he predicted I'd end up unsuccessful and alone. My chest feels hollow, my knuckles tight around my phone, and guilt swirls deep in my belly as my mind stabs itself with memories.

Memories in which I put myself first and her second.

Memories in which I treated her the way I hate to be treated.

It's too much right now. Too much to unpack where I've gone wrong.

I couldn't bear talking to Lewis earlier, emotions flaring bright when I'd just learned he'd won the same grant I'd been rejected for, but the cocktail of anger, disappointment, and jealousy has lost enough of its sting and made space for a slew of questions. After his betrayal, I don't think the promises we made to each other late last night still stand, but I want answers and I want him to know how much I'm hurting.

Instead of heading home, I turn back to campus.

The Sawyer's summer picnic is still in full swing. The lanterns have blinked on, strings of light crisscrossing above the food sections, and alcohol has turned up the volume on people's conversations. Some of the vendors are already packing up, but the lines for drinks are long. I push down one of the main footpaths, past an area of the green that has been turned into a dance floor, and there he is at one of the metal tables—elbows angled, head in one hand, the other tapping his phone whenever the screen switches off. The lit screen gives me flashes of him: eyebrows pressed into a frown, downcast mouth, the smudge from my fingers dark on his chest.

Seeing him sets off a flurry behind my ribs, like my body hasn't learned yet that we can't reach out to him anymore. Next to him, Brady talks as she spins her straw through the shrunken ice cubes of her drink.

My sneakers crunch over the gravel as I plot a path toward them, and a few steps before I reach the table, Lewis looks up, then jumps to his feet.

"Frances— Jesus, I was worried." His eyes trace over my face, his hand twitching up as if he's about to touch me.

I take a step back. "I want to know why."

"He was worried you didn't get home," Brady chimes up behind Lewis, who must have given her an excuse for his sullen mood.

My gaze remains fixated on his face. "Why didn't you tell

me about the grant? I want to know what else you didn't tell me." My anger has evaporated, and it has left behind a deep aching pit in my chest. "If this whole fake-dating business was all a game to you. Why you didn't think the grant was important to mention when we agreed to give us a chance last night." My voice cracks and I press my lips together, not willing to let him see me like this. Not anymore.

"No, I—" Lewis starts.

"Oh. My. Fucking. Golgi." Brady shoots out of her chair, her eyes wide and pinballing between Lewis and me.

Right. Brady.

I forgot she didn't know about our charade. Two weeks of painstaking care to make this relationship seem real so Lewis's and my reputation wouldn't suffer and I just spelled it out for her. *Fake dating*.

Brady cannot know. It doesn't matter that the Sawyer's is over and Lewis and I are, too—it could still mean the end of our careers. I wait for a rush of nerves but, after everything that has happened this evening, I can't bring myself to care anymore.

Brady's voice is shrill when she cries, "I was right. I *knew* there was something fishy going on, like how Lewis never mentioned you were together until this trip and I barely saw you at our hotel, and never in the mornings . . . And how excited you were to meet Professor Alderkamp, as if you wouldn't have had any other opportunity to meet her, even though Lewis has been in touch with her for so long. It was all . . . Right. There."

Brady pauses, her gaze frantically jumping between us. "But you guys were also so cute together and looked so happy. Like, Lewis lit up like a Christmas tree every time you were around, and I wasn't sure— I thought nobody would ever fake date in real life! Oh no, I said something about the two of you having a *just one bed* situation, didn't I?" She clamps her hands over her mouth. "Why didn't you tell me?" she adds, squinting at Lewis.

He juts out his chin. "Brady," he says without averting his eyes from me, "I'll see you at the hotel later, okay? I'll explain, but please. Not a word to anyone."

"I'd never." She sounds appalled as she gathers up her tote bag and empty glass. After she pulls me in for a hug and says her goodbyes, she mimics zipping her mouth shut before she trudges away.

"Do you want to sit down?" Lewis offers cautiously as he motions toward the chairs.

I shake my head. "I'm not staying. I just want answers."

He nods, slowly. "I guess I should start from the beginning. I met Rosanna when she was visiting for a talk at the institute in Berlin last summer." He hooks his fingers into his collar and lifts it away from the nape of his neck, as if to grant himself a little extra space to breathe. "At first, she only wanted me to be her postdoc since her current electrophysiologist was leaving. But we started brainstorming from there, realizing we could merge the focus of our research in a much bigger way. To study memory in a multi-methods approach. I pushed to include MRI and computational modeling. I was thinking of you and everything I'd learned from your papers." His somber tone brightens with excitement about the project, but only for a beat. "So we wrote the grant together, Rosanna and I, and I thought maybe, in the unlikely case we won it, I could contact you. To see if you wanted to handle a part of the project."

He holds my gaze and I swallow thickly. It's scary how much our dreams of the future are aligned, how similar we are in our goals. Some twisted part of me melts because he wrote me into his grant, because he thought my research was valid, useful, necessary.

But it also makes me sick, getting pushed into somebody else's grand scheme like this—again.

"And yet I had to find out about the grant from Rosanna. So what happened?" I prompt, crossing my arms.

"The Sawyer's happened. Our plane ride happened. You happened. You sat down next to me on the plane, and I honestly forgot about the grant because there was no space for it." He bites his lip and his voice goes quieter when he adds, "There was only you, and how much I wanted to be around you. And by the time I heard the news, I was already in so deep. Everything I said these last days is true, Frances. I care a lot about you. I just didn't know what to do."

"You care about me, so much that you were planning to keep this a secret?" I push down all the unwanted feelings his words trigger and focus on his betrayal instead. "How long have you known?"

He lowers his eyes. "Sunday night."

"Sunday?" I press out. The donuts, the weekend in the Catskills—they weren't a lie. But everything after?

"You were there when I unlinked my emails from my phone. I didn't check my inbox until after we got back to the city." He's looking at me now, lets me see the trouble stirring in the blue of his eyes. His hands lift for a moment, but then he sinks them into the pockets of his jeans.

"So, your notebook going missing was a really convenient distraction to keep us focused on something else until the end of the Sawyer's," I observe. "Did you think you could keep the grant a secret until we were back home? Were you ever going to tell me, or did you plan to ignore it like you did four years ago?"

"No, I . . ." Lewis frowns. "I wouldn't do something like that on purpose. I really did lose the notebook. You know I was desperate to get it back. I didn't want it to mess up either of our careers."

"Whatever the deal with the notebook was, the fact still stands: You decided to keep the grant a secret."

"Only until I knew what was going to happen with us. I was going to tell you, Frances, you have to believe me. I thought I could figure out some kind of solution before it messed anything up . . ." He gulps. "And we weren't sure what was going to happen after the Sawyer's anyway. What's the use of talking about this grant if I was only going to get a few more days with you?" He presses his lips together. "I'm sorry for how it happened—for not telling you when I know I should have."

"Regardless of what was or wasn't going to happen to us after the Sawyer's, how did you think you could solve this?" I ask him, words brimming with hurt. "Did you think I'd leave to some faraway lab and you'd hire someone else? Or were you going to sit me down and offer me the position? None of these options sound like a good solution to me. And what about letting me drive and just wanting to be along for the ride?"

"Frances, you have to understand. I was terrified of messing things up. When it comes to you, I don't know what to do." His voice is gritty as he presses his index finger and thumb to the bridge of his nose, and when he lowers his hand again, the half-moon dents of his fingernails are imprinted into his skin. "I've *never* felt this way before. Attraction, sure. Appreciation, maybe comfort, too. But not this endless wonder. Like I'm a kid again, going to bed after the best possible day, but scared to fall asleep because I don't want it to end. That's what it feels like when I'm around you."

The space behind my ribs feels raw, exposed. Lewis admitting his feelings for me hurts just as much as the explanation of his lies. I hug myself tighter, trying to minimize the area of impact.

Lewis leans forward and catches my gaze. "If you'd think about it—think what we could achieve together. Scientifically. And with our lives. At the end of the year, we could already be living in the same city if, you know, you decide to take the job."

I shake my head, his suggestion like a punch out of nowhere. How can he still think there's a good outcome for both of us in this situation? "Have you been listening at all?" I blurt out. "You know I won't. I'm not going to depend on you. This is my job and my career, and I won't take handouts."

"But isn't it different this time? It's a lab you've dreamed of working with, a professor you know you get along with—who you've been wanting to work with, no less. You'd be responsible for your work package of the grant. I wouldn't be your boss, just your colleague, really. You'd still be in the driver's seat."

Lewis's inability to understand that the damage is done is like a screw winding tighter and tighter. He's pushed us down an impossible path, one we can only navigate separately now.

I shake my head, more insistently this time. "It doesn't matter. Whatever study I run, whatever conference I go to or colleague I talk to, whatever paper I publish, I'll always think it was all because I fucked the right person."

His hands fly up as if I physically lashed out. The crease between his eyebrows deepens. "But that's not how it works," he argues back. "It's not like I can give you a job just like that. Despite all the nepotism in science, you'd have to interview, Rosanna would have a say in it . . ."

"Don't you think I know all that?" I bite out.

"So why doesn't it change your mind? Why isn't it enough?" Lewis counters, and as his hands reach for the back of a chair, his emotions are all right there in the white of his knuckles. "If we break up, would that be your solution? I don't want to come between you and what you love. Tell me what it is you need me to do, and I'll do it."

The screw winds so tight that I splinter around it. "I need you to leave me alone. I need you to not fit me into your five-year plan to professorship. I need you to understand you can't make choices for me."

"Frances," Lewis says, exasperated. "Let's take a step back for a moment. This is not about fitting you into my plans. I care about your reputation, but I care about producing good science, too. Don't you?"

A dry laugh claws out of my throat. "Stop making excuses for yourself in the name of science. No wonder people leave if you mess up this badly."

The words rush out of me before I fully parse their meaning. Like running a bit of code I came up with, just to see if it works. Except there's another human being at the other end, one who flinches and then looks at me incredulously, a muscle in his jaw dancing to a beat I cannot hear.

My stomach feels like it's climbing up my chest, and I want to pull my words back.

"I'm—"

"You know what," Lewis snaps, and something cold slithers down my spine. His face is all angles, like he desperately wants me out of his space. "You're right. I'm done. You can put this into your long list of failed experiments. It takes more than a week of play-pretend to fall in love."

And with that, he steps around me. He shoves his hands into his pockets, as though he needs to restrain them from reaching for me. When he's stalked past me, Lewis turns around once more.

"Have a safe trip, Dr. Silberstein."

Chapter Twenty-Six

The evening has taken away the protective layer of my skin, leaving behind a raw, sulking mass of inadequacy. Each step farther away from Lewis deepens the crack in my chest and makes me sick with guilt for what I said, but I force myself to breathe through it and remind myself of what he did—what he kept from me.

What he said yesterday about how he feels isn't important. How *I* feel isn't important.

Not when he wasn't honest about something so big, pushing me back into the corner I'd been fighting my way out of ever since my breakup with Jacob.

For about ten minutes after I leave campus, I'm in denial about everything. Ten minutes, or about as long as it takes to get to my studio and realize that my fingers have twitched for my phone too many times to count, eager to call Karo so she can make sense of everything for me.

Except I've already messed up her honeymoon.

Except what she said boils down to: Grow the fuck up and handle your problems on your own.

Shame pinches in my stomach as I think about Karo, and when I've toed off my sneakers at the door, I finally allow my brain to flip through the last years. Our almost daily phone calls, my short visits to Berlin, our trips together. I was proud of myself for keeping such close contact with her, my anchor point amidst all the changes. But through the new filter her words have given me, I see that all these memories are tinged in my work. Ranting to Karo about failed experiments, racing to meet conference submission deadlines while sitting at her kitchen table, and pushing off visits because I had too much to do. A trip with Karo tacked onto a conference abroad, off-loading my worries onto her while she was supposed to celebrate her honeymoon with Lennart, fitting her in around the biggest constant in my life. I used her to fill up my social battery and to solve any emotional problems without caring for her needs. Karo cheered me on toward my goals, but I'd stopped asking about her life and what future she was dreaming of.

I think back to my relationship with Jacob. How he'd become so focused on himself and his career that he only cared about my use for him and nothing else. Now, I'd done the same with Karo—I'd taken my own sister, her kindness and emotional support, for granted.

And for what?

An offer to work in a lab with a professor I admire and a topic I care about. A way to tackle the research questions that have hovered out of reach, a way to finally make a difference.

Yet all I feel is this churning sense of dread. A scratching doubt. That whisper in the back of my mind.

Has any of it been worth it?

Was it worth all the stress, the late nights and long weeks? Packing up my suitcases over and over again? Never making a home anywhere because soon I'd be moving to a new place? Prioritizing my data over making friends, over finding true connection? Yanking a colleague into this ridiculous charade that risked both of our careers? Hurting my sister?

I want to cry, but I'm too stunned, too disappointed, and too disgusted with myself to give in to the urge. I'm not ready to reevaluate the last five years yet, and even less ready to get close to that tender spot behind my ribs that pulses whenever I think about Lewis. But as I put myself under the icy spray of the shower, I realize that there's one thing I *can* change. I can show Karo how much I care about her. That she's not my emotional trash can but the most important person in my life.

My flight gets into Seattle at midday tomorrow, just a few hours after Lennart leaves back to Germany for the summer concert series his orchestra is playing. Two weeks of uninterrupted sister time. Two weeks that'll hopefully allow me to make up for all the ways I've been absent.

I have eighteen hours to push all these overwhelming feelings down, so I can focus on Karo. I can pile up the weariness, the anger, and the disappointment and deal with them at a later time.

For now, all that matters is my sister.

Karo doesn't come running toward me when she spots me in arrivals at Seattle-Tacoma International Airport. She doesn't do anything at all, no excited wave, no upturn of her mouth, just a slight turn of her body in my direction showing that she acknowledged my presence.

My hand is clammy around the handle of my suitcase, thoughts flitting nervously through all the options: Can I still hug her, or do I just stop in front of her and say, *Hi*? And: How have we coexisted for thirty years in this world, but never had a proper fight?

I suspect the answer to the latter can be traced back to Karo's patience and goodwill.

Next to me, a couple falls into each other's arms, and ahead, a girl with pigtails waves a star-stickered and glittery *Welcome home* cardboard sign to someone walking behind me.

I stop in front of Karo, her fist tight around the strap of her tote bag. Except for the red around her irises and the smudged mascara, she looks less tired than when I saw her two weeks ago. Skin tanned, the red in her hair faded, and the strands sun-kissed.

"Hey," I say when too much time has passed for her to hug me, and it sinks in that I won't get a whiff of her citrus shampoo and a tickle of her short curls against my nose. That she won't dislodge the sob out of my chest that's been stuck there since our call yesterday.

I didn't really think all that pent-up frustration she had about me would solve itself that easily, but I'd still hoped we'd be okay as soon as we saw each other again. Now I recognize how naive I was to think she'd help me navigate through this, when that's exactly what she blamed me for: loading any emotional labor onto her shoulders.

"How was your flight?" she wants to know, her voice strangely monotone.

I nod. "All good." The leftovers of my allergy pill cling to the edges of my brain, slowing me down. *Snap out of it*, I tell myself. It's on me to make things right.

"What about Lennart?" I ask back. "Did he get out okay?"

Karo swipes her finger over one eye, smudging the mascara a little more. "Yeah, his flight left on time."

I want to squeeze her elbow, give her some kind of reassurance, but she only turns her head and declares, "I need coffee."

I swipe my credit card for her oat flat white and my triple-shot latte before we pick up the rental car. I know how much she hates driving—we both do, really—so I wordlessly take the key, and while I adjust the seat and mirrors, Karo connects her phone to the sound system. She turns up the volume when we roll out of the airport, filling the terse silence with strumming guitars and a deep male voice.

Loud music, windows down, conifers lining the road and infusing the air with their crisp scent—it's how I'd pictured this trip when I planned it with Karo half a year ago.

But now the trunk holds all the unsaid words between us, my throat burns with the emotional pain I'm trying to swallow down, and my chest is a pressure chamber of sadness.

Awkward, barely speaking—that's how we start our trip together, the first one in more than a year. I don't know if I can handle two weeks of this, but I've already caused an oil spill on Karo's honeymoon with all my preventable problems and work-related worries. I won't spoil the second half of her holiday if I can avoid it.

When Karo has fallen asleep that night, I scroll down in my Notes app until I find the wishlist she has Lennart and me synched in on so we don't accidentally give her books she's already read. I buy credits on my audiobook app and download the top title on her list, a sweeping historical romance by an author called Rosalind Bellamy. Ahead of our drive out west, I head to the car early and hook up my phone to the speakers, but when I realize where we are and remember what started my sister's obsession with books when we were teenagers, I download another book instead.

Over the next few days, we make our way around the Olympic Peninsula, listening to all the angst and heartbreak of the *Twilight* saga. Back in the French mountain town where Karo had her concussion on that long-ago ski trip, I scoured the library and bookstores, trying to find her favorite books in a language she could read, finally succeeding with a copy of *Eclipse* that was almost falling apart. Bella, Jacob, and Edward got her through the confusing and lonely days of amnesia, and now they help me get her back, too.

Between the fresh mountain air, the shock of the cold Pacific, and the rhythm of our hikes, I don't bring up our fight, and I push down all thoughts about Lewis. But as our trip goes on, I try to steer our conversation away from the things that need to be sorted out in the moment, and to the things that matter. When I ask about her life, Karo is cagey at first. From her honeymoon to her doubts about her job, from her and Lennart's decision to try for a baby, to the spiciest books she's read this past year, I don't run out of questions, and though she only answers a third of them, hesitantly, sometimes monosyllabically, I'm content to listen, to have my sister back and learn about all the ways she's changed when I was busy looking elsewhere.

One afternoon, after a three-hour-long hike, Karo stops me in front of a store window stacked with donuts. "Franzi, hang on a second." Her hand grabs my underarm, and it's the first time on this trip that she touches me casually, like it's no big deal. The first time her voice doesn't sound compressed, and her gray eyes look at me level, without darting away.

It makes me hopeful. It makes me ignore the warning bells that ring in my head when my nose detects the sugary fragrance. It makes me suppress memories of the last time I had donuts, and how Lewis had been there for me then.

I let Karo pick the flavors, and she carries the greasy brown paper bag back to our rental. We take a dirt road off the highway and polish off our donuts while we watch the fog swirl low above the churning waves of the ocean. I only realize my mistake when we're on the way back. Something gives in my chest and the bridge of my nose begins to tingle, the donuts cranking open a valve. This time, I know what's coming, and I quickly wipe the powdered sugar and butter off my fingers, before the first tears appear. A little croak spills from my throat.

Then I lurch forward, the windshield and dusty black hood of the car coming closer and closer until the seat belt digs into the space between my breasts.

Karo breaks into a full stop in the middle of the highway.

"What are you doing?" I cry.

"What are *you* doing?" she shouts back, fingers white in their clasp around the steering wheel, and eyes wide as she stares at me. "Your gasp gave me a heart attack. Are you okay?"

I check the rearview mirror, but behind us there's only the empty stretch of tarmac below a cushion of gathering clouds. Only when I've smacked the button in the console to turn on the hazard lights, do I wipe the palm of my hand across my eyes.

"Franzi, are you okay?" Karo repeats, more insistently this time.

"Yes. No," I press out between two giant sobs that feel like someone has taken a sledgehammer to my chest. I've been holding everything in for the sake of Karo's and my relationship but now it comes crashing out in my tears, like an overstuffed piñata. Lewis's betrayal, my guilt over how I ended things with him, even more guilt about how I've treated Karo. And though I've tried not to think about work after Karo blamed me for having such an unhealthy relationship with it, there's that, too: my failed grant, Rosanna's job offer I can't take, and the general panic I feel when I think about my future because it will mean uprooting myself again when I'm not sure I can take it anymore.

"Franzi, you're crying." Karo lets go of the steering wheel and shakes my shoulder. "What does that mean?"

"I'm okay," I wheeze out. "I just feel like I messed everything up." Behind the stream of my tears, I imagine her rolling her eyes, wondering if it's about my code or my job again, and I quickly add, "But it's okay. I can ha-a"—a sob makes me hiccup—"handle it."

Karo leans over and drops a roll of toilet paper from the glove box into my lap. I trumpet into a tissue as fat drops of rain start pelting onto the windshield, drumming on the roof of the car. "I'll figure it out. We don't need to talk about me," I assure her, and this time it sounds believable, voice sans snot and teary cracks.

Karo knits her eyebrows and squeezes my knee. "Of course we do, silly," she says softly.

I press my lips together. I don't want my thoughts and anger and sadness to come spilling out. I can't, not when I've witnessed how much it hurts her to shoulder them all the time. "No, Karo. Seriously. If anything, we need to talk about us. About how I've been treating you."

She looks at me skeptically.

A car whizzes by on our left side, splashing water against the windows. "Are you okay to drive?" I ask. "Should I . . ."

Karo slowly turns the key in the ignition, and with her eyes on the road and hands on the wheel, I hope that this can finally be the space where we can talk.

"I'm so sorry," I tell her, noting how her shoulders inch up, and my heart twists. Maybe I've read her wrong. Maybe it still isn't the moment.

But then she gives a minuscule nod that tells me to continue. "I'm really sorry for how I've treated you. I thought our closeness was special. How we kept in touch even when I was living on the other side of the world. But I can see now how I've taken you for granted, all these years, and how it must've been really hard from your side." My tears are threatening to come back, but I swallow them down. "I promise it won't get to that again. I promise I won't bug you with my stupid problems anymore, and I'll make sure to ask you about yours and everything that's going on in your life."

"It's not like I don't want to hear about your life anymore, Franzi." Karo sighs. "But the way we worked, it was all you and never me. Sometimes one person needs to lean on the other for some time and that's fine. I was fine having your back while you figured things out. But I realized I was becoming this one-dimensional side character in your life. The one you call when it's not going well, while you were getting more and more stuck on this path you'd determined for yourself."

"I'm so sorry, Karo," I tell her, nestling up with my back against the door. "All I ever wanted was to learn more about what happened to you in that ski accident. You asked me all these questions, over and over again, and at some point, the answers I gave you stuck, and everything turned out fine, but it's not like that for everyone. So many people out there have long-lasting complications after accidents, or other memory issues. Epilepsy, dementia, Alzheimer's. People whose memory gets scrambled, who forget more by the day or can't hold on to any new information. It's heartbreaking to see a person disappear while they sit right in front of you. This is who I'm doing my work for. I never meant to hurt you in the process."

The rain drums down strongly now. Karo increases the speed on the windshield wipers. "I know that this is your *why* and I'm not telling you to change it. But I worry about you. You're willing to sacrifice so much for this. Ever since you broke up with Jacob you got so hung up on your career. I get that you needed to fight for it and stand up for yourself, but suddenly nothing else mattered anymore."

My first instinct is to deny it. As Lewis once hazarded, I'm a bit allergic to criticism. But truly, she's right. As I crumple up the greasy paper bag that's left over from the donuts, I force myself to say, "Maybe, yeah. I think after Jacob, and how he took advantage of me, I overcorrected."

Karo sets the indicator to turn off the main road, deeper into the forest where we've rented a tiny house. "It was like the places and people you passed were props in your journey to success. But now—I don't know. It sounded like this time in New York you stopped being just Dr. Silberstein the scientist but gave the rest of yourself some space to breathe, too. Like you were finally making memories instead of just studying them."

She shrugs, but her words hit me, hard. "I guess I thought something in you had finally shifted. That we could turn the page to the next chapter, where you were doing better, finding balance for yourself and caring about things other than work or proving Jacob wrong. Where I could share my own problems and ask for your advice, too, and where we could be silly sometimes. So, when you called and it was all about solving amnesia and success again, I snapped. And I'm so sorry for the way I did, in a moment that was hard for you." Stopped at a traffic light, Karo's eyes leave the road for a moment, glancing at me. "I got scared when I sensed you moving backward to the place you've spent the last five years in. One where you doubt yourself constantly, forget about yourself and everyone else, and don't find peace. I don't like to see you in that place.

"But obviously none of that means you're not allowed to talk about yourself anymore. That's nonsense. Especially because, well . . ." She gesticulates at my tear-streaked face and the wad of tissue tucked into the middle console. "Clearly something's up. So, tell me what happened?"

"What about you, though?" I divert.

Karo rolls her eyes. "We talked about me for the last week. I don't know what else to tell you. I need to get back home and live a little before I can tell you more."

I study my beautiful little sister, my best friend; how every few seconds her eyes pivot over to me, the gray tinted with warmth and care.

"You're not happy with your job anymore?" I insist. "Maybe we should talk about that."

"It's not that I'm not happy, it's just . . . I've gotten to the point where it has started to feel boring. I love the books, and my colleagues, our campaigns, but I feel like I've gotten all I need out of the job. And it's hard, because I don't know what's next for me. I've always admired how adaptable you are, and I wish I had some of that, too. It might make changing jobs easier."

That same adaptability Karo is talking about is the exact reason why she's the only person I confide in—I've perfected this skill to the point I don't put down roots anywhere anymore. But maybe this is something I can help her with. "We can look for other opportunities when we're back at the cabin," I offer. "Get your résumé up to speed. I can . . ." I falter because the constant changes in my life are so second nature that it's hard to verbalize them into one concrete piece of advice. "Coach you through it. What's holding you back?"

"I don't know," she says, voice soft.

"Start from the beginning," I tell her, borrowing the words she's calmed me down with time and time again, "and then I'll tell you if it's fixable."

Later that evening, after brushing up her professional social media profiles and scrolling through job portals to identify vacancies that spark some kind of excitement in Karo, we sit down to veggie burgers and a truckload of fries at the local diner. On the short way over, I've caught her up with the bits and pieces about the Sawyer's she didn't know about: running into Jacob again, our hunt for the notebook, my breakup with Lewis, the strange surprise at discovering Vivienne's kindness, and how unmoored I'm starting to become when thinking about my career choices.

Because I'm worried it'll push us back into the pattern we're trying to work ourselves out of, I've decided not to tell her about the panic attacks until I've made a therapy appointment back home. Once I know I'll get the professional help I need, I can be vulnerable about it without giving her the feeling she has to carry this on her shoulders, too.

"Okay. Let me sum this up," Karo says, dragging her fry through the puddle of BBQ sauce on her plate. "You either take the job, which would give you the opportunity to live close to the guy you fell in love with, or you don't take the job and you'd have to find a new lab wherever, plus you'd be far from the guy you fell in love with. Those are your options. Correct?"

"Taking the job is not an option, because I wouldn't take myself seriously," I confess as I peel the sliced pickle off my patty and stack it on the side of my plate from where Karo transfers it onto her burger. "It doesn't feel earned. I'll always question whether I deserve to be there and I can't live like that. I'm proud of what I've accomplished, and I've worked too hard to be put in that position. It's like Jacob all over again."

"Except it's not, is it?" Karo tips her head to the side, as if something just occurred to her. "You left Jacob because he put you second, took advantage of you, and never recognized that you wanted to pursue your own dream. But now? It seems to me like you're giving up your dream *and* Lewis because he happens to be involved in an opportunity that would have come to you anyway—you said so yourself that Rosanna was impressed with your work before she ever knew you were involved with Lewis." Karo tracks my movements as I take a big bite of my burger, and when my mouth is too full to say anything, she gives me tough love. "Lewis took advantage of you one time and from what you told me, he's been making up for it ever since. He recognized his mistake, he admires your work and credits you for it, and he wants you to pursue your dreams—so much that he'd be willing to break up with you, just so you get to be comfortable in the job he offered you." Karo purses her lips. "That doesn't sound like Jacob at all. It sounds like he cares a lot about you."

Her words make me swallow hard. "I'm not sure he still does," I say, a horrible feeling tugging at my gut when I remember how I pushed him away. "And also, if the job depends on *him*, then, well . . ." I shrug. "Then it's not the dream job. I admire Rosanna for what she does and would love to work with her, but the real dream is getting a stable position, so I can work on my own research," I explain. "All without help. I talked to someone in Australia—"

"Franzi, no. Australia? Is that what you want?"

"It's what I have to do."

"I've never understood why you'd be willing to move across the world every few years for a job that gives you so little in return."

"It's . . ."

It's because I've spent so many years trying to answer these questions, I want to say, *that I can't give up now. What if nobody else will ask them? What if nobody else will answer them the way I do?*

We only ever remember the big names, Albert Einstein and Rosalind Franklin and Galileo Galilei and Marie Skłodowska Curie. But thousands of scientists could've made a different decision in their own research, given up or investigated something else. And what if that would've become the missing piece in the bigger puzzle? What if them not getting answers to their little questions would've prevented us from landing on the moon or figuring out the structure of DNA?

The longer I talk to Karo, the more I realize that my reasons for not wanting to give up my research are more complicated than that. It's not only about my questions, but also about sunk costs and hunger for recognition and maybe a bit too much ambition than is good for me.

"It's science, yes I know," Karo says. "A bit of a cult."

I shake my head. "It's the only way I can still make a difference."

"Is it, though?" Karo asks me. "The only way?"

Chapter Twenty-Seven

After we leave the Olympic Peninsula, Karo and I make our way north to Victoria Island, talking and joking our way back into a relationship that feels balanced. With a few exceptions, I manage to keep Lewis out of my mind. But occasionally he pushes back to the forefront of my thoughts: in a bookstore when I spot a copy of the hefty book he brought to the cabin, when we go on a hike he recommended and, worst of all, when we arrive in Vancouver, where I picture a younger version of him at every street corner. On the last morning of our two-week-long trip, before Karo and I board separate planes taking us back home, we meet Brady for brunch, but, to my relief, she avoids any mention of him, and bonds over books with Karo instead.

The Netherlands welcome me back with a gray and wet August, one with countless days of fizzy rain and a dull sky. On my first day back at the office, I type out an email to Rosanna, thanking her for our conversations and stating that I won't be interviewing for the postdoc position. I've had weeks to think it over, and although working with her was—is—my dream,

I have decided that it's not worth putting myself in a position where I'd doubt my worth every second. Giving up on this dream feels less groundbreaking than I thought it would. It's just another email. A few strokes of the keyboard, a snap of the enter key.

The clock on my project, and my job, is ticking, but over the next few weeks, I try to put my head down, get through the time I have left at work, not think about Lewis, and figure out what's next for me. I fall into a rhythm of work, exercise, job hunting, a few hours of unwinding before a fitful night of sleep and then the cycle starts all over again.

Although I haven't experienced any more panic attacks, the constant buzz of my thoughts prompts me to finally make a doctor's appointment a few days after I get back, and once there, I ask for a referral to a therapist. Theoretical knowledge about fear responses and the pathways of emotion are one thing, but I need professional help to get out of my habit of pushing down unwanted feelings and distracting myself with work instead. I can't rationalize my way through life when sometimes it just is the way it is—messy, and full of surprises, good and bad.

Karo and I talk often—not daily, like we used to. I don't give her a rundown of my job search, the faraway labs I'm considering, but instead coach her through her own insecurities and practice interview questions with her. In the evenings, I listen to the historical romance audiobook I downloaded back on our trip, so I understand which brooding looks and stolen touches she gushes about on our calls, and the day after my first therapy appointment, I finally tell her about the panic attacks.

With the start of fall semester approaching, email traffic picks back up and clogs my inbox at a speed I can't keep up with. I mark all department-wide emails as read without even looking at them, but in the two weeks after I'm back, three emails stand out.

One, an invitation to virtually present my research at a lab at Monash University, to which Tegan, the postdoc I met at the Sawyer's, has added a note: *It's not quite your research, but they're looking for a postdoc, so if you do well, they might consider you.*

Two, Brady sending the first chapter of a new story she started—not fan fic, but her own, about a biomedical scientist who is forced to collaborate with a werewolf to find a cure for a rare disease. I zoom through it on my lunch break, and when I email her back, demanding more, I notice that she sent the chapter to Lewis at the same time as me. And my longing for him flares back up.

Three, an email from Rosanna Alderkamp that comes in right as I'm changing out of my bathing suit at the local pool. I hadn't expected to hear from her anymore when she already sent a kind response right after I turned down the position. Once I'm fully dressed, I find a bench in front of the pool complex and open the email.

Hi Frances,

New developments on the postdoctoral position that will open in the lab. While still involved in the project, Lewis has stepped down from the hiring process, citing a conflict of interest. He mentioned this caused your reservations in interviewing for the position. Interviews will be handled by a colleague from the imaging department and me, and we'll do a lab culture / compatibility check with two other postdocs from the group.

Shall I disregard your previous communication?

Talk soon,

R

Rosanna sends a copy of Lewis's grant proposal along, "at my discretion," so I can see what the research would entail.

My first read through has me crying.

From hope or heartache, I don't know. The research entails something wildly promising, as if Lewis had pulled the next steps I wanted to address out of my brain. Like me, he must have written this proposal last winter. It shows that he hadn't only read my work closely, but also understood me, *saw* me, before we even met. The grant is a glimpse into his brilliant mind, and I race home, where I reread it obsessively, masochistically, until my eyes want to bleed.

Karo was right: It *is* different this time. Rather than brush over my name, like Jacob did, Lewis's appreciation for my work is all over his grant. But not only that. Back in New York he said he only ever wanted to see me succeed, and Rosanna's email is yet another sign of that: He listened to my concerns and is willing to sacrifice his control over the project to clear the way for me.

Two days later, I give my virtual presentation to the lab in Melbourne. Tegan introduces me, and I get some interesting questions from the rest of the group, and before I finish the call, I get invited to an official job interview. As I exit the meeting, I already know I'll cancel it.

I don't want to move to Australia. Despite what I told Karo, I don't want this to be the only way.

It's midnight when the call ends, and I begin pacing around in my office, limbs tense and brain swirling with indecision. A postdoc in Rosanna's lab with Lewis's money or moving all the way to Melbourne on my own terms.

None of the options feel right. In the past, whenever I reached the end of a contract, I usually had the next opportunity lined up; a new open position at a lab or a successful grant project. The thought of moving halfway across the world wouldn't have even made me blink, whereas now it overwhelms me with a fresh burst of anxiety.

I know I need to make a decision soon.

Unsure how else to tackle my problem, I stop in front of my whiteboard, which is scribbled dark with crossed-out revision points from my last paper. I wipe it clean.

For about half of my life, I've been trained to look objectively at my experiments. Consider all questions and biases, shift my perspective, and let the data drive me. So, it's no surprise that after taking stock of my current life, I realize that something needs to change.

I thought I'd done the right thing after breaking up with Jacob five years ago. When my heart felt like one giant bruise, I pushed back all the way. I decided I'd work tirelessly and pour everything into reaching my goal.

Get tenure and make a difference with my research. No matter what.

But I've run out of breath in my blind sprint toward that goal, and it's gotten pretty lonely here, too. I've lost track of myself, again, except this time I only have myself to blame. I've pushed people away and put everything else—happiness, stability, whatever else I wanted—on the back burner, convinced it would pay off when I finally reached the finish line. My self-worth is so dependent on work that any major setback—a grant rejection, learning how much better Jacob did for himself—felt like a demonstration of what an absolute failure I was, and pushed me to lose control.

After scribbling all of this onto my board, I'm still not closer to finding a solution for what to do next. But there's someone, I remember, who might provide me with a sense of direction. Someone who's arrived at a point in her career she seems happy with, someone who offered that we could talk.

Despite the late hour here, it's early evening on the East Coast, so I hunt for the Sawyer's program on my messy desk and find Vivienne's number on the last page.

"Frances," she greets me happily when I tell her who's on the line. "So nice of you to call."

I only manage a little bit of small talk before the reason I'm actually calling tumbles out of me. "What did you mean when you said you didn't change your mind? Back on that last day of the Sawyer's? We were talking about ambition, and . . ."

" . . . how hard it can be to balance that. Yes, I remember."

"Which is something I've been failing at, big-time. So, it resonated, and it stuck. And confused me, because, um, I mean . . ." I search for a way to say it politely. "Jacob is your fiancé *and* your boss, isn't he?"

On the other end, Vivienne makes a little noise of disbelief. "He's not—though I can certainly see how it would seem that way because he handles all the politics and leadership nonsense. But no, he's not my boss and has never been," she continues, which I'm grateful for. I don't know what to say. "It wasn't an option for either of us. Even if that meant staying long distance until we finally got funding together at the beginning of this year. You know, we applied for a joint grant two years in a row, and they got turned down. He absolutely would've had the resources to hire me on money he got for another project, but we both didn't want that for our relationship. So we tried again, and this time it worked. Now he runs the lab and manages the people, but I steer the research because that's my specialty and . . . Well, it works for both of us."

I cringe inwardly, ashamed that I made assumptions about her that would make me furious if I were in her shoes. All this time I was worried about Jacob treating her how he'd treated me, when he seems to have learned from our relationship, like Vivienne said he had.

Maybe it's time for me to learn from it, too.

"What would you have done if your application wouldn't have been successful?" I ask.

"Honestly? I would've probably stayed in Paris, and tried for funding some other way," Vivienne muses. "Even if long distance is horrible and it seemed silly to put ourselves through that any longer when I could've just worked for Jacob."

She's silent for a beat, and I wonder how things would've played out if I'd drawn such a clear line five years ago. Karo showed me that boundaries are for keeping people in your life, not to push them out. Maybe, if I'd said something earlier—if I'd given Jacob the opportunity to back off when he took over the wheel—our relationship would've taken a different course. I'll never know, but I *do* know I don't need to repeat my mistakes.

"I get it," I say.

"I thought you would," Vivienne replies and I can hear the smile in her voice. "Look, it wasn't an easy decision and for a while I felt like I couldn't find a way to make everything work that I wanted. But in the end, it's the same as running an experiment. So often, it feels like they're not working out—that we went wrong somewhere, made a mistake. But if you really think about it, we always get an answer. No matter how confusing the results, how unexpected, we get an answer to the question we were asking at that moment. And especially when they're unclear, they tell us, we need to take a step back and reevaluate. It's like shining a flashlight into the dark. If there's nothing in our cone of light, we know not to shine there again, but move elsewhere." After a moment of silence, she adds, "Or maybe we just need a different flashlight. A new perspective."

I let her words sink in. Maybe it's time for me, too, to throw out my old flashlight and try a new one.

At the Q and A event, after receiving the news about my last rejected grant, I'd told the students to put their eggs in many baskets, to find connection, and grow outside of work, because that's how you manage the setbacks. Maybe the time has come for me to heed my own advice and learn how to look out for myself.

Therapy has helped with that. Opening up in my first two sessions was hard, but I've realized I don't want to pack down so much of myself anymore, especially not for a goal I'm not sure I'll ever reach.

What I want is to put down roots, to hammer nails into the walls of my living room and hang up pictures rich with memories, to make friends I can cook dinner with, people whose lives I can see change right in front of my eyes and not through biannual updates in nondescript conference venues. I want a life that's hard to pack up, one that is full and grounding and confusing and messy, and very much not only about work.

I still want to make a difference, but the *no matter what* needs to go if I want to last.

Maybe I can put up boundaries. Not only for Lewis, if he'll still have me, or for me and Karo, but for my own sake, too, so I get to have the life I want, with a career that works for me. It's something my new therapist hinted at in our last session, but I only grasp it now. Maybe I'm not stuck with the two options I drew out on my whiteboard.

"Is this about the grant with Lewis?" Vivienne asks, tracking the direction of my thoughts.

"Yeah. That and everything else, too." I bite my lip, and then the admission finally comes slipping out, the one that has been bouncing around between the walls of my skull since my last grant got rejected. Or maybe even longer than that.

"Vivienne, I love my research, but I don't know if I can keep it up. I think I'm tired of academia. Of always having to think about the next next thing and feeling like I can never catch my breath."

She's silent for a beat, then: "I can try to help. You know, from one academic to another?"

When she said she'd like to be friends all those weeks ago, I didn't think I'd end up asking her for relationship and career advice, but here we are. Talk about surprise stops along the way.

"How about friend to friend?" I ask back.

Chapter Twenty-Eight

I've never been a firm believer in Murphy's Law. The statistics of anything going wrong that might go wrong just didn't line up for me. But some sources say that aeronautical engineer Edward Aloysius Murphy Jr. meant the words that were later named after him as precautionary advice: *In designing any plan, if anything can go wrong, it might.*

When I came up with the plan on how to move forward, and with all the chaos of my flight to New York still fresh in mind, I took extra care. I came up with contingencies for anything I thought could go wrong: Book a hotel for the night before, buy flexible train tickets, pack an extra outfit just in case. But despite my plans B and C, Murphy's showing me the upper hand again. Getting to the Codify offices in Amsterdam for my job interview at Maria's e-learning start-up has been an adventure, to say the least.

Some kind of track problems delayed my train to Amsterdam, turning the two-hour journey into a five-hour one, which made me arrive past check-in hours. Thanks to an emergency number and a tired but kind receptionist, I managed to get into my room for a few hours of sleep. This morning wasn't any better, though. A coffee spill on my blouse led to a last-minute outfit change, which made me run late. Then, on the way over, it started raining and I got something in my eye and rubbed it, losing my contact lens in the process. A half-blurry sprint later, I finally arrive at the offices on the second-to-last floor of a renovated warehouse. I have just enough time to swap my remaining contact lens for my glasses and to pull my drenched hair into a quick braid, which drips cold water onto my neck, before Maria meets me at the reception desk, her HR person Henrieke in tow.

Wary of what else Murphy might be coming up with, I tell myself to breathe when I follow them into the conference room where my interview will take place. I really need this job interview to work out. I'm not sure if a position in Maria's tech ed start-up is the answer to all of my problems, but it doesn't involve a move halfway across the world, provides the combination of stability and purpose I crave, and makes me excited about the future. Plus, I've started learning Dutch, and now I want to leave this country even less.

"We're having some problems with the screen in here today," Maria mentions apologetically.

Of course. But this is an obstacle I can deal with. I smile with relief. "I brought my laptop just in case."

Despite the IT problems, Maria and I hit it off, like at our first meeting back at the Sawyer's picnic, and throughout the conversation, I get more and more excited about the job. I can see myself relocating to Amsterdam and building a life here: wandering along the picturesque canals with their crooked houses, riding my bicycle in the crowds of aggressive cyclists, trying out all of the cafés I've bookmarked on my phone on past day trips here.

Maybe, if tomorrow goes well, even with Lewis at my side.

When Karo told me a few weeks ago her interview at an audiobook company was scheduled for the same Thursday as mine with Codify, I booked train tickets to Berlin so we could celebrate the changes in our lives together. I'd also made the decision to seek out Lewis at his office the next day—tomorrow. The silence of the six weeks since the Sawyer's has been brutal and I miss him and I need to tell him how sorry I am, even if he might not feel the same.

My interview finishes without any other complications, and I make the mistake of thinking the statistically unlikely chain of events I've dominoed through since yesterday might be over.

But Murphy isn't done with me yet. Instead, he reveals the final trick up his sleeve.

After the interview, when I've packed up my laptop and said goodbye to Henrieke, Maria leads me out of her office and back into the elevator. "Do you have any plans for the weekend?" she asks, leaning against the wall and pressing the button for the ground floor. "I have to say, I was surprised you agreed to today's interview, what with Lewis giving a visiting lecture in Maastricht. I thought maybe he was there to see you?" When I don't respond, Maria shrugs and keeps making small talk, the LED screen behind her counting down the floors we're passing. Six, five. We're at four when her words catch on.

"What?" I blurt out, mind racing.

What is Lewis doing in Maastricht, the small town I still call home in the southern Netherlands? He has no business there. Soon, *I* won't have business there anymore.

He has business here, in Amsterdam. So what's he doing *there*?

"Rosanna likes to use me as a sounding board for all her experiments. Or practice for tricky mentoring conversations," Maria tells me. I guess that's what she had started talking about while my mind was short-circuiting, but I'm only half listening while I contemplate what Lewis could be there for. To grow his network in the Netherlands? To show to all my colleagues how his approach to our research topic is better than mine?

Or maybe, a small voice pipes up in a dusty corner of my brain, *he's there for you.*

"I'm sorry, I need to check something real quick." I scramble for my phone in my pocket, have a short but nerve-racking battle with two-factor authentication, scroll down in my inbox, and there, among all my ignored department-wide emails, it is. An announcement for a guest talk by *Dr. Theodore L. North, research associate at Berlin School for Mind and Brain*. In bold, underneath, is today's date, the location, and the time of his talk.

12 p.m.

Which is in two minutes.

Please RSVP to join the borrel outside the lecture theater afterward, it continues, and of course the link for the drinks and snacks has expired, with the deadline long gone.

Where I am in Amsterdam is about a two-and-a-half-hour train ride sandwiched by two ten-minute bike rides away from where Lewis is lecturing, so even if he talks for a full hour, followed by questions, snacks, and drinks, there's no way I will make it on time. Not to mention the promise I made to Karo about celebrating the changes in our life together.

"Frances?"

"Huh?" When I look up, Maria is standing in the open door of the elevator, a man in a suit waiting behind her.

"Are you alright?"

"Yes. Sorry about that." I follow her through the vast space of the lobby with its concrete floor and pendants of geometric lights.

If Lewis is there for me . . . I swallow, my heart beating a staggering rhythm. That would mean he's not in Berlin, where I planned to meet him tomorrow. I won't get to ask him whether he would give us another chance. I won't find out if he's still as hung up on me as I am on him.

"Thank you for coming here," Maria says and steps around an exposed metal column. I almost walk into it, my brain quieted by the news that one key player in my whole plan is not where he should be.

"Shit squared," I mutter to myself, impatiently following behind Maria even though I'm completely at a loss what to do.

If I don't go to Berlin now, I'm putting Karo second. Again.

But Lewis . . . I need to not let him down, either. No matter what it is that he has to say, I need to be there and listen. After a lifetime of not being enough for his parents, struggling to connect to his brother, and only ever being able to rely on himself, I need him to know that it's worth putting himself out there.

In the absence of a good mitigation strategy, I improvise. After I thank Maria for the interview and we say goodbye, I dash through the rotating doors into the rainy afternoon, and as I sprint back to the hotel to pick up my backpack, I throw my original plan out of the window. A breakneck-speed ride on a rented bike later, I'm back at the main station in Amsterdam, hopping onto the train as the doors slide shut. On my phone, the live stream of the lecture theater shows Lewis in low-resolution, and my visual cortex fills in the pixelated gaps of the video: the tight expression that camouflages his nerves, the scatterplot of freckles on his nose, the soft swoop of his hair. The sound quality is so bad that his voice cuts out every few seconds, but that only instills a stronger sense of urgency in me: I need to see him with my own eyes, bask in the real sound of his voice.

I take a deep breath before I call Karo, pushing Lewis and my racing heart aside.

"How did it go?" I ask her, as soon as she picks up. My voice sounds winded.

"I just got home," Karo responds with a laugh. "It went on for longer than expected because we couldn't stop talking and then they gave me a tour of the place. So . . . it went well? I think?" She goes on to tell me how they introduced her to what would be her team and how she gelled with them immediately.

"Karo," I squeal, "this is amazing." My phone vibrates against my ear, notifying me that the delivery I'd ordered from the hotel elevator is almost at her place. "Hey, I got you a surprise—there's someone going to ring your doorbell in about," I check the app, "a minute, so can you get your ID ready?"

"Um," Karo starts, but thankfully follows my instructions when the door buzzes. A muffled conversation and the clipped sound of a closing door later, she's back on the line, voice incredulous, "Franzi, why did you get me a cocktail delivered?"

"Well." I hesitate. "There's been a change of plans. Before I tell you why, I want you to go out onto your balcony, kick back in your hideous rattan chair, and tell me how your interview went."

Our chat about her interview fills an hour of my painfully slow train ride, but when I finally tell her what's brought the change of plans about, she falls quiet for a moment.

My stomach drops. Did I just mess up the last four weeks of progress?

"I'm so sorry," I tell her, "I know there's nothing more selfish than to skip out on a weekend with your sister because you're still heartbroken over some guy."

"Oh, Franzi." Karo emits a long sigh. "I told you. It wasn't so much about you being selfish, but about you pushing for things you'd convinced yourself you wanted without considering the harm they were causing you. If you're going after something—someone—you *actually* want, I am nothing but proud of you."

The encouraging tone of her voice makes me feel raw. Grateful. "Thank you."

"And he's clearly not just some guy," Karo continues. "Thanks to you, I've done my bit of going after what I want today. Now you do yours. Go and tell him how you feel."

Chapter Twenty-Nine

The auditorium is empty. At least I think it is at first, until I spot the back of a head in the first row. Golden waves, messy, like they've been disheveled by a set of nervous hands. Their sight sets off a tingling in my fingertips, a tightening of my throat. My eyes trace the outline of his body, over the dark green shirt collar peeking out underneath his blazer, down the sloped shoulders and to the elbows on the fold-out table, his forehead sunk into the tent of his fingers.

He doesn't notice me. It almost makes me turn around, because what if he's just here, exhausted after his lecture, not wanting to talk to anyone? But the need to know is stronger than my fear of rejection, and when I take the first step down, the other ones are easy, as if my body wants to be close to him, no matter what.

The tension grabs hold of his shoulders when he realizes someone is here: the shift in his neck, the way his fingers pinch the bridge of his nose. His blazer rustles when he pivots his knees into the middle corridor and turns around.

When his eyes find me, a little nick burrows into the gap

between his eyebrows. Almost imperceptibly. I drink up his face as I take each step toward him, his scent once I'm close enough, his voice when he says my name.

He doesn't look angry. Just . . . Tired. Disappointed. Weary. But he's never been as beautiful as he is now, because he's here, finally close enough to touch.

What if this is the last time? What if he hears me out, only to shake his head and tell me we're not on the same page? That I'm too late? That he didn't come here for me?

A million things I want to say to him swirl through my mind, but caution has me start slowly. "What are you doing here?"

"I gave a guest lecture," he replies and sweeps his arm through the air as if to include the whole auditorium, the university. "It's not *all* I wanted to do. There was something else I was hoping to talk to you about after everyone left, but you weren't here, so . . ."

I'd forgotten the hum of his voice. The sound of it feels like stepping into a warm kitchen after a bike ride through the rainy Dutch winter.

"I'm sorry," I tell him. "I had a job interview."

He continues as if he didn't hear me, "So that's what I'm doing here. You weren't here so I gave my guest lecture. I guess everything I had to say was pretty old news to you."

There's a strain in his voice, the one that makes his laughs go dry and his words sound a little painful. I didn't think I'd ever become the target of this version of his voice.

"It was," I say, but before I can lay out my next words, Lewis beats me to it with a sullen, "Gee, thanks."

"No, it's . . ." I bite my lip, trying to figure out how to tell him that I've combed through his papers to get a little piece of him, something just for myself, and with every reread

I missed him more, his sharp mind and his meticulousness and laser focus and drive and his soft laughs and his patience and—

He's turned away from me and is sitting with his head in his hands again. And all of this is going so wrong, and I still don't know what he came here for, but I do know that if I don't speak now, he might walk out of my life and I might not get this chance again. The thought sends my heart into a panicked staccato, and my motor cortex scrambles some random signals to open my mouth.

"I read your grant."

Weird opener. But okay. That's where we're going.

"And it's brilliant. I can't believe how fucking brilliant it is and I'm almost jealous I didn't put it together except I know with you it's in capable hands," I go on, voice overflowing with excitement for him, "and I didn't say this the first time, even though you massively deserve it, but congratulations."

"You did tell me," he murmurs, almost too low to hear.

"What?"

"Congratulations. Then."

I cringe when the words loop back through my mind. *Congratulations on your fucking grant.*

"Not for real. Not seriously. Listen. There's something I came to say to you, too," I begin the speech I should have rehearsed better on the train. "Usually, this time of year—the summer—is what I love most about work, because I get into this flow where I feel like I'm part of this huge dialogue in science."

Lewis tilts down his chin, but at least he's letting me get the words out. I suppose it's all I can ask for after everything I said in anger the last time we spoke.

"But this summer, no matter how hard I chase it, I can't get into it. It doesn't feel right anymore."

"I'm sorry you feel that way," he says, but there's frustration lacing his words and tightening his jaw.

I didn't expect him to be so closed off and it almost makes me abort the whole mission, but I push on.

"No, you don't understand. Research doesn't feel right anymore because it's not. Not without you. There's this giant Lewis-shaped hole. Like I lobotomized you out of my life but did the worst possible job of it. I still get these phantom pains, as if you're sitting next to me, commenting in the back of my mind. Snarky words when I'm doing a sloppy job, jumping to conclusions too quickly, or spinning my results into a neat little story."

Now that the first bit is out, I allow myself to finally lift my gaze from where I've been staring at the floor and find him looking at me with a furrowed brow.

"I'm sorry for what I said. I pushed you away and I'm so sorry that I did. How I did it. You not telling me about the grant hurt me, and when I found out, I saw myself being sucked into someone else's agenda again and could only think of pushing back. I'm sorry for what I said to you. It was horrible and, more importantly, so far from the truth."

Something flashes behind Lewis's eyes, but his face remains impassive, and I can't tell if he's battling with his emotions quietly or if all I have to say leaves him cold. I touch my chest, right where fear drills a hole into it.

"I think I was scared," I go on. "Of you. How you're able to see through me and understand me. I was afraid of everything I was feeling for you and all the ways it could go wrong. But it's like you said. No matter how much we try to plan and control as scientists, sometimes it takes a leap of faith."

I feel like that first day we met on the plane, trusting another person with my panic as we were hurtling through the sky. But I have to do it, *say* it, even if it feels like free-falling into the unknown.

"So I guess, here I am, doing just that. Betting on all the ways it might go right. Because I love you."

I barely hear my own words over the deafening thud of my heart, but they're out. Lewis blinks slowly, and lifts one hand, just to hook it into the pocket of his blazer.

I'm not sure what I expected him to do after my confession, but it wasn't this: Lewis jumps to his feet, so fast I step back in surprise, and heads to the lectern, where he smacks a button until the projector whirrs back on. The last slide of Lewis's talk lights up on the wall, a photo of his lab, the logos of all the research foundations supporting him, and the special thanks to his colleagues who contributed to all the data he presented.

"You asked me what I was doing here, so I'd better do what I *actually* came here to do, which wasn't my guest lecture." Lewis taps another button and the slide switches to a new one, blank except for the Sawyer's logo at the center of the screen. "At the start of the summer, when I boarded that airplane to the Sawyer's, I was ready to just survive the trip. You know, with how little I like networking and with how nervous I was to see my brother again." Lewis pauses, and in the silence my memory overlaps with his. His hands in mine on a shaky flight. "And somehow, you made everything I was dreading so much fun. And I wasn't sure if it was just that—that you were a distraction, a happy one, and I got swept up in it."

Oh. A distraction. Is that really all I was for him?

Lewis frowns down at the keyboard, and I watch him inhale once, twice, while the fissures slowly crack through my heart.

It's okay, I remind myself. *We survived worse. Jacob, all the rejections, that brutal night in New York. We'll survive this, too.*

"I got invited for this lecture, and I thought maybe you

were behind it, but I wasn't sure. I gave myself an ultimatum then. Promised myself I'd accept this invitation and that I'd sort through . . ." Lewis swallows, his gaze still cast down. "Everything. How to reconnect with Ben. My feelings for you. How to tell you how sorry I am."

One hand cups the back of his neck as he smiles wistfully. "But in the end, it was one endless wait. I admired you ever since I first came across one of your papers in grad school, and I was attracted to you the moment you sat down next to me on the plane. I knew you were never just a distraction. I think the coin dropped when we were at the graduation party, and the person I was looking for in the crowd wasn't my dad so I could avoid him, or Ben to figure out how to talk to him."

Lewis finally looks at me then. "It was you," he breathes out. "It was you, but I was too scared to recognize it."

My gut untwists slowly, tentatively.

"It's that eerie feeling you get when you plan out an experiment and list your hypotheses," Lewis continues, "and everything turns out right as you predicted. It never happens. You know it doesn't. So when everything falls into place—against all odds—you question yourself. You go and look for the error in your data, the bug in your code, the fault in your logic. You question yourself until you go mad. You try to find what you did wrong because there's no way that something this special can be this clear and simple. And yet."

A blush spreads over his cheeks. "That's how I felt about you. Feel about you," he adds, and it's that sentence that brings the swirl of my emotions to a standstill.

I am here and Lewis is here, and his gaze is filled with something that manages to be enormous and intense and tender all at once.

"Falling in love felt like an inevitability, but everything after? It's hard for me. I've been talking to Ben a lot, when he visited me. My therapist. My sister. And I've been thinking about what I told you that first evening we had dinner. That love is accepting someone without revisions. Maybe it's something I wished for all along, but now I know it's bullshit. Because we change, all the time, and relationships require communication and compromise and change. You can love someone, all their marvelous and flawed sides, but sometimes you also need them to change their stubborn ways, even if it's just by an inch. Because life *is* a fucking peer-review process. You mess up, and you're lucky if someone tells you and invites you to do better the next time. *That's* love. Because it's the way you build things that last.

"So that's what I came here to tell you, really. It's all I could think of doing." He huffs out in exasperation. "Do you know how hard it is to respect you and leave you alone but also not let you go? To show you that there's space for you in my life, that I want to fold mine around yours? It's impossible. An unsolvable problem, really. So I thought I'd do the only thing I knew how, which is talk about brain waves and memory tasks first and see if you'd show up. I needed to be here as loudly and quietly as possible."

Lewis switches to a new slide in his PowerPoint, this one with a paragraph of text.

While North and Silberstein has its issues, I can see the effort put into this collaboration. Although the origin of this work might go against standards of scientific integrity, I recognize the potential it holds and, moving forward, I'd like to make a few suggestions on how these strengths can be pulled to the forefront. These changes are substantial enough to warrant a major revision, but I'm convinced that they can be tackled.

My eyes fly over the words. Lewis isn't here to tell me that we end here, or that we ended in New York. He's not here by accident. He's here for me.

Understanding takes hold and dominoes through my body, quieting my heart and soothing my stomach. I'm still free-falling, but now he's falling with me, holding my hand.

"Did you—" I start, and need to steady my voice. "Did you write me a revision letter?"

"I did."

I lean my hip against the side of a chair, crossing my arms in front of my chest.

Lewis's eyes track over my face, the blush on his cheeks deepening, as though he's overcome by the same excitement I am. "You cannot imagine how much I missed seeing you squint at me like that. There's something you don't agree with. What is it?"

"Why does your name come first? In our collaboration?"

He shrugs. "Alphabetical order, I guess?" Pulling out his notebook from an inside pocket of his blazer, he scribbles something onto the page. "I'm adding it to the list of revision points." After setting down the pad, he taps the keyboard again, revealing a numbered list. "Here are all the ones I already came up with, starting off with number 1. I'm sorry. So sorry for not telling you about the grant. Historically, when I've been honest with people, they didn't stay around through the tough parts, so I was scared to pop that bubble we had. I didn't want to lose you. But that doesn't change the fact that I'm sorry for not telling you about it."

Lewis falls silent, giving me time to read.

1) I will always tell you how sorry I am for the times I've hurt you, starting with keeping the grant from you and for pulling a Jacob on you. From now on, I'll tell you about complicated things as they come up.

2) I promise we'll figure out a way wherever you end up. At a distance or right here, I'm happy if you'll have me.
    a) We might have to fine-tune our communication a little bit.

3) I will hide all your contact lenses so you need to wear your glasses, and I'll make sure you see clearly with them.
    a) At the risk of sounding like a mind-body dualist here, but I'm obsessed with you, Frances, in and out.

4) I will hold your hand and tell you to breathe whenever you need me to. Let's remember that not everything in life is a variable to control and I get that that's a scary thought, but also: look where serendipity has brought us.

5) I promise I won't push you away when things get tough. Whenever we let each other in about what went on in our minds, it was scary but it always turned out for the better. So how about, moving forward, I'll make hot chocolate and we talk things through?

6) I will help you paint your walls and nail pictures into them wherever you live. Evon if it's a rental and for a limited time, I want you to feel at home wherever you are. I promise I'll restore it back into original condition afterward.

7) I will continue asking you to explain to me everything I don't know (and everything I do), be your safe place to land whenever your determination gets the better of you, and keep asking for all the nerdy jokes.

As I'm reading, Lewis leaves his place at the lectern and comes up the first few steps of the lecture theater. When he stops on the step below me, my pulse is close to tripping over itself from wonder.

"Related to point 3 . . . May I?" he adds, gently touching the metal-wire frame on my temple.

I give him a small nod because I don't trust my voice right now. A smile creases the corners of his eyes, and it warms me within my heart as he gently pulls my glasses off. When they're clean, he returns them to me, then holds up his notepad. "I knew you'd have suggestions, so . . ."

I pull the pencil stub out of the spiral bind of the notepad and add to the list.

8) I will set boundaries in my life, so I get to keep all the things that I love in it, and that, first and foremost, includes you. I'm done pushing people away for the sake of my career.

9) I will not allow you to cut off your hair, ever, but I will give you back your favorite T-shirt if you let me steal other ones.

10) I will engage with you in scientific discussions for as long as you want, but I will also ask you to tell me about your

feelings when I know that you're deflecting. I'm here to take care of you, too, Lewis, so let me make the hot chocolate sometimes.

11) I will help you shorten your abstracts and let you use the wrong emojis because these are things you really don't need revisions for. They make you the way you are and that's a good thing.

12) But I also promise to encourage and support you when you need to make changes. Sometimes things need to get hard before they get better, and I will stand beside you while you figure out your relationship with Ben. I will hear you out so we can solve complex situations together. Caring for someone is communicating with them and finding the best way forward as a team, and I promise to make you all the grilled cheese sandwiches so we get there together.

13) I promise to pay attention to you every day and tell you all the ways in which you are enough.
    a) Just to name a few right now: your curiosity, attention to detail, that grumbling laugh.
    b) Also, that move of your hand.

I hand Lewis the list. Although I saw him reading it upside down as I was writing, he goes through it once again, eyes sharp with focus. He nods as he reads through each item, his cautious smile burrowing deeper.

"Can I?" he asks then, waiting until I hand him the pencil.

"Um. Sure."

Lewis draws a *14)* at the bottom of my list. He tilts up the page so I can't see what he writes, and I push up onto my toes to get a glimpse, but it's only when he finally hands me the note that I get to read his words.

14) I promise to tell you every day that I love you.

"Starting with now," Lewis says. As he takes me in with an infinitely tender expression, he pauses his gaze like each part of me is something precious, Eyes, cheeks, lips, jaw, the frame of my glasses, and back to my eyes again.

"*Ich liebe dich*," he whispers. "I love you."

My heart balloons and this time, I let it fly.

I tug at the paper, drawing him into me until his right hand curves around my hip. The notebook page crumples when I flatten my palm against Lewis's chest, and the fingers of my other hand find the nape of his neck, curl into his hair. But before I can move in to kiss him, I remember there's something else he needs to know.

"One more thing," I tell him. "Relating to point 8, setting boundaries. I won't be taking the job."

Lewis's face falls. "I don't understand. The job you want, the funding, it's there. Even if it's just to tide you over until you get your own grant, I checked with HR—I wouldn't be involved in the interviewing process. Getting the job wouldn't have anything to do with me. I made sure, I—" He drags his hand over his face, then fixates on me with what looks like desperation. "What do you want me to do, Frances? Tell me and I'll do it."

"You don't have to do anything, you've done enough. This is not on you, but on me. It's my decision how to move forward, and I've decided I won't be taking the job. I need to do this for myself. I need to figure out what's good for me."

Lewis squints his eyes pensively. "So, what you're saying is . . . you'll have me, but far away? Did you get any news from the lab in Melbourne?" His hand lifts to the back of my head and he unfurls his fingers, pulling me closer.

"Hold on, no." I stop him. "Let me finish explaining."

I take a step away, even though I'd love to stay nestled up to him. But I need to look at him for this, need him to see me. I need to have this conversation without hiding.

"I'm not going to take the job with Rosanna. In fact, I'm not going to take any other job in any other lab," I tell him, and it's the first time I've said it out loud. It's scary and unfamiliar, and my heart beats furiously in my chest, but it also feels right. "I'm leaving academia. Hopefully, if it all works out, just for a little while. If they'll have me, I'll work four days a week as a researcher at Codify, Maria's start-up. And if I miss academia, I'll apply for another round of grants, with Rosanna as my mentor, with a project that's really mine. If it doesn't work out, well, I gave it one last shot. But if it does . . ."

"You'd have enough funding to build up your own research line next year, in Amsterdam," Lewis finishes my sentence for me.

I nod slowly. "I need to learn how to set boundaries for myself and my career. Like, what I'm willing to do for it and where I need to draw a line for my own sake."

He brushes my hair out of my face and I can't help but lean into his touch. "I'm proud of you for doing what you need to do, Frances. I'll be here to help whichever way I can. And when you get the job, Maria is lucky to have you."

"*If* I get the job," I correct him, because even though

I feel good about today's interview, I don't want to get my hopes up.

"Nah. *When* you get it." His confident tone infuses my chest with a calm energy. Then, his face splits into a shy grin. "Amsterdam, huh?"

His smile is infectious. "I thought it'd be good if I was close," I muse. "You know, in case you ever need last-minute help for overly long abstracts."

We stand there, drunk with happiness. Now that I can look at him more closely without fear, I notice the dazzling pop of blue that are his eyes and how long his hair has gotten since I saw him last.

"Can I kiss you now?" he murmurs.

I nod.

And then he does. As his lips move over mine, I can't believe I ever wanted to run away from this. Now, all I want is to lean in. To run headfirst into that *us* we've started to build. Some may call it Murphy's Law, and others serendipity, but the fact is that sometimes our plans don't work out and sometimes they surprise us, leading to something beautiful.

When I draw back, I take Lewis's hand and interlace our fingers. We're back where we started, with his hand wrapped around mine, reassuring me with a quiet comfort. "So, about item 14 on that list . . ."

"What is it?"

"I'm not quite sure I understand what you meant."

"Maybe you'll get it when I say it a few more times," he whispers into the pocket of space between us. I want to cartograph the crinkles that form around the corners of his eyes and build a home in the soft hum of his words. "I love you, I love you, I love you."

He presses our interlocked hands to his heart, trusting me with the steady beat of it.

Epilogue

Seven Months Later

It's Friday, the middle of the day, and someone pounds on the door so hard I worry they'll punch a hole through it. But then the lock turns and the door opens. *Thud, thud, creak*, go the stairs, and Lewis appears in the center of my oddly shaped living room, rain dripping from his hair onto the collar of his denim jacket. The dusting of red at the top of his cheeks tells me he hurried here, but the hammer he carries in one hand, and the brown paper package in his other are entirely confusing.

"Have you checked your email?"

All of this plays out in less time than it takes my mind to resurface from the code I've been writing. I blink at Lewis, the urgency in his voice slowly filtering through. Apparently too impatient to wait for me to catch on, he's already crossed the room to where I'm sitting at the kitchen table amidst a sea of research papers, a ring-bound manuscript of Brady's finished first draft of her novel, orange Post-It notes, and three cups with varying quantities of leftover coffee.

"Did you steal Brady's book again?" he asks as his hands hover over the cluttered surface.

"You read too slowly," I point out.

"I'm just making sure she's getting all the science right."

"Lewis, it's fantasy, not her PhD thesis! It's not like there is an objectively true explanation for how werewolves evolved."

"Whatever," he grumbles, and finally seems to find a somewhat clear spot to drop his hammer on, effectively messing up my carefully laid-out chaos.

"Now, Dr. North," I growl at him, but he sweeps me up with a hand around my waist. His hair smells fresh, like the rain that started pelting down this morning right after he left to give his lecture.

"What are you doing here?" I wonder. "Should I be worried?"

But the look in his eyes is fierce, not troubled.

"You," he says decidedly, "should check your email."

"Oh." I gulp down the burst of nerves his words set off.

When I submitted my second grant with Rosanna two months ago, I started treating my inbox like a bomb that's about to go off. At first, I was ready to just abandon it, but I've been working on my coping mechanisms with my therapist. Now, I open it only when I feel centered enough to deal with the havoc it could wreak.

Even though I have a safe job at Codify, and I enjoy working on the module that'll teach our younger users how to code a simple memory game, it's Fridays when I can't wait to get out of bed in the mornings. When I get to stay at home, work on my independent research projects or prepare new applications with Rosanna. On Fridays, it feels like my whole heart is in everything I do: the mind-bending questions and the dreary formatting of figures alike. Turns out that leaving academia has reignited my love for it, now that it has become a choice. Now that I've understood it's not just about answering my questions but getting to ask them in the first place. I miss the wonder and confusion in my day-to-day, the exhilarating feeling of thinking about things nobody else has thought about before.

I still want to make a difference, but the process of getting there has become almost as important.

After the rejection of the first grant, I struggled to keep up my hopes for this second one. It comes with more funding and, in consequence, is more competitive. To prepare, I squeezed in time during the winter holidays; on the train ride home to my parents' before Christmas, on the flight to New York where Lewis and I celebrated New Year's with Ada and Ben (and I snuck off to have brunch with Vivienne the next day). But I'd kept my laptop closed that weekend in January when Karo and Lennart came to visit and my sister shared the news that she was pregnant.

Angling my laptop toward me, I finally compute why Lewis has left the lab at this random time on a workday.

The results must be out.

I'm scared, to say the least. Because if this doesn't work out, maybe it's time to give up academia for good. Staying at Codify would be a nice kind of future, but I don't think it's the one I ultimately want.

"Give me your hand," Lewis orders gently now. Surely he would tell me if it was bad news. He wouldn't leave me hanging like this, would he? Or maybe he doesn't know yet, either?

"Tell me if you know already." Fizzy unease pumps through my veins and makes my fingers jittery. Some grant agencies announce the awardees publicly at the same time as they send out the individualized decision letters. "Or wait, no. Don't tell me."

He only nods at my laptop and waits as I swivel the cursor over the mail icon at the bottom of my screen. Once. Twice. By now it has almost become a routine, Lewis holding my hand through something I'm afraid of, me saying, "This doesn't change anything between us," and him patiently replying, "It doesn't."

"And if it's a rejection," I continue with a glance at the hammer, "please don't destroy my laptop."

Today's email changes things between us. Massively.

Lewis cheers and I can't believe my eyes.

"You knew!" I stab an accusatory finger at him.

He catches my hand and ghosts his lips over my knuckles. "Only that there was an email. Rosanna wouldn't let me open it with her. But I had a hunch."

"This is insane," I say, eyes drawing back to my computer screen and the number with enough zeros to cover research expenses, publication costs, salaries. Mine and two PhD students. For the next five years. "I can't believe this."

Lewis looks at me, eyes sparkling and voice brimming with pride. "You did it," he confirms, then lets go of me as he hands me the package he brought. "This is for you." I tear through the paper and find a picture frame inside, holding a simple line drawing of a brain. One hemisphere is chaos, a thread unspooled and muddled up, the other one a clean rendering of cortical ridges.

"You know what this means," Lewis says. His eyes are a mirror for the happiness pumping through my body with each beat of my heart.

"I do?"

"This is your home now."

With his words, the realization hits me. This one-bedroom apartment on a second floor of a narrow building in De Pijp is, in fact, my home now. Permanently.

"You're right," I say and look around. The crooked living-room wall with a slowly growing collection of Polaroids and postcards, the herringbone parquet flooring, the backsplash of pale yellow tiles in the kitchen. And beyond that, too; the market popping up every day down the street where one of the green grocers has started to recognize me and helps me practice my Dutch skills. Mila and the rest of my friends at the bouldering gym who I meet for climbing sessions, and for coffee, walks in the park, and Friday night drinks. All of it feels like I'm slowly arriving somewhere. Five years of funding means I can take the time to settle down for real. "This is my home now."

Lewis brushes a strand of hair behind my ear. His voice is quiet as he says, "Ours, if you want it to be."

I look down at the artwork Lewis has given me, and when he hands me the hammer and I spot the nail he has taped to the handle, I finally understand.

"Are you asking to move in with me?" My voice is hoarse with emotion.

"If you'll have me."

My eyebrows draw together. "What about your place?"

"This place is nicer. Farther away from work, which is probably only good. You have a bigger kitchen and I like that third step that is a bit creaky," he reasons. "And, well. The loft."

He's right. Nestled under a gabled roof, the loft may be my favorite part of this whole place. It reminds me of the bedroom in Lewis's friend's cabin in upstate New York. And in times like these, when rain cloud after rain cloud moves over Amsterdam, the *pitter-patter* on the roof makes it cozy and magical, like sleeping in a tent. Minus the damp clothes and back pain the next morning.

"I know things are moving quickly. That you only moved in a few months ago. But I'm living here half of the week anyway, and wish I was here for the other half. There's more than enough space for the two of us, and with the extra money—"

"Lewis," I stop him and squeeze his hand. The bliss of this day is almost too much for me to handle. Not just one dream come true, but all of them. I hold on a little tighter to his thumb, to reassure myself that all of this is real. "There's nothing you have to convince me of."

"I don't?"

"Unless you made plans to persuade me over a home-cooked dinner, in which case I'll gladly have you convince me."

He ruffles my hair and kisses my temple. When he draws back, his eyes are dazzling, the crinkles around them full of delight. I take his hand, grab my present, and pull him to the bottom of the stairs leading up to the loft. There's a little nook in the wall that I'd planned on placing a vase of flowers in, but it's tall enough to fit the picture frame. Something more permanent.

When I've hammered the nail into the wall, Lewis hands me the frame, and he closes his arms around me as I hang up the fine copper wire.

"Welcome home," he says.

Acknowledgments

As someone who reads the acknowledgments of every book religiously, getting to write this section is a true pinch-me moment. The day-to-day of putting words onto the page can be lonely, but in the four years since Frances first nudged into my mind, this book connected me to so many kind, smart, beautiful minds. Whether you contributed to the making of this book by spurring me on, giving me advice, reading carefully, or using your expertise to get this book into the right hands, please know you have my eternal gratitude.

To Hannah Todd, my agent: From the moment you gushed in your email about the glasses micro-trope that Lewis and Frances have going on, I knew you were the person this book needed to get out into the wider world. Thank you for believing in me and this story, for patiently answering any questions I have about the opaque world of publishing, for your enthusiasm, your optimism and groundedness. I'm so excited I get to navigate this dream with you to guide me.

To Elizabeth Hitti, my editor on the US side: Your perceptiveness and enthusiasm, your careful questions, insights about character and emotional turning points, your vision of this story—they've taught me more than I ever could've asked for. Thank you for being so committed to Frances and Lewis; for pushing me to transform their story and myself in the process.

To Aubrie Artiano, my UK editor. Thank you for showing this manuscript all the care and love, for sharing my sense of humor, and for reminding me that the side characters in these books are the main characters of their own stories.

Thank you also to Elinor Davies, Valentina Paulmichl, Hannah Kettles, Tian Zheng, Virginia Ivaldi, and everyone else at Madeleine Milburn; Nathaniel Alcaraz-Stapleton, Mina Yakinya, and the team at Janklow & Nesbit UK; to Camila Araujo, Heaven Jenkins, Zakiya Jamal, Lara Robbins, Amanda Hudson, and everyone else at Atria Books; and Holly Humphreys, Sophie Dawson, Elle Bloom, Shannon Hewitt, Yasmeen Doogue-Khan, and the rest of the team at Head of Zeus; and Sarah Horgan and Monika Roe for your gorgeous cover illustrations. Dr. Kelcie Willis, thank you for the sensitivity read and your helpful notes on Frances's character.

Thank you, Cat, for letting me tell you this story in its most incoherent, bare-bones, and rambling form, thank you for your open ear whenever I needed to talk something through, for ignoring the many side characters named Brendan and those that disappeared halfway through the book, and encouraging me to keep writing instead. The first hurdle to writing any book is getting that first draft down on the page, and I couldn't have done it without you.

Vojta, I'm so grateful we became friends in the middle of writing this book. Thank you for reading early, for asking about these characters as if they were real, and for indulging me with everything Aaron Tveit related.

To Margot Ryan. Thank you for taking a chance on me. You showed me how to get from the flawed version on the page to the ideal version in my head. Thank you for tirelessly rereading drafts of the manuscript and query package, and for holding my (virtual) hand all throughout querying. Thank you also to the SmoochPit community at large: to the organizers for all your hard work on this program, and to my fellow 2023 cohort that made querying less daunting. To Clare Gilmore, for writing the most extensive and insightful "How I Got My Agent" post, and for providing feedback on my query letter; to Carla Calvo, Ellen Kirkpatrick, Chelsea Lankford, Michelle Mitchell, and all the writers I met along the way, for inspiring me to keep going and giving feedback to drafts and other materials of this book. Sonia Tagliareni, I'm so happy we get to be each other's sidekick on this publishing journey. Thank you for bracing the editing-cave with me, and yapping about tea in the quiet moments between deadlines.

To my friends, Sophie R, Marlene, Sophie F, and Lotte; the couch people, Vanessa, Jaun and Egg; and to the CN lunch group, Olof, Vaish, Till, Seb, Michele. Thank you for pulling me out of my head and into the real world whenever I needed it. A special shoutout to Seb and Danielle—your reenactment of Frances and Lewis's meet-cute still lives rent free in my mind.

To my family, thank you for raising me to be a reader. Mama and Papa, you introduced me to the written word and the magic found inside a book with every bedtime story you read to me. Sissi, Oma Freia, and Oma Elisabeth, for taking me to the library when you picked me up from school to borrow all the books I could get my hands on. Leon, thank you for teaching me to read way ahead of time so I could have my own adventures.

To Julio, thank you for your endless support in everything I do. From taking me on my first writing date at the NYPL to telling me all your research ideas, indulging me when I wax on about tropes, and making me dinner when I'm on deadline (and when I'm not). Our love story is my favorite of all.

And finally to you, dear reader, thank you for picking up this book. It's the greatest honor of all to accompany you on your commute, sweeten your Sunday morning, or be your space to wind down at the end of the day. I wrote this book when grad school was hard, and all I wanted was a joyful story in the context I knew so well. I hope I made the hours spent with this book worth your while.

About the Author

Hannah Brohm penned her first novel when she was a teen, and yes, it was about vampires. After studying psychology in university and graduating with a PhD in neuroscience, she rediscovered her passion for storytelling and swapped writing articles about brain science for swoony romance novels. Born and raised in Germany, Hannah lived in Portugal, the Netherlands, and New York, before moving to London, where she now lives together with her husband and an ever-growing collection of books and handknit sweaters.

Thanks for reading!

Want to receive exclusive author content, news on the latest Aria books and updates on offers and giveaways?

Follow us on X @AriaFiction and on Facebook and Instagram @HeadofZeus, and join our mailing list.